T0032643

*Praise for Max B......*

"Flagrant, shameless, high-voltage, and sometimes just consummately silly. I can't think of another translator who could have pulled this off, but like any great writer who feels they have total license to do whatever the hell they want with their language, Lethem creates what the narrator describes as 'a language that constitutes the topography of its own world,' not striving for an accurate period reconstruction, but an archaism that's invented, anachronistic, bastardised, defiantly inconsistent and totally, gloriously fun."

**—Daniel Hahn**

"An heir to Rabelais, Cervantes, Sterne, and Swift, Besora has conceived his novel as a giant neo-baroque container with room for everything and more besides. The combination of events, registers, genres, and characters is manic in its variety."

**—Pere Antoni Pons, *Ara***

"Like *Don Quixote*, this is a chivalric novel, seasoned with the humor of an author with wit in spades. Besora grew up with the toxic style of the great US underground cartoonists, the 'Weirdo' gang, and you can tell."

**—*Time Out***

"This novel is here to atone for a glaring oversight in the history of Catalan literature, reviving a tradition that has seemed all but dead since the time of *Tirant lo Blanc*, since any language deserves, at the very least, two great satirical novels; and this one is so Catalan it hurts."

**—Montserrat Serra, *Vila Web***

Copyright © 2017 by Max Besora
Translation copyright © 2021 by Mara Faye Lethem

First edition, 2021
All rights reserved

Library of Congress Cataloging-in-Publication Data: Available.
ISBN-13: 978-1-948830-24-9  /  ISBN-10: 1-948830-24-8

*This project is supported in part by an award from the National Endowment
for the Arts and the New York State Council on the Arts with the support of
Governor Andrew M. Cuomo and the New York State Legislature.*

NATIONAL ENDOWMENT for the **ARTS**
═══ arts.gov

**NEW YORK** STATE OF OPPORTUNITY. | **Council on the Arts**

*The translation of this work has been supported by the Institut Ramon Llull.*

**LLLL institut ramon llull**

Printed on acid-free paper in the United States of America.

*Cover Design by Tree Abraham*
*Interior Design by Anthony Blake*

Open Letter is the University of Rochester's nonprofit, literary translation press:
Dewey Hall 1-219, Box 278968, Rochester, NY 14627

www.openletterbooks.org

The *ADVENTURES* and *MISADVENTURES*
of the *EXTRAORDINARY* and *ADMIRABLE*

# JOAN ORPÍ,

*Conquistador and Founder of New Catalonia*

Max Besora

TRANSLATED BY MARA Faye LeTHEM

**OPEN LETTER**

LITERARY TRANSLATIONS FROM THE UNIVERSITY OF ROCHESTER

# *Preamble*

Everything we know about the figure of Joan Orpí del Pou (Piera, 1593–New Barcelona, 1645), founder of our country, we know thanks to the historian and geographer Pau Vila, who states, in his rigorous, severe biography—the only one to date—that Orpí was "a Catalan man who went through a lot and managed to come through it all."[1] However, that study was the last of any research into this personage—a Catalan lawyer who worked for the Spanish Crown, became a conquistador and, finally, founded New Catalonia on the other side of the world—as the Chronicles of the Indies and modern historiography have, generally, shrouded him in silence.

About a year ago, however, destiny or providence brought to my hands an unpublished volume that shed further light on our character's story. It was while I was in the Archives of

---

1.　See *Joan Orpí, l'home de la Nova Catalunya* (Ariel, Barcelona, 1967) and the later edition, expanded and translated into Spanish by Pau Vila himself: *Gestas de Juan Orpín, en su fundación de Barcelona y defensa de Oriente* (Universidad Central de Venezuela, Venezuela, 1975).

the Indies in Seville researching some *relaciones de servicio*[2] from the conquest, when a sheaf of old papers tied together with a goatskin cord fell to the floor. The text had a printed cover but the pages inside were written in a shaky hand faded by the passage of time. The poorly cut and glued paper and the lack of stains made it clear that it was an unpublished document. After a few months of furious literary archeology, during which time I deciphered and copied the text, I came to find some wholly surprising results. The book was written by an anonymous soldier who, during the 1714 Siege of Barcelona, had transcribed his captain's oral narration of the life and adventures of a man named Joan Orpí, who had lived in the century prior. The manuscript was not published or distributed in its time, nor in the centuries that followed, remaining forgotten in that dusty corner of the archives, until I "stole" it in order to make its contents known to both the scientific and lay communities.

Now, would it be accurate to call those soldiers from 1714 "historians"? The answer is uncertain. In fact, it's more than likely that this document is as dubious—if not more so—as the Ossianic poems, the *Fragmentum Petronii*, or Scheurmann's *Der Papalagi*, and we have made that clear in this critical edition, in which the dates do not always match up with the accepted timeline. It is precisely in such manuscripts as ours, which is to say deriving from an oral source, that such historiographical problems often crop up. How much truth is there in this document? To what extent does literature reflect society and to what extent does history? How does literature transform our perception of history? These questions, while perfectly legitimate, open up a whole can of worms, since any

---

2.    *i.e.* Reports delivered to the Spanish Crown in order to obtain recognition for successful missions and compensation in the form of pensions and other rewards from the royal authorities.

close inspection of history books soon reveals divergences. *The Adventures and Misadventures of Joan Orpí* blurs the distinction between poiesis and mimesis (or what boils down to the same thing: invention versus history, because they are but two faces of a single coin), and employs an extraordinary variety of narrative strategies including the picaresque, rumors, decrees of the period, annotations, chronicles, legends, official government papers and files, myths, letters, fables, songs, contradictory narratives ranging from popular to elitist, hegemonic and counterhegemonic, with trips down to various hells, legal treatises, the Byzantine or chivalric novel[3], records, polemic tracts, catechisms and sermons, the rhetoric of the heroic epic, biography, allegory, satire, and, of course, the historical events of the conquest of America that later would become legendary in the conquistadors' own words, in *The Chronicles of the Indies*.

In short, this text offers a wide range of narrative resources that fill in the blanks left by Pau Vila's biography, and show Joan Orpí moving between two very different times: Catalonia on the Iberian peninsula and New Catalonia on the American continent; modern Europe and "primitive" America; the Baroque world and the incipient Enlightenment; the mechanistic and the magical views of the world; always between two spaces, constantly fluctuating between the real and the imagined. This ambiguity allows us to use this historical personage as an instrument for reinterpreting the subject in history, for rethinking the relationship between the colonizer and the colonized, as well as the figure of a person made metaphor who must face up to the failure of a utopia and accept

---

3.  The subtle distinction between fantasy and reality, on which the power of conviction of many chivalric novels lies, was due to the audience's demand for guaranteed true events. Often, in their prologues, they claimed to be adaptations of some original document or a manuscript happened upon by chance.

*Sic transit gloria mundi*, a person who created an alternative historical reality.

To conclude this introductory note, we want to point out that we decided to revise the manuscript, transporting the narrator's voice to modern Neo-Catalan and leaving only the dialogue in the original language, to avoid losing contemporary readers' interest. That said, we have kept the changes and annotations to an absolute minimum, except for the footnotes (which meet the criteria for the quality and precision demanded by the Academy) used to correct some historiographical errors or simply insert information to allow modern readers to judge for themselves.

Walter Colloni
Professor of Neo-Catalan Postcolonial Studies
Universitat de Sant Jeremies
New Catalonia

4.   *i.e.* The original cover to the manuscript. The printing house of Sebastià Comelles was famous in its day for publishing the works of Lope de Vega and Avellaneda's apocryphal third volume of *Don Quixote*. However, neither the font size of this manuscript's title nor the metal type match with the Barcelona printer's typical style. Not to mention that the rest of the text is written out by hand. As such, we've deduced that this cover is merely an intellectual forgery, as I explain in further detail in an essay entitled "Joan Orpí: History or Literature?" (Edicions La Parranda, 2097).

*Dicere etiam solebat nullum esse librum tam*
*malum ut non aliqua parte prodesset*
Gaius Plinius Secundus, *Epistulae*, III, v. 10

The *ADVENTURES* and *MISADVENTURES*
of the *EXTRAORDINARY* and *ADMIRABLE*

# *JOAN ORPÍ,*

Conquistador and Founder of New Catalonia

*September 10, 1714,*
*The Siege of Barcelona*

A group of infantry soldiers and their captain opt to smoke and drink in an abandoned theater rather than be stationed at the walls, firing against the Bourbon troops. Bombs fall on the city night and day, ceaselessly. Everything is ruin and desolation. Death hangs gloomily over everyone, scythe at the ready.

"What mindless suicide!" one of the soldiers suddenly exclaims. "We shall die as rats yf we continue on this way. A pox upon the Hapsburgs and a pox upon the Bourbons: *Ni dieu ni maître!*"

"Die as dogs, jolt-head!" chides another soldier. "I should beat thee down at present! For at least we shall make history! They'll write book after book about us, they will erect museums, make paintings, write poems in our honor . . . we shall be heroes of the fatherland!"

"Aye, if there's any fatherland left," grumbles a third infantryman.

"I had rather be a living deserter than a dead patriot," muses a fourth soldier.

"That's enough! Quiet, all ye!" bellows the troop's captain. "Chance to die and chance to live but, in any case, remember that the fatherland doesn't always coincide with the territory. I wot the tale of a man named Joan Orpí, who refounded our Catalonia on the other side of the globe, less than a century hence. On my word."

"Incredible!"

"Cock and pie!"

"And what befell henceforward, Captain?"

"And what befell henceforward, bid ye? Well, in 'is quest to try that all, he lived a thousand and one adventures," declares the captain. "Ye shant find these in any book of history, yet they be no less memorable or less important. *Au contraire.* Would ye care to hark, and forbear complaining for a time?"

The infantry soldiers smile like children, nod their heads, and perk up their ears. They pour more wine and pass around tobacco. The captain/narratorlights his wooden pipe and begins his declamation.

"Who was this adventurer what founded a New Catalonia thousands of leagues away, yet went to the diet of worms leaving naught a trace in our history?"

"Joan Orpí!" one soldier shrieks.

"Precisely! Who traversed seas fill'd withe mythical monsters and virgin forests at risk to his life (and the lives of many others) for a fistful of gold coins and (perchance) posthumous glory . . . ?"

"Orpí . . . !" bellows a soldier.

"The selfsame! And who risk'd chicaning the very Catholic Kings and came cross't near as many enemyes as friends?"

"Christopher Columbus . . . ?" ventures another soldier.

"No, ya beef-head, none other than Joan Orpí! At least that was what I was told by a corky criollo from the Yndies I happen'd upon one night when tippling in Seville. He quoth

4

to be a 'friend of a Catalan conquistador, humble altho an old Christian[5] and a nobleman of New Andalusia in the Americas, later founder of New Catalonia.' Thus he even spake Catalan."

"Hold up . . . one moment, Captain!" says one of the soldiers. "Canst thou truly trust a brandy-face? Art thou convinsced the criollo was whom he sayd to be and that he werent lying with a latchet? How many years pass'd betwixt these events and the telling of them? And, once for all, why have I this tic in mine eye each tyme I get nervous?"

"Enuf tilly-tally, soldier, and merely heed the tale," orders the captain, in a didactic tone. "Whence my 'informant' explaint this historical drama to me, the criollo in question were four sheets to the wind. Nonetheless, I didst believe him. And knowth ye why? 1) For the criollo spake Catalan, and 2) for I be a man of faith (faith in the imagination, to be clear!). And now, allow me begin with Chapter XVI, of whych I am inordinately fond."

---

5. *i.e.* In the sixteenth and seventeenth centuries, the subject of blood purity divided the Hispanic world into new Christians, in other words, those descended from Arabs or Jews, and old Christians, of pure Christian blood.

*Chapter XVI*

In which young Orpí celebrates Carnaval
with his fraternity and ends up
dressed as the Stag King

I shall begin with a day when Joan Orpí was celebrating Carnaval. Following the parade, our young hero ended up in a cemetery, where a band of joyous revelers were engaged in a wide range of obscenities. Some were licking others' anuses, some were eating fruits and tomatoes they'd rubbed on their genitals, and others were drinking sacramental wine and masturbating and dancing to the improvised music of drums and tambourines. All were dedicated to the collective ritual, singing, shrieking, praying, making offerings and insinuations, muddy and half nude . . . ducks and rabbits fell at their hands . . . hens were violated and eviscerated . . . some slathered themselves with the blood of the dead animals—

[One instant, Captain . . . halt! Forbear the tale!]

"How now?" he asks, irritated.

"For the lyfe of us, we cannot fathom why thou beginnst with Chapter sixteen. Would logick not state the first Chapter?" asks one of the soldiers.

"Yea, start withe the first! The first!" cry out other soldiers.

"How's that? Doth ye seek the typical story with a beginning, middle, and end?" asks the captain, perplexed. "Dunderheads! Don't ye know that true literature is only true when written against itself? Why put plot over language and form?"

"Here we hie again," complains one of the soldiers. "Art thou one of those pedantic academics, ay? For if that be the case, I prefer to be killt by enemy troops . . ."

"Numbskulls!" bellows the infuriated captain. "When I speak of going against the narration I don't mean there shall bee no story, no adventures, no characters! I speak of the need for a hybrid construction, plurilingualism, exaggeration, hyperbole, pastiche, and bivocal discourse to bring together what convention & morality strive to keep separate. Literature must be a frontal attack designed to suspend all rational judgment in order to reinvent it each second anew!"

"I cannot bear these sermons . . ." says one of the soldiers.

"If he keeps up this proselytizing, I'm outta hither . . ."

"Yawn . . ."

"Fine!" exclaims the captain in exasperation. "Okay, Okay, fine! Quit thine complaining! I shall beginne at the beginning, as you wish! But no more interruptions, I'll lose the thread, and judge me not for mine invention, but rather for the grace of my wit, glossed in three books and their corresponding Chapters, which one of ye shall 'copy' anon. And that's an order!"

# Book One

In which is narrated, with great gusto and an eye on posterity, Orpí's infancy and childhood, first in the town of Piera and anon during his studies in the city of Barcelona, where he had varied experiences, as many good as bad, which taught him that life is no bed of roses but rather a long ordeal where one learns from hard knocks, and as such and befitting his story shall be explained perhaps not exactly as it truly happened, but at least quite similarly.

## Chapter I

Thus begins the story of Joan Orpí,
indubitably some sort of premonition
of his later life of adventures

It is said that while Joan Orpí's birth was a bit strange, it was highly spectacular, regardless. And if you don't believe me, listen to this: It all began in the small Catalan town of Piera, one evening of the Year of Our Lord Jesus Christ MDXCIII (if I've got my Roman numerals right), when an old, ailing pigeon, wet from the falling rain, flying hither and thither from clouds filled with electrical activity, soared through the trees and sown fields, made three shaky circles around the church bell tower, and floated through the heavens of smoking chimneys in a prodigious final flight, until its wings could take it no further and, finally, amid hoarse *glook-glooks*, it landed clumsily on the angular sill of a window where, agonizing in horrific pain, it consumed its last moments of life in absolute sepulchral silence.

That window belonged to the home of the Orpís, a family of respectable wealth and notable local pedigree, and inside the room the light given off by three candles revealed spread-eagle legs covered in varicose veins and hair, trembling from the effort of bringing a new soul into the world. Mrs. Orpí was about to birth an infant in such a way that would become legend, and fodder for numerous sessions of rumor-monger-ing in the town of Piera (at least for the duration of Sunday afternoon).

"Push . . . ! For the love o'God, Eulàlia, push . . . !" shouted old Orpí.

"This child be driven by the Devil, my beloved . . . !" she bellowed, the birth being such great torment that she couldn't help dire prognosticating.

The woman had flooded the bed with excrement, blood, and other fluids, and was straining her nether regions to get the baby out of her womb once and for all. So loud did she bellow that it seemed the sky would crack and splinter into a thousand shards. Alerted by the hollering, a throng of curious neighbors had gathered outside the house and were pointing their fingers at the window of the Orpís' home.

"Even me bottom is set to essplode!" she shrieked, her eyes rolling back in her head. "Ay, God's loaves and fishes . . . I'm dying hither!"

"Come now, woman, don't scream so, thy serenade of hur-tling and shouting shall bringeth all Piera here!"

"Sssh! Quit thy rubbish talk, Pepet," ordered the woman. "This birth art an executioner come to take me!"

"Peace be quiet, woman, prithee, any moment now he'll be out in the worlde, a perfect right genius . . . wid a moustache andall!"

"And who woulde have thou believe my baby art a boy-child, big lump?" asked the woman, pushing

"Come now, woman . . . caint ye see we needs an heir to tend these lands?"

"Always with your mind on coin, vile leech! Whilst here I beest dying of excruciating pain! My wish is a girl and she shall be called Maria . . . hither, thither, and yon!"

"Over my dead bodikins! Firstmost a male heir . . . it's the least thou canst do!" countered her husband. "And we shall name him Joan, as my father (who art in Heaven), whether thou liketh it or not! I'll respect thine pain, at least respect mine legacy!"

"If that be true, then thou oughten warn all those whores of yours since, out of respect, thou should lyest only withe your wife!"

"Darent ye commence that ole song & dance, Eulàlia!" bellowed her husband, feigning indignation. "Let us get this birth over withe . . . or I'm like to faint!"

"Oh, yea, sure, when I rayse the subject of the bawds ye frequent in Barcelona, out comes the broom and, flish-flash-flish-flash, thou changeth up the subject right quick . . . ya swine!"

"Eulàlia, cry thee mercy . . ." said her husband, kneeling by the bed. "Quit gabbering and push . . . for the love of all that be holy!"

Just then, at the eleventh-hour, the town midwife rushed in. She was in such a rush that she came wearing just her nightgown and slippers. "Let us see if we caint get this here show upon the road, milady!" she barked with a macaronic howl as Eulàlia's husband crossed himself. But despite the best efforts of that expert in births natural and unnatural, it didn't seem the child would be born that night, nor that the storm had any desire to wane; quite the contrary, the sky spat out its fury harder than ever, with clouds colliding violently and creating brutal electric jolts that fell upon the earth, cleaving mountains, burning forests, and splitting trees in two. So great was the storm that one of those streaks of lightning fell right atop the Orpí home, hid in the chimney, snaked down like a bulimic cosmic worm and burst through the fireplace into the living room, where it hit a dog in the snout. The electrical charge set its pure canine instinct into motion, and it bit one of the servants who was stretched out on a straw bed; the young man leapt up from the pain and banged into a shelf above him, and from the shelf fell a pot containing two thousand Catalan reals, ten gold maravedis, thirty billion castellanos, forty of Barbarossa's pfennigs, eight liards, five hundred deniers, five croats, two-hundred pounds, eleven 1/3 trentíns, and a bunch of counterfeit money (plentiful as it was throughout the country in that period), of which one coin went flying and, tracing a perfect semicircle, landed in the mouth of the woman giving birth. A curious detail: throughout this entire chain of circumstances, the lightning's electrons had transferred from one object to the next when they touched, and the coin the woman swallowed sent an electric charge through her entire body, helping her with the final push needed for her to expel—with a shy "oh!"—the newborn from his maternal cave, whilst the coin emerged from her nether-slot in a wholly ultranatural way.

*Plof.*

Thus was born Joan Orpí del Pou.

## *Chapter II*

In which young Joanet sees his siblings come into the
world, learns to speak, takes a fancy to a word, and has a
divine revelation

The curious reader must undoubtedly be astonished after
hearing tell in the previous (which is to say, the first) Chapter
how highly diligent Joan Orpí came into this world. By now,
kind sirs, you may very well have formed a hasty judgment
against the author here narrating. However we must demand
a bit of patience before a condemnation *in saecula saeculo-
rum*, and open hearts before the pages ye shall hear forthwith[6], withholding judgment for the time.

House Orpí, located beside the market on Carrer Major
de Piera, was enormous, and little Joanet, crawling, would
lose himself amid the muddle of people coming to and from
between that large house and its stables. At first everything

---

6.   *i.e.* Here the narrator feigns speaking directly to the reader, in a recourse
typical of literature of the period, using forms more appropriate to oral than to
written narration.

was sounds: the clink of the haulers' bells, the barking of the dogs, the neighing of the horses, the shouting of the dayworkers. Then everything was legs. Then he discovered that atop those legs were people. Then, that people had different faces. Then he learned to differentiate the faces. We could also add that his mother's wasn't particularly pretty, but she was his mother. And we can also say that his father's resembled an irascible owl's, but he was his father. And we shall say no more on this aesthetic matter.

Little Joanet was surprised to realize that he would not be the king of the castle much longer, since he soon had a front-row seat to the respective births of his siblings. The first, Francesc, was born as naturally as breaking wind, right in the middle of the living room. Their mother heard a *Plaf!* from between her legs as she dined, and the newborn was already on the floor. The second, Maria Anna, emerged as Eulàlia headed to church for Sunday mass: *Plof.* The third, Joana, was born just as the first. The fourth, Jaume, slipped out from between Eulàlia's legs exactly as the second had. The fifth . . . ah, no, there was no fifth.

Meanwhile, little Orpí learned to speak by imitation, like monkeys do, and those first childish sounds distinguished truth from error, a truth that would always be increasingly more uncertain and lost. When writing, there were some letters that gave him more trouble than others, to be frank. For example, he found it easier to write an "A" than an "R," as strange as that may seem. There was a reasonable explanation. The letter "A" reminded little Orpí of a house:

The "R," on the other hand, didn't remind him of anything, and was therefore harder to learn. In any case, once he knew how to say whole words and link them up with other words, and even write them down on a piece of paper, it seemed that all the mysteries of the world could be resolved. At one point he learned a new word he was terribly fond of. The word was *sensual*. Ever since he learned it everything seemed to be sensual. When he saw a pretty tree he would say "that tree tis verily sensual." If he saw a pig splashing around in its own excrement, he would say "all that tis highly sensual." If he happened upon one man killing another, he would say: "now that tis quite sensual."

One day his father said to him, "Joanet, why dost thou call everything sentsual? Art thou an ydiot or wut?"

Since the boy was unsure as to how to respond to that question, old Orpí gave him a cuff to the head that sent him facedown onto the ground. Some time later, our young hero swapped out the word sensual for another word he liked even more, *strumpet*, which he had heard directed at one of his sisters. From that day forward he found everything quite entirely strumpet. One Sunday when Mrs. Orpí brought her five children to church, something highly unpleasant happened due to Joanet's obsession. Whilst everyone was praying, and it came time for a communal amen, Joanet exclaimed *STRUMPET*. So loud and so clear that everyone was shocked, all their mouths shaped like Os. The sin did not go unpunished. They washed out his little mouth with soap and gave him thirty thwacks on the bum. After that, the little boy from Piera seemed to have learned his lesson about obsessing over words, because he didn't open his mouth for a week. His family, seeing him sit there agape for hours, thought the boy had been struck dumb. But after a sennight they saw that his dumbness had been a mirage because a few days later, upon seeing some vultures devour a calf, little Joanet exclaimed: "all that tis verily sensual and quite strumpet!"

His sisters, Maria Anna and Joana, grew up surrounded by their mother and the kitchen servants, while his brothers, Francesc and Jaume, followed old Orpí out into the fields when it came time to thresh the wheat, or to the market when it came time to sell the grain. But our Joan was different. And that wasn't just a gratuitous conviction but a prophecy, as we shall soon see.

One day, the Orpí family was leisurely headed to the holy mountain of Montserrat—like the upstanding Catalans they were—to light some candles to "The Black Virgin," as she is widely known. Joanet, who was just eight at the time, asked, "Who be that blacke woman?"

"The Virgin, mine son, the Vyrgin of Montserrat," answered his father.

"Art there more blacks in the worlde, Father, beyonde her?" asked the boy. "I finde her a tad affrightening."

"There be many blacks throughout this worlde, mine son . . . and they feast upon menn! Yet there be but one holy black Virgyn," declared his father, making the sign of the cross.

As the entire family prayed some very heartfelt Ourfathers, little Joan approached the holy-water stoup, set into the wall of the church beside the entrance. There he entered a small, roundish room filled with ex-votos: crutches left by the lame, wax arms left by the maimed, shrouds covered in dust and mites, and icons of the saints. Impressed by the uncanny look of those prosthetics hanging from the walls, the boy had the stirrings of a nervous attack and, while his little brain practiced cognitive free-association exercises and his body shook epileptically, a celestial light appeared at the back of the room: it was the Virgin of Montserrat, dressed in a freshly-washed blue sheet and with a crown of gleaming light around her head. She spoke with a voice from beyond the grave:

"Joanet! Hark carefull! Twas I which sent the lightning bolt what aided thine mother on the day of your accouchement! Tis thee, Joan Orpí, was birthed for to rule a distant New Land. Thine divine destiny awaits!"

"Caint hear ye, milady. Furthermore if ye came to eat me up, I muss say that I am in disaccord with said culinary policy," said the boy, who, terrified by so much negritude, had shat himself.

"Whosoever hath told you such a thing?" said the Black Virgin. "Hush thy blathering piehole and heed these instrucktions on how to effect your fate: thou hast but to light three candles for next year's harvest, two candles to put paid to brigandage, and seven further candles to honor the lord our God who hath wroten thine eternal glory in the firmament. Ah, and lest I forget . . . thou mustesth eat grass!"[7]

"But, milady . . . that be a lot of candles! I haven't the coin!" said little Joan, scratching his moist ass. "Moreover,

---

7.   *i.e.* This final recommendation, curiously, is the same one the Virgin of Lourdes gave to Bernadette, in the nineteenth century, in a typical case of divine plagiarism.

I understandest nary a word of what yee proclaimeth. And furthermore, mine father saith that black people, like milady, doth eat menne even though milady protesteth the contraire."

"Yee art a bastard ratbag! And thou hast besmirch'd thyself!" scolded the Virgin, strict as a police officer, and pinching her nose. "Thy cheek is thy whole face! Many a manne would slaye fer a miracle such as this, yet thou speaketh of the price of candles? Pish posh . . . skinflint!"

The Black Virgin vanished into the ether, and our hero ran, diarrhea streaming down his legs [insert disgusted facial expression here], to explain the miracle to his mother and siblings. However, no one believed him. In fact, they laughed in his face. When he explained the story to his father, he received such an ass-whooping that our young hero refrained from revealing his divine visions to anyone else ever again. And that brings us to the end of this second Chapter, pleading with our beloved readers, should they encounter some historical inconsistency herein, to please forgive it, for memory is not always exacting but wit will never fail us. And now, let us advance to the third Chapter.

## Chapter III

### In which young Orpí sees a circus show
### and decides he will become a knight-errant

In those good old days the town of Piera was indeed the most boring of all places in that hemisphere of the (mapped) earth. Since nothing ever happened there, those rural folk took even a fly's negligible trajectory for entertainment, or watching the cows chew their cud (the latter sufficient activity for the whole family). One day, however, a traveling circus came to town. The bizarre delegation came through the streets playing drums and fifes[8] so off-tune that the children who'd come to receive them turned around and ran back, covering their ears. The circus convoy was filled with costumed people and cages with strange animals inside: there was a camel, a bear, and even an orangutan. No one had the faintest idea where those beasts were from, because the itinerant circus people spent their lives traveling from one place to another and collecting the most improbable things.

---

8.    *i.e.* High-pitched flute of the period.

The circus was soon set up beside the Santa Maria church. After paying their three maravedis, the audience was welcomed into an enormous red tent by a string of outlandish characters performing feats of juggling, and a fat sweaty barker: "Stepeth right up, folks, see the arcane marvells of this w'rlde: Savage beestes of Africa, swashbucklers from the Indies, the whoreson of James I the Conquerer, a wilde issue discover'd in the Pyrenees . . . stepeth right up!" The people of Piera, wary yet curious about the strange get-ups those circus folk were wearing, gradually approached the tent, where they were received by a midget with pierced ears who immediately charged them the entrance fee.

"Tisn't cheap," said one townsperson.

"Eyen sharpe, or thou shalt turn round to discover theyth knick'd your snickerdoodles," complained another.

Girls and boys, men and women, young and old, all of Piera ended up inside that improvised circus tent. First, out came the animals. The bear had learned to juggle, the orangutan could write profanities on a chalkboard in a lean scrawl, and the camel smoked a pipe. Then out came the players. The supposedly savage boy appeared before the crowd with an acrobatic flip as the master of ceremonies declared that he'd been raised among wolves in the forests of France. But actually he was no child, just the same midget with pierced ears who'd worked the door, naked and smeared with mud to look more feral. People started to whistle and shout "whadda ripoff" and "skullduggery!" while the midget stuck out his tongue and gestured obscenely. Then out came a man dressed in a tunic and fake gold crown who assured the crowd he was the last descendant of James I of Aragon. His only evidence was some unintelligible murmuring that the ringmaster claimed was in Valencian, however no one could be entirely sure. Then came a man they called The Fakir, who could fold himself up like a rag doll. First they stuffed him into a box, then they made him walk over a carpet of nails, and then he swallowed a ball of fire that killed him immediately. His corpse was dragged off quickly as the crowd gleefully applauded. Then the ringmaster said:

"And now tis time to introduce one of the lastest of adventurers returnt from the Newe World. Ladies and gentlemen, the authentic hidalgo Hierro Azul de los Llanos Castrados, Kinge and Lorde of a thousand castles and a thousand armies on Terra Firma!"

A rickety, gangly man, who seemed to be starving to death, took the stage. He was dressed in a rusty suit of armor and when he unsheathed his sword, its weight sent him down flat on his hindquarters. The audience all laughed. But the ringmaster was not amused in the slightest and he quickly waved out the princess, a fat dirty woman wearing a pink dress that was too tight in various places. When the princess knelt down to help her knight, the back of her dress ripped open. The audience laughed again. When they were both back up on their feet, they acted out a story of princesses and knights, while another man narrated:

Once upon a tyme, there were a knight, named Sir Hierro Azul de los Llanos Castrados, very noble in his personage who, after instating a Theocracy in his kingdom, christened Jauja Valley, was keene to wedde. Yet there wart nary a princess in that realm, merely corrupted sauvages. Accordingly, he took up sword & steed and set out in search of a robust ladee of royal lineage who would do. In the magickall lands of El Dorado, he discover'd a castle built of gold with a princess lock'd up in the highmost tower. The knight did his darnedest to breeche its walls and rescue that damsell but an armey financed by the king of the castle kept him at bay. Hierro Azul foughten the thousand and three soldiers, smiting them all with a single blow of his sword. "Milord," did sayeth the sergeant to the king, "Hierro Azul is invincible! He slayt our entire army withe a single blow!" "How now?" did saith the King, "Ynacceptable! Thou art degradedeth to latrine-cleaner!" Then the King started the catapults. Three million rockes, as big as cathedrals, fell upon Sir Hierro Azul, but they broke into tiny pebbles the size of shirt buttons with a syngle swash of his sword, fore he were invincible. Then they dispatch'd a monstrous, fire-breathing dragon, likewise payd for by the King, to eate the knight, but it were Sir Hierro Azul which ate the monster in a single bite, having not eatene prior in that day. Then, Sir Hierro Azul entert the fortress, lopped offe the regall head with but one finger and leapt up into the gilden tower fore to recover the princess, who was named Magdalena Morena de la Sierra. After a brief, hackneyed exchange of platitudes, the princess did consent to marryeth that gent. Before leaving, Hierro Azul knock'd down the castle withe one lunge, plunketh the precious rubble into a satchel, and knight and princess bade offe hence the Lands of Jauja, whereuponst they lived happily ever after much as the clams of yore, thus & so & blah-blah-blah, we finde we hath reach'd the ende of our tale.

Everyone clapped while the two actors, who played the knight and the princess, struck the attrezzo, cursing their nomadic life all the while. But it was the boys and girls in the audience who were the most spellbound by the story. And little Orpí, restless by nature, was no exception. Heroic dreams twinkled inside his skull:

"Henceforth, Papa, for mee, tis knighthood or bust!"

"You ginormous son of a bobolyne!" bellowed his progenitor, slapping him on the back of the neck. "I forbid thee even think such claptrap. What thou must do is attende school so thou canst keepeth the books and maketh some coin forr the family busyness!"

And, well, his house, his rules. And thus little Orpí began his studies, as you shall learn in the next Chapter, which, as you shall soon see, starts on the very next page.

*Chapter IV*

In which young Orpí
does not seem a particularly gifted scholar,
so his parents seek out a tutor

The school, located on the outskirts of lower Piera, near the
Casa de les Voltes, turned out to be an uninteresting place for
little Joanet. Any chance he and his friends got, they shoved
aside their Latin notebooks and covertly opened up the chivalric romances that were fashionable at the time, such as
*The General History of Sir Partonope: Count of Blois and Emperor
of Constantinople*; *The Four Books of the Virtuous Knight Amadís de Gaula*; *The Adventures of Esplandián*; *The Tribulations of
Valiant Gausbert Calostre*; *The Ballad of Merlin the Wise and His
Prophecies*; *The Book of the Assiduous Knight Arderique*; *The
Quest for the Holy Grail, with the Marvellous Feats of Lancelot
and of Galahad His Son*; *Sir Silves of the Forest*; and *Yvain, the
Knight of the Lion*, among others. One of them would read and
the rest listened and all of their imaginations were lit aflame,
making them feel they themselves were knights trained to kill
Turkish armies, and hydras, and gorgons, and forest gnomes,

and titans, and dragons, and that they were destined to rescue princesses and make friends with flying unicorns.

Subdeacon Jaume Amades was a Satanic-looking clergyman, white with dark circles under his eyes. He always brandished a boxwood stick for those distracted students. When he saw little Joanet reading instead of working, he would grab his stick and . . . thrash his buttocks! The teacher had earned a fearsome reputation.

"Let's see now, Joanet: What is one + one?"

"Three."

*Bam!* Another blow to the buttocks.

"Pray let us try it again: One + one?"

"A hundred!"

All the children laughed. *Bam, bam, bam.* Three blows and Joanet was sent into the corner.

There was no way in hell he could study with all that thrashing, and little Orpí started to skip school. He preferred to watch the hustle and bustle on the main street and in the town square. His mouth would drop open as he watched the peasants loading up the beasts of burden with sacks of grain, the fishmongers and butchers shouting, the pilgrims doing penance on their way to Montserrat, the vendors with their thumbs on the scale, and the men-at-arms who protected the area from bandits and highwaymen. Sometimes, they would catch a few and hang them in the main square, where their corpses would sway for days, little kids throwing rocks at them, until they started to rot. These sorts of extracurricular activities were turning little Joanet into a slugabed of brobdingnagian proportions.

Desperate, ole Orpí hired a roving tutor to teach his son something of value. The young squire, a short, squat, bald and fat-faced man, turned out to be one of those know-it-alls who called themselves humanists and suggested alternatives to the ecclesiastical education methods employed in schools. The wiseacre windbag believed that education must be active, not passive. Influenced by Erasmus and his thesis on the *Plan des Études*, he emphasized ancient texts while appealling to the boy's intelligence and respecting his individual freedom. The Orpí family didn't give a toss about those new methods as long as Joanet started using his brain for once. The tutor put into practice his teaching method: translate, repeat, analyze, and recompose, in that order of importance. Picking up Homer's poetry, young Orpí was thrust into translating from Greek to Latin (and not the degraded Latin of the Middle Ages, but Cicero's!), as he recited the verses aloud, poeticizing the plot of his own education. The tutor explained nothing because, according to him, there was nothing to explain.

Or to put it another way, *"Non est discipulus super magistrum nec servus super dominum,"* declared the teacher. "Whych is to saye, thy intelligence shall be not subordinated to mine, but rather we must commence upon a plane of equal and equitable ignorance. Got it?"

No, little Orpí didn't understand a thing, but together, teacher and student, they read and translated Seneca, Plutarch, Diogenes Laërtius, Herodotus, Xenophon, and other Greek, Latin, and Corinthian classics, and they studied the sacred texts directly without the clergy censorship.

"*Mort principium est*, young Speusippus[9]," said the highly metaphysical tutor.

"*Quot erat demonstrandum*," replied Joanet. "*Amicus Plato, sed magis amica veritas!*"

The boy from Piera soon forgot Catalan and spent his days mumbling unbearable Latinisms, with his nose in dictionaries, overwhelmed by a *désir de savoir*. His newfound love of logos made young Orpí the perfect subject for such an all-encompassing education, but at school little Joan was also quickly excluded, for knowing too much. The other kids taunted him and the teachers flunked him in every course (except for Latin) because they considered him a brown-noser.

One day, his father asked him, "Son, what didst thine tutor teach thee today?"

"I knowth not what thou dost mean withe that question, father, since as Sextus Empiricus wrate, and I paraphrase: If all that is taught can be both true or false, and both conditions are subject to doubt, I can only conclude that naught can be taught.[10] And I wouldst also append: *O miserum te si intelligis, miserum si no intelligis!*"

In the face of that mysterious response, old Orpí chose to smack the boy. He was beginning to suspect that the private lessons were transforming his son into a truly unbearable pedant. What's more, old Orpí discovered that the tutor, arriving home from the tavern fuzzled, would enter the bedroom of his eldest daughter, Maria Anna, to do unmentionable things. One day he decided to hide in his daughter's armoire, watching and waiting. Two hours later he caught the *dominem* with his pants down, *in flagrante*, in front of Maria Anna, who looked upon the scene as if she'd stumbled into the wrong theater.

---

9.   *i.e.* A disciple of Plato.

10.   Greek philosopher and doctor. From his book *Against Professors*.

Old Orpí thought that the perfect excuse to fire the pervert. And so he did: he fired him immediately. Despite the professionalism of the tutor, who pulled up his skivvies and left the girl's chambers with all the aplomb the situation demanded, wagging tongues say that he left Piera crying and cursing his fate. Whatever the case, that was the end of young Orpí's humanist education and the start of his laboring on the family lands, which as the eldest son were to become his, until one fine day . . . one fine day, as I was saying . . . bah, now I've lost my train of thought! Probably best then just to skip directly to Chapter V.

## Chapter V

### In which we tell of Joan Orpí's adolescence
### and his discovery of a "vagina dentata"

Ah, yes, that's what I was going to say. Take a good hard look at Joan Orpí, and then look again: at thirteen years of age, he is a daydreamer with raging hormones, neither here nor there. More tall than short, more thin than fat, and with cheeks more red than pale. His face is banana-shaped and his big eyes—the color of an absconding mutt—don't miss a beat, despite being hooded by bushy, undomesticatable eyebrows. Honestly, it's best not to even mention his moustache: it just began to sprout one day and didn't stop until someone took pity on him and taught him the art of shaving. Regarding his aquiline nose, on the other hand, everyone had some sort of opinion. He is slim of body but brisk in his movements, sending his messy hair flopping over his forehead. In sum, young Orpí most resembles a bundle of hairy bones with legs.

We now find our young hero in tender adolescence, an age in which hormones accelerate, an age in which everything seems bright and magical, an age in which boys start to feel something growing in them. And I'm not talking about their brains. Thus our hero was faced with an important enigma:

what was the purpose of that hanging bit taking up space between his legs? For some strange reason, it seemed to have a life of its own and would grow big and shrink as it saw fit, and sometimes, upon first waking, he would find it throbbing beneath sheets all mucked up with a white, gummy substance. The whole business was quite disconcerting to young Orpí.

One day, as he was walking through the orchards on the outskirts of Piera, he saw a very lovely young girl by the name of Gisela Coll de Cabra, a neighbor from town, washing her teenage thighs on the riverbank. Dressed though she was like an ordinary peasant girl, in the eyes of our hero she seemed a true damsel. As it was hot, the young woman was splashing water into her low neckline onto breasts white as cheese, and our hero noted that bit between his legs rapidly inflating. As he watched her, mouth agape, for a good long while, he stuffed his hands into his pants and pulled on his pud in a fit of instinctive onanism. Gisela Coll de Cabra, seeing him shaking behind a bush, waved him over with a wag of her finger. Our young hero, nervously buttoning his pants, obeyed.

"Whatsoever were thou up to backe there, ye swine?" she said, realizing the state of affairs. "I see yer full-mast, eh? Yer knick-knack, yer gimcrack, yer crimson chitterling . . ."

"I . . . I . . . didd-nnt knowe . . . I didnt knowe that . . . that sooo . . . so very many . . . names existed . . . fore . . . fore . . . that 'bit' . . ."

"What's wrong wid yer mouth? Are ye dumb or wut? Ye shud see all da t'ings one canst do wid dat dere 'bit'!" she asserted, laughing joyfully.

"Are thee no vergen, Gisela?" Orpí asked naively.

"Ha, ha, ha . . . ! Only virgin I knowe is atop Montserrat. Point a fact, the right whole virtue business war invented by da churche to controlle girls. I caint even recall when mine hymen braked, all I knowe is the one who did it war indowed withe a giant prick, and I shriek'd like a sow withe pain & pleasure! Ere since I nair misst a chance ta fadoodle. Dost thou wish to learne to fucke?"

"Verily . . ." panted our hero, his knick-knack still pointing at the heavens beneath his pantaloons.

"Firstmost, ya gotta warm up what's betwixt these ham-hocks," she ordered, didactically pointing to her crotch.

That said, wanton Gisela took his hand and stuck it under her skirts. Young Orpí felt something akin to a hidden crea-ture, although he couldn't say whether it was a rough rat or a soft ferret. In any case, he was convinced it was alive because it was quite damp. When he looked under those skirts all he saw was this:

Seeing those teeth on the girl's erogenous zone was such a deep disappointment to the young Orpí that his crimson chit-terling immediately and irremediably deflated. And not only that, but he also came to the conclusion that what Gisela had between her legs was nothing less than a kraken. And thus, he rapidly reached yet another conclusion: Gisela was in grave danger as long as that monster was stuck between her legs like a leech. So our hero grabbed a boxwood stick, lifted up all those skirts and petticoats and then started beating the girl's crotch, thinking that he would save her from being devoured by the fearsome beast.

"What be ya doin', ya son of a camelopard! Ya stunted speck of shit!" bellowed Gisela Coll de Cabra, leaping out of the brambles to avoid the stick. "Hallp . . . hallp me this ydiot is set ta kille me!"

Hearing her shouts, a group of young men from a nearby town came to her aid, singing a song the whole while:

♪ Come round, ye lads, and gather ♫
Damsell in distress there bee!
Tyme to saveth her honour
♪ Yea, her honor and her glory ♫
For we art the hardy foes
of abstemia & anemia
We art the favored sons
we make a right goode team, yeah!
Come round, ye lads, and gander
Fore this here coprophagist
is beggin' fer a lather
Let's check him off our list!

Young Orpí thought those young men were coming to help him kill the skirt monster, and he devoutly joined their song. But soon he realized they were not coming to his aid, nor did they want him in their choir. The young men pounced upon him and gave him such a drubbing it is quite easy to picture what state he was in afterward. However not as easy to imagine was the state Gisela Coll de Cabra would be in. After she thanked the vigilantes, that selfsame swarm of fiery lads raped her, one after the other, until they were sated. After the brutal attack, Gisela joined a nunnery, where she lost her mind, convinced she was fornicating with the Devil. So she took her leave of the convent, returned to Piera, and ended up selling vegetables at the market in the square. But that's a story for another day.

## Chapter VI

In which young Orpí attempts every trade
to no avail and, finally, has his fate
determined by his father

Our hero, traumatized by his terrible first sexual encounter,
had taken a quite solemn vow of chastity, swearing that he
would never again venture a hand under a petticoat and that,
henceforth, he would only serve the glory of the Lord Our
God. And as such, he applied himself strictly to the fiercest,
most refined methods of *askesis*.[11] He no longer read chivalric
novels, instead reading the rosary and books of saints, and
spent his days praying like a bedlamite. However, it turns out
that working the land like the rest of his family was no job for
our hero. Workdays at the Orpí farm, despite the hired hands,
were arduous: reaping and threshing the barley, feeding the
animals, tilling the rough fields from sun to sun, cleaning the
stable, negotiating the tithes, paying the workers, husking the
corn, fixing the tools, fertilizing the fields, taking the goats
out to pasture, milking the cows, planting the vegetables, etc.

---

11.  *i.e.* Philosophical/religious term that refers to the use of abstinence to
control passions and lascivious thoughts.

Not to mention that in winter it got very cold, and in summer it was altogether too hot for such undertakings.

One day, when little Joan's mother caught him praying to the Virgin of Montserrat after the Angelus[12] hour had already passed, she said, "This lad is not befit to worke the lands. All the livelong day besotted with religiouse books, and allways praying Ourfathers. Alas and alack . . . we might haven a chaplain in the familly."

"Or a right sissyboy. In that case, it'd be best to kill 'im," complained his father. "Whatevere sort of milk dud he be, something must bee dun withe 'im."

So they brought Joanet before the town priest, a dark, twisted man. The priest interviewed him personally to see if his was true Christian faith or a passing fancy, for the boy's little head was filled with a mishmash of Biblical proportions.

"Come nowe, Joanet, whom dost thou ween created the worlde?" asked the priest.

"Well, I reckone at first all was chaos, when, 'ittle by 'ittle, sollid material started to amasse and . . ." our little hero interrupts his narration to look at the statue of Christ with its sad eyes and bloody wounds and then continues, ". . . a solid mass, as I was sayething, whence da utmost worms of very life itself aemerged & turnt inna angels, and one of those wurms was God, whom created thee world."

The priest gave him a clout on the head.

"Joanet, that's hereticall & impious! Repeat after mee: dost thou accept Jesus Christ as thine son of God and dost thou believe in the shrift of sins, the resurrickion of the body, and life everlasting?"

"Methinks that Jesuset wuznt nary hoping ta start a sect,

12. *i.e.* Midday. The hour when workers prayed and entrusted themselves to the Virgin.

iths only a dolthead could believe all that pike 'bout virgins having chillren what don't emerge whence that hairey monster betwixt their legs. Whomever whatsoever wishes to swallow that story, may. Moreover I've a bridge to sell to them."

"What breede of byzantine discussions art thine, sinner! Come now & recite the Apostles' Creed: *Credo in Deum Patrem omnipotentem, Creatorem caeli et terrae,*" stuttered the priest, "*et in Iesum Christum, Filium Eius unicum, Dominum nostrum, qui conceptus est de Spiritu Sancto, natus ex Maria Virgine . . .*"

"Borne to a vyrgyn?" asked Joanet. "Tell me another one!"

"Do not blaspheme!" croaked the priest. "Come now, bade us continue: . . . *passus sub Pontio Pilato, crucifixus, mortuus, et sepultus, descendit ad inferos, tertia die resurrexit a mortuis, ascendit ad caelos, sedet ad dexteram Dei Patris omnipotentis, inde venturus est iudicare vivos et mortuos . . .*"

"You cain't possiblee ween that, Father," said our little hero, "not a person alive believeth that story 'bout dying & coming back ta lyfe. And me, I'm quite fonde of alle that up in Heaven, some eight years backe the Virgin of Montserrat appeared befor mee & gave me all sortes a bizarre orders, but she never did sayeth a worde 'bout nay communion o' saints nor remissing o' sins nor resurremption o' flesh nor lyfe everylasting."

"Son of a trollop! Tis people such as ye who shall breake the *unanimitas*! I should washe yer mouth out withe cow patties! Begone or I shall 'ave you denunced fore the Holy See!" barked the enraged chaplain, ejecting him from the church with a bonus kick in the behind.

Old Orpí, seeing that the boy was useless both as a priest and as a peasant farmer, thought of enlisting him as a soldier. All of Piera's human rejects ended up in the town's military.

Most of them were mental deficients who spent their days fighting with each other or playing craps. Normally they would bet their horses or their weapons or their wives, but eventually they'd almost always end up killing each other for some reason or another. Young Orpí joined the ranks at the age of fifteen and a mere two days later was already a compulsive gambler. He bet his sword and lost it before he'd even learned how to use it. He bet his saddle and lost it. Finally he bet the family home and lost it. When the soldiers came to make good on the debt, old Orpí beat them off with a hoe and quickly pulled his son out of the military.

One day, a cart filled with bohemians arrived in Piera, pulled by two old mules and followed by ten mangy, barking dogs. There were more than thirty people inside that cart, but less than fifty. They quickly set up a makeshift market in the town square. The oldest among them, a fat, blind woman, read people's futures from the lines on their palms for a quarter real, and mapped out their astrological charts for the modest sum of one real. Joanet's mother brought him there so the old pythoness would tell him his future, to see if they could shed some light on the boy's fate. As the woman read the lines on Joanet's small hand, she spoke in thickly accented Spanish, filled with Zs and splattered with *caló*.

"For Undivel's[13] sake! Thiz boy 'as a complicated future, murky and far-flung, in that order of importanze and thiz I decree. If ye want to know more, zen ye muzt pay two more coinz."

"These chancers allways wanteth more coin," complained old Orpí, who decided instead to see if he could place his son as an apprentice in some trade.

Father and son knocked on the doors of every artisans

---

13. *i.e.* In Caló, the language of Spanish gypsies, God.

guild in Piera: stablemen, cordwainers, apothecaries, carpenters, shipwrights, blacksmiths, tailors, cutlers, furriers, matmakers, perfumers, bakers, sifters, equerries, etc., but none of them wanted anything to do with young Orpí because every guild had a very strict admission policy: if you aren't the son of . . . you simply weren't admitted.

"Blasted artisans!" complained old Orpí. "They cling to their titles like Jews to gold."

"Indeedy, father," said young Orpí. "I swere for as longe as I liveth to be mercyless against evil & fraud, and that no one mann under me shall go hungerly mere fur being poore or withoute pedigree, fore I shall allways protect the simple, oppressed man, punish all infamy, and allowe reason to triumf."

His father, a sensible man, saw that his son had what was commonly called a "sense of justice." That was when old Orpí had an idea. Which we shall reveal to you, dear reader, but not until the next Chapter.

## Chapter VII

### In which young Orpí heads to Barcelona and along the way meets a priest who turns out not to be one

Seeing that Joanet would never be a farmer, nor a priest, nor a soldier, nor anything to put food on the table, his father came to the next logical conclusion:

"Sith yee be good for nuthing save reading fruitless books, thou shallt go to Barcelona & study thee law. Let us see if thou art quicker with thy tongue than with a hoe."

Barcelona! Seat of knowledge and all the pleasures of the fatherland! Glorious womb whence sprung splendiferous Catalonia! Our young hero could scarce believe his ears! His siblings couldn't believe it either, since Francesc, Maria Anna, and Joana were all better intellectually endowed than he; but such were the advantages of being the oldest son and heir.

Young Orpí dressed in his Sunday roast clothes: he put on some perfumed linen breeches, a new flannel shirt, his well-shined lambskin boots, and a white silk tie that was the envy of his schoolmates. He combed his hair with lamb grease like a prince, put on his red, velvet-lined dress coat and placed a feathered cap on his head. He lashed a dagger to his belt and, protected from the possible inclemencies of the voyage by a dark cape and a wide brimmed hat, he entered the court-yard of his home thus lavishly dressed. There he embraced his mother. She gave him a scapulary, which our hero hung around his neck, as well as a bag containing black bread and goat cheese for the road. Old Orpí gave our hero a small leather bag filled with gold coins, which were to last him the entire school year in the city, and a letter of presentation for a friend of the family, Antoni Carmona, who lived in Barcelona.

"Mind you look after yerself, mine son," said his mother. "And forget ye not that desperation be the work of the Devil. Stay brave."

"Yes, Mother, I have not fear of falling, nor of being beaten & robbed, insulted & disrespected, spat upon or condemned. Faith and mirth for living shall be my weapons," he said, attempting to mount a horse gracefully, yet unfortunately tumbling off the other side of the saddle. "I shant let meself bee hoodwinked, Mother," he continued, leaping onto the horse again, this time with better luck. "The roads of life bee per-ilouse, but I promise, saintly mother, to return to Piera some day, made the very Duke of Life! Knight of Jesus Christ . . . ! Victor over Death . . . ! Lord of the Counsell of the Celestial State and Cabinet . . . ! Protector of the Innocents . . . ! Subject of the Armies of Our Lo—"

"Desist thy prattling, son," interrupted his mother, "and be on thy way alreddy."

With that maternal decree, our hero leaves Piera at day-break beneath a stagnant sun, before the rooster cockadoodle-dooed. He heads away from the church and the town castle, crossing the Guinovarda gully and riding along the highroad leading to the king's road between Solsona and Barcelona. But after five hours of galloping through the groves of a very dense wood, bridging pits and ravines, young Orpí found a fork in the road, a Pythagorean Y. Saddened by the impossibility of taking both paths, he was still for a while, overcome by Herculean doubt over which he should choose. Finally, or perhaps impartially would be a better choice of words, he took the left path, which was much less overgrown than the one on the right. Our dear readers will soon be able to judge for themselves whether he chose well. After some time at a trot, young Orpí came across a priest and a dwarf who were idling beside a civilized fire on which a pungent chicken broth was bubbling.

"May the Lord keep you and save you and laud be to Saint Anthony, guide of pilgrims!" was young Orpí's greeting, as he dismounted his horse and removed his hat.

"We'll see about dat," grumbled the dwarf. He had a tiny nose, a twisted back, and a bushy beard.

The priest, a thorny, disagreeable, and ecclesiastic figure, said, "On all the demons, arsworm, quit thy pessimissity and welcome this here gallant and marvellously dressed young man! How dost thou, boy! Whence come ye and wherefor art thee headed?"

"Mine name be Joan Orpí, of the Orpís of Piera, mine journey takes me to the capital, for to study at university. Mine illustrious parents (may God preserve them inn 'is glory) hath gaven me a bag rife with coin to keep me in vittles for what be left of the year."

When the priest and the dwarf heard that, they looked at each other and an evil gleam lit up their eyes, which seemed for an eternal instant to house ten thousand miniature hells.

"Be seated here besydes us, young Orpí, and honore us with thine presence at our meal," said the priest.

Our young hero sat between those two men and, accepting a wooden plate, served himself some food. While the three men wolfed it down, young Orpí kept staring at the dwarf.

"I reckon I knowe thee from somewhither. Didst thou perchance work in a circus that came through Piera many a twelvemonth ago?"

"Indeedy doo!" said the dwarf. "I did at one time but no longer, for that circus folded due to tha proprietor's naturall death by murder. Mine name art Triboulet Dvergar the Distasteful, descendant of the illustrious Triboulet family which worked in the Court of René I of Naples, Louis XII, and Francis I, and what did inspire the great Rabelais for his Pantagruel, at thy servyce."

"A right bizarre name, if ere I hearde one. And ye, Father, to which order are ye sworn?" asked Orpí.

"Betwixt *vois et mois*: the habit makes not the monk," the man said, opening his cape to reveal a collection of lethal weapons. "Antoni Roca,[14] at thy service. Sworn to nay religious order, rather I doth devote mine time to the lucrative taske of marauding."

"I cain't believe mine eyes . . . art thou the famous highwayman known as 'the furor of Catalonia'?" asked Orpí, awestruck. "I was quite convinc'd you were naught but a tall tale! What a thrill to discovere thee here all alone!"

"I be far from alone," said the fake priest. "I have a band of eighty menne with me."

"I behold no menne," said Orpí.

Hearing that, the fake priest whistled and from the bushes, as if by art of magic, appeared a band of men wearing shepherds' cloaks and carrying knives, daggers, blunderbusses, and crossbows with arrows in place.

---

14. Here we find the first chronological *décalage* that we must clarify right away: the bandit Antoni Roca did indeed exist, but was executed in 1546, whereas Joan Orpí was born in 1593. Therefore, such a meeting was impossible and, as a result, suspicion persists as to the authenticity of the entire document.

"These be myne menn: Underdogge (hello!), Brau (good day to you!), Pastoret (howdy . . . ), Langue d'Or, a professional jokester (ça va?), Matamoros (greetings!), Peu Leuger (Gascon, at your service), Denejat (hello!), Slim Jim ('cause I be trim!), and . . ."

The priest-bandit paused to think. There were so many men in his band that he couldn't remember all of their names, so many that he started to get them all mixed up, and even began to wonder if he wasn't losing his head.

"Fain to meet ye," said Orpí, waving kindly to them all.

After the meal, the priest lit up a pipe and said, "I knewe an Orpí, he wart a count complete with castle, a well-to-do man t'anks to the high tariffs he charged his serfs. A despot and a sciolist, twasnt helde in high regarde. Yet the worst waer when he established a *droit du seigneur*. So, by law, every virgin in the region were passed through bye his 'shotgun' afore marrying."

"Yoicks, wut a horriblis personage!" exclaimed Orpí.

"Forsooth," said the priest. "But it did came backe to bite him in the ass. Long story short: suffice ta saye that the count went above and beyond his duties. In essence, he stucked his you-know-what whence it nair belonged."

"And what happened thence?" asked our hero.

"Well, one fine day, the menn of the town ambuscaded the count as he strolled through the gardens beside the castle, and stoned him right to death. The lesson of the story being: don't wish for more than you already have. War that Orpí, perchance, thine kin?"

"Be content with your lot, thou art everso right, illustrious & most reverend Sir Roca," agreed Orpí. "But that Orpí of whom thou speaketh was no kin of mine; this is the first ere I heard that story, and all those of mine house, by my troth, are honorable persons."

"Bully for you. Regrettably, these are harde times," said the fake priest. "Being a bandit taint all it were cracked up to be. Far too much competition, ya knoweth?"

"Of course, of course," stated Orpí, knowingly.

"As ye shall seeth anon, I'm an honorable person too . . . it's just that ere so oft I needeth to make some bank."

"Of that I am holy convinc'd!" said our hero, who, satisfied by the soup, settled his butt cheeks down onto the parched grass of the forest floor.

"And by mine word I'd like naught more than to bade thee continue along thy road without a hitch. Needless to quoth!"

"Thank thee, thank thee. Thou art awlfully kind, Sir Roca."

"But now understand this: I must feed my men and clearly thou art transporting more coins than any single man needs. As such," said the priest, pulling out a harquebus[15] from his baldric, "as we sayeth in these parts: your money or your life, if ye be so kindly."

"What? Mine God! But . . . but wherefor?" exclaimed our hero, with a start.

"Because I sayeth such," ordered the fake clergyman.

Young Orpí was not a man of arms, and when he pulled his dagger from his belt the dwarf was able to take it from his trembling hands without him even realizing. Our hero put up no resistance after that, but did emit a ton of very real swearwords, moans, and tears, as he handed over the sack of gold coins, clink-clanking inside the little leather bag, to the fake priest.

"We oughten kill him," said one of the thieves. "He's awrfully loud."

"No," replied Triboulet the Dwarf. "We shall leave him live, as we art pinchers but not murder'rs. However, we shall hold on to his equestrian vehicle."

---

15. *i.e.* Gun of the period.

In the face of the dwarf's decorum, young Orpí came to the conclusion that there were bad people and worse people in these worlds of God. But nevertheless, he grumbled, "And what shall become of me, oh woe is mee, with neir money nor steed?"

"I shall give thee a mickle of counsell, completely on the house and only slightly theological," responded the fake clergyman. "Do what everyone doeth and hath done in ev'ry single period of history: Steal all thou canst, wise up, do not steppeth on a crack, and get a damn clue! And let us hit the road anon, it's late and threatens to rain!"

That said, the highwaymen gathered up their pots and took Orpí's horse, then disappeared into the depths of the wood.

"Blast mine luck!" complained our young hero, as he began to walk through the wood without looking backward, since returning home was not an option. What would his family and the people of Piera think if they knew he'd let himself get robbed like a greenhorn? He preferred the uncertainty of the road ahead than the shame of having to backtrack. And thus, in that sorry state, young Orpí continued on, through the darkness of the heart of the wood, until . . . until the next Chapter.

## Chapter *VIII*

In which young Orpí wanders through the woods,
finds a clutch of horny witches, and goes to hell

The uncertainty of the road ahead, when one has no concrete destination in sight, stretches the minutes into hours and tribulations into eternal torment. And as this story of young Orpí lost in the wood is ever so sui generis, we shall tell it in the following manner. During those next few days our hero slept hidden amid the brush. Sometimes he took the advice of the vicar-highwayman and stole the occasional hen from a farm before slipping back into the wood, but generally he was hungry, cold, and altogether melancholy. One night as our hero walked chip-chop-chip through the overgrown sward, he heard rustling noises beside a river. As he approached a clearing beswirled in fog, he discovered ten naked women dancing around a bonfire: pastoral devil worshippers celebrating a black mass.

The assembled women—most of them old, poor, and soft in the head—were smearing unguents all over their faces, anuses, and pustulous vaginas, as they kissed each other lasciviously, and sang out in Frog: ♪ 𝔍'𝔞𝔡𝔬𝔯𝔢, 𝔐𝔬𝔫𝔰𝔦𝔢𝔲𝔯 𝔏𝔲𝔠𝔦𝔣𝔢𝔯 ♫

Young Orpí, singularly innocent, went over to them in search of aid.

"Good even, ladies. Ye wouldn't happen to haveth a bit of bread fer a hungerly soul? As mine luck would hath it, dread highwaymen pilfred mine coin & steed and anon I nar starving right to deathe."

Seeing him, the witches took him for the sabbatic goat they'd been invoking since dusk with their black magic and, without hesitation, they pounced on him like a herd of ravenous wolves, ripping off his clothes and preparing to rape him. One sucked on his nipple, another stuck a rough tongue in his mouth, yet another tore his underwear, and there was even one who drank the blood of a dead rabbit while smearing it all over herself. As they raped him, the sodomitic enchantresses made our hero drink a potation containing old women's molars, thornapple, belladonna, fly agaric, cascall, old hen schmaltz, and arsenic. Those herbs, rich in an alkaloid called atropine, acted quickly on the nervous system of our young hero who suddenly saw a crater in the earth open before him, as the sky darkened with shadows. Poor Orpí fell into a very pungent, sticky place. Everything stank of roasted flesh and all that was heard were souls shrieking in eternal pain, brought about by a perpetual flame that burnt their impious asses. One of the many souls there, by the name of Pere Portes,[16] approached our hero and spoke to him.

"Milord, I seeth that thou art a newcomer to the Kingdom of Hell."

"Helle? Holy Mother of the Vyrgin of Seven Sorrowes! I reckont I war somewhitherelse!" exclaimed young Orpí.

"Ssshh! You can't invoke saints & virgins down hither! And as fore thy location, in his *Aeneid*, Virgil placeth it in the Sybil's cave. The *Orlando Furioso* sayeth it be beside the source of the Nile. Others doth claime its entrance be at Bouchet Lake, in Auvergne, or Lake Avernus, or at the Gole dell'Infernaccio in Italy. Others ween it in the Alt Urgell, in the town of Segur and the Baix Empordà or the Torrent de l'Infern in Tavèrnoles, just ta nameth some local places; Mount Etna be a hellmouth, too. I could verily bee hither alle the day long listething names till blood cometh out mine nose."

"Thank ye for thee unnecessary inf'rmation," said Orpí. "I caint reckon iff I done kicked the bucket or wut, but I doth not like this lodging in the slightest. And it's too muggy."

"Exactly, exactly! I totally concurr. Methinks they shouldst pop the doores (wherever they be), and aire this place out. Helle is verily an academy of heat."

As the two men walked amid the fires and scorched souls, they greeted Gilgamesh, Seth, Odysseus, Hermes Psychopompos, Virgil in Hell, and a bunch more illustrious figures, all surrounded—poor things—by flies, excrement, and flames. Then, continuing along on their infernal Grand Tour, Pere Portes showed Orpí some rooms equipped with all of the latest generation of torture instruments and filled with souls shrieking in perpetual suffering. Then Satan himself materialized before

16. A famous character in Catalan literature, from the anonymous work *The Strange Case of a Man Named Pere Portes, from the Town of Tordera, Who Entered and Exited Hell,* written in the year 1611.

the two men. He was a hideously ugly being, all reddish and covered in spikes, accompanied by an entourage of incubuses and succubi.

"Verily well, I see we hast a new guest at our hallowe home!"

"Thou art mistaken," said Orpí. "For I'm not meant to beest here."

"That's what they all say!" bellowed the Devil. "Thou dost not repent thine sins, henstealer? For if ye plan on accreting up worldly riches & accolades, then this hither shall surely bee yern final stoppe."

"How canst I repent, when I've committ'd no sinne?" responded Orpí. "And seeing ath I be in charge of mine own selfsame, therewithal I'll beest leaving on mine own two feet withoute running it by anyone."

"Aha, crappy peasant, bethinks thee escape soe easy?" roared the Beast. "I'll lash thee so harde thou shallt ne'er feeleth thine posterior again, and then thou shalt knowe who's in charge of thine own selfsame."

Just as the Prince of Darkness was about to stick his pitchfork into him from behind, young Orpí ducked out of the way and, with a quick goodbye to ole Pere Portes, he slipped like a hare through the tortured souls. The Devil was close on his trail until, there in the distance, Orpí saw a light and the light turned out to be the mouth of a cave, a yawning mouth amid the rocks. And through it, our hero managed to escape certain eternal damnation amidst the fires of hell.

## Chapter IX

In which young Orpí is nigh nearly beat to death,
first by some entirely nasty priests
and then by a frenzied ascetic

When young Orpí awoke from that subterranean reverie, he
heard a rowdy group of pilgrims coming along the forest road
playing handbells. When he realized he was nude, he covered
his pudenda with dried leaves. Following the clip-clop clip-
clop of the horses, our hero discovered a two-wheeled cart
in the middle of the road, driven by three vicars who were
headed to the city. Beside the cart walked two young aspiring
priests, one dressed as a cretin and the other a numbskull,
complete with dunce caps, who were shaking bells. And a
little farther on were two penitents accompanied by two friars who whipped their backs. And all these men of God were
drinking wine and singing pious songs to praise their Lord:

> ♪ Lift your cups, brethren, let us toast ♫
> fill our cups to the brim
> mull our wine, drink it in
> we'll warme ye right up to the holee ghost

𝔒𝔥, 𝔱𝔥𝔢𝔶 𝔠𝔞𝔩𝔩𝔢 𝔲𝔰 𝔱𝔥𝔢 𝔠𝔬𝔲𝔫𝔠𝔦𝔩 𝔅𝔯𝔬𝔱𝔥𝔢𝔯𝔥𝔬𝔬𝔡
𝔴𝔢'𝔯𝔢 𝔠𝔬𝔫𝔟𝔦𝔫𝔠𝔢'𝔡 𝔦𝔱 𝔟𝔢 𝔫𝔬𝔱 𝔰𝔲𝔭𝔢𝔯𝔰𝔱𝔦𝔱𝔦𝔬𝔫

𝔣𝔬𝔯 𝔴𝔢 𝔡𝔞𝔯𝔢 𝔱𝔬 𝔡𝔢𝔠𝔩𝔞𝔯𝔢 𝔱𝔥𝔞𝔱 𝔊𝔬𝔡𝔡 𝔟𝔢 𝔤𝔬𝔬𝔡
𝔥𝔢'𝔰 𝔡𝔦𝔯𝔢𝔠𝔱𝔬𝔯 𝔬𝔣 𝔬𝔲𝔯 𝔥𝔬𝔩𝔶 𝔦𝔫𝔮𝔲𝔦𝔰𝔦𝔱𝔦𝔬𝔫 . . .

𝔥𝔢 𝔠𝔬𝔪𝔪𝔞𝔫𝔡𝔢𝔱𝔥 𝔴𝔢 𝔡𝔬𝔱𝔥 𝔡𝔯𝔢𝔰𝔰𝔢 𝔦𝔫 𝔰𝔞𝔠𝔨𝔰
𝔶𝔢𝔞, 𝔱𝔥𝔢𝔶 𝔠𝔞𝔩𝔩 𝔲𝔰 𝔱𝔥𝔢 𝔠𝔬𝔲𝔫𝔠𝔦𝔩 𝔅𝔯𝔬𝔱𝔥𝔢𝔯𝔥𝔬𝔬𝔡
𝔶𝔢 𝔨𝔫𝔬𝔴𝔢 𝔲𝔰 𝔟𝔶 𝔬𝔲𝔯 𝔣𝔞𝔪𝔢 𝔬𝔯 𝔴𝔢𝔩𝔩 𝔶𝔢 𝔰𝔥𝔬𝔲𝔩𝔡
♪ . . . 𝔞𝔫𝔡 𝔞 𝔴𝔬𝔯𝔡 𝔱𝔬 𝔱𝔥𝔢 𝔰𝔦𝔫𝔫𝔢𝔯𝔰: 𝔴𝔞𝔱𝔠𝔥 𝔱𝔥𝔶𝔫𝔢 𝔟𝔞𝔠𝔨𝔰! ♫

One of the vicars started dancing an entirely lay fandango with the two sacerdotal aspirants. Upon hearing the festive music, they promptly hitched up the skirts of their habits to shake legs so white and covered in varicose veins that even God shielded his eyes.

Young Orpí made sure this time that they were true clergy and not highwaymen in disguise and then—despite the risk of catching his death of a cold—went out into the very middle of the road, lifted his hands, and yelled, "Halt, for the love of God!"

"*Vade retro, Satana!* Who art thou?" shouted one of the vicars. "And why goest thou nude through these worlds of God verily like an Adam without an Eve?"

"Gentlemen, be not misled by mine unfortunate appearance," said Orpí, whimpering. "For I be but a young student robbed of mine steed and maravedis, and violated by witchkind. I demand succor on compassionate grounds, for I be heavily burden'd . . . !"

When he described all the vexations he'd suffered, the three pious vicars, who'd been drinking wine for hours and had just witnessed an execution by the Inquisition, quickly came to the conclusion that that young ne'er-do-well was actually possessed by the very Devil himself because of his terrible stench.[17] The clergymen got out of the cart and began to chase him through the forest howling, "*Horror diabolicus! Death to the Antichrist . . . !*" and throwing rocks and sticks for a good long while. Since they were not able to catch him, the vicars returned to the cart to drink even more and continue mocking the two costumed novitiates.

Saddened by the vicars' response and wounded by the rocks they'd thrown at his head, young Orpí wandered like a specter through the wood for a week, nearly spent and covered in scabs of dried blood. His clothes were so tattered and his face so dirty that he looked like a wild beast, and that whole aesthetic question made him so sad that he wanted to die. But without coin or steed he had no possibilities of improving his appearance, and he was plagued by hunger. Luckily, wandering through the wood, he came across an old hermit with a long white beard, originally from Germany, who had been a soldier in Flanders and was now living a true life of spiritual retreat in the forests of Catalonia. The hermit invited him into his humble cabin, which he'd built with his own hands, and where he lived in holy solitude. There he cured our hero's wounds with St. John's wort. It so happened that the ascetic was an expert in humors[18] and remedies: he had elixirs for toothaches and rheumatism, he could heal smallpox, fevers, vomits, adolescent acne, chillblains, fistulas, hemmorhoids, myopia, glaucoma, scabies, and mange. He could even set your colon back in place if it was slipping out your back end.

Orpí explained all his misfortunes as the ascetic listened absently.

---

17. *i.e.* It was believed that smelling bad was a sign of demonic possession.

18. *i.e.* According to classical physiology the human body is comprised of four humors: phlegm, blood, yellow bile, and black bile, associated with phlegmatic, sanguine, aggressive, and melancholic natures, respectively.

". . . and I war totes nekkid ere the flames begunne and the earth opened up and I spyed Lucifer and errebody and all at one I felle faint and all becamme black and when I didst awoken from mine voyage down into Hell, well, as I said, I founde meeself in the middle of the greenwood just as my mother brought me into this world (I blush just thinking about it!) and that war when I heard the cart of the vicars what wanted to slay me because they were convinced I was the Devil. By the way, what sect be thou a member of?" asked Orpí while the hermit cured his wounds. "The Ionic, the Cynic, the Pyrrhonic, the Sceptic, the Epicurean, the Eclectic?"

"I am simply *Sklave*[19] to the Author of Life, yon dead and crucified."

After healing our hero, the hermit, who was a man of few words, invited him to stay in his humble shack for a few days to recover. Young Orpí gratefully accepted the offer. He dressed in a sack like his host and teacher, and imitated everything that holy man did. The only meal of the day was a soup made out of roots, and that vegan diet led young Orpí to a kind of spiritual sanctity he'd never before experienced. Our hero stopped washing, let his beard grow out and, in a matter of weeks, looked entirely undomesticated. He felt filled with joy, and quickly assumed the life of a mystic of the forest. He would pray alongside the ascetic every morning, afternoon, and evening before a cross that hung in the cabin.

However, one fine day, when his body had grown accustomed to that diet of rhizomes, young Orpí's guts began to move. He let out a burp and some little farts followed by a liquid bowel movement so noisy and rank that all the birds in the forest took flight at once. And all because of that raw food diet, which had literally destroyed his stomach and sphincter,

---

19. "Slave" in German.

his nether regions now were all bescumbered. The sound of his flatulence and the stench of his excrements alarmed the vegan hermit so much that he jabbered, "*Um Gottes willen!* Canst thou notte goe to the *Toilette* & aire out yer backeside, ya swine?"

Having said that, the hermit then reached the harsh conclusion that so much flatulence could truly only be the work of the Devil. He grabbed the bread knife and prepared to eviscerate our hero in order to get the Evil out of him. Since he couldn't reach the other end of the table where Orpí was, he began to pursue him, running circles first left, then right. "Comme hither, I'll get the deville out of you!" ordered the ascetic. "I didnst mean it!" bawled Orpí, "I verily swear I have no suche demon in mine body . . . it's all the fault of eating soo many roots!" he said, his haunches all dirty as he ran round the table, until he got up on a stool and leapt out of the shack through a back window. As soon as he got up, the hermit appeared behind him again, brandishing the knife, "Thee shant escape mee . . . *Schwein!*[20]" After running like a hare for a while, his ass smarting from the gas and excrements that continued torrentially from his posterior, young Orpí managed to lose sight of the hermit, escape the forest, and run like a decapitated turkey for a long hour through the brambles. It was then another hour in the dark through a series of marshes before he came up against an enormous rock: that rock was part of a wall, and that wall surrounded the city of Barcelona.

## Chapter X

In which young Orpí tries to enter Barcelona
but is denied everyhow and is almost
devoured by the plague-stricken

Young Orpí did what everyone does when trying to enter a
civilized place: he searched for a door. When he found one,
it had two *guàrdies del morbo*[21] armed with harquebusses
blocking his way in.

"Not so fast. *Quo vadis*?" said one of the guards.

"Joan Orpí del Pou, from Piera. I've cometh hither to study
at the university."

"Poppycorks!" said the other, kicking him in the ass.
"Studying be for those with wage, or for priests, not foreign
vagabonds."

"Aye," added the first guard. "Besides, haven't thee heard
that there are epidemics everywhere? As they say in Girona:
*Gloriós Sant Roc, guardeu-nos de pesta i de foch.*[22] And now,
avaunt, for thine odour be unendurable."

---

21. *i.e.* Guards that kept infectious diseases from entering the city.

22. Glorious Sant Roc, pray let us not expire protect us from the plague and
fire.

Young Orpí, whose clothes (really just a sack) were indeed still covered in shit, was easily confused for a plague victim. He moved away from the door and watched as a ton of elegant people came in and out: hunters on horseback with wolf-hide coats, soldiers armed with long rifles, muskets, pikes, cutlasses, and halberds, vendors pushing carts of fruit, and hideously homely Sisters of Charity. Saddened at not being able to enter the city, our hero approached a group of tramps by the wall who were grilling an obese black rat, in a cloud of horrific pestilence.

"Good tidings, godly folk. Couldst ye tell me how I canst enter the city and not be mistooken for a plague victim?"

It should have been abundantly clear to him that those people were not normal folk. Yet, in fact, unbeknownst to Orpí, he'd ended up in the middle of a group of lepers whose black bile was making all the humors of their bodies emerge in horrible secretions of blood and pus. Both the men and the women were gangling and bearded, and each missing at least one limb. This one an arm, the other a nose, another's eye hung from its optic nerve, and one was just about to expire, still standing up. They shared everything, in a true brotherhood of scabies, lice, and purulence. A man with his face deformed by fatal tumors, his body covered in infected scabs and with two gangrenous stumps for arms, came over to our hero and began to kick him with shoes full of holes. Young Orpí kept him at a distance with a stick. In the commotion, a circle of bloodshot eyes and deformed bodies formed around our hero, staring at him suspiciously. The plague victims, seeing him so young and tender, approached slowly with the innocent intention of eating him alive (despite his lower half being covered in shit), but our hero, agile as a cat, slipped through the legs of the crowd, leaving them disappointed. Driven mad by their hunger, they pounced upon the most cadaveric of their fold, to tear out his cheeks (which were, according to some, a real delicacy). The sacrificed tramp fell to the ground squealing like an eviscerated pig and the others leapt upon him, devouring the poor wretch, every last bit, even his testicles.

A bit further on, young Orpí saw a series of men and women impaled on pitchforks and others swinging from the trees in iron cages that were usually reserved for insolent children, disobedient soldiers, thieves, and vagabonds. Some of them were dead, others were still stammering.

"Esteemed criminals," began Orpí. "Wouldst ye bee so kinde as to tell me how I might enter the city?"

"Ooyyyy, dat's *très difficile*," said one.

"Specially if thine purse clinketh not," specified a second.

"As they sayeth in olde Castille: ¡*dineros son calidad!*" exclaimed a third.

Young Orpí, sat beneath a tree, depressed. He didn't know what to do and wanted only to cry. Just when he was about to give up and return to the forest to live like a wild beast, someone called to him.

"Pssst! Pssst! Joan Orpí de Piera! Over here!"

He turned and noticed the same dwarf with pierced ears who had robbed him in the wood a week earlier, calling to him from a cart, waving with his hat. He was richly decked out in a black velvet shirt with sleeves embroidered in white; a gold embroidered vestaloon, a hat with a duck-feather plume, and a large gold chain hanging from his neck, crowned with a precious stone. There was definitely a slight patina of distinguished nobility in that there small personage.

"Triboulet!" exclaimed Orpí, picking up a rock to get some payback with the dwarf. "Thee damn crook, behold what thee've done to me . . . I shalt kill you!"

"One moment!" The dwarf stopped him. "Recall yon I saved your life. Tweren't for me, those highwaymen would have surely finished thee off."

"Alright. We'll leave the subject of murdering thee for anon then."

"What's more, I must confess I nowe longer live in penury. Turns out I did leave behind the life o'the highwayman and reinvent myself. Since they put mine boss Antoni Roca in the clink, I did pick up the dice and start to play craps professionally, and God knoweth I was born for it: I bee now filthily rich and liveth quite the noblemans life!"

"Isn't that lucky for you, halfman," said young Orpí. "But that doesn't make me want to breaketh thine neck any less."

"Listen, Orpí, let us not be cross wid each other, naught goode shall nair come of it. Behold thine owne luck: I be not only rich, but a good person. I shall retornne the maravedis I didst nick from you, plus interest. And I'll even throw in this: ask for any one thing and I shall grant it."

"I wish to enter the city."

"Wish granted. Hoppeth onto mine coach."

And thus Orpí, at the ripe old age of sixteen, entered Barcelona hidden in the back of Triboulet's carriage, and there witnessed what occurs in the next Chapter.

## Chapter XI

In which young Orpí sees the city of Barcelona
for the first time and then engages in his first
duel to the death

Once he had made it through the walls bedecked with flags,
gleaming pennants, and multicolored oriflammes, young Orpí
stuck his head out of the coach, which was moving slowly
along barely lit streets, and observed the roar of the metropo-
lis. As they drew closer to the Cathedral, the streets grew
more lively and filled with people: illustrious ladies hidden
behind the curtains of small carriages led by dapper pages,
knights sporting shields, haughty royal guards armed with
musketoons and advancing to the beat of a drum's forward
march, Frenchmen, Hungarians, Milanese, Pythagoreans,
Peripatetics, magicians, lunatics, dukes and counts, plebians
and courtesans, donkeys shooing away flies, beggars begging and dogs scratching their mange. All that and more, and
young Orpí took everything in as if he were discovering an
unknown continent.

Triboulet the Dwarf offered our hero a room at the inn
where he was to stay that night, and Orpí accepted. Once they
were washed and dressed in new clothes, they both went out

for a walk, straight up Carrer Nazaret to Carrer del Carme and through the Porta Ferrissa. The poorly laid-out streets of Barcelona were filled with knaves, bald women hiding in doorways, soldiers armed to the teeth and itching to kill and pulverize, rickety young squires, pulpiters predicting the imminent apocalypse atop rotten wooden crates, contorted old men splashing in the mud with sows, sailors flirting with prostitutes, and orphans stealing everything in reach and then sitting on the docks to look at the caravelles moored in the port and skip stones. Then young Orpí and Triboulet the Dwarf passed through the Plaça del Blat,[23] where they watched the market vendors burdened down with work and misery, and saw alleys filled with urine and animal blood from the furriers' guild. A cloud of tavern inebriation and fried fish floated in the dense, suffocating air, making our hero want to vomit. Beggars deformed by disease dragged themselves along and were spit on by porters hauling carts filled with sacks. Everything spun, distracting and stunning young Orpí amid the constant muddle of shouting whores, coachmen spurring on horses, disoriented newcomers, servants bustling about on impossible errands, Trinitarian friars trotting to church, argumentative commentators passionately yakking about the latest news of the Court, domestics smoking at windows, poor widows asking for alms, vendors squawking out the latest deals in a thousand different languages, folks outside the city walls plotting thwarted revolutions, and tightrope walkers and acrobats charming their spectators.

"Bade us go to the Plaça del Rei to visit a friend of mine," said Triboulet the Dwarf.

The friend turned out to be an old comrade, the famously fake vicar Antoni Roca, who had been captured by the

---

23.  *i.e.* Today the Plaça de l'Àngel.

authorities and was now being executed for his crimes. The prisoner was transported, half naked, on a small donkey along Carrer de la Bòria, where a considerable throng was shrieking "death to the highwayman" and throwing feces on him as he passed. The bandit endured that public shaming stoically, dignified as a duke. Once they reached the Plaça del Rei, they set up a platform and placed the prisoner on it. Then the executioner arrived. First he burned Roca's skin with red-hot tongs. That pleased the mob, who roared fervidly as the whole plaza filled with the stomach-churning stench of roasted flesh. Then the executioner took a hammer to his arms and legs, breaking them with catacracks that echoed throughout the plaza (ovation from the crowd). Then he cut off Roca's hands, and liters of blood splattered those sitting in the front row (more ovations). Then he ripped out his eyes, which he threw to the plebes, since some collected them recreationally. Finally, Roca's throat was slit and he was beheaded as the crowd exploded with joy. Then the former highwayman was quartered with a hatchet, his body parts hung in different places throughout the city, and his head placed at the main gate into Barcelona. Seeing his fate, a clergyman named Pere Giberga[24] intoned a popular ballad:

♪ With his pair of sizzling plyers ♫
Z'executioner didst relish
Thus and so with his screwdrivers
Yea, the dude war oh so zealous

Then he wipt out a hot poker
ye malefactors heed this day,

---

24. *i.e.* Popular poet of the period who, in 1544, published *Cobles novament fetes contra tots los delats de Catalunya sequaços de Antoni Roca*.

"Hear ye, hear ye! Tremendilious! Exquisite! Truly a sight to see!" exclaimed Triboulet the Dwarf. "That there be what I do call a death wit' erry honour!"

"I doth deem said expiration abominable," said young Orpí, vomiting on the street after all that human butchery.

"Don't be such a priss! Come now, bade us returnne to the inn and rest."

As they were passing beneath the window of a home, someone threw out the day's trash (excrement, chicken bones, banana peels, and watermelon rinds) and our hero was once again soiled from head to toe, so much so that he was forced to wash yet again. That very night young Orpí went with Triboulet to a renowned casino in the city, where the crème de la crème of the local villains, prostitutes, artillery-men, and bohemians gathered. While the dwarf bet more and more bags of gold, our hero observed it all from a distance. Finally, five hours later, someone shouted, "Damne ye cozeners! That there gnome be bamboozling!"

"My lordling, that accusation be not reasonably proven," said the dwarf. "Furthermore, I may be short, but from where I doth stand thou art ugly as a toade and thine breath stinketh most foul."

And chase him they did, indeed, but they couldn't catch him. With Triboulet vanished, young Orpí found himself alone as could be against that gang of furious gamblers who wanted back the money the dwarf had swindled from them.

"Mine pockets be emptee, kindly sirs. And now, if ye will excuse me, *adieu*."

"Nay, nay we shant excuse you," said the chief victim, grabbing Orpí by the arm. "As thou refuseth to cough up the coin, I, Ernest of the Cirrhotic Liver, son of Bernat of the Cirrhotic Liver, grandson of Prudenci of the Cirrhotic Liver, great-grandson of . . . etc., doth declare mine honor besmirched. I hitherforth demand full & complete legal recompense from a juridical perspective, *ipso facto*."

"I knowe not what thou meanst," said young Orpí, linguistically befuddled.

"I meanst a duel with swords, right here, right now."

"But I hath no sword!"

"No problemo," said Ernest of the Cirrhotic Liver, grabbing one of his friends' weapons. "Here, now thou doest."

And thus our hero found himself, through no fault of his own, in his first official duel. The circle of people around him were shouting "death to the huckster" and "kill 'em" and "slit 'is scrawny throat" and things of that nature. Young Orpí couldn't see how he could possibly get out of there alive and his heart began to beat faster and faster. Cirrhotic Liver leapt toward our hero, leading with his sword. Orpí, petrified, knelt down fearing the worst. But as luck would have it, his sword was facing out and pierced his adversary's thigh like a spear.

"Ay, ay, ay . . . ! Lorde holp me, I'm dying . . . !" shouted the villain.

But the villain didn't die. Young Orpí himself, along with some others, helped carry him home, where a doctor dressed and cured his wound.

"So, all's fair in love and craps? Bee we even lyke Steven?" asked our hero later.

"Even Steven," said Ernest, "for at the morrow I hath an entrance exam at university and I shant have time to killeth thee anywise."

Orpí, flabbergasted, said, "What a fit of happenstance, I hath come to Barcelona to study at the university, too! I wish to becomme a civil attorney."

"Heavens to murgatroyd! I too wish to be an attorney, albeit a canonical one!"

And that was how Joan Orpí made his first friend in the city. When our hero returned to the inn that night, he found no trace of Triboulet the Dwarf. The next morning, he had gathered up his things and was just about to leave, when he was violently stopped by a hand. That hand belonged to an arm and that arm was the property of the hostel's owner, a man named Guiseppe Gorgonzolla, who had yet to be paid for the accomodations.

"I thought mine friend hath already paid thee," said our hero.

"*Cosa dici? Quell'amico?*"

"The dwarf I did arrive with yesterday."

"*Non inventare storie perché non ho visto nessun nano,*" stated the innkeeper, boiling with rage. "*Escaguitxa come tutti gli altri o chiamo a la polizia, mafioso!*"

Young Orpí patted his pockets, which were entirely empty.

"I hath suffer'd excoriation by highwaymen! Defilement by hags! Pursucquition by psychopathic friars! And just yesterd'y I near nigh perished in a duel!" he whimpered in his defense.

"*Bugiardo! Malandrino!*" bellowed the innkeeper, holding him back as he called for the militia of the Mossos de l'Esquadra.[25]

---

25. The (peninsular) Catalan regional police force, originally dating back to the eighteenth century during the reign of Philip V.

Our hero was arrested, despite resisting with all his might, and what happened next will be explained *tout de suite* in the very next Chapter.

## Chapter XII

### In which young Orpí is locked up in jail
### and meets some rather odd characters

Our poor hero was thrown like a sack of potatoes into a dark, smooth, ugly, useless, nasty, and poorly ventilated cell, with two other prisoners.

"Fine folk, why for art ye locked up here?" asked Orpí, lifting his head off the ground.

"Point of fact: we be harden'd criminals," said one of them, a man with a very long beard that hung off his face like a curtain covered in spider webs. He smiled, revealing teeth yellowed by tartar and desperation, in equal parts.

"Speaketh for thineself," said the other prisoner, who was dressed as a woman. "For mine presence here be a miscalculation. I am none othere than Queen Cleopatra. Ergo, I'm innocent."

"Yeah, sure," added the first. "And I be Charles V . . . tommyrot! All and sundry here shall be condemned according to Title XXXI Law of Registry VII, what reads:

to the pillory ( . . . ) in the sunn, smear'd with honey to be devour'd by flies or whipp'd or openly branded with hot irons to teach a publick lesson to the pilferers & purloiners with lash wounds or other means so they may suffer anguish and shame.

Upon hearing that, our hero broke down in tears, defeated by his ill luck.

"Cryeth not, young leman," said the prisoner in drag, whom we shall call Cleopatra from here on out, to avoid misunderstandings.

"Fear not, kid, I've here the solution to our problems," said the other, stripping down to reveal decrepit skin covered in hundreds of tattoos.

"Zoinks, what a noisome bod," complained Cleopatra, in an effeminate tone.

(S)he and Orpí approached to get a better look at all those permanently inked characters covering the bearded man's body.

"They appear verily like hieroglyphics," murmured Orpí, trying to decipher them. "Beyon that, I be harde pressed to unriddle 'em."

"A month hence, anoth'r prisoner did make these drawings," said the bearded man. "From mine chest to mine pinky toe, he didst draw an unexpurgated scheme for abscontion from this here prison."

"Impressive!" exclaimed Cleopatra.

"But if thou hatheth a map, why hath thee yet to abscond?" asked our hero.

"I canst see mine back or mine asse without snapping my spine . . . that's why!" exclaimed the bearded man. "Now, if thou & Cleopatra would do mee the indulgence of reading mine body, all three of us could vamoose this dark, smooth, ugly, useless, nasty, and poorly ventilated place. Shall we?"

Our hero and Cleopatra looked at each other for a few moments, their eyes questioning, and then nodded without needing to say a word. They started with his chest. Moving aside the old man's beard, a drawing showed a cell with a single floor tile that opened. So all three men started to search for a loose slab. A few minutes later, Cleopatra exclaimed, "Come hithere, post-haste!"

Between the three of them they managed to move the heavy stone and to their surprise they discovered a small blackened tunnel, which they hid inside. After crawling on all fours for a short time, they emerged in something like a laundry room. No, that was exactly what it was: a laundry room. Our hero and Cleopatra looked at Bewhiskered's next tattoo, inscribed on his ribs.

"Curiouser," said young Orpí. "The inking depictes thee exact place whence we now befindeth ourselves and, conform with these indications, we must openne a weeny window to our right."

And so they did. They opened the window to their right and went into an interior courtyard filled with garbage that they trotted right through. Following the directions on the tattoo located on his triceps and latissimus dorsi, they turned left and then right until they reached a gallery at the extreme south of the prison. Once there, Cleopatra and Orpí again took a look at Bewhiskered's body. On his gluteus maximus the tattoo showed a shortcut through the prisoners' yard. So the three crossed it, from one end to another, waving to all the inmates who were playing dice or sunbathing, until they reached a small door, off limits to prisoners, which they nonchalantly opened. That door led to an office where they encountered the jail's bureaucracy, but few of the bureaucrats lifted their heads from their classified papers and, when they did, they didn't show the slightest interest in the fugitives. Having crossed that area, Cleopatra and Orpí went back to Bewhiskered's tattoos. The drawing continued along his sartorial muscle and quadriceps femoris and seemed to be depicting a leap. So they leapt over the wall in front of them, without any of the soldiers on guard seemingly interested in their fugitive affairs. After leaping over the wall, now outside the prison, the three inmates found themselves on a large esplanade. The tattoo at the height of Bewhiskered's biceps femoris directed sprinting to the nearest forest, and in that manner all three absconders pranced along until they found themselves amid magnificent trees where birds happily trilled.

After a few seconds of catching their breath, they continued following the instructions found on Bewhiskered's tibialis anterior, which proposed skirting the forest, descending to a nearby stream, and entering a sewage pipe. The three of them followed these directions without a single moment of hesitation and, after checking the tattoos, they advanced through a long tunnel, feeling their way until they saw a light at the end. When they reached the surface, they found a wall, which they gamely jumped over; then they went through a room where a few workers had their bespectacled eyes fixed ocularly on piles of papers on their desks; then they crossed a courtyard filled with men who, strangely, waved at them; then they went down through a gallery, then around an interior courtyard; then they entered a small window into a laundry room, where there was an open floor tile. They descended through it, finally crawling through a tunnel until they resurfaced in a room lined with bars.

"Tis right bizarre," said Bewhiskered. "I hath the sensation I've been heere before."

"I understandeth not a thing. Heeding the tattoos, we did everything right," said Cleopatra.

"Zounds!" exclaimed young Orpí. "We art back whence we did start! We be back in our cell!"

Indeed they were. The tattoos on Bewhiskered were actually part of an elaborate prank among the wardens. One, pretending to be a prisoner, had tattooed the old man with a round-trip route. The three buffoons had managed to escape the prison and return without realizing it, while the guards on every shift had a hearty laugh at what idiots the three jailbirds were. And that was how, on that day, young Orpí learned not to do what everyone else does, but rather the exact opposite, and he fell asleep in that dark, smooth, ugly, useless, nasty, and poorly ventilated cell.

## Chapter XIII

In which diligent Joan Orpí begins his university studies
and comes to realize that a fine sword
is a good as a fine brain

The next day, young Orpí was released from prison, after his
bail was paid by the nobleman whom his father had assigned
as his guardian: Antoni Carmona, an affluent, young hunch-
back. After Carmona helped Orpí get installed in the pigeon
loft in his house, he accompanied him to the University of
Barcelona, making a tour of the city. They passed the seaside
wall and the Sant Ramon bastion where, from the watchtower, guards kept lookout for attacks from Turkish pirates.
They passed the fishermen's market filled with pungent salted
sardines, smoked fish, dried cod; they passed more stands
where they sold salted pork leg, mutton and lamb, veal and
sheep; they passed baskets filled with grapes, calabashes of
weak wine, bundles of hay, barrel hoops, and millstones. Then
they walked to the Shipyards, where they could watch galleys
small and large being built with the cheap labor of hundreds
of prisoners.

"More boats be made in Katalonia than in any oth'r kingdom or province on the Peninsula," said Carmona, scratching his hump, "but the Kingdom of Castille hath banned our trading with The Indies. If thou don't want to end up sentenced to the galley ships like these men, or in the lockup again, thou best study thine darnedest."

"By all means," agreed young Orpí, marveling at the architecture of those urban buildings and the market in the plaza by the port, with its stands and awnings set up to keep the midday sun off the fresh tomatoes, peppers, eggplants, and parsley.

Next they passed the Torre de les Puces[26] and both men walked up the Rambla dels Estudis[27], alongside Capuchin and Carthusian monks, gentlemen, knights, and garlanded damsels who stopped to look at the shops selling kitchen supplies, silverware, tapestries, and sweetmeats. They also saw some doctors wearing beak-like masks to prevent contagion from the plague-stricken they cared for at the Hospital de la Santa Creu, where consumptives and asthmatics shared scabies, viruses, and other pestilence. Orpí and Lord Carmona arrived at Barcelona's Studium Generale. The two-story university building, located at the top of the Rambla was adorned with the crest of Charles V.

"Above all, Joanet, pay close attention to thine lessons and waste not thine time carousing," advised his guardian. "Thine father bid me keep a close eye on thee."

Young Orpí nodded as he entered the cloister of that monastic building. Once inside the Aula Magna, the university rector, a Peripatetic humanist theologian by the name

---

26.  *i.e.* Later called the Santa Madrona bastion, at the end of the Rambla, at the city's wall.

27.  *i.e.* Name of the current Ramblas, which run from the Plaça Catalunya to the Statue of Columbus.

of Cosme Damià Hortolà, gave the opening speech. Then a man named Rafael Vilosa, who had earned his doctorate at Salamanca, began handing out the course program. The *ius commune* included Roman law, an introduction to Canonical law, and some broad strokes on feudal law. That first day, young Orpí already had to familiarize himself with Accursio's *Magna Glossa*, Penyafort's *Summa Iuris*, Azzone's *Summa Codicis*, the *Corpus Iuris Civilis*, the *Justinian Code*, and Roberto Maranta's *Aurea Praxis*, some *consilia et responsa* (legal rulings) and the constitutions of Catalonia.

"All that be mere duck soup," said Ernest of the Cirrhotic Liver, whom Orpí had found again and now sat beside in the Aula Magna. "I had the goode fortune to meet the famous jurist Celse Hugues, an extremely erudite womanizer. He doth question many of the immutable laws sold by these 'word peddlers' knowne as salaried professors. Whom dost thou hath for criminal law?"

"Master Lluís de Peguera," said Orpí. "I must read his *Liber quaestionum criminalium* over this next sennight . . ."

"Ah, that one's a doozy . . . he be the worst of all the professors. He allways assignes his own books obliging us to runneth out and buy them. Sure coin!"

"Sooth is I'd rath'r readeth *Lazarillo de Tormes* or *Guzmán de Alfarache*, they art more of a comfort to me, being as they be comickal & simple."

"Very well & goode, Orpí," said Cirrhotic Liver. "But surely this be enoufh class for the present day, we needeth a little drinky-poo more so than a lesson from the Council."

Young Orpí ended up in a famous tavern called the Thirsty Student, surrounded by itinerant artists, wanton poets, and law students like him who belonged to the Brotherhood of the Nocturnal Academy, where everyone was known by pseudonyms like Temerity, Chaos, Shadow, Fear, Silence, etc. There they mingled with other fraternities and unaffiliated followers of the licentious life, drinking and singing until some students from the Cordelles Jesuit School came in, looking for trouble. The conversation between the two fraternities soon soured.

"Look to it," said one of them. "These greenhorn *gaudints* think they hath the same rights as soldiers. Be there any man more pedantic & bamboozling than a lawyer?"

"And furthermore, they're singing bits of the *Coena*, a book Rome hath long included in the *Index of Banned Books*."

"Were I to choose, Id send them all to work in the stables *ad hoc*."

"For thine information, we lawyers hath the same rights as soldiers," bellowed Cirrhotic Liver. "And withall, in mine humble opynion, ye traitors should allst be ympaled throughout the anus."

In less than a minute everybody was fighting. Chairs and beer steins were flying, asses were hitting the ground, things were shattering, mouths were bellowing . . . t'was pandemonium! Young Orpí, who no longer knew if he was striking his own team, the opponents, or himself, ended up on the floor. Someone was just about to run him through with a sword when his friend Ernst of the Cirrhotic Liver stopped it, swashbuckler that he was.

"How is it that thou art more inclined to the sword than the toga?" asked our hero, as he dodged a flying beer tankard.

"The pen & the sword art compatyble occupations," said Cirrhotic Liver, smashing a chair onto a man's head. "How other canst thou explain Garcilaso de la Vega's end, in 1536, following the siege of the Le Muy fortress in southern France?"

Thenceforth young Orpí made that declaration of principles his own, considering a good brain as valuable as knowing how to use a weapon. So he began to practice the art of fencing with Cirrhotic Liver, and in a matter of a few weeks he was already besting his friend in the use of black swords.[28] But that was the only ambit where he bested him, because as for studying and good grades, his was not the door to knock on.

After drinking beer every afternoon with his friends from the university, young Orpí would stagger home in the wee hours to the house of Lord Carmona. His room, in the pigeon loft, was cold and dirty. As its name indicated, all of the city's pigeons came there to roost and our hero had to share his room with all those repulsive birds and their horrible guttural noises and their shit everywhere. Add to that, dear reader, the fact that young Orpí's university studies were a bitter pill for him, and thus he spent the following months drinking from afternoon to night in the taverns and, upon returning home to Lord Carmona's house, shooing away pigeons and pissing in a wash-basin for lack of a latrine. After tolerating the situation for some time, his clothes stinking to high heaven, young Orpí gathered up his belongings and left that house to move into an inn where his friend Cirrhotic Liver was living with some other students from the university. The change was significant. From that point on, he discovered true college life in all its splendor. There were parties every night and the young student's diet consisted entirely of alcohol and opioids. All the funds sent by his family were spent on these and other dubious objectives. In fact, our young hero, impetuous and naive, became a true rapscallion thanks to the company he kept, a parasite of the night who couldn't get enough gluttony and wassailing, plotting out hole-and-corner routes to attend all sorts of parties, and generally laboring harder to earn a degree at the school of debauchery than at the school of wisdom, as we shall see play out in the following manner, forthwith:

---

28. *i.e.* Name for the swords used in fencing.

## Chapter XIV

In which young Orpí finds the fantastic
world of bodily pleasure hindered
by a serious erectile problem

It is in this student context that young Orpí discovered Barcelona's extensive spectrum of opportunities for distracting the mind with a focus on the body. One day, Cirrhotic Liver brought him to Carrer dels Mirallers, famous for hosting, in buildings with red markings, most of the city's prostitutes. A very lively street that welcomed sailors into dance halls with open windows that secreted various types of music and joyful laughter. The smell of fried food melded with cheap perfumes, and women with cheeks aflame, dressed to attract attention, drank and smoked to the health of those who sought them out. They swirled through the narrow streets, gesturing with a finger or a wink of the eye, offering up tongue-in-cheek propositions and scrumptious suggestions to the men in need of their humanitarian services. Dark doorways were marked by the carved stone face of a bearded man, the unmistakable sign for a brothel.

"Yee've gotte the typical harlots," explained Cirrhotic Liver in a didactic tone, while young Orpí listened attentively, "the hookers (these ones ye see here, on the street) who accepte any client, howsoever disfigured or bestank. Then ye have the escorts (the most dear), or the strumpets or the ladies of the evening, who for two copper coins will let thou verily do it all, such as that wench over yon," he said, and pointed to a doorway, where a man was mounting one of these professionals from behind. "Then there be the call girls, who deliver and the . . ."

"Enuff!" exclaimed our hero, quickly losing his patience. "Mye God . . . this be Sodom and Gomorrah!"

"Yea, and there be plentee for all," said his friend. "Even priests doth come here on the down low to wet their willy ever and anon."

"I hath ne'er seen souch lewdness in so few square meteres . . ." murmured our hero.

"It's not 'bout seeing it, Orpinet, it's 'bout givin' it ye olde whirle," said his friend, waving goodbye as he took one of those young ladies by the arm and disappeared into a building. "Standeth thither not with thine mouth hanging open! Hie and selecte one!"

Our hero wandered a few yards on, stopping at the Carrer de les Trompetes in front of doorway where a slovenly and malformed woman, heavily made-up and perfumed *ad nauseum*, stood. Her plunging neckline revealed perfectly round breasts as she signaled with her index finger for the young man to approach. The big-bosomed woman was very depleted and wore cheap lace lingerie. Unable to escape, Orpí was dragged toward that apparition with red-painted cheeks who, in a shrill voice, warbled out a song:

♫ 𝕸𝖆𝖗𝖗𝖞 𝖆 𝖗𝖎𝖌𝖍𝖙 𝖌𝖊𝖓𝖙𝖑𝖊𝖒𝖆𝖓 ♪
𝕬 𝖕𝖗𝖎𝖓𝖈𝖊 𝖎𝖓 𝖙𝖍𝖊 𝖇𝖔𝖚𝖉𝖔𝖎𝖗
𝖆 𝖕𝖊𝖗𝖋𝖚𝖒𝖊𝖉 𝖜𝖊𝖆𝖑𝖙𝖍𝖞 𝖘𝖕𝖊𝖈𝖎𝖒𝖊𝖓

who'll neva call ye whore
He'll pay for every last whim
as long as ye doth werk that willy
Fill yer cup up to the very brim,
And ride ye like a right filly
Oh, ye and we shall have it all
we shall drippe with jewels and lace
When that fine man comes to call
And doth see our lovely face-es!
But if by chance things should sour
And he doth beat us for mere sport,
ye know we shant eere cower
but stab him in the ven'eral wart-s
That's how a lady doth behave
Oh, yes, that's how a true woman be.
I'll keep my secret to the grave
Oh don't ya wanna marr-rry meee!

The prostitute, who was named Roberta, continued to sing as she dragged Orpí up the creaking stairs of a crumbling building, to a desolate room that smelled of human genitalia and sweat, where the only furnishings were a bed and a basin to wash your private parts.

"Up and at 'em," said the slattern, pinching Orpí's bottom before sitting on the bed to take off her shoes. "Let us commence to fuckeing, since these days of marital abstention are when I hath most work, not counting the fourty days fore Christmas, the eight ere Pentecost, Sundays, Tuesdayes, and Frydays during Lent and etcetera, etcetera. So let's get a move on!"

Without further ado, the woman brusquely took off all her skirts and petticoats, allowing a glimpse of her body, as deformed as it was ghostly, slathered from head to toe with cerus.[29] She had been destroyed by the various diseases inherent to her profession, was covered in folds of fat, varicose veins, and stretch marks, her breasts hanging down to her belly like two cattle-bells. Our Orpí was shocked, his mouth agape, upon seeing, for the second time in his life, the monster women kept between their legs.

Roberta the prostitute pulled down his stockings and britches and her eyes grew wide as saucers.

"For Mary Magdalene, patron saint of all whores!" she exclaimed, her face in front of Orpí's prick. "What a truncheon! I've ne'er seen one quite so well endowed! Let us hop into bed forsooth, ya rascal, but take care whenst thou cume as I don't wish to nurse no babies, ya hear? Point a fact, tis best thou weareth a Venus glove[30] and we'll be safe from French caries[31]."

Having said that, she started to rub on our hero's lobcock, but it failed to respond in the slightest.

"How now, don't thee like wenches?" asked Roberta, polishing young Orpí's arborvitae so hard that it got all wrinkled and small like a chickpea. "Thou arent no invert, be theu? Watch out cuz the *pecado nefando* will get you burnt up at the stake, eh? Or be thee fond of beasts, perchance? I once knew a peasant who had a comely younge wife and still fellt in love with an ass. One day they caught 'im mounting it from behind and the poor manne ended up roasted like a chicken by decree of the *Fuero Juzgo*."

"Nay, that's not it, ma'am," he said, ashamed. "But heretofore I doth hatte an egregious experience with a lass from

29. *i.e.* A cosmetic made of lead to "whiten" skin, since paleness was a symbol of distinction in the period, that had serious health consequences.

30. *i.e.* Condom of the period, invented by the Italian surgeon Gabriel Fallopius in the sixteenth century.

31. *i.e.* A term for syphilis.

mine village, and thereupon 'that bit' hasn't risen to the occasion."

"Aha, I see . . ." the whore murmured pensively, rummaging in her bag and pulling out a card. "This be a rite typickal case of sexual trauma. But I hath the remedee thou seeketh, discombobulated young man. Lucky for thee, I'm half strumpet and half saint: here, take this card."

---

### Alfons The Healing Wizard

Solves all health and love problems, unites couples, ex-couples and lovers in general. For divorces, getting rid of overzealous lovers, attracting the love you seek without collateral damage and side effects. Increase feelings and the desire to be loved, faithful and obedient. Deflects bad vibrations and the evil eye, increases sexuality and cures male impotence. Salvages businesses and companies and all with immediate results and 100% guaranteed in two days time. And if you're not completely satisfied, we'll return a part (to be determined) of your money.

---

"Get thee to see this man, he'll fix the problem with your lobcock . . . and then returnne to finish thine task industrious[32] and payeth me mine due!" she said.

Our hero, tying his breeches, swore that as soon as he was cured, he would come back. And thus, still pursued by the laughing stammer of the prostitute as she twirled her hair on the bed, he walked through the door of that room, with all the dignity the occasion demanded, in search of the healer.

---

32.  *i.e.* Diligently and assiduously.

## *Chapter XV*

In which Joan Orpí seeks out a remedy for his problem and
meets up with an old acquaintance who dares to play God

As he searched for his genital cure, night fell upon our hero;
all was solid blackness and Orpí moved slowly now along
the city walls, toward the Raval, careful to avoid scallywags,
through farm patches and corrals[33]. He was feeling his way
along when suddenly a light appeared from above: it was the
healer's home. He knocked on the door but got no answer;
nonetheless it was ajar and our hero took the license of
entering.

There were open books everywhere in that marvelous
room: copies of the Kabbalists and the ancients such as
Heraclitus, Parmenides, Democritus, Lucretius, and Plotinus;
among the moderns there was the omniscient Ramon Llull,
his disciple Ramon Sibiuda, and the magnanimous Coperni-
cus in an atmosphere crammed with dusty objects including
armillary spheres, test tubes, barometers, and varied mystical
and orphic devices appropriate for the hermetic disciplines.
Young Orpí heard someone singing in another room.

---

33. *i.e.* In that era, the Raval was still outside the city walls.

♫ How fare the gods? ♪
How fare the elves?
All Jotunheim groans,
Isn't it rich?
Loud roar the dwarfs
masters of the rocks on the ground
by doors of stone[34]

When he entered he saw a tiny being jumping all around the room, doing some sort of arrhythmic tap dance.

"This cain't be . . ." murmured Orpí.

The other man turned upon hearing his voice. And indeed, there in the middle of that room was none other than Triboulet Dvergar the Distasteful.

"Orpí, what bringeth thee here?"

Two years had passed since our hero had seen the dwarf and he was shocked by his decline, which included a three-day beard, a hole in the crotch of his trousers, and a deerskin hunter's cap askew upon his head. Orpí explained the sorry incident with the lady of the night and his sexual problem.

"There be a facile solution," declared the dwarf, who had a pet snake and an amulet coiled around his neck. "What thou needst is this potion, made with extract of the *Cantharis vesicatoria* fly; the cantharidin produces a congestive action upon thine member. Just drink up the brew and watch as it sharpens thy cutlass!"

"Thanks be to thee, Triboulet," said our hero, putting the flask in his pocket for safekeeping. "Gosh, I never would have tooken thee for a homeopathic wizzard!"

"Natch," said the little man, with a bow. "Every dwarf has

---

34.  *i.e.* Fragment of the Völuspá, Scandinavian mythological poem of *The Poetic Edda*, bastardization of the translation by Henry Adams Bellows.

a bit of the magician in him. Bye the by, what bee the name of the prostitute who recommended you mine Gay Science?"

"Roberta, methunks."

"Ahh, mine belov'd Roberta . . . !" murmured the dwarf, who then proceeded to explain to young Orpí how, after fleeing the casino over the whole bamboozling business two years earlier, he came to realize that he needed urgent psychological help. He found the answer to the meaning of life alongside an old alchemist who took him in and taught him demonology, scatology, angeology, and sotierology, and all the secrets of the arcana. "There be no accidents, mine friend," his master teacher told him one day. "Tis fate in control, and as such, in an order'd huniverse, coincidences forme part & parcel of the Great Creator's cosmic plan." And having said that, destiny or the aforementioned fate played the master alchemist a dirty trick: he took two steps and slipped on a banana peel, breaking his neck in the fall and dying instantly.

"A strange manner of exit. So be this the house of thine master teacher?" asked Orpí.

"Precisely. He passed last winter but I continue his work and successfully so. Followe me," said the dwarf, returning to the first room, where he showed Orpí a glass vessel our hero hadn't noticed when he came in.

"In this vessel," explained the dwarf enthusiastically, "I hath managed . . . to create life! Employeing more than nine-score forms of traditional divination, which include bibliomancy, chrysopoeia, crystallomancy, gyromancy, and philomancy and symbolic arithmancy gathered from Agrippa, the Pre-Socratics, and the atoms of Democritus, Heraclitus's doctrine of flux, the 'everything in everything' of Anaxagoras, the sublime plurality of worlds from Epicure and Lucretius, Zoroaster's *Chaldean Oracles*, the *Asclepius* by Hermes Trismegistus, Lucifer's autobiography *The Book of Fallen Angels*, the *Tabula Smaragdina* of Jabir Ibn Hayyan, Ficino's *De Vita Coelitus Comparanda*, and others . . . in order to rehabilitate matter and present it as one of the three indivisible foundations: hyle, nous, and God . . . in brief, utilising the splendid dictates of mathematics, physics, proto-critics, anti-systematics, and other pantomimes . . . I hath broat forth a homunculus through various surgickal experiments combining suche elements as saliva from an empty stomach plus Paracelsus's recipe using a bag of bones, spermatazoides, skin fragments, and animal hair."

"Wondrous!" exclaimed Orpí, drawing near to the vessel until he could make out a figure small as an acorn, in the shape of a human and with yellowish skin, moving amid the coagulated fluids. "But this be wholly antinatural! Anticlerical! A direct attack on the idea of divine creation!"

"Contemporary alchemists hath lost faith in imagining creation *ex nihilo*," complained Triboulet. "They no longer believeth that metals can transmute, or that the elixir of life be more than mere chimera. False, I sayeth! Not only be it possyble but here is the upshot . . . the stone of the philosophers! And that's not the word of some sciolist nerdde, but a verittable prophecy."

"Mine eyes cannot believe such a marvelle . . . what sort of magic be this?"

"Pray let me elucidate: if we assume that the univerce be infinite (in other words, eccentric, where everything be centre and there be no peripheries) and no physickal division betwixt the sublunary & supralunary spheres, then one canst extrapolate that there be no difference between the world comprehend'd as a totality and divinity. Ergo, God canst not have created the universe, nor life, for God be a tautology and existeth not. Even mine mother (God rest her soul) could apprehend that."

"Heretic! Nigromancer!" exclaimed Orpí. "I doth still believe in virgyns and miracles! Listening to thee, theurgic demiurge, leadeth mee to ween that, afore thine intervenchun, the world didst live with a veil over its eyes. And forbye, I reckon thee be more scharlatan than magician."

"I fancy the wurde 'scientist,' if thou donst mind," said the dwarf, scratching his beard. "Lyfe be as a hieroglyph concealing a series of enigmas that must allways be kept secret, but evene *vox populi* sayeth tis highe time to repudiate the ancient Aristotelian-Thomistic ways in favour of empyrical nahledge."

"I cann't graspe half the things thou sayeth, halfman, but I can tell thee that playing at Prometheus be verily playing with fire," said Orpí. "Specially in thys era wenne so many art burned at the stake. *Deus factus sum*: pilfering the divine flamme to bestowe it upon man must have consequences, beyond besmirching thine home and leaving it in vast disarray. This playce be a righte shambles!"

"Bogg off!" Triboulet exclaimed angrily.

As the two men argued, the sound of horses' hooves was heard outside. A few moments later there was a knock at the door, accompanied by a barking voice: "Open up, that's an orrder!"

"The Mossos de l'Esquadra! What didst I tell thee, halfman?" said Orpí. "They'll lock us up or send us off to the galleys and it be all thine fault! Let us skedaddle 'fore we're arrest'd! Every time I seeth thee, bad things happen!"

"Relax, Orpí," said the dwarf, grabbing his homunculus and putting it into a small box. "Thou must fleeeth out the left door and I'll take the right. As thou shalt see, Orpí, there be a price to pony up for everything in this worlde and by and large the price is incredibly steep. We only survive if we createth anoth'r being in our image. And now I bid thee farewell."

Having said that, Triboulet the Dwarf vanished through one door and young Orpí did the same through the other, again pushed out into the harsh darkness of the night without knowing where to go. Patting his pocket as he headed away from the house as it was looted by the police, he found the elixir against impotence the dwarf had given him and then he had a clearer idea of where to direct his feet: he would finish what he'd started with Roberta the strumpet.

## Chapter XVI

### In which young Orpí celebrates Carnaval
### with his fraternity and ends up
### dressed as the Stag King

It was our hero's last year of university and, having failed
almost all his subjects, he found refuge only in debauchery.
Calends, Whitsunday . . . any excuse for merrymaking was a
good one and, particularly, Carnaval, which lasted three days,
beginning on Carrer de la Palla and ending where shrimps
whistle. A grand procession of parade figures featuring dev-
ils, dragons, giants, and cardboard horses were followed by
brotherhoods dancing to the beat of drums along the city
streets, illuminated by countless torches. The festivities also
included Tarasques, hoop games or pala mall,[35] bull fights,
minstrels singing and dancing the *contrap*às, sotties with
some people dressed as demons and others as madmen, yet
others as funambulists with bells on their legs, reciting gibber-
ish and repetitions, dizzying lists and satirical allusions to the
clergy as they threw fireworks. The celebration also included

---

35.  *i.e.* A game similar to today's croquet.

jousts, circus numbers, tastings, and executions left and right of the riffraff filling the city's prisons. Just then there was an announcement, along with trumpet fanfare, of the execution of ten dangerous highwaymen who had their flesh torn off with pincers, then were hung by their arms, had their genitals amputated, and finally were quartered. The whole city was in motion: the Frogs were bustling about angrily because they'd been forbidden to carry weapons (crossbow, lance, or shield), while some gentlemen idled, walking their purebred *doggos*, and some Holy Thursday penitents who'd gotten the day wrong and were dragging themselves through the streets flagellating their own backs with iron whips until they bled while the ning-nang of cathedral bells could be heard in the distance. A band of musicians, strumetty-strum, blowetty-blow, advanced as costumed people danced around them in a muddle of arms and legs in sweet harmony.

So, as the multitude partied down the streets of Barcelona, young Orpí and his brothers in the fraternity of the Nocturnal Academy got drunk on *piment*[36] in one of the taverns in the Born, on Carrer de les Mosques. There they could listen to parodies of the Easter Week Sermons improvised by fake priests in chaps, and guilds planning all sorts of hooliganism, and singing old Goliardic songs.

♪ Vivat nostra societas! ♪
Vivant studiosi!
Crescat una veritas,
floreat fraternitas,
patriae prosperitas.
Vivat et Republica,
et qui illam regit.

---

36. *i.e.* White wine infused with honey and spices.

𝕭ibat nostra ribitas,
𝕸aecenatum charitas
♫ quae nos hic protegit.[37] ♫

"Hold up, waite a minute," said Cirrhotic Liver. "This song is passé. We hath no patrons. Nor do we believeth in the Republic or the Church."

"Nay, but *protegit* rhymes with *regit*, man!" said a student from the University of Salamanca who was on an exchange in Barcelona.

"Hey, guys, why donst we procure a few kiloes of oranges and bombard the home of the dean, Abbot Cuckhold?" said one who answered to the name of Fear.

"Goode idea," exclaimed another, whom they called Shadow. "There be no body more vain and orgulous than the dean."

"Any day now he's like to ban laughing in the university, as Plato attempted in his Academy," put forth Silence.

"He hath already separated the liberal artz (doctrine, theory) from the mechanic artz (painting and sculpture), which methinks deeply grosswitted," noted young Orpí.

"And how they maketh us read the fourth eclogue of Virgil's *Aeneid* as a proffecy of the coming of Christ is right bunkum!"

"They do the selfsame with *Genesis*, melding theological trut' and sense to validate their monopoly on knowledge and gette a paycheck at the end of the month!"

"The university bestinks of fustylugs!"

"And withal, we liveth amid the darke ignorance of Vatican idolatree!"

---

37. Long live our association! / Long live those who study! / May the single truth grow, / may brotherhood flourish, / as well as the prosperity of our homeland. Long live the Republic, / and its governor. / Long live our city, / and the generosity of its patrons / who take us under their wing.

"Let's do up his house in oranges and fecations!"

"Let us play pranks & capers!"

That being decided, the student fraternity filled up baskets of rotten oranges and even some excrement from a sick dog, and went to the dean's home, near the Rambla. When they got there they threw the oranges against the walls of his house while singing lewd songs. The darkness of the night helped the student gang, which even painted obscene drawings on the walls and smeared feces on the door. In fact, the "oranging" was a tradition repeated each Carnaval for centuries, even though it had been prohibited by the Consell de Cent, and the dean had long grown sick and tired of those nocturnal serenades come February.

"How now, students?" the rector bellowed like an ass, sticking his head out the window as a bag filled with liquid diarrhea splashed his clenched face.

The students, scattering, were relentlessly chased by the Mossos de l'Esquadra. Luckily, young Orpí was able to camouflage himself amid a group of people coming down the street singing songs and dressed up as cows, monkeys, goats, and birds.

Someone handed a deer mask to Orpí and they covered him with an animal hide. Following the cavalcade, laughing, baying, bellowing, our young hero ended up in the cemetery, where the entire gang of joyous revelers engaged in the most varied array of obscenities, with the invaluable help of copious amounts of alcohol. Some licked others' anuses, others ate fruits and tomatoes they'd rubbed on their genitals, and yet others drank sacramental wine and masturbated and danced with the improvised music of flutes and tambourines. Surrendered to the collective liturgy, they offered up their bodies, standing, kneeling, opened legs, nipples pointed skyward. Most of them were peasants who worshipped the trees and the rocks . . . the fake beards, gleaming silk clothes, masks with giant noses, feather headdresses, goat horns, and silk masks stimulated the sinners' lust and everyone sang, shrieked, shouted, offered themselves up, muddy and half-naked . . . ducks and rabbits fell . . . some hens were raped and gutted . . . some smeared themselves with the blood of the dead animals . . . women spread their legs revealing hairy, damp vaginas that were penetrated and hosed down with industrial quantities of semen . . . anuses dilated and bled as a squad of policemen in rooster costumes sang *Nun, Little Sister, we'll bust yer teensy hole* . . . ! and she, coquettish, lifted her habit to flaunt a round, white ass while another woman shat in the mouth of a large peasant man who opened his jaws (somewhat repulsed) as one of the roosters jerked him off . . . and in that widespread transfiguration of pagan inversion, our Orpí was the Stag King, brandishing, like a knight his lance, his now definitively cured foreskin, prepared to meet all the indecent demands of the lovely courtesans in heat that Carnaval night, if not for—exactly—if not for the fact that the Mossos de l'Esquadra interrupted that colossal orgy and everyone scattered into the foggy night as quickly as they'd come.

## Chapter XVII

### In which young Orpí finds his first job
### as a lawyer and ends up getting a bit scalded

Truth be told (because here we tell no lies), we would need a few hundred more pages to explain in full how our hero managed to finish his law studies, being as he was so feather-brained. But, for the time being, suffice to say that he finished them, and he finished them well, in other words, *in utroque jure*,[38] not with *cum laude* but definitely with *sapere aude*. And, indeed, he'd become a true *legum professor*.

The next period in Orpí's life worthy of telling took place the year after he earned his degree, when we see him walking through Barcelona's streets toward the Tribunals. A friend from university had procured him a penal case at the Courts, in defense of alleged witchcraft. The courtroom is brimming with people, and our hero sits at the atrium awaiting his clients, whom he has yet to meet. When Orpí greets the accused his eyes near nigh fall out of his head. They are seven women, and none other than the seven witches who had raped him four years earlier in the wood.

The trial was presided over by a prelate judge and two Inquisition judges, and got off to a bad start.

---

38.  *i.e.* With a degree in canon and civil law.

"Zhese women art witches, milord," said the prosecuting attorney, a long-bearded Frenchman who went by the name of Pierre Pathelin.[39] "It is *très facil* to establish. Zhey all hafth a verry small mark on their shoulders, reveal'd ere rubbing wifth holy water. Ergo, they art demonically possessed practitioners of *la sorcellerie ad cursum Dianae!*"[40]

The lawyer pulled down the shirt of one of the women, showing the judge and audience the fateful mark. The two Inquisition judges kissed their portable crucifixes and Holy Oils as they sensed the Devil's proximity. The attendant public, a mix of vagabonds and housewives, let out *ohs!* with a mix of shock and shuddering. But Orpí, despite having been violated and visiting hell itself because of their psychotropic potions, couldn't quite believe the whole scene, since he was well versed in distinguishing reality from daydreams.

"Maywith it pleaseth the court," said our young hero, whose pulse was accelerating each and every minute he had to tolerate that fallacy, "methinks the unequivocal accusation by Barrister Pathelin forsooth consummately equivocal. These women mere be persuad'd they art witches, but in sooth they art nowise, they giveth ear to superstitions and blasphemies[41] and maketh them their own. They dost ween they descrye the Devil when they doth not, since in reality they mere hallucinate with strange herbs. They appear to fly thru the skies but in sooth they doth not. This fancifull daydreaming, joined with the barmey convicktion they canst make hail and smoke plumes, be naught more than jejune malarkery. Moreover, we stande requisite to elucidate the classic contradistinction

---

39. *i.e.* Pierre Pathelin is the protagonist of *La Farce de Maître Pathelin* (1464), an anonymous work featuring a dishonest lawyer.

40. *i.e.* An expression used by demonologists to refer to the coven, relating to the pagan cults of the goddess Diana.

41. *i.e.* Curses.

betwixt witchcraft and sorcery: witches engageth in satanic ministree hence renouncing Jesus Christ; sorceresses be mere ladies who art benamoured of drugs, like these ones hither."

"For Saint Raymond of Penyafort . . . I acutely objecteth!" exclaimed the prosecutor.

"Objecktion sustain'd . . ." said the judge, waving his hand as if to say "we'll put that on the way back burner," weary of holding court over the same cases day after day, while one of the two Inquisitors recited, in a whisper, versicles from Apocalypse and Psalm 50 from the Bible, which begin *Miserere mei, Deus.*

"This dandiprat lawyer be unfitted fer the fearsome trut'," continues the prosecution. "Howbeit this heretical crime seemsth comprised of autarkic acts, they doth all converge into one selfsame *iter criminis*. If the bench doth allow it, we hath testimony from an attestor who hath seen and heard tell that these wymmin be all witches."

The witness in question turned out to be a young thief who had been tortured so badly that he no longer had eyes. The boy confessed to having seen those women with the Devil, but his confession rang as false as the supposed chastity of a priest. It was obvious he'd been forced to confess a lie in exchange for a pardon.

"Prevarication!" bellowed Orpí. "This man hath been coerced civly and creminally! The farce of Barrister Pathelin art pathetic!"

"No, lord!" the prosecutor cried in his defense. "Didst thou or didst thou not see these energumen[42] fornicating amongst themselves and subsequentlee with the Devil?"

"Yea," said the boy without eyes.

"Canst thou now seeth? This poor rogue prevaricatith not,

---

42. *i.e.* Possessed by spirits.

Your Honor," stated Pathelin. "Civil legislation has for centuries prescrib'd death sentences for sodomee. As far back as the 1189 *Fuero de Cuenca* it was decreed that: 'Burne whosever shalt descend into sodomitic sinne.' And tis understood that here no appeals shall be entertain'd from convicted confessors nor others whom, by common law, art deny'd appeal *in criminalibus*."

"Hear, hear!" cried the public. "Sin . . . ! Blasfaemy . . . ! Burn at the stake . . . !"

"If it pleaseth the court!" exclaimed Orpí to quiet the room. "This be pure poppycock! *Lectura facilis*! There art no justice in this! Not only are they wyping their arses with the law, and transgressing the universelle dyrectives of natural law and *jus gentium*, but moreover flouting the legal & moral framework of a fair trial for all."

"Milord, with full justiceness discharg'd, let us signeth what we must and get this here show on the road!" replied the prosecutor.

"Silence every-one!" shouted the judge, his wig slipping on his head to reveal a mortifying baldness. "Silence in the court, I sayeth!"

In those years, the courts had a bad rep because they allowed exploiters to take advantage of people and grow rich through prevarications, acting under the *Saepe contengit* that allowed them to sentence in the blink of an eye. Finally, it was announced:

"Bailuff!" bellowed the judge. "Get thee to the Nuncio and bid him publish, upone mine orders, the promulgation of capitall punishment by dynt of rigorous execution in eight days time. And one more thing: have this courtroom scrubb'd of any and all traces of eville spirits!"[43]

---

43. *i.e.* The act of cleansing, or purifying, has historically been associated with witchcraft.

And thus the accused were condemned and, after the authorities of the Holy Office read a pronouncement, they were hung in the Plaça del Rei the following week.

"This here proclivitee for slaying people is the stuff of savage no-nothyngs," said Orpí to a man next to him, as he watched the executions. "Ramon Llull did stateth clearly in his *Art of Contemplation*: the trickery of false testimony and the trickery of bad judges and lawyers causeth the entyre world to be corrupt and disturbed. At least these women shall finde rest in the next world. Meantime, I must commence the search for a new job gyven that no one in Barcelona will hire me as a lawyer."

"Thou canst sayeth that again," said the tall, bearded man beside him, in Spanish. "I doth divine thou art a person with an ethical sense of justyce."

"For I art an attorney, and most of all a goode person," said Orpí before switching into Spanish, "Mine name is Joan, what be thine, good sir?"

"Miguel, from Alcala de Henares," said the man, bowing. "Yet I sweareth that never hath I seen a city this fair, fountain of courtesy, shelter for strangers, hospice to the poor, land of the valiant . . ."

". . . these acts of death bringeth not distinction to any land," said Orpí, interrupting the man. "But far be it from me to leave thee with a bad memory of the Catalans, so prithee accept mine invitation to a tipple."

Our hero and the Castilian sat down at a tavern and proceeded to converse at length. It turned out the Man from La Mancha was a famous writer of plays, poetry, and prose. Seeing the pessimistic tribulations that had young Orpí lamenting, his Castilian friend gifted him a copy of his latest work: *The Ingenious Gentleman Don Quixote of La Mancha.*

"Truly, if thou doth savour reading 'uninhibited prose,' kind sir, I promise that at the very least thou shalt obtaine a few chuckles from these exployts."

"Thanks be to thee, ever so clement!" said Orpí gratefully. "But what I doth need art a job, not entertainment."

"Worry not, kind sir, for I hath a Castilian friend who is a soothfast man and liveth in these parts; and while I beest poor as a churchmouse, he art rich & affluent, and moreover he owes mee a favour. Let us visit him anon and thou shallt seeth . . . thou shant want for employ."

No sooner said than done. The two men walked to pay the gentleman a visit, as we shall see in the coming Chapter.

## Chapter XVIII

### In which young Orpí enters the service of a gentleman
### and realizes that being rich is better than being poor

The man who hired our hero goes by the sickly name of Manuel de Rubeola. And despite claiming to be an "old Christian" from a family of low-ranking, titled nobility, and the distant cousin of the cousin of the cousin of Isabella I of Castile, he was in sooth a Sephardi descended from Jews, whose name was originally Yehuda Abrabanel. He had become moderately wealthy with his crafts business and, in order to avoid expulsion from the Iberian Peninsula, lived under a Christian identity, contravening, in this case, the Jewish proverb that says "By his name shall ye know a man."

"I need an attorney to looke after mine finanzes," said Mr. Abrabanel in Ladino-inflected Spanish. "If thou entereth into my zervice thou shalt ne'er again have ekonomic problems. Hath ve a deal?"

"Yessir," said Orpí.

Our hero thanked Miguel de Cervantes and bade him farewell to continue on his way to Italy. Orpí and Mr. Abrabanel quickly got into a groove and our hero worked for his new employer handling his tributes, the taxes, and tariffs of his property in Barcelona and the small palace he had in Girona, as well as his letters, provisions, commands and commissions, collecting his employer's debts and resolving all the legal hindrances that arose: "Here thou hast the property survey, five t'ousand six hundred pounds in gold, in renewal of the hereditary lease for thine palace and to refreshe the memory of the allodial lord of the rights conferr'd from the landes and assets subjekt to the rule of milord." Or "Whatsoever alienations for foriscapi be owed and in what summes?" *Et cetera, et cetera.*

The sumptuousness in which Lord Abrabanel lived made a huge impression on young Orpí. His enormous estate was built with Sevillian marble floors, had flatware made from silver from the Indies, and many mahogany chairs, gilded curtains, and other luxurious brocades. The Sephardi enjoyed the good life, and dressed in very expensive Neapolitan silk robes and the latest velvet shoes imported from Germany, and as Orpí came and went from his various properties in his carriage pulled by Arabian horses, the nobleman spent his days sniffing snuff, uncorking bottles of fine wine, and playing cards with the friends who came to visit him on the only day of rest he allowed himself, which was Saturday, when he sang *zemirots*[44] at the breakfast hour.

Lord Abrabanel also had six servants in his service. Two of them had been imported directly from the Indies, along with a butler named Josué Mandinga, a Black from Cuba sold as a slave in the Canary Islands whom Lord Abrabanel had bought at a very dear price. Mandinga, following the orders of his lord, was dressed in the latest style, with buckled shoes, pink stockings, a red dress coat, and a white wig that contrasted spectacularly with his face dark as night, revealed only when he smiled and showed his perfectly white teeth.

---

44. *i.e.* Jewish hymns.

"Whither goe't milord, I too chall go," the Cuban would say.

The Sephardic businessman had, among other luxuries, a small private orchestra of musicians who played *sarabandes* and *saetas* at dinner: oboe, harpsichord, viola da gamba, two transverse flutes, marine trumpet, and a violin whose precise, energetic strokes got everyone dancing to the music. The indigenous maids with pierced ears danced, Josué the Cuban danced, and young Orpí danced. It was a celebration every night!

As the months passed, Lord Abrabanel grew fond of our young attorney, so much so that he treated him like his protégé. Our hero dressed in the French style, with his face covered in white makeup of flour and rice powder, his cheeks painted red, a fake beauty mark on his right cheekbone, and a white wig as enormous as it was ludicrous, all imitating the lifestyle of his lord. He spent a good bit of his salary on visits to the tailor, buying ostentatious regalia with neck ruffs to express a bold, self-assured masculinity. He wore his wigs long, as was the fashion of the time, and had a beard in the shape of a spade. And what he didn't spend on clothes and accessories, he spent on prostitutes or revelries with his friends from university. At that pace, he had little savings, but that didn't seem to bother our hero much, because since becoming acquainted with that new world of luxury and wealth, he resolved to become rich no matter the cost.

In the service of Lord Abrabanel, Orpí seemed to have a promising future, but bad luck once again found our hero from Piera and, on the rebound, the country as a whole. The agrarian economic crisis that Catalonia was experiencing caused the banks to fail; the failure of the banks provoked a currency crisis that was the ruin of the artisanal sector and at the same time made prices shoot up, and soon everyone stopped paying tariffs. It was every man for himself. Lord Abrabanel was racking up more and more debts and soon was so insolvent he was unable to pay them. First he had to sell his palace in Girona for next to naught. Then he let go the orchestra and sold his carriages. After that came the servants, all except for Josué the Cuban. Then the law went for his jugular, because he was a Jew. One day our hero confessed, "Milord, I've come to fetch thee, for I've something paramount to inform."

"Whatsoever iz the matter?" asked Abrabanel.

"If I err not thou art soone to be without a penny to thine name. Thou hast spent oodles & oodles, and the usurers be all over us like a veritable shiver of sharkes. They demandeth compulsoree payment on debts, forthwith. Thou hast spent a tonne living a pipe dream. Basically, thou art flat broke. And furthermore, I heard tell in the courts that the authorities seek to *regaliar-vos*[45] and expel thee from the Penynsula for being a Jew!"

"Juanito, don't you go vorrying 'bout me," said the man. "Spain no longer views anykthing as ugly, infamous, and offensive as deskending from a line of Jews. Not blasphemers, thieves, highwaymen, adulterers, nor the sacrilegious. Not since the ekpulsion edict of 1492 hath there been such persekution with this 'blood purity'. But don't you vorry, I'm forsaking this דרפס (land of rabbits),[46] and heading to Italy, vhere I haff powerful friends. But vat shall thee do now?"

"Mayhaps I shall request work at the Diputació del General. Becoming a government bureaucrat behooves anyone 'ankering for a decent salary at the present daye."

"Oy . . . thou needest connections to get vork there. Ye best

---

45.  *i.e.* Take away privileges.

46.  *i.e.* Hebrew name meaning "Sefarad" that denoted the Iberian Peninsula following the expulsion of the Jews, in 1492. From this name comes the later deformation into "Sephardim" meaning descendants of the Jews of the Peninsula.

skip town, for this kingdom is of interest only to government spekulators. If thou wants to live vell, thou must be either a politician or a highvayman. Thou hath been loyal to me, Urpín and, as the saying goes: 'Whosoever is a friend to everyone is either very poor or very rich.' I've on good worde that a spot for a government attorney hath opened up in Seville. That be the city where all good things are happening now. I vill write thee a fine letter of rekommendation."

As young Orpí gathered up his papers, Lord Abrabanel waved him down to the courtyard of the house, near the stable. There a powerful white horse was waiting for him, snorting impatiently, its nostrils intermittently flaring.

"This pureblood is my gift, Urpín. He vill be more faithful to thee than any woman. His name be Acephalus (to differentiate it from Bucephalus, Alexander the Great's steed)."

"Thanks unto thee, Yer Worship," said our hero, thrilled and hugging his benefactor.

And thus, mounting Acephalus, Orpí tearfully bade farewell to Abrabanel, who had been like a father to him. He also said goodbye to Cirrhotic Liver and his other friends from the university, with whom he'd shared many a late night, amid sad rejoicing. It had been five years since he'd arrived in Barcelona as a boy, and now he was leaving a grown man. When he passed by the two soldiers guarding the entrance to the city—the same ones as on the day our hero had first come through its gates, one of them barked, without recognizing him, "*Quo vadis?*"

"Joan Orpí del Pou, Esquire," shouted out our hero, who wore a large wide-brimmed felt hat adorned with two peacock feathers, a leather doublet, silk stockings, velvet breeches, pointy shoes, and was shrouded in a cape, all his fine clothes giving him the appearance of an absolute gentleman.

"Fare thee well, milord," said the soldiers, as they stepped aside with a theatrical bow and Orpí's *equus caballus* let out flatulences in the soldiers' face and neighed showing bright white teeth.

With Lord Abrabanel's letter of recommendation safely tucked away in his bag, our hero headed toward Piera to bid farewell to his family as he dreamed of a dazzling future in the service of the crown, as an adviser to the Court, or a magistrate in the Royal Audiencia.

## Chapter *XIX*

In which young Orpí, in this final Chapter of Book One,
returns to Piera and is beset by great misfortune

Our hero returned to his hometown along the same road with
which he had taken his leave of it, and there Piera appeared
amid the iridescent halos of morning clouds. He rode Acephalus slowly through the narrow streets as kids followed him
laughing and he greeted first the bailiff, then the barber, then
the blacksmith, as they all wondered how the feebleminded
elder son of House Orpí had managed to turn himself into
such a success. However, when he reached his home, he was
greeted with bad tidings. His father had fallen ill with gout and
was in bed about to receive last rites.

"Father," exclaimed Orpí, kneeling beside the bed. "Whatso
. . . whatever's wrong with you?"

"What dost thou think be wrong with me?" he bellowed.
"I'm dying, that's what! Years of study and thou still be the
same nincompoop as ever! And wherefor art thou going,
dressed as a pansy? Now I seeth whichfore thou never mar-
ried . . . thou art a right pouf!"

"Father, don't get madd with me, and prey listen: I hath found work in the Court," said Orpí, pulling off his French wig. "I planne to travelle to Seville and become a gentleman. Now that I hath earned my degree, I am prepared to adminst'r our lands here, in Piera. I shall do it all."

"Not on thine life, goldbrick!" said his father in a cold, mercantile voice. "Thy younger brother hath demonstrath'd much more love & commitment to these here lands. Furthermore, you hath ne'er had nor the strength nor the skill to work them. Twill be thine brother what taketh the reins. I've already made mine will."

"But father . . . with mine studies I clearly be the best choice! Besides, in cumplyance with Catalan customary law, I be the bona fide heir!"

"Wastrel scattergood heir, tis what you are! Contumacious pettifogger, slugabed, dastard! I'd sooner give all my worlldly goods to the mule . . . surely she wouldst do a better job! I shall tell thee one thing, son: since thou hath always had bats in thy belfry, there is but one future for thee: a bad one! Now let me croak in peace, gottdamn it!"

Indeed, after that parley, ole Orpí shuffled off this mortal coil with a smile from ear to ear, widely regarded as virtuous and held in eternal memory, in name of the Holy Trinity, Father, Son, and Holy Ghost, amen. The family kept watch over his body throughout the night and the next morning; at the cemetery, a family friend, Father Francesc Vicent Garcia[47] officiated the burial, even ending on a sonnet:

Those whose wish is to be read must have memory,
those whose wish is to be soldiers, speak of war

---

47. Known as the Rector of Vallfogona (1582-1623). This fragment is from the poem "A la vanitat del món i engany."

and go forth, if gallant, as did Absalom;
and forget thee not how labor glory be
hold most holy those who work the land therefore,
all is but appearances till Kingdom come.

After singing a very heartfelt *Teu Deum laudamus* with his family members at the grave, our hero made a barefoot pilgrimage to Montserrat to honor the memory of his father and, while there, ask the Black Virgin to bless his trip to Seville. Fate is cruel when it takes a beloved relative, and Orpí needed someone to mitigate all that suffering. Lost in his thoughts, disconsolate, sad, and lonely, he had not a shoulder to cry upon. As he ascended the sacred mountain, he decided to wash the wounds on his feet in a spring. Beside the fount he found a skull with *Praeter nomen inane, nihil* inscribed on its forehead. That made our hero ponder life's disillusionment. As he was about to pick up the skull, he heard a commanding voice from behind him.

"Who traveleth along this *Strasse*[48] that bee mine alone?"

When Orpí turned, he found himself face to face with the same German hermit he'd met in the wood five years earlier.

"Meester ascetic! Dostt thou not remember me? I'm the man whose wounds thou cured some twelfemonths back in thine cabin!"

"I hath no recollection," said the old man, who was naked but whose private parts were covered by his long white beard. "Whence doth thou come and where art thou heading, *Jugendlicher*?"[49]

"I now be a lawyer and I seeketh the Virgins blessing and interdicktion for mine good fortune and gaynfull employ in

---

48. Street or path, in German.

49. *i.e.* Youngster, in German.

Seville, since mine father hath no use for mee in Piera."

"Heading downe south be a blighty ill-fated voyage, mine son. Few reach there, and even fewer return," said the old hermit. "And as the Bible dixith: *Peregrinus, sicut omnes patres mei.*"

"I'm not afeered of nuffin', meester asceetic," confessed Orpí.

"Mere becaws thou art too full of yourself, like ev'ry young gent," said the hermit. "Go ahead . . . *laufen Sie*[50]! But befor thee splittest, bestowe an alms: a long hundredweight of pork to the monastery!"

Orpí agreed to the hermit's wish and, after praying to the Virgin, returned to Piera with his feet once again bloody. The penitence and high levels of Catholic faith seemed to have an effect on that gallant young man, who, upon reaching his hometown and placing some flowers on his father's grave, was seeing everything through rose-colored glasses. It is well known that faith moves mountains, and Orpí had his cup filled to the brim.

Once in Piera, he wanted to depart for Seville posthaste. He bid farewell to his mother, who gave him clothes, money, victuals for the road ahead, and a piece of advice:

"Fyrst & formost, son, bee mindfull of the highwaymen, the shysters, the bohemians, the heretics, the rapists, the energumen, the thieves, the crooked, the plague-stricken, the sadists, the overbold, the 'ostile, the snobs, the improodent, the habituat'd, the wretch'd, the pedantic, the wiseacres, the curmuggenly, the simple-minded, the 'pologists, the unworlde-ly, the feather-'eaded, the clever, the onlookers, the bullies, the poets, the pernickety, the simple and the scoundrels, the swagger'rs, the bootless, the affright'd and the fickle, the

---

50. Run along, in German.

priggish, the cynics, the foul-mouthed and the foul-minded, the incompetent, the equivicators, the spoiled, the extravagant, the pusillanimous, the braggarts, the insolent, the supercilious, the organised and the disorganized, the peevish, the fantasts, the egotistickal, the nonplusss'd, the malleable, the naive, the egocentric, the naughty, the temerarious, the beguiling, the narcissistic, the witty, the parsimonious, the smug, the oversplendid, the weak and the fungus, the Franks and the French, the brilliant, the yronic, the punctiliouse, the normall, the observant, the cockproud, the sated, the multiloquent, and, above alle, the dimwitted!"

"Indeed I shall, mother."

Then he said goodbye to all his siblings.

"Seconde & formost," they recommended, in unison, "rather than retornne home without a farthing to thy name . . . don't come home at all!"

"Thanks unto ye, brothers and sisters. I love ye, too."

And, forthwith, Orpí felt the need to leave. He packed up a dozen indispensable books into a bundle, which was his only baggage. Wearing breeches and a black leather baldric across his chest, his cape and hat, and with two blunderbusses on his belt, he left the town of Piera as the churchbells rang out. It seemed as if with each chime they were saying, "Ge-ron-i-mo and a-way you go!" And thus, away he went, forward never rearward, amid an earthly solitude, spurring on Acephalus and vanishing into the fog of a chilly morn.

When he'd been trotting through the mountains for a couple of hours, our hero heard the noise of rocks splintering. As he approached he was met with a fantastic surprise: a giant named Trucafort[51] was playing ball with a rock as enormous as the Barcelona cathedral. Upon seeing Orpí, he asked, "Whence comest thou?"

"Out of your mouth," replied Orpí.

"And wherewith didst thou live? What didst thou drink?"

"My lord, of the same that you did, and of the daintiest morsels that passed through your throat I took toll."

"Yea but," said the giant, "where didst thou shite?"

"In your throat, my lord," said Orpí.

**[Hold on a moment, Captain! A giant? Stop the tale right this instant!]**

---

51.  *i.e.* A character in Catalan mythology.

**1714:** The infantry captain pauses
In the telling of his tale and
engages in a fairly intellectual
discussion with his soldiers:

As bombs fall on the city of Barcelona, and explosions and harquebus fire are heard, inside the half-destroyed theater the Captain stands before his soldiers, with eyebrows equal parts inquiring and shocked.

"Whitherfor ye dareth heckle mee yet again, comrades? Wouldst ye like me to start dysciplinary proceedings?"

The soldiers exchange glances, murmuring inaudibly and shaking their heads repeatedly. Finally, one of them says, "Esteemed Captain, your tale is highly entertaining, that none would dare to call into question," stated the soldier, seeking out the approval of his peers. "Be that as it maye, thou must conceedeth that . . . that there be certain inconsistencies in thine story what make it implausive in the superlative, if thou alloweth."

"Inconsistencies, ye say?" bellows the captain, as his pipe turns intermittently red then black, after each puff of smoke that covers his irate countenance. "Malarkey! Expounde!"

"Milord and Captain, you see . . . all that about Orpí encount'ring the Devil, the Black Virgin appearing befor 'im at Montserrat, his be'olding the creation of a wee being through the art of nigromancy, meeting the most renown'd poets and writers . . . and now he doth happ uponst a giant in that ultimate part, which seems verily to hafe been lifted from *Pantagruel* by the great Rabelais!"

"How dare ye . . . !" exclaims the captain, wiping dust from his dress coat from a recent bomb, launched by the Borbonic army, that collapsed part of the theater's ceiling. "Very welle, perchance I plagiarized Rabelais. Soe what? In this bastard genre that is the *romanzo*, invention (utopia) is merely possible based on the memory (the story) of a 'could be' since we haven't access to the historical figure, as there be no-one who can confirm the truth of what happened. Eversuch, the very idea of originality is absurde. Ergo authorship is banal and any statement of authenticity or originality is spurious. And shud some other author, some other day, plagiarise us, it shall mean we've done our job well."

"Be that as it maye, what mine comrade meant," says another soldier, "is that thine tale, Captain, converts the past into a yarn, mixing the mythickal with the historickal. I mention it in case someone later complains that our text doth not depict the unequivocal historical truth that embodies our national espirit."

"Ye must knowe, dear soldiers, that the telling of history be not one-sided."

"Still and all, this telling lacks level-headedness, sycological truth, conscience, realism . . . !" says a third soldier. "And it be entirely too long on dirty jokes! Tis near nigh bereft of the moral conventions befitting the bourgeoisie who art the readers of these sorts of stories. In a nutshelle: thine tale be insufficiently mimetic (and, thence, insufficiently commercial!)."

"Ye packe of mindless nitwits!" swears the Captain. "What hath mercantilism to do with true literature? Here what's required is merely a pact betwixt the printed worde and its reader, by dint of a paineless 'act of faith.'"

"But, Captain," says one of the soldiers, "this rumoured 'act of faith' be impossible if we cann't find in thy tale the fullness, order, and unity requisite to all creative workes."

"What be this, are ye now literary critics?" asks the Captain sarcastically. "Didn't *Don Quixote* already eclipse the Aristotelian-Horatian tradition? Don't be moralistic!"

The soldiers exchange glances, their expressions repulsed and confused, as the harquebus shots from both armies boom outside the theater.

"Having reached this point, Captain," says another soldier, "I now surmize that the criollo what told thee this story war lying and, in consequence, thy tale be false."

"Yes and no! Just like the Epimenides paradox! Here we speaketh nothing less than the truth by lying . . . and I wouldst be lying if I told the truth!" exclaimed the Captain, filling his wooden pipe with more tobacco. "Traditionally art hath been understood as imitation of or feyning reality, but which reality doth we referr to? The empirical reality ye all quest after in this tale shall only be creat'd when ye wish for it . . . and twill be neither truth nor a lie, but 'nother thing entirely! And now desist thine chatter, for we could argue this till our brains explode. So let us return to the adventures of Joan Orpí, if ye don't mind. And even if ye do . . . !"

# Book Two

In which the highly eventful travels of Joan Orpí are related: first on horseback from Barcelona to Seville, in which he will make many good friends and very few enemies, and a second voyage by sea, indeed quite rough and even more eventful. So patience, dear reader, we are only at the halfway point of this adventure and, despite an expeditious telling, the life story of the man who became a lawyer by family decree and finally an adventurer in the new world—in other words, a conquistador—by divine decree, is not going to fly by quick as a wink.

## Chapter I

### In which Joan Orpí faces the first pitched battle of his lifetime and miraculously makes it out alive

Very well, fine . . . we'll set aside the giants and focus on Joan Orpí's departure for Seville. We shall now say, to all those who still want to listen, that such a long voyage as the one our hero undertook to the south of the Peninsula was no joke. In those days one lived on constant alert, weapons at the ready, prepared for probably dangerous encounters. The fears were real. Between the bloodthirsty Barbary pirates who patrolled the Catalan coasts by sea and the treacherous highwaymen on terra firma, it was rough going.

Orpí was a scant four leagues from the Via d'Igualada, the kingsroad that linked the Court to Barcelona, when he came across nothing less than a troop of Nyerros dressed in lace-up espadrilles, barretines, and britches, and armed with pistols, pouches, and shotguns, galloping out of a blazing forest, playing bugles and rattles. Their leader stopped in front of our hero.

"Pray God keep thee safe, gallant pilgrym. By what name be thee known?"

"Joan Orpí del Pou, at thy service," he said, removing his hat in greeting.

"Good tidings, sir. Mine name be Perot Rocaguinarda[52], in the employ of the Duke of Pudding, on the French side. We beseeketh a band of statist Cadells what wish him harm. Our lord hath been challeng'd by an unimpeachable herald and we must obtaine justice. We knoweth yond the Cadells hath a *fautor*[53] somewhither 'round these parts."

"Ah, well I knowe naught arent that. All I know is that ye art Nyerros, since the dog insignia be embroidered on thine baldrics."

"Spotte on. I descry thou art a well-informed man. So what beest thou: duke, marquis, counte, viscounte, baron, knyt, or squire?"

"Null of the above. I be a graduate in law from the University of Barcelona, and destin'd to Seville in seek of gainful employe."

"Goode on thee. Thanks be for the particulars, lawyer. And now, necessarily: thine money or thine life."

"I doth protestest!" said Orpí.

"Protest sustained," said the highwayman. "Thine fine raiment leeds mee to surmise thee hath coin."

"Fearest thou not royal perogative?" said Orpí, using his legal skills to save his skin and the little money he had.

"Not evenne in the slightest," said Rocaguinarda. "The jurisdictional manner in whiche the Principallity hath been carved up means that the viceroy hath neither voice nor vote in matters involving determined noblemen. We be untouchable under his wing."

---

52.  *i.e.* A Catalan highwayman, famous throughout Europe, who even appears in the second part of *Don Quixote*.

53.  *i.e.* A peasant accomplice who hides highwaymen.

"Excepting when assaulting a royal officer on a king's road or in the course of a Peace and Truce, is that not so?"

"Precisely," agreed the highwayman.

"Well that being the case, I art verily a royal officer," lied Orpí. "And if I be not mistaken we findeth ourselfs uponne a king's road and, if I be not mistak'n, we art in a period of Peace and Truce. And, if I be not mistaken, vilating the Peace and Truce of God sygnifies infringin' a royal order and whosoever doth imfringe uponst thus and so, art then considered 'expell'd by Peace and Truce' or, in other words, legally outside the law. And be I not mistaken, no man canst make use of weapons in the absence of a war justifying such weapons under *Princeps namque*—in other words, with the country under invasion, nor for illegal pilferage of any sorte. And if be not mistaken, I hath not a thing furthermore to adde."

"Blowe mine buttons . . . thou maketh a good point! Begge pardon the interruption," said the highwayman. Quite befuddled by all that legal information, he gave a long whistle and disappeared along with all his men, in the opposite direction whence they'd come.

Joan Orpí continued along his route, pleased and proud of having gotten rid of those marauders by using his wits and the little he'd learned at law school. But, after only ten minutes of riding, he came across another troop of highwaymen heading toward him.

This time they were Huguenots of the sect of Luther and Gascons traveling together who'd clearly come from looting a convoy of the king's money and cargo from the American continent, because they had all sorts of precious metals peeking out of the pouches strapped across their chests. Someone blew a goat's horn and the troop halted. The captain, who wore the symbol of a Santiago piglet sewn into his habit, marking him as a member of the Cadells, approached Orpí.

"May the Lord blesse thee and keep theeee, Mr . . . ?" asked the highwayman, a tall, lanky, one-eyed man, known as Barbeta,[54] who, due to his profession, was wanted for murder, misdemeanor rape, and maxdemeanor theft.

". . . Joan Orpí del Pou, at thine service."

"The good time of day to thee. Thou didnst happ to espy a bande of Nyerros passing here, heading north, if it be not too much to ask?"

"Well, the sooth is I didst beholde them," said Orpí. "And I wouldst posit they be no more than a half-league from hither, giveth or taketh."

"Thank thee kind for the information. We bee up in arms against a feudal lord who has harmed mine own lorde and we wilt safeguard his honor with blood and guts."

"Very well, valorous luck to thee and until we meeteth again," said Orpí, preparing to leave.

"Not so fasteth," said the captain. "How canst I know whither thou speaketh the truth or a bald prevarication?"

"I see not wherefor I shud prevaricate, since I beest a just person, inside and out."

"I shall bee the judge of yond in any case," declared the captain. "Until such tyme, thou shalt come with us as our

54.  *i.e.* Historic highwayman by the name of Pere Barba (Guimerà, sixtenth century-Barcelona, 1616)

guide. If we donst find the Nyerros, you're a dead man. Hath we a deal?"

"I object!"

Despite his strident objection, poor Orpí had no choice but to accompany the band of Cadells toward the north, when what he wanted was to head south. As he reluctantly rode, a civilized pony came over to him, and atop the pony was none other than the dwarf, Triboulet the Distasteful.

"Not thou again!" exclaimed Orpí. "Thou art as a carbuncle on mine posterior, dwarf. Each time we meet I know something bad is bounde to happen."

"Orpí, don't look daggers nor speaketh so ille of me!" exclaimed the dwarf. "Methinks tis fate, or destiny, what bringeth us together."

"We could also deem it 'rotten lucke,'" added Orpí. "Dost thou mindeth telling me what thou doeth here, a highwayman again?"

"I canst explain," said the dwarf. "What happen'd wast, after fleeing mine own laboratory pursu'd by the Mossos de l'Esquadra in Barcelona, I did hide in the forest whither this band of Cadells did trapp me like a wild beeste. They did spare mine life in exchange f'r the secret to a joyous life."

"And what be yond secret, halfman, if't be true thee knoweth it?"

"The secret is not to gette ensnared in aught too boring," said the dwarf, undaunted. "In any case we shant be bored soon, of that I canst assure thee."

Ten minutes later they saw a cloud of dust approaching; the dust cloud transformed into miniature shadows; and the miniature shadows turned out to be the band of Nyerros they were looking for.

"Wait here," the captain ordered Orpí.

"Never fear, that I shall."

Soon that valley became a battle scene. The two bands clashed in a combat with a horrific shootout, the screeching of the dying, the clanking of swords, bodies falling from horses, and splintering skulls and teeth. It was a mortal combat that lasted as long as a dog's piss, an absolute slaughter that left no man standing. When the lethal dust cloud dissipated, Nyerros and Cadells had finally avenged the honor of their lords, but they been all made mincemeat. The only man left standing was our Joan Orpí.

## Chapter II

### In which Joan Orpí finds three traveling companions without even trying

Everything was left in shambles. More than eighty Nyerros and Cadells were now being devoured by vultures that'd quickly swooped down for their next scrumptious cadaveric hors d'ouevre. When Orpí was just about to flee the scene, he heard a cry for help. As he approached the mountain of inert bodies, he discovered a hooded highwayman, with restless, bold eyes, who had been badly hurt but was still alive.

"Who bees ye?" said Orpí as he treated the wounds of the highwayman with the covered face.

"What dost thou care?" said the mysterious survivor.

"Insolence! When I've only come to thine aid. I shall run thou through with mine sword!"

Before our hero managed to unsheath his weapon, the highwayman had already cut his belt and Orpí's pantaloons were at his ankles, revealing underwear badly in need of a wash. The highwayman let out a rather effeminate laugh.

"One moment, thine jauntiness & grace with thine sword art beyonde compare, but something be fishy hither," said Orpí, pulling away his adversary's hood in a lightning-fast motion. Our hero was totally surprised, and not just partially. A petite young woman with intelligent eyes stared back at him threateningly.

"Thou . . . art no highwayman . . . thou art . . . a highway-woman!" he said.

"Martulina the Divina, as I be knowne. What's wrong, bub, never seen a girle before?" she said, undoing the knot in her hair as long, golden locks fell to her shoulders.

Orpí didn't know what to do or say. He noticed that the highwaywoman seemed too young to be a mother and too old to be a girl. She was some sort of sexless, narrow-hipped lass, covered in grime and with tobacco-stained teeth.

"Look, bub," said Martulina, "there be soldiers who battle highwaymen, highwaymen who are sent to the galleys, soldiers who turn into highwaymen, and highwaymen who turne into soldiers."

"Yeah, sure, but . . . thou art a woman!"

"Harping on gender again, art we?" she exclaimed. "I suppose thee bethinks I doth belonge at home, washing clothes and cooking for mine own husband, tis that it? Well, I hath not a husband, nor do I seeketh one! Mine lyfe is far remov'd from traditional patriarchal roles as all distinktion betwixt menne and womenne be based in an abuse of social authority, dost thou understandeth? Grrrrrrr!"

"Don't get all riled up, woman . . . " said Orpí, trying to calm her down. "I've ne'er bespied a woman brandishing a swarde, but I don't presuppose thou art the last nor the first to doth soe."

"Thou presupposeth correctly," declared Martulina. "History be fill'd with warrier women: from Athena and Zenobia to Queen Boudica, the Valkryies, the Amazons . . . fistfulls of eggzamples whence to choose! And, admit it, I doth brandish a sword a mite bit better than thee," she said.

"I admit it," conceded Orpí.

"I've allways been more skilfull with a weapon than with the laundry, to be frank. Pointe of fact, I'm wanted for triple murd'r bye the Audiencia of Barcelona, and near nie tooke the axe when, at the last minute, they didst proffer a pardon in exchange for enlysting with the Nyerros. However now there be no Nyerros nor any Cadells (them being all butchered) so, officially, I seem a deserter. Either I abanden Cataloonia or I shall end up swinging from a noose in the Plaça del Rei. They make no gend'r distinctions whence it comes to that, ye knowtice?"

In the face of such overwhelming logic, Joan Orpí and Martulina the Divina set off together, although for different reasons, on the long road south. They trotted over a plain, they mounted a hillock, they descended into a valley, they crossed a fresh, clean river, they passed three thousand heads of livestock, they looked up and saw a group of vultures flying by, they came across a procession of penitent Capuchin monks, they spanned a small bridge and on the other end they found a hunter who sold them two dead quails and a hare.

That evening, as they cooked the victuals under the generous shelter of a holm oak, they heard a deafening sound coming from Orpí's satchel.

"Good Lord, what be that horrendous noise?"

"It doth come from thine bag," she said. "Some sort of sorceree."

Orpí opened up his satchel and there he discovered, to his great surprise, Triboulet the Dwarf curled up inside like a worm.

"Dost thou mind telling me what thou art doing here?"

"First of all: hi," said the dwarf. "And, next of all, seeing that matters were upon the verge of hairy with those two gangs, I did decide to seeke refuge in thine satchel. Furthermore, I heardeth the plan to head south and I'm all in. I shall wend with ye guys to Seville. Se-vi-vi-vi-lla, tra-la-la!" sang the dwarf, laughing and clapping his hands as he leapt from the satchel to the ground.

Then Triboulet snatched one of the paws off the hare they were roasting and chomped it down noisily until not even the bone was left.

"Good Lorde, that's revolting, dwarfman!" complained Orpí. "Canst thou not wait for us all to dine cheek by jowl, half-savage?"

After dinner, Orpí asked the dwarf, "Thou didst tell how you escaped from thine lab, but I hath yet to learne the fate of thine Homunculus . . ."

"Oh, I carry 'im with me at-all times, in dis here little leather bag," said the dwarf, opening it up to reveal a deformed little being, as tiny as a chickpea and as repulsive as a fetus. "The poor little guy canth speak yet, but he singeth like a troo nightingale."

No sooner had he said that then the Homunculus began to modulate in a thin, raspy little voice:

♪ So yeaaa they call me Homunculesss ♫
Yeah, that's right, hot off da press
I cou' whistle, I cou' dance, now ya hear me sang,
Yeah it aint no thang but a chicken twang.
Mine Creator was forever dreamin'
Of that day I came inta bein':
Simple parts join'd with a dash of grace divine
Thou got thouses, now I gots mine
Cuz Imman intellectual with a fly IQ
Displayin' strong emotions
like I loathe you.
Yeah, sassite, they call me Homunculus

No, not yer average abunculus
In fact this little man is hyper-magnetic
While others, they call him supremely frenetic.
Mine Creator, yeeeah, in His infinite wistdom
Done gave me a closed digestive system
Now Im not made a no clay
Not sprung from no gard-enn
Make sexual reproduction passé
So go on and put away that hard-onnn!

And while that strange creature sang, Triboulet the Dwarf started to play a *sac de gemecs*[55] and Orpí and Martulina frolicked in a highly entertaining little dance as the night sky rolled out a carpet of stars. And that was how our hero continued on his journey to Seville with two unexpected friends (plus a singing Homunculus) who would be of great help to him, because as we all know, "a life without friends is no life at all, it's just passing days." And now, let us journey on to the next Chapter.

---

55. A type of bagpipe native to Catalonia.

## Chapter III

### In which Orpí and his friends, on their way south, happen upon a depressed knight

The three friends arrived bright and early to the capital city of the Kingdom of Valencia, where they purchased new provisions for their journey. The city was an unbridled hustle and bustle of buying and selling, where vendors feathered their nests. Triboulet and Martulina visited the Serranos Gate and the Silk Exchange, while Orpí bought some books by Roís de Corella and Isabel de Villena at rock-bottom prices. After resting one night in the city, the three friends continued southward.

As they were crossing a desert, the sun roasting their heads, they saw a man approaching at a gallop, gleaming like a star. He shone thusly because he was wearing an old-fashioned suit of armor, with a lance and standard and a shield with a noble crest. Let's clarify, now that we've reached this point, that a knight such as that was an anomaly in the landscape, because the only knights left by that point were in fairytales and in engravings like the one reproduced below.

Be that as it were, the anonymous knight, upon seeing Orpí and his companions, spurred on his horse and, with his lance pointing straight at their noses, he hurled himself fast as lightning on the attack. The three friends didn't know what to do or where to hide because they were surrounded by desert. But as luck would have it the horse stumbled, and both beast and rider fell on their asses. The tremendous racket of the metal plates of armor crashing against the ground echoed through the entire desert and a couter, his sword, surcoat, the crest atop his helmet, and one of his shoes trimmed in metal went flying through the air, along with many of the screws, rings, hooks, straps, and buckles that held together his suit of armor.

The knight tried to stand up but the thirty kilos of metal he was wearing made that impossible without the help of Orpí and his companions. When he was finally standing on his own two feet, the knight began to cry. It was a remote, childish, metallic weeping, since he was still wearing his helmet. The anonymous knight introduced himself as Grau de Montfalcó from Castle Pink, son of Gausbert de Montfalcó of Castle Pink, and he ceased to be quasi anonymous *ipso facto*.

"Mayhaps thou'd feel better if thou tookest off all that scrap iron," said Martulina.

"Nay, I doth never removeth mine armor, not even to sleep," said the slightly effemininate Sir Grau. "Nor mine helmet, Knight's Honor. As the great March[56] did sayeth:

> As armour forged in steel crunches with a blow
> And that made of iron is pierced at the slightest
> When joined together they withstand every test;
> et cetera, et cetera. . ."

---

56. *i. e.* "Tot entenent amador mi entengua," by Ausiàs March.

"Quitte bawling like some Amadís de Gaula, man, pastoral novels are for spinster aunts," said Orpí, trying to cheer him up. "Bucke up, any day now thou shalt find chivalrous virtue & a princess's love and some minstrel shall singeth thine exploits."

"Nooo!" howled the knight from inside his helmet. "Nowadays minstrells only chase skirts. Tis all 'thine gams art golden' and 'thine locks be the fount of mine adoration' and corny stuffe of that manner. I shall end up having to pen mine own exploits, like a regular olde picaroon. Thou may as well just kill me now! As Tirant sayeth: Oh, fortune, so displeased with me, sometimes exalting me and othertimes bringing me so low!"

"Knyght, picaroon, pastor or pilgrim, it be all the selfsame as long as there's adventure," mused Orpí.

But Grau de Montfalcó seemed to suffer from severe depression and he was not listening to reason. So our hero decided to camp out beneath an olive tree for the night. They invited the knight to sup with them and treated him with the kindness and care that any sensitive person needs in such moments of existential anxiety. Before a controlled bonfire (where Triboulet was roasting some partridges), the knight, continuing to wear his armor and helmet in everlasting perpetuity, confessed his traumas:

"Ere since I was a wee tyke I was ever bein' told that I had to do as mine father dictat'd," murmured the knight in a metallic voice. "First they hadst me castrat'd to see whether I had what it tooketh to be a *capon*,[57] but uponst seeing that I wouldst never be a soprano, or even so much as a mezzo-soprano, mine father did decree I wouldst be what mine

---

57. *i.e.* Also known by their Italian name, *castrati*, these were boys who underwent orchidectomies so that their singing voices would always stay high, to better reflect the apogee of sixteenth- to eighteenth-century Italy.

grandfather and great-grandfather hadst been, viz., a knight. I desir'd to study medicine still & all thee wate of family tradition did make me what I be at the presente: a walking anachronism. From hither to thither, I doth ride from one ende of the earth to the other, casting 'bout fer someone to smite in a duel, seeking bewitch'd damsels, obsolete tournaments, and giants and dragons in distant caves knowing, as I knoweth, that suche things existeth mere in dreams and in books."

"Thy frustration bee understandable, friend," said Orpí. "We all hatheth ambitions, but some art more realistick than others. As a knave, I too did dream of becoming a knight, since they appear a good mite better in books than they doth in realitee."

Having said that, Orpí pulled out one of the many books he carried in his satchel.

"I recommend thou readeth yond *editio princeps* of a highly popular book: *The Ingenious Gentleman Don Quixote of La Mancha*, by a writer I knewe briefly in Barcelona. It doth stand up very welle against Martorell's *Tirant*."

"Tis right naybourlee of you. But I ne'er wanted to be a knight, nor an ingenious gentleman, nor any suche thing!" lamented Grau, putting away Orpí's gift. "I've abhorred violence ere I was a child, the sight of blood makes me faint, and I canst barely lift my broadsword and make a thrust!"

"Thou must 'kill thy father,'" said Martulina the Divina. "That be the only way thou shalt be free to choose what thou truly desireth, without the weight of family pressure."

"She's got a pointe," added Triboulet the Dwarf. "I killt mine with a hammer blow at the ripe age o' six . . . and ever since I've had the best of luck!"

"I meant symbolically, half-idjiot," clarified Martulina. "As a fledgling, they bade mee dress as a gurl, and do all that whiche little girls do (mend, scrub, bake), till one day I did choppe mine hair off, pluck uppe mine things, and hitt the road. Disguised as a knave I canne liveth out mine dream of swashing a sword and having adventures."

All these group confessions seemed to cheer up the knight of Montfalcó a little, although it was hard for the three friends to tell since with that helmet on they didn't know if he was smiling or still crying. Finally the knight decided to take it off, revealing a glimpse of his chubby, oval face and his hair, white and fine as a baby's. He looked like he'd never hurt a fly.

"Thank ye, friends," he said with his effeminate voice. "Thine kinde words hath persuad'd me to make a life change. I vow[58] never again to be who I be not. If tis alle the selfsame to ye, I shall accompany ye along on the present pilgrimage, seeing as ye be the sole friends I hath in this worlde."

Thus, with the addition of an existentially unshackled Grau de Montfalcó, Joan Orpí's companions on his journey to Seville became three instead of two. Ay no, four—I can't forget the Homunculus!

---

58. *i.e.* Vows were a common recourse within the knightly realm.

## Chapter IV

In which Orpí and his friends meet up
with a sect of mystics and take part
in a remarkable competition

While Orpí and his friends rode south, along the patrol road,
they stopped their horses at a watering place where the following sign was posted:

**FIRST ANNUAL CONGRESS OF THE ENLIGHTENED**
**INSCRIPTION: 10 MARAVEDIS**
(INCLUDES A GLASS OF PLONK
AND AN OLIVE)

Behind the sign there were many people milling about,
and when they saw the riders approach they invited them to
partake of the refreshments they were serving. So Orpí and
his friends mingled with the pilgrims. Our hero soon realized that he was in the midst of a meeting of madmen. And
we say that because, in one of the circles that had formed, a
group of people were watching an orgy between a eunuch,

a hermaphrodite, an eighty-year-old woman, a monkey, a huge dog, a goat, and a four-year-old child, the old woman's great-grandson.

"Slip 'er the ole church atop the belltower!" shouted one onlooker.

"Now . . . squeeze & dig!" yelled another.

"Here cometh the twitter-light, tinting the worlde with darkness!" exclaimed another further on.

Orpí, horrified, asked one of the spectators in Spanish, "Pray telle, what sort of diabolickal gathering be this, sires?"

"This be the Annyual Conventicle of Toledo *dejados* or *alumbrados*, disciples of Isabel de la Cruz," said one man.

"Our objective be acheeving mystickal ecstasy through amourous rites. We doth rejecte the concept of sin, preferrin' coitus and orgazm as the supreme union with divinity," added a second man.

"We donst subscribe ta tha worship a saints, 'r fryars, n'r the adorayshun a relicks 'r Catholisism in generall," informed a third.

"We sweareth to forswear wage, coin, and power," affirmed a fourth. "And to disrate pain and suffering in fav'r of the earthly plaisures."

Orpí and his friends observed the various circles. In some, there were people fornicating, in others the mystics whipped themselves mercilessly, and in still others they ate the excrements, pus, and vomit of the dying. In one of those circles there was an adage and proverb contest. The winner was to receive the prize of a sexual experience with a pony. Triboulet the Dwarf, who was competitive by nature, entered the circle, where a "dexado" was waiting for him. They began to battle, face to face, barking proverbs and adages at each other in the middle of the circle, one in Spanish and the other in Catalan:

"A fool and his money art soon departed!" said the dejado.

"A leopard can't change his spots!" shouted Triboulet.

"Napple a day keeps da doctor away!"

"There be reason in the roasting of eggs!"

"Durly bird catches da wurm!"

"Half a loaf is better than none!"

"Play wid fire, and you'll get burned!"

"Make hay wile the sun shines!"

"Necessity is the muther of invention!"

Triboulet the Dwarf's mind went blank, but he opened up the small bag where he kept his Homunculus and the little being, in his high-pitched voice, yelled out:

"Spare at the spigot, and let out the bung-hole!"

"More den one way to skinne a cat!"

"Watch da donut, not the hole!" said the "dexado."

"Patience be a virgin!" continued the dwarf.

"Whem da catz away, da mice'll play!"

"Squeaky wheel secures the grease!"

"When it raineth, it poureth!"

"Strike while the iron be hot!"

"A bird in thine hand tis worthe two in thine bush!"

"Look beforst leapeing!"

"Speak soft and carry a nice stick!"

"Idle hands conclude the devil's work!"

"In the land of the blind, the halfman is king!"

"The worst men giveth the best advice!"

"Even a broken whore's right twice a day!"

"Enuff . . . !" shouted Orpí, weary of so much folly, as the two competitors panted and drooled from their efforts. "Enuff, enuf, ennnuf of this infernall paremiology! This be a conventicle of ninnyhammers, not mystics!"

Just then a tremendous din of galloping horses was heard. A band of armed men appeared out of nowhere shouting,

"Death be to the heretics! Alle hail the Golden Fleece![59]" while they ruthlessly swung their swords and decapitated the *deja-dos* and everyone ran around shrieking and bloodied from the attack of the fearful swordsmen who . . . [60]

---

59. An order of chivalry related to the Hapsburg dynasty.

60. Unfortunately this Chapter is unfinished because the ink on the original manuscript faded beyond recognition. Nonetheless, Joan Orpí and his friends survived the adventure, since we see them all again in the next Chapter.

## Chapter V

### In which Orpí and his friends
### are robbed by thieves
### and then celebrate St. John's Eve

Making their way south, the four friends traveled around the city of Cordoba and came across Andalusian goat herders lying pastorally beneath the trees together with their herd (with whom they made many happy memories), sport hunters on horseback with their dogs running behind them; soldiers in regiment, solitary pilgrims, and highwaymen hiding in that parched and shriveled landscape where every cave was a castle and every hill a watchtower. The friends navigated towns, rivers, and streams with their eyes peeled and the triggers of their harquebusses at the ready, just in case.

When night fell, Orpí and his friends decided to stop and refuel at a small rancho[61] made up of improvised tents. No sooner had they arrived than they met three shifty-looking didicois dressed in old rags. Amid *ceceos*[62], they invited them

---

61. *i.e.* Gypsy camp.

62. A dialectical phenomenon native to some southern parts of the Iberian Peninsula.

into a ruinous *cortijo*[63], saying they wanted to invite them to supper.

"Come in, have a zeat, fellowz."

Once everyone was inside, the three gypsies pulled out their flintlocks from beneath their capes and politely demanded money from our hero and his friends.

"Didicoi shysters," declared Orpí.

"Vile geneaology," agreed Grau de Montfalcó, weeping in fear.

"Tis but an expression of the class struggle," explained Martulina the Divina. "The Roma art poor people rebelling in defiance of their poverty."

"Ye seeketh fortunes and adversity," said Triboulet the Distasteful. "But mistake me not: fer I be one of ye, I steal to live and thusly live carefree. I gette ye!"

The muggers, ignoring them all, went ahead and shot their weapons, but the flints were too worn and none of them worked. The three scalawags then tried to run out and steal their horses, but when one mounted Acephalus, the steed bucked and threw him off while relaxing its sphincters and impregnating everything with a gut-churning odor. The didicois, relinquished and repentant, confessed, "Hey, man, even though weez pickpockets we too be childrenz of Undivel.[64]"

"Luck favorz the bold. We make our way, bezeeching and eyez peeled for something to znatch, but we don't want to zin no more."

"We're thievez because nobody done never teached uz nuffin, to uz gypzies. We don't know how to read nor fright . . ."

Orpí, seeing that the didicois had good hearts, gave them the following sermon:

---

63. A type of traditional dwelling in southern Spain.

64. Caló for God.

"Sirs, I wilt admit I didn't understandeth a word of thy very particular mumbo jumbo, but as a lawyer, I wilt telleth thee plain: highwaymen, thieves, sluggards, and murderers shouldst beest punished with the full force of the law. However, as sure as mine name be Joan Orpí, the good are allways rewarded and ne're suffer, and ingenuity and fine intentions can transmute evil into productive peace. So let us forget this incident, for verily no wanion has transpired here."

The three thieves, hearing that speech and the name of the speaker, gratefully said, "What a fine lezzon of mannerz you sirz have gived us. From now on, we zhall try to be zomewhat better peoplez. And what a conzidenze about yer name, zince today iz Zaint John!"

"Itz June 24th!"

"Zinging, dancing, and bonfire! Pilgrimz, ye art welcome to join uz!"

Without any ill will, Orpí and his friends followed the pious, reformed gypsies to the middle of their camp, where a crowd had formed to celebrate our hero's saint's day with some hundred-odd people who, despite being poorer than a skunk's misery, invited them to eat a stew containing the spines of animals they'd hunted, goat anus, and extremely hot Arabian spices, and everyone enjoyed the feast, happy and sated. Then they were enjoined to partake of a spicy black broth, made specially for that celebration, called *cornezuelo*, made from a fungus of the Claviceps family that has psychotropic properties. With an enormous bonfire burning in the center of the circle of caravans, they began to sing *jácaras* and dance in an improvised, eclectic, and detached way after drinking that broth. Some of them rolled around in the mud like happy sows, others leapt over the flames shrieking and laughing, others tore off their clothes and danced half-naked, gyrating their hips.

Driven mad by hours of frenetic dancing, most of them fell to ground out of pure exhaustion. Others, their thoughts still flummoxed by the effects of the lethal fungus, had visions of another world. Amid the general hallucinations, Grau de Montfalcó thought he was a hen and was clucking in a corral amid other hens, until the rooster approached and pecked him in the foot. Martulina the Divina was dancing and kissing a very dark gypsy girl, giving free rein to her natural instincts. Triboulet the Dwarf had fallen into the stew and was imagining he was at a Turkish bath surrounded by concubines, while his tiny Homunculus hopped through the bread crumbs on the ground and envisioned himself on the surface of some imaginary planet. Our hero, on the other hand, was having a bad trip and, dancing and dancing, he'd ended up in front of an abandoned house. And the house had stuck in his mind. And now, instead of a head, Orpí had a house. And inside that house, no one was ever home.

## Chapter VI

### In which Orpí and his friends meet an Arab who tells them a ghost story

The next morning, when Orpí and his friends awoke, they saw that the improvised camp had disappeared and the gypsies had vanished as if by the art of magic.

"Damn tinkers! They hath bilked us!" bawled our hero. "But unaccountably, they forsooke our ducats and took merely our shoes . . . what bisarre folk!"

So, barefoot as your average penitents, Orpí and his friends continued their route toward Seville, where they stopped at a convent to ask for some soup. There they were given shoes and that very afternoon, crossing over two gigantic mountains traversed by a timid brook of crystal-clear water, our hero said, "Methunks we've been here before."

"Cain't be," replied Martulina. "Hange on, now that thou sayeth that . . . yond brook ringeth a bell."

"Alass & allack!" cursed Orpí. "We hath gone in circles! Did thou not say thou knew the way, Triboulet?"

"I lied," confessed the dwarf, laughing the whole while.

A fog was now spreading through the precipitous mountains, surrounding the small group lit only by a big, round, full moon that was partially blurred by the mist. Suddenly, a long, high-pitched howl broke the silence.

"Awesum, just what we needeth: wolves," complained Grau de Montfalcó, furrowing his brow. "We shll be eat'n alive if we don't doeth something!"

Too late. A shadow appeared before them, spinning in circles, emerging and vanishing amid the rocks.

"They art surrounding us!" carped Martulina, who'd pulled out a slingshot and fired a rock at the beast, who let out a quite unbeastly "ow!"

"Ow?" asked Orpí. "Wolves don't say ow."

The friends approached the wounded body stretched out on the ground, and discovered a man covered in wolf hides.

"This poore man besuffereth *mania lupina*," said Orpí, medically. "He most lik'ly wast bitten by a wolf, like the King of Arcadia,[65] and did turn into a lycanthrope."

At that, the wolfman, who wasn't dead, leapt up and bit the person closest to him, who was poor Grau de Montfalcó.

"Owwww!" Grau cried out in pain as Orpí and the others pounced on the stranger and tied up his hands.

When the biter came to, he spoke like this: "انت مجنون!"[66]

"What sayeth he?"

"That must bee the language of the licanthropes," concluded Orpí. "We must heal Grau rapid or he shall turnt into a wolf as well."

"No! He be a Turk!" exclaimed Triboulet the Dwarf, drawing his dagger.

"أيها الملاعين!"[67] he said before continuing in Spanish. "I art no wolfman and no Turk! More like a yunicorn with this

---

65. *i.e.* Orpí is alluding to Ovid's *Metamorphoses.*

66. *i.e.* "You're crazy!" in Arabic.

67. *i.e.* "Damn idiots!" in Arabic.

141

noggin bumpe from yon rock ye threw at mee! I art Valle del Omar Sha-Rif and a Moslem from the Penynsula, a physician by trade. Free me and, while I healeth thy friend, I shall tell ye mine peckuliar story."

A little while later, they were all sitting around a campfire on which Triboulet the Dwarf and Martulina were cooking, lovingly, two hares they'd caught a few hours earlier. While they all gorged themselves, the Arab tended to Grau de Mont-falcó's wound and told his story.

"As a man of mine wurd, I shall begin at the begynning. I am a Moor, *Allah is xabidor*,[68] borne and raized in Alhama, a city of the Kingdom of Granada, and did study to be an algebraist[69], as ze Arab triumfs in those lands art numerous and varied, in the fields of architecture and bricklaying, agrickulture, medicine, and craftwork. Mine medical renown anon reach'd the ears of a deep-pocket'd gentleman, whose saintly wife, Doña Inés, grewe very ill after a tumble offe a stallion. As the Averroists, I doth not believe in eternal life, notwithstanding I did sweare to remedy his bryde and thus I did, and they both didst marvell, and hence I did becomme their doctor. However a remarkible friendship aroseth twixt Doña Inés and I, so remarkible that mine orbs didst growe more and more captivat'd with each passing day as I look'd beponst her, 'til her splendour seemed to me commensurate to, and even greater than, the majestick gardens of Aranjuez (which, as all civilised men knowe, art the most lovely in this worlde). Altho her husband didst discover our secret love, and one night he did kille Doña Inés as she sleept and had me arrest'd and condemn'd to death by hanging. But, by the prophet Mohammed, whilst I did awaite mine fate in

---

68. *i.e.* "Only Allah knows," in Arabic.

69. *i.e.* Surgeon specialized in bone fractures and dislocations.

pryson, induring a mickle of tortures, one night before me didst appeare the ghost of Doña Inés, who open'd up every door to me, allowing mee to escape. I fled yond city, into the mountains, where I did contrive to catch a wolf to sate mine hunger. And then I didst rid mineself of mine vestiments so as to elude discoveree, then did sheathe mineself with the skyns of that beest. And tis thusly how I came to be thusly: in these mountains, in this solitude amongst these crags, amidst this snow, distanc'd from mine longe life of anguish, ever glancing o'er mine shoulder, for the long arm of justice be long. Ere-since, mye Doña Inés doth appear to me each night—prithee may the Prophet keep her in his Garden—and tis as if I twere wedded to a zombee. That be alle, peoples of the northland, I canst tell ye of mie story, whose ending I shall leave to the heavens, to the earth, and to thine goode guidance."

After hearing the end of Valle del Omar's sad and moving biography, Orpí and his friends dried their tears. And it aroused such tenderness in them toward that poor man that they invited him to continue along with them to Seville in search of a better life. However, dear reader, that is a story not for this Chapter, but the next.

## Chapter VII

In which we learn of the arrival of the six friends
to the city of Seville and
Joan Orpí receives some bad tidings

The five friends (plus the Homunculus) finally reached the city of Seville. It was all flower-filled balconies, narrow cobblestone streets, churches with gold and polychrome altars and Solomonic columns, and it was all immobilized by a lethal heat that made the excrement and urine on the streets boil with an unbearably noxious stench. Our band led their horses up-up-up a long, narrow street of white houses, crowned with a small church. Then they went down an even narrowerer street to the Torre del Oro and from there, to the Puerta del Arenal. A raging sun beat down, and throughout that entire trajectory they didn't see a single soul. The city seemed to be abandoned. But as soon as the sun set behind the mountains and the chiming of the bells of the Giralda were heard, the whole city suddenly filled with people and the roar of human life: royal soldiers, hidalgos, gentlemen, ladies of the upper bourgeoisie, black slaves imported from Africa, natives from the Indies wearing loincloths and feathers on their heads who looked at everything with terrorized eyes, carriages and carts passing up and down, taverns opening up their doors, churches ringing their bells, *sopistas*[70] singing amusing syllogisms for their *sopa boba*, villains plotting swindles beneath bridges, sailors flirting with ladies of the night, and citizens of a thousand different nations.

"What a lotte of people there be in this city . . . and suche rejoicing!" exclaimed our hero.

Where so many people came from not even God knows, but the city of Seville turned out to be a very lively, jovial place, a marvel where it seemed all dreams could be realized.

Orpí and his friends entered one of the many taverns that lined a square, where they heard a music entirely new to their ears, with intense guitar strumming, shouts, faces that clenched and softened, shrieks and vibrant stomps. A dancer moved her skirt as if two flags were waving at once and a man bellowed as if his liver were being pulled from his mouth, and everyone accompanied the musicians with rhythmic hand clapping. When Orpí asked Valle del Omar what sort of music that was, the Moor answered, "*Fellah-mangú*, mine friend. The song of the Moors and the journeymen gypsies."

"Thou dost call it *falamengu*?" asked Orpí.

"Yes, flamenco, or some such," he said.

---

70. Poor students who sang in exchange for a stew made of leftovers.

While Martulina, del Omar, and Grau had some tapas and Triboulet the Dwarf joined in with a dancer, our hero headed, thinking positively and wasting no time, to the local government office. He was prepared to ask for the job that his former mentor in Barcelona, the Sephardi Yehuda Abrabanel, had assured him his letter of recommendation would secure him. When Orpí reached the secretary, he removed his hat in a wide bow and said, "Hello, esteem'd secretary."

"My name iz Zeñó Ernesto, not zecretary."

"Very well, *Ernesto*. I come sent by Manuel de Rubeola, of Barcelona, bearing a letter of commendation for the post as administrator to thee royal tobacco shoppes," he said, in Catalan-inflected Spanish.

The secretary Ernesto laughed so hard he almost choked.

"Lookee here, Catalan, the man whoze name thou bandy about be a huckzter and a Jew. He'z wanted by the law, underztand? If he zhowz hiz face in Zeville, he shan't live long."

"Art thou saying I don't get the job?" asked Orpí. "I have a law degree, eh? Can I speak with whomever's in charge around hither?"

"Law degree zchmaw degree! Skedaddle!"

When our hero returned, entirely woebegone, to where his friends were waiting for him, he found Martulina the Divina in a sword fight with five rogues at once and the tavern in shambles.

"Wouldst thou mind telling me what the heyeck be going on here?" asked Orpí, fighting by the young woman's side.

"Thy friend, the dwarf," she said, stabbing an opponent. "He groped his dance partner and now thirty of her brothers, cousins, and uncles be intent on cutting us down to size to safeguard her honour. It seems she was unmarried and the didicois have very strict laws regarding such matters."

"Aha," said Orpí, as he brandished his sword left and right.

Meanwhile, squads of fearsome musketeers began to arrive, breaking up the bar fight with shots of their muskets. Orpí and Martulina slipped through the backstreets before they could arrest them. Not long after, they found Grau de Montfalcó sitting on a wooden bench.

"Friends, sorry that I didst not lend a hand," he said, crying inconsolably. "Ye know I canst bear violence, I'm ever so sensitive."

"Wherefor art del Omar and Triboulet?"

"They hath vanished into the thicke air."

"Well, that's juste great."

The three friends searched for somewhere to spend the night. Once they were installed at a *posada*, they went out to a *mesón* for supper.

"Friends, I feele lost," confessed Orpí. "Turns out I have not the job I was expecting to gette. No matter thine university degree, if thou hath no godparents nor goode contacts these days, thou art a veritable no-body."

"Chinne up!" exclaimed Grau de Montfalcó. "Surely only good canst befalle us from now on! Don't ye agree?"

Orpí and Martulina looked at each other with their eyebrows raised, not at all convinced.

"Be thou a lump or what?" said the girl. "All we've had are catastrophes!"

"One moment," reflected Orpí. "Grau maketh a point. We must not allow ourselfs to lose hope withe such insouciance. As Doménico Cavalca sayeth: he who doth not work hath no right to eat. Morrow I shall get busy pursuing a jobbe, and ye guys aught followe my lead!"

Thus, with a clear plan, the three friends finished their supper and then snuck into a new comic play, entitled *Don Gil of the Green Breeches,*[71] in a corral in the Plaza Alfalfa, and then later they went to sleep, and then later . . . I'll explain what happened then later.

---

71.  *i.e.* By Tirso de Molina (1579-1648).

## Chapter VIII

In which Orpí searches for work everywhere
and finally tries his luck in a bookstore

During the following weeks, our hero devoted himself heart
and soul to his search throughout the city for paying employ-
ment. He asked for work at the port as he watched steve-
dores and sailors hauling sacks to and fro, he asked for work
from the Genovese bankers and at the markets, he asked
the carpenters, the makers of sails, the tavern keepers, the
apothecaries, and the gunners, but he received no positive
response. Finally, one day he entered a house of books called
Cromberger Press.[72] The old, antiquated place was crowded
with used, damp-smelling copies, disorganized on shelves that
went all the way up to the ceiling in endless dusty towers.
On one of the shop's walls, Orpí noticed an engraving by Jan
van der Straet that showed Amerigo Vespucci discovering an
America represented by a naked feral woman, as seen in this
reproduction:

---

72.  *i.e.* For years this Sevillian press had the exclusive monopoly on sales to
America, thanks to the favor of the King.

Rummaging through the shelves, our hero also found a copy of *Les Grandes Voyages* (1588) by Theodor de Bry, which depicted the natives of the New World as savages and cannibals. The darkness inside the shop, lit only by a weak oil lamp on the counter, prevented our hero from making out a figure seated in an armchair, right behind him, in the shadows. Orpí rang the bell on the counter several times, until the figure spoke.

"Good tidings, sir."

Our hero turned with a start, and discovered a wrinkled old man whose eyes, behind small glasses, were fixed on an enormous tome propped up on his lap. He was surrounded by mountains of books on both sides.

"Good tidings be to thee too, sir, deare bookseller!" exclaimed Orpí, removing his hat courteously as he picked up a random book to touch its dried pages and theatrically smell its binding, as he took a breath to begin the declamation of his curriculum vitae. "Ahh, what scent these longevous books doth have, both nauseating and intoxicating! Mine name be Juan Urpín, a name that perhaps means nothing to thee and as such I shant repeat it (for the moment), but thou shouldst know that tis destiny or fate what brought me here. Being as I art learn'd and well-read, I specialise in the selling of books long and short: entertainin' books such as pastoral and byzantine novels (which, lest we forget, traditional rhetoric considers the highest and most noble literary genre) and chivalresque novels (somewhat out of fashione nowadays), almanacks and books of vet'rinary science, breviaries & missals, albums of stamps and crestomathies, dictionaries & grammar books, collections of maxims & adages, books with complex characters and simple ones, violent novels for manly men and romances for restless women, epistolary collections and ancient history, eclectic medickal treatises, esoteric kabbalistic volumes or gardening manuals, expensive books with elegant covers for the rich and cheap reading copies for the plebes, notebookes for students and teachers, pens & pencils for the erudite and the ignorant, new editions for those who are uppe on the latest of trends, old books for the carefree, and *editions princeps* for those seeking ancient treasures, and even the most heathen on the trail of secret, arcane, or directly heretical books included in the famous *Index Librorum Prohibitorum*, whence the Holy See did gather all the volumes the faithful must not read under threat of mortal sin. I canne furthermore sell with equal utmost ease and sweet diligence books of military strategy as of theology, maps, or imagery, since, as an accredit'd attorney, I be a great expert in sundry subjects, from Greek and Latin to the most scientific wizdom and voguish educational postulates, and I be also capable to presage, just by looking at a customer's face, what sort of book he seeketh, and whye and whatfore, whether he shall treat the book well, as if twere 'is son, or if he shall tear it up at his first need for a bonfire, whethere he shall use what he gleaneth from his reading for Good or for Evil, since it is knowne that litterature, of all the arts and branches of 'nowledge, be verily the fertile mother of all wisdom, the fount of all relative to human experience and behaviour and, just as God omnipotent playeth with his creation (that is to say, us), the writer canst employ his skillful techniques to do as he wishes with his protagonists, so that if, for example, *this* were a novelle and not pure, concrete reality and I were the writer, I couldst decide for thee whether or not to grant me this job, and maketh all sorts of introspections into thine mind, but as such writing, just as reading, be a ne'erending story, pray let us goeth straight to the bunche of sublime and original ideas I hath in mine brain for rest'ring thine business its erstwile glory and sheen, i.e. a nice coat of paint on these mouldy walls engulf'd in centuries-olde dust, or swapping out these disgusting, opaque windows for clear'r ones, believe me, fore henceward passersby wouldst see thine intellectual business from outside and all come running in, anxious to educate their souls to the fullest, and now we couldst move right into discussing the salary that, in mine opinion, such a person as meself, Doctor of Law, shouldst receive, seeing as knowledge doth not make one rich in this worlde."

The old man, who'd been listening to our hero with all the patience in the world, got up from his armchair and said, "Young man, I hath not the faintest idea of whiche thee speak. I don't work here. And without further adoo, goodbye!"

And, taking a bow, the old man put on his hat and left the shop with quick little steps, looking over his shoulder in the hopes this lunatic wasn't following him.

"Who goes there?" said the true bookseller, a man with terrible teeth and overpowering halitosis, emerging from the back room where a bunch of people were working at a press. "Who art thou?"

"Good tidings to thee, dear bookseller!" exclaimed Orpí once again, putting on his hat only to take it off again, and picking up a random book to feel its dry pages and theatrically sniff its binding in a repetition of already rehearsed gestures. "My name is Juan Orpí, a name that perhaps means nothing to thee and as such I shant repeat it (for the moment), but thou shouldst know that I hath come here because I wish . . ."

"Enough blether & blather!" barked the bookseller. "What dost thou want?"

"Work," mumbled Orpí.

The old man put down the stack of books he'd been carrying and inspected our hero's hands, his physiognomy, his teeth, and finally, the width of his skull with a measuring tape.

"Dear lad," the bookseller finally said. "I seeth in thee a very particular, very decisive character, to put it one way, and yet thou hast an incorruptible streak of idiocy. And even if thou hast read all the books of all the world's bookstores, thou cann't force the rest of humanity to accept what thou believest to be literature, but rather tis thee who must accept what humanity believes literature to be."

"I comprehend thee not . . ."

"In short: thou art no good for selling books, only for buying them!" said the bookseller, vanishing into the mountains of books and returning, a few moments later, with a pile of volumes that included books of proverbs such as *Filosophia Vulgar* by Juan de Mal Lara; epic poems such as *La Araucana* by Alonso de Ercilla and *Pharsalia* by Lucan; Latin texts such as *The Golden Ass* by Apuleius and Ovid's *Metamorphoses*; novels of chivalry from the Carolingian and Arthurian cycles, works of philology such as *Arte de la Lengua* by Nebrija; satires such as Martial's *Epigrams*; picaresque novels like *La Celestina* and *Guzmán de Alfarache*; political science books like Boccaccio's *The Fall of Princes*; pharmacopeias such as *Exposición sobre las preparaciones de Messue* by Antonio Aguilera; books of theoretical and practical law like *De justitia et jure* by Soto, *Recopilación de las Indias*, and *Censuras del derecho*; books of oddities like Pierre Bouaisteau's *Historias Prodigiosas*; of geology like *Quilatador de plata, oro y piedras* by Juan de Arfe; encyclopedic works such as *De propretatibus rerum* by Bartholemeus Anglicus; works of ancient history like those by Xenophon and Herodotus and more modern history like Ocampo's *Crónica General*. A total of more than ninety volumes, which ran the entire spectrum of erudite literature being read at that time in Europe, were sold to Orpí at an exorbitant price, and he left the shop loaded down like a mule and without a pot to piss in, while the bookseller stood behind the counter, unable to stifle his laughter.

## Chapter IX

### In which Orpí finds himself with girl troubles
### that he shant escape easily

Having failed in his attempts to find work in Seville and having spent the little money he had on books, we find our slacker hero barely scraping by. One day he enters a courtyard so his horse Acephalus can drink from a generous spring. It is then and precisely then that he hears a woman's infinitely lovely voice singing a popular song to the gentle strumming of a lute:

> ♪ 𝔐𝔶 𝔥𝔲𝔰𝔟𝔞𝔫𝔡 𝔥𝔢 𝔴𝔢𝔫𝔱 𝔱𝔬 𝔱𝔥𝔢 𝔍𝔫𝔡𝔦𝔢𝔰 ♫
> 𝔗𝔥𝔢𝔯𝔢 𝔦𝔫𝔱𝔢𝔫𝔡𝔦𝔫' 𝔱𝔬 𝔟𝔲𝔩𝔨 𝔲𝔭 𝔥𝔦𝔰 𝔠𝔬𝔣𝔣𝔢𝔯𝔰:
> 𝔥𝔢 𝔡𝔦𝔡𝔰𝔱 𝔠𝔬𝔪𝔢 𝔟𝔞𝔠𝔨 𝔴𝔦𝔱𝔥 𝔪𝔞𝔫𝔶 𝔰𝔱𝔬𝔯𝔦𝔢𝔰,
> 𝔅𝔲𝔱 𝔫𝔬𝔱 𝔞 𝔩𝔬𝔱𝔱𝔞 𝔡𝔬𝔲𝔤𝔥 𝔱𝔬 𝔬𝔣𝔣𝔢𝔯 . . .

Suddenly, the music stopped and a voice asked, "Dearheart, dost thou seeketh company?"

Orpí looked up and saw a tall lass with generous bosoms in a window above. She was gesturing him over with a finger, as she gazed upon him with eyes of honey. Our hero did not refuse the invitation, subscribing to the proverb that says "always choose a girl who's thin and fresh, she'll be fat and sullied soon enough." He climbed the stairs and found the singer waiting for him on the first floor. After removing his cape and hat, he was invited in for coffee served in silver cups imported from Mexico. While the girl with carnal lips filled his cup, Orpí suddenly found himself with a female leg upon him, its stocking lowered past the knee, and a high-heeled shoe now resting on the parquet floor. Our hero then looked up and found himself practically inside a plunging neckline with a red rose nestled in its brown and freckled cleavage. Orpí plucked the rose out with his teeth flirtatiously, and the rest was history. After a few hours of sexual gymnastics on a noisy mattress, the girl made known her undying love as well as her first and last names:

"Úrsula Pendregast, daughter of mine noble father Arturo Pendregast, granddaughter of Calixto Pendregast. Not to mention mine mother was a countess. So basically, I've got certificates of pedigree on both esides. Would't thou care to esee them?"

"No thanks," said Orpí, who looked the girl over carefully and couldn't see nobility anywhere.

"Ay, mye leettle Catalan, thou esetteth my heart aflame!" said the woman from Seville, phony as a three-dollar bill.

"Quit yer carping, maiden, when all candles bee out all cattes be gray. Thou art very pretty, but yore love be feigned."

Just as the girl was about to continue with her list of supposed illustrious relatives, a tall, bearded man abruptly appeared in the room with the tragic expression of a cuckhold: her husband.

"Feculent sow, daughter of three-hundred squalid 'arlots! Tis the fifth tyme I find thee with another gent! This time I'll kill thee . . . trollop!"

"Ceese and desiste, Gregorio!" she shrieked.

*Malgre lui*, the deceived man's most striking feature was his missing left hand, amputated after he was bitten by a wild boar, but that didn't stop him from drawing his sword with his right and, with the fury befitting an enraged cuckold, he went straight for Orpí, who was still in his underwear, and found himself forced to defend the woman who was now crying inconsolably between the sheets. As the two men clanked swords, Úrsula came up behind her husband and broke a flower vase over his head. He fell to the ground like a sack of potatoes.

"That's all eshe wrote for yond nutjob."

"Yeegads, yee've slain him!" exclaimed Orpí.

"As the esaying goeth: Ye who gallivant off to Peru, esshall get what's coming to you!" she said, impassive. "Now I canst collect the twelve thousand *arrobas*[73] of fine gold this *perulero*[74] bastard found in the New Worlde, plus the widow's pension, to pay for all these *alhajas*[75] thou eseeth here."

Allow us here to clarify an important detail for the reader: it turns out that the ubercuckold Gregorio Izquierdo was a soldier of fortune from Seville who had gone to the Indies and found a treasure in a tributary of the Amazon River. His wife, meantime, had been gathering up a collection of lovers to fill her lonely nights. But none of those lovers had had the bad luck that Orpí did on that fateful day. And now you shall see why I say this.

"I'm outta here," said our hero, pulling up his britches.

"Hold it right thither, dulbert!" she said, lighting up a filtered cigarette. "Listen to what we'll do. Thou esshalt embark for Caracas, where this pig Gregorio keeps his riches, and

---

73. *i.e.* A measure equivalent to 138 kilograms of gold.

74. *i.e.* A man who had made his riches in Peru.

75. *i.e.* Furniture.

with this letter I give to thee, essigned by him, pretend to be my husband and grab all the treasure he's got holed up there. Nobody knows what he looks like anyway. If thou canst pull that off, forty percent of the treasure will be all thine. If thou don't agree to my pleading, I'll delate[76] you to the Holy eSee. Have we gots a deal?"

Orpí read the letter, which said:

*I, Don Gregorio Izquierdo, do hereby certify on this day—*the date was here—*with my name and on my honor, that all that is under my name belongs to me alone. And that only with my signature and my presence can my gold be withdrawn from the bank.*

And it was signed:
*Don Gregorio Izquierdo*

"I object!" exclaimed Orpí, waving the letter in the air. "This be all highly illegal! I shall report your misdeeds to the Royal Guard!"

"Objection overruled, lawyer," she said, laughing with a devilish smile. "What makes thee think they'll believe an unemployed Catalan over an esSevillian lady? If thou don't help me with my plan, I'll tell the authorities that thee killed this gachupín[77]. And beliefee me, around here they burn people for much less."

"Why donst thou go to the Newe Worlde thineself to find that blasted treasure?" asked Orpí. "Thou art his wife!"

"Dost thou take me for an idiot, Catalan?" she said, smiling.

---

76. *i.e.* Report, inform on.

77. *i.e.* A Spaniard who had spent time in America.

"Gregorio put all the treasure in his name, as the document esstates. He didn't trust me een the esslightest (with good reason). Moreover, only edesperate men travel to America, and Iym a distinguished laydee."

Our hero, realizing he'd been had, exclaimed, "With permission, in sooth thou art a scheming scallywag and a witch."

"Permishon denied . . . doth we have a deal or not?" she asked, putting out her cigarette in a ceramic ashtray. "We'll both get rich. It's a win-win."

Our hero imagined himself in a hypothetical future, covered in gold and living nobly, and we have to admit he didn't hate the idea. He put the letter from Don Gregorio in his jacket pocket, and left with his thoughts divided. If he didn't do what Úrsula Pendregast asked, the city's authorities would soon find him and charge him with murder, since a Catalan in that Spanish landscape was like a fish out of water. Orpí quickly returned to the inn and immediately gathered with his two friends, who hadn't found work either, to explain his sudden change of plans.

"And whatsoever shalt thou do now?" whimpered Grau de Montfalcó, in his falsetto voice.

"They'll hang thee, Joanet," said Martulina the Divina. "Thou must leaveth Seville ASAP."

"Impossible, there be soldiers of the Crowne from here to Barcelona all along the kingsroad," said Orpí, and with the letter signed by Gregorio Izquierdo open on the table, he made a decision. "I hath no choice but to do what that witch says. By passing for Gregorio Izquierdo and getting his treasure, I canst return to Catalonia and start a new life with every 'I' dotted and every 't' crossed. Wouldst thou like to accompanee me?"

"I'm afearedt of the sea . . ." said Grau. "I prefer to start a new life in Madrid and study to become a docktor. The south hath brought us only misery & desperation."

"Well, count me in," said Martulina the Divina, who had the true soul of an adventurer. "I'll dress as a man as before, and thus pass unnoticed."

That very night, Orpí wrote a letter to his mother, which read:

Dearest Mother,

I am writing you from Seville, where things hath not gone as I hath hop'd. I 'ath not found work and, therfor, I'th decided to sette sail for the Newe World, whense I hope to soon return with riches and honours. Fear not, Mother, for I shall make do just as I hath up til now. If perchance anyone asks after me, tell them that I'th gone to the Indies.

With love and gratitude,
Joan Orpí del Pou

## Chapter X

### In which our hero sets sail for the New World under his new false identity: Gregorio Izquierdo

The following morning, after bidding adieu to Grau de Mont-falcó, who was emigrating to Madrid in search of a better future, Orpí and Martulina headed to the Arenal district, where a forest of masts swarmed and all sorts of people boarding and disembarking from the caravelles and galleons moored at the docks at the Guadalquivir River, donkeys carrying boxes of contraband books to the boats casting off for the Spanish Indies, navigators and sailors marching in formation to the naval school, all singing songs and smoking American tobacco, missionaries dusting off their cassocks, artisans, African slaves in chains, manufacturers, gentlemen, feathered natives of the New World, adventurers, musicians, merchants, students, and royal soldiers everywhere. Orpí looked at the officers' jackets and braids with a mix of fascination and fear, not because of his support of the monarchy or lack therof, but because if they discovered that he was a Catalan, noticed his accent, they would arrest him. So the two friends, while striving to go unnoticed, got busy finding out what they needed in order to get onto a ship bound for America.

After much asking around, they ascertained that they would need an authorization issued by the *Casa de Contratación*, where all travel permits were obtained, where one paid the fare and taxes, where the shipping quotas were established, and the import and export taxes collected, the boats inspected and charged the King's fifth on all precious metals arriving from America. When Orpí and Martulina reached there, they saw a sign that read:

---

EMBARKING PROHIBITED TO MOORS, CONVERSOS OR RECONCILED JEWS, BLACK SLAVES, HALFBREEDS, MULATTOS OR BERBERS, HERETICS, APOSTATES, LUTHERANS AND THE SONS OF SUCH. ALSO DENIED PASSAGE ARE FOREIGNERS, GYPSIES, CRIMINALS, AND LAWYERS. ONLY OLD CHRISTIANS ACCEPTED.

---

When our hero saw that, his heart sank to his feet.

"Lawyers too? We're off to a great start," he complained in his native tongue.

"Friends," said a man in line with them. "Ye be Catalans, is that not so? Well, allow me to tell ye that Catalans art not allowed on Spanish boats, as foreigners."

Orpí and Martulina looked at each other with nervous eyes when another man chimed in.

"Relax, man, in pointe of fact, by law, they art allowed. While there be much controversee on the matter, those born in the kingdoms of Castille, León, Aragón, Valencia, Navarra, and Catalonia art not considered foreigners. Foreigners be the French, the Genovese, the Portuguese, the Germans, and the

Italians. But really, if sooth be told, all sortes of riffraff manage to slip through."

"For a mere two thousand maravedis, thou canst become a rankless soldier," said another.

Our hero decided to enlist as a soldier so as not to raise suspicion. Martulina followed her friend's lead. They both stood before some men in patent leather hats and black jackets who were writing down names on various lists, depending on availability of the ships.

"Name?"

"Ummmm . . . Gregorio Izquierdo," declared Orpí, closing his eyes and thinking of the many possible ways out of the deceit he was entering into.

"Whence dost thou want to go?"

"New Andalusia."

"As a soldier for His Majesty's government?"

"Yes, sir."

"Doth thou knowe how to read and write?"

"Yea. And mine only belongings in this world be abstract thoughts."

"Here we go again! I see thou art a dyed-in-the-wool intellectual! A convinc'd humanist! Very well indeede! Dost thou have thine own steed?"

"Yea. He's parked outside."

"Then thou canst embark as a distinguished soldier, with four bars, on the *Argos*, already *despalmaó*[78] and chartered on course for Cumanagoto."

"And where be that?"

"The Indies, where else? Some selfless humanist you are! Goe on now, and may God keepeth you safe!"

"Damn know-it-all bastards . . ." grumbled the soldier as

---

78. *i.e.* cleaned and greased

he received the next passenger, not realizing it was Martulina dressed as a man.

"I'll go aborde the *Argos* as well," she said, making her voice as deep as her vocal cords would allow. "José Isla, at His Majesty's service. But as a rankless soldier, as I cant read."

A sailor with red cap accompanied the newly-named Gregorio Izquierdo and the newly-named José Isla to the dock and pointed out their ship to them.

"I shud warn ye, friends," said the sailor, "first get yer hands on some *matalotaje*[79] lest ye starve to death on the journey."

After buying victuals for the long voyage, the two friends boarded the boat as our hero spelled out its name under his breath: "A-r-g-o-s . . ." as he thought about Jason and the Argonauts. They had to bunk with some twenty-odd other soldiers, and their long lances, muskets, swords, daggers, banners, drums, and trumpets, in one corner of the hold. The vessel in question turned out to be a 400-ton floating wreck patched up with rotted barrel wood, a twisted keel and leaks sprouting everywhere. But the vessel, despite being as small as a breadbox, had a captain, a coxswain and a boatswain, two advisors, eight merchant captains, an oarmaker, a surgeon, ten peasant farmers, a priest, a shipwright, a cooper, ten crossbowmen, a scribe, a bailiff, a doctor, a barber, four trumpeters, five bombardiers, seven oarsmen, eight bowmen, three steersmen, a seneschal, a black cook (who was the skipper's slave), and one hundred fifty-two rowers.

As the sailors and apprentice sailors herded onboard goats, hens, and other animals destined to feed the crew, they trafficked in ropes and assured the right of cabotage before setting sail. Our hero, unaccustomed to the hustle and bustle

---

79. *i.e.* provisions

on deck, then approached the ship's captain, Ninus Mandari-nus, who was smoking a pipe in front of a map held open on a desk by an astrolabe and a compass, contemplating it all with the passiveness of authority.

"Prithee, milord & captain, dost thou know if this ship will be moving a lot?" he asked in heavily accented Spanish.

"What dost thou expect, ya greenhorn! Already *catting*[80] before pushing off?" said the captain. "*Marededéu de Mont-serrat. . .*"

"Egads," said Gregorio when he heard the captain's excla-mation. "Art thou a Catalan?"

"Yes and no. I was born in León but worked in the port of Barcelona for many a twelvemonth," he said, fiddling with an astrolabe that allowed him to calculate the route to Terra Firma. "But don't go around saying that there are Catalans on these ships, it doesn't go over well at all with the guys from Castille. And thine name be . . . ?"

"Juan . . . I mean . . . Gregorio . . . Gregorio Izquierdo, sol-dier at Your Majesty's service," said our hero, finding the new name that had been forced on him strange in his mouth. He touched the letter from Úrsula Pendregast, which had turned our hero into another man.

Suddenly, a deckhand who had just turned the small hour-glass that counted out the half hours, began to sing.

♪ Haul on the bowline, the old man is a-growlin, ♫
Haul on the bowline, the bowline Haul!
Haul on the bowline, so early in the mornin'
Haul on the bowline, the bowline Haul!
Haul on the bowline, it's a far cry to payday,
Haul on the bowline, the bowline Haul!

---

80. *i.e.* Sea-sickness in the pidgin language used by sailors of the period.

And thus, on that cool, clear morning in 1623, the fleet lifted anchors followed by a deafening boom of cannons that echoed through the dirty streets of Seville's port district, frightening off a cluster of pigeons, while the sailors hoisted sails as they sang in unison: *Bu-iza, bu-iza!*, and a crowd of the curious watched from the wharf as the galleons were set in motion. The *Argos*, bedecked with banners and pennants of the Crown, followed the fleet, with the admiral at the bow, along the Guadalquivir River, dodging the hellish traffic of warships, frigates, galleys, merchant barges and fishing schooners that came and went. And that was also how, reluctantly, Joan Orpí—ah, make that Gregorio Izquierdo—set forth on a long sea voyage that would take him far from the Old World, to a distant and uncertain future, a place where many went but from which few returned. And if by chance readers want to know how his adventure continues, they must keep reading, in this new Chapter which features new vim and vigor.

## Chapter XI

### On how Gregorio Izquierdo, aboard a ship, discovers the brutality of life

The *Argos* traveled down the Guadalquivir, passing the dangerous sandbar at Sanlúcar de Barrameda, ascending along a narrows, and then heading into the open sea. Only then did the hull star to really move; it wasn't properly ballasted because all the cargo was up top. The ship was leaning this way and that: hens, shoes, sacks of grain, drums of water (and rum), everything rolled up and down the deck. The boat's pump worked tirelessly to keep the water level down, but that didn't stop the entire hold from giving off a pestilent odor. Soon, the heat, the cramped quarters, all the people and the smell from the bilge created an unbearably noisome stench.

Among the crew there were three Capuchin friars from Toledo and a Jesuit priest with a dingy cassock by the name of Pere Claver,[81] who incessantly read his worn out copy of Ignatius of Loyola's *Spiritual Exercises*, two agents of the Crown

---

81.  *i.e.* Pere Claver (1580-1654) was a Catalan Jesuit missionary who fought against slavery in the Americas.

from Madrid, three *cargadores*,[82] two *caballeros de industria* or soldiers of fortune, and a whole cast of characters from all over the map: Sicilians, Napolitans, Aragonese, Andalusians, who didn't believe in virgins or saints, motherless adventurers, single gals in search of a pedigreed husband, converso and "reconciled" Jews, heretics, apostates, Lutherans, foreigners, convicted murderers (who'd perhaps been granted amnesty), forgers, adulterers, traitors, perjurers, *criadas*[83] and a bevy of *llovidos*[84] passing themselves off as pureblooded Christians. In other words, all the scum and undesirables for whom there was no place on the Peninsula were now settling in as best they could into that wooden world, some packed in right on top of the others in a sizeable tangle of legs and feet.

The ocean voyage turned out to be a true ordeal, despite the best efforts of the extremely capable Captain Miruelo, grandson of the famous captain of the same name who had led the first voyages of the most famous conquistadors. The hold was so cramped that burps, vomits, and farts mixed in a nauseating symphony. The rats were right at home amid the feet of people sleeping on the floor, and sometimes bit the random ear. The lucky folk slept in some sort of sacks suspended in the air, called *chinchorros*,[85] an invention from the New World, but that only amplified the swaying to and fro. There was no escaping that floating prison.

Gregorio Izquierdo and Martulina were among the less fortunate, since, being some of the last to board, they'd had to settle for a spot on the bilge, where water seeped in through the holes in the poorly caulked vessel. Add to that, dear

---

82. *i.e.* merchants

83. *i.e.* prostitutes

84. *i.e.* Those traveling without a royal permit.

85. *i.e.* hammocks

reader, the diabolical rocking of the waves and you can easily imagine that what spurted from the crew's black mouths wasn't precisely words. And while that floating city was supplied with pork and beef, cheese, olive oil, garlic, fava beans, yams, vinegar, sugar, Mexican chili pepper, honey, dried fruits and nuts, and water, no one on the crew would have dared to taste even a bit of bread on that gyrating vessel, not for all the gold in the world.

"This boat stinks of death," said our hero. "Its air be vile and pestilent."

"Indeed, this *mare coagulatum* has little in common with dear *mare nostrum*," concluded Martulina.

After a few days of sailing, the nausea lessened and everyone seemed to have grown used to the ship's rocking back and forth. One evening, the valet lit the deck lanterns that illuminated the binnacle, as well as an improvised altar. Being that it was Saturday, it was time for the group prayer. One of the friars delivered the Christian doctrine for the entire crew, hats in hands.

"*Pater Noster, Ave Maria, Credo, Salve Regina.*"

Then the shipwright said, "Art we all here?"

"May God be with us," said the Capuchin.

"Star of the Sea, guide our voyage," stated the shipwright. "Guide our voyage, Star of the Sea."

Then they all started to joyously sing the Hail Mary and

other litanies. Some sailors played their lutes and tambourines, and some crewmembers were inspired to sing prayers and dance between the main mast and the quarterdeck of that small floating city with comical pomposity, while others played *flux* (with marked cards) and yet others organized cock fights. Of all the passengers, it was our hero who had made the best use of his time over those ten days.

"Martulina, I've been reading *Aethiopica* by Heliodorus, *The Travels of Sir John Mandeville*, and *The Description of the World* by Marco Polo," said Gregorio Izquierdo, sitting on one of the cannons on deck. "And I hath reach'd a conclusion: once I akquireth my part of the original Gregorio Izquierdo's treasure, I'm going to write travel books and descrybe all the marvells of this world."

"But half of those books art lies!" exclaimed Martulina.

"Not lies. Alonso Pinciano articulates it in a rather more favourable light, in his *Philosophia antigua Poetica*, whence he speaks of literature, saying . . . that the object is neither to lie, which would coincide with sophistry, nor is the object history, which would leade the material toward the historic; and, neither being history, because of a proximity to fables, nor lies, because of a proximity to history, the object must be verisimilitude which embraceth all. The resulting art is superior to metaphysics, for it contains much more and extends to what is and what is not."

"Don't lecture me, Orpinet, I get dizzy just hearing thee . . ."

And that was the end of that oh-so intellectual conversation between the two friends, because suddenly a strong eastern wind kicked up, as the *Argos* turned toward the southwest, near the African coast, and then toward the west, and the Canary Islands. With the ship's rocking, the nausea returned as fast as it had disappeared. And with it the vomiting and diarrhea. But we'll abstain from any further commentary on that gastronomical affair and move right along to the next Chapter.

## Chapter XII

In which our hero falls in love for
the first time in his life, with a damsel
with an extremely long name

After sailing for seven days, the *Argos* stopped at the island of Lanzarote, an obligatory sojourn, along with the rest of the fleet. The apprentices climbed the riggings to let down the sails and roll them up, singing happily, pleased to spend a night in port before setting back out into the open ocean sea, toward America, and the crew disembarked to stretch their legs and buy staples before the long voyage.

From the stern, Gregorio Izquierdo contemplated the hustle and bustle of the port as he chewed on an apple. Then he watched as, amid the havoc of people boarding and disembarking, a pedigreed woman boarded, dressed in fine clothes with a red velvet bodice, colorful embroidered silks, and a damask overskirt studded with silver and covered with a mantilla of white-blonde lace. She was riding a white donkey and kept the flies off with a fan in the Sevillian style, followed by a servant with thick hair cut in straight bangs and a lady-in-waiting with a peeved expression. Seeing her, Gregorio fell in love at first sight. Leaping on deck, he asked the first sailor he found who that princess was.

"She be no princess, she's a noblewoman of known lineage and engaged to be wed," replied the sailor. "Her name is Doña María Fernanda Esmeralda Brunilda Isegarda Sigismunda Regenta Magdalena Grande de los Cerros Medianos de la Onza, third daughter of the Governor of Tenerife, also known as 'The Nun' for her chaste, pure reputation. But take heed, she art accompanied by her fearsome, mannish *dueña*[86], named Olga, who won't let any man near her."

The next morning, the *Argos* lifted anchors followed by two more Spanish caravelles, and the fleet entered the vast Atlantic, heading southwest to the sixteenth parallel, where the winds would push the boats toward the Lesser Antilles. As the ship rocked with a gentle sway, our hero could only think about being alone with Doña María, who was followed everywhere she went by the enormous Olga, her equally enormous shadow keeping the maiden safe from lascivious gazes and attempts by the sailors and officers to proposition her.

One evening, when Gregorio was wandering about on deck, he heard a sweet voice singing from the ship's stern. There he went and there he found Doña María, sitting alone and melancholy, reciting in half-song a poem by Sor Juana Inés de la Cruz.

> But where does mine sweet fondness
> For mine native land carry
> Mine thoughts and divert
> Mee from my subjecte?

---

86.  *i.e.* The role of *dueñas*, soubrettes, was often described by writers of the period, almost always satirically.

Our hero, after making quite sure that the fearsome Olga was nowhere nearby, approached her and, continuing the poem of Sor Juana, declaimed:

"I daresay that mine intent be none other
milady, than to prostrate myself
at thine soles that I kiss
despite so many seas."

"Who goes there?" asked Doña María, confused by his sudden appearance.

"Merely a well-read soldier," said Gregorio. "But one thing be sure: a voice such as thine, those eyes the color of the heavens and thy pearly white teeth, milady, be worth more than the entire ocean and all its fish bathed in gold."[87]

"Pish posh!" exclaimed the lady, fanning herself.

"What brings a distinguished lady such as thineself to a place such as this?"

"I wish'd to be a nun but couldn't bear the thought of being locked up in a convent. Then I wish'd to be an actress and sing aria in the grand theaters of Europe, but didn't have the requisite voice talent. As a girl I was only taught how to be a wife. As suche, I am headed to America to marry."

"I hath heard telle that in those lands there be spiders as big as thine lovely head," said our hero, inching closer to the lady.

"Deer mee . . . that's horrid!" she exclaimed, making room for him where she was seated, as she nervously rubbed at a small stain on her skirt, which didn't actually exist.

"And terryble fish they call 'shark,' with jaws big as a donkey's that gobble up menne two by two," he continued, putting his arm around her.

---

87. *i.e.* All these elements of courtly love are common to the Petrarchanism of the period.

"The horror!" she said, removing the arm.

"And plagues of ynsects what rip your skin off in strips," Gregorio went on, stroking Doña María's hand.

"Stop it!" she shrieked, with a slight chuckle. "With all these monsters I shant be able to sleep tonight!"

"They've also discover'd the tomato, the yam, and the prickly pear, which are very ambrosial foodstuffs," he said, trying to kiss her. "Almost as tasty as your lips, milady."

"Go no further, insipid soldier, I don't even know thine name!" she pulled away, acting offended but still playing along.

"Mine name be Jua—Gregorio Izquierdo, but since meeting thee, oh, Lady María!, I am aflame with love and sickness, whych are but one and the selfsame," said our hero, and, following that briefest of incursions into the territory of more intimate feelings, kissed the woman's hand. "Thine beauty, thine Christianity, and thine honor art worthy of a queen, a queen of this world and the *plus ultra*."

"Take it eazy, soldier boy!" she said, pulling away her hand as one of her shoes slipped off and fell to the floor, whether in error or feigned error it was not clear. "I am on mine way to the Americas to enter into an arranged marriage with a criollo nobleman, the son of a conquistador. He may be ugly, but he shant be poor."

"What goode be money without love?" he declared, picking up her shoe. "On all my travells round the sun, and travels through hell, I ne'er saw such solemn beauty as I doth now see befor me. These must be love's deliriums, what maketh me see such perfect loveliness."

"Ah, thou art verily a snake charmer! Thine focus is on conquering women, not landes and treasure troves!" she exclaimed, blushing with modesty and lifting her overskirt to her knees so that Gregorio could put her shoe on her foot.

"However, thou must desist in thine aspirations of unbridled concupiscence toward me, for they be neither decent nor decorous."

"Very well. Then yf I cannot have the tempting fyre of thine love," he said, clambering up onto a ledge and preparing to leap overboard, "I shall end mine life this instant!"

"Madman . . . !" she shrieked, grabbing him by the pantaloons.

"Twixt decorum and fervour, what law be more just than the law of love?" said our hero, pretending he was about to throw himself into the ocean. "Fare thee well, for time is brief and I am nothing, milady, if I doth not please thee. Forgive my ruffling of thine chaste sentiments. And now, farewell . . . !"

"Don't overleap!" she shrieked, immediately covering her mouth, surprised at herself. "Must I barter my willpower to save thine life?"

"Milady, thee mustest loveth me, by choice or by destiny," he said resolutely.

"Thy path from the house of respect to the house of pleasure appeareth a shortcut. Doth thou aspire to employe sensuousness to put paid to mine chastity?" she asked, smiling and handing him her handkerchief as a token. "But if that willst save thee from death, sobeit. But don't push thy luck, okay, soldier boy? I'm a proper lady!"

Our hero followed her to his cabin with the silk handkerchief at his nose, while the other soldiers and sailors watched him, sidelong and envious. His room was small and Gregorio hastened to remove the diamond-studded cross she wore around her neck, the bodkin that held up her hair, her pearl earrings, then lifted up her blonde-lace mantilla, tucked up her red velvet bodice and unlaced her corset, moving on to unfasten the false sleeves of her blouse and her embroidered gloves, unlacing her shoes quickly, lowering her damask overskirt and rigid pannier, removed her stockings, half stockings, and g-string . . . and when our hero, bursting at the crotchseams with passion at the glimpse of the intimate contours of the honest damsel, and just as he was about to consummate that amorous act, hastily lowering his drawers, there came a shout from the crow's nest on the main mast.

## Chapter XIII

In which the ship carrying
Gregorio Izquierdo is attacked by a
very famous and vainglorious
English corsair

"Shippe at starboard!" bellowed the lookout, from up high in the crow's nest.

A flag appeared on the ocean horizon. Then two masts. Then three. Everyone was nervous and apprehensive, since in those days there were many regular squadrons of pirates and corsairs waiting for their chance to board the Spanish vessels coming to and from the Indies. The crew busily squirreled away jewels and money; animals were hidden in the ship's catacombs; the women were shouting "why oh why did I ere board this blasted boat!," the civilians took up their blunderbusses and swords, the Capuchin monks prayed the *Ave maris stella* and made the sign of the cross repeatedly over their chests, the crossbowmen got into position on the deck, while the soldiers prepared the cannons. It was a chaos of running up and down and terrified expressions.

"My God, I hope it's a Spanish ship. The las' rover attack

cos' us forty tousand gold florins a damage," said one of the sailors.

"If all we lose is money and not our lives . . ." added another, loading a cannon with gunpowder.

"Itz da *Bucintoro*, from Venice!" shouted a third.

"Nah, itz duh *Miñona* from England!" bellowed a fourth.

"Tamee looks like the *Cagafogo*, from Portugal!" shrieked a fifth.

"As it a Franch flag, or Hitalian?" asked a sixth.

The mysterious vessel looked like a merchant ship but, when it got close to one of the brigantines that followed the *Argos*, they hoisted their colors, revealing the red cross of Saint George.

"Yer all wronge, chumps . . . it's the *Dragon*!" said the pilot. "English corsairs!"

As the enemy ship drew closer to the Spanish fleet, Captain Nino bellowed out orders in the pidgin common tongue to the boatswain and sailors:

"Cast off th' cargo! Steer th west cuarta t' southeast! Release the mizzenmast! Women t' th' hold! Crump th' clew lines t' th' spars o th' topsail and th' velancho! Let leese th' sheet 'n th' tow sails! Load th' falconets and th' pasamuro! Get those mololas off the deck! Lead rowers: get rowing! Helmsman, yaw to the right! 'Prentices, lash th' cable! Everyone, prepare fer battle! N' be careful not t' wag aft!"

Despite the captain's orders, the enemy ship was much faster and soon overtook the two Spanish caravelles that trailed the *Argos* and, burning their waterlines with cannonballs, sank them both. After that nautical murder, the corsair ship came up right alongside the *Argos*. Bombing attack, bombing counterattack, it was a humdinger of a hullabaloo.

Gregorio Izquierdo (pulling up his pantaloons and still "standing at attention") and Doña María came out on deck and face to face with that mayhem. The crew was overcome by terror as projectiles fell on the ship, hammering sails and timbering, sinking the forecastle, perforating barrels and sending bits of human flesh flying through the air. The corsairs' cannonballs decimated both the main mast and the foremast. The thundering sounded like the end of the world and the stench of burnt flesh and gunpowder scented the atmosphere, drying out the throats and stinging the eyes of those preparing for hand-to-hand battle. When the powder was exhausted, the real combat began, amid a cloud of gray, and it was a furious one. The corsairs besieged the ship with gunfire and swords, killing, torturing, burning, and destroying willy-nilly and many promptly died. Artillerymen, cannon loaders, and soldiers fired at the enemy at close range, and every shot of flintlock and harquebus found a body to fell, leaving cadavers everywhere. One of those bullets hit a barrel of gunpowder, which detonated. Amid the enemy fire, some continued to battle the corsairs while others rushed to put out the flames, hauling buckets of saltwater amid the horses trotting spooked and chickens running around frantically. The British had them outnumbered, but the Spaniards didn't back down and fought fiercely for as long as they could. Even the women and Father Claver joined in. Olga, Doña María's lady-in-waiting, was run through with three swords but still had time to deal a fatal punch that exploded a corsair's head; Martulina the Divina slit corsair necks with the delicacy her profession required, and our hero wielded two harquebusses at once and was shooting without even taking aim first. The battle was such a chunky bone-broth of blood and guts that even the fish in the ocean looked on gobsmacked.

Before long the entire deck was a vast puddle of death. Both sides had lost more than half their men, but the Castilians had finally surrendered. The pirate captain quickly appeared onboard the *Argos*: it was the famous English corsair Francis Drake[88], also known as "El Draque"—the Dragon. Despite his long shadow and his formidable reputation, his physical appearance was that of a stocky, short man with proper British rosy cheeks.

"Goodevening, ladies and gentlemen. I am not a rover, nor a 'bucanerow.' I am the most British privateer from the East to the West coast," he said displaying a document with the English royal seal. "Mine name art Francis Drake, at your service. I request thy peaceful surrender."

"What's this Brit sayin?" asked the boatswain.

"That we should surrender without a fight," said Captain Nino.

Forthwith, Francis Drake proceeded to tally up his wounded. His men set him up with a table and chair on the deck of the *Argos*, as they served him his five o'clock tea and a string quartet from the Royal London Symphonic—which the famous privateer always brought with him—played chamber pieces by English composers such as John Dowland, Robert Johnson, Holborne, and Pilkington for lute, zither, and harpsichord. As the music played, Drake dipped his silver quill and, between sips of tea, wrote:

### Corsair accounting book:

| | |
|---|---:|
| ear | 600 |
| left arm | 500 |
| right leg | 400 |
| one eye | 100 |
| one finger | 100 |

---

88.  *i.e.* Here the narrator has, once again, committed a flagrant anachronism. Francis Drake died of dysentery in 1596, while Orpí crossed the ocean, according to Pau Vila's biography, around 1623, making this historical encounter impossible.

"Whutz he doin' now?" asked a sailor.

"Counting his dead and wounded so his Queen, ole Betty, will pay him back for the money he's lost," said another.

"Hang me if I understand a thing," said our hero. "Whence doth this whole song and dance come?"

"The British, they like to do things their own way," added Martulina, cleaning the blood off her sword. "They even have the rudder on t'other side of the boat, just to be different from everybody else."

After jotting down all the losses on his side, Francis Drake greeted the captain of the *Argos* very courteously and with numerous curtsies, and then the corsairs proceeded to grab everything of value on the ship, such as jewels, paintings, furniture, animals, and rum, as well as kidnapping all the women onboard under thirty years old, for their pleasure and for ransom.

"No!" exclaimed our hero, seeing that they were also taking Doña María Fernanda Esmeralda Brunilda Isegarda Sigismunda Regenta Magdalena Grande de los Cerros Medianos de la Onza, along with other women.

"Fear not, my love!" she said, cutting off a lock of her hair and giving it to him, while a corsair grabbed her and threw her over his back like a sack of potatoes.

"I doth protest!" exclaimed Gregorio Izquierdo, pulling out his inner lawyer from inside his soldier's shell, as he clung to the lock of hair. "The ocean is considered, ere Roman times, *res communis omnium*, and as such thou hath no ryght to this kidnapping!"

"Sorry, barrister," said one of the corsairs, carrying off Doña María. "Danger has jurisdiction over the ocean sea and all the lands of the world."

"I maye be violated," said Doña María. "I may be killed, but we'll always have our bryef amorous time together!"

"Damn mine luck . . ." grumbled our hero, struck melancholy by the whole affair as he watched the corsair ship head off with his beloved, who waved goodbye to him from the other deck.

## Chapter XIV

### In which Gregorio Izquierdo hallucinates sirens, all due to his heartbreak

After the corsairs' butchery, everyone who survived had to lend a hand with the cleanup and repair of the ship, and to gather up some survivors from the two caravelles that Francis Drake had sunk. Meanwhile, the *Argos* had sprung leaks all over from the fearsome hurly-burly .

"We're sinking, amirite?" asked a sailor.

"I shant abandon this ship, even dead . . ." said the captain. "Worke that pump! Bail, for fuck's sake, bail!"

Finally, the holes made by the cannonballs were patched and the water in the bilge was cloudy, a sure sign it wasn't coming in from the ocean sea. The masts were repaired, the sails sewn up, and order once again reigned on the vessel. In fact, the fair weather conditions were too fair. The wind had vanished and the ship now looked like an eggshell bobbing in a puddle of oil. Everything was static.

"Accurses, we're in a calm!" lamented a sailor.

"I seconde that emotion," said Martulina. "Calm means calamity. Without wind, we'll rot here, in the midst of the ocean sea."

"I prefer death to the loss of mine divine lady Doña María Fernanda Esmeralda Brunilda Isegarda Sigismunda Regenta Magdalena Grande de los Cerros Medianos de la Onza," was the depressed mantra of Gregorio Izquierdo, sniffing the lock of his beloved's hair.

That calm meant not one, but numerous misfortunes. The first was that it brought a plague of rats onboard the *Argos*. They pissed everywhere, gobbled up all the food, and gnawed on the boat's timber, causing new leaks, and they got into scrapes with the handful of hens the corsairs hadn't stolen or killed. The heat would soon rot the meat and vegetables in the hold. Someone had the indecent suggestion of eating the horses, but our hero said he would rather die than devour his loyal Acephalus. Then some of the crew started to chow down on the leather of their shoelaces and clothing. One of the sailors even took a bite out of Martulina's military jacket.

"This jacket is property of the Crown, tis not for eating," she said, pricking the famished sailor with her sword as a warning.

In the end, since the clothing was hard to digest, they concluded it would be better to eat the rats themselves. Soon there were specialized hunters who sold them to the crew for half a ducat. More than three thousand rats were roasted on the grill. The problem with that rodent diet was that it brought with it an even more serious problem: scurvy. The gums of the infected were so badly inflamed that you couldn't even see their teeth. The disease claimed nineteen lives, and the corpses were thrown into the open sea, where the aquatic fauna ate them up. After that, no one was interested in eating more rat.

"Now we' well and truly done fo," said a Cuban sailor. "Nada de food in ten 'hole day."

The wind still didn't blow, and those who drank seawater

all ended up sick. Some began to die of starvation. One day Gregorio Izquierdo, who was famished like the rest, in desperation ate a bit of leather from one of the boat's masts, and in ten minutes' time his belly began to emit horrific sounds and he had a frantic need to void his bowels. The *Argos* only had two latrines and both had been destroyed in the battle with the corsairs. There was only one solution. Our hero grabbed one of the rope ladders on the main mast, clambered up to the ledge of one of the crossbow holes on the poopdeck, lowered his drawers, and shat into the ocean, in full view of everyone.

"I'm sorry . . ." he apologized to a sailor who was staring. "It's imperative."

"As Salazar says, *Muita vegadas chega a merda ao ollo de o cu*,[89]" quoted a sailor.

"How right he was, and emfatickly. This fylth is a shameful mess. By law, there should be decent toilets aborde these vessells. I shall present a formal complaint to the *Casa de Contratación* when I returnne to Seville."

And it was as his sphincter relaxed that our hero heard a song emerging from the deep ocean. He tried to find the source of that strange melody, and glimpsed a movement in the waves. Looking closer, he thought he saw the body of a woman with bare breasts and a fish tail, diving in and out of the waters. Gregorio Izquierdo's pulse began to race.

"Milady Doña María Fernanda Esmeralda Brunilda Isegarda Sigismunda Regenta Magdalena Grande de los Cerros Medianos de la Onza, my beloved! Lord in heaven . . . she's been turned into a siren!"

---

89. "Many times the shit reaches the hole of the ass," *Navegación del alma*, Eugenio de Salazar, 1600.

Everyone on deck ran over to where our hero crouched, his ass still in the air, squinting out at the ocean.

"How now, a siren!" said a sailor, "Dats a valrus!"

"You're 'allucinatin', Orp . . . oop, I mean Gregorio," said Martulina the Divina, "Hunger can make ya see things what isnt dere."

"Cant you hear her?" he said, reverting to Catalan in his hallucinating state, and trying to jump into the water while the others held him back. "It's Doña María who warbles thus . . . ! Raped and murdered by the savage corsairs, she's become a siren! Thus I shall become a *felo-de-se*[90]!"

It took a few sailors to keep our hero from such an idiotic death and, a few moments later, he regained his senses, pulled up his drawers, and ran to search for a book. Then he recited the following to the curious:

"Listen, Columbus wrote, in his ship's diary on January 9, 1493 that: 'On the previous day, when the Admiral went to the Rio del Oro, he said he quite distinctly saw three sirens, which rose well out of the ocean sea; but they are not so beautiful as they are said to be, for their faces had some masculine traits.' In other words, sirens!" declared Gregorio Izquierdo. "Ugly as sin, but sirens! Otherwise it's surely one of the monsters catalogued in Saint Isidore of Seville's *Etymologiae*."[91]

---

90.  *i.e.* An Anglo-Latin term for one who commits suicide.

91.  The references to fable reinforce the mythical view of the conquistador and were generally common in that period, as seen in the aforementioned *Etymologiae* and in the various chronicles of the conquest. Although, truth be told, by Orpí's time, that mythology was a bit passé, frankly.

"That be a blunder," said Captain Nino, who had approached to see what all the fuss was about. "In sooth they were manatees, cetacean water mammals. The females have a pair of knockers on them that can easily be mistaken for a siren's."

"Art thou sure?" asked our hero, stricken by the sad reality.

"Entirely so. I recommend you cease the reading of so many fantastickal books, since they are comprised largely of calumnies," said the captain. "But at least we'll be well supplied with grub for some time . . . bring out the nets!"

After fishing some of the quasi-sirens, the entire crew enjoyed a piscivorous feast beyond their wildest imaginings. Luck seemed to have returned to the *Argos*, since that same night a north wind began to blow and the ship set sail once more.

"Thar blows de Galerne!" said a deckhand.

"Tis the angels puffing to billow the sails from the clouds," said the Jesuitic Father Claver.

The crew sang a *Te deum laudamus*, and some other prayers and litanies, sated with their solid food and happy to be alive and on their way. But their adventures were not over, as our readers shall learn forthwith in the next Chapter, upon turning the page.

## Chapter XV

In which our hero befriends a slave and
frees many others from the same condition

The next day dawned shrouded in thick, thick fog. The *Argos*
seemed to be floating among clouds and the blue of the sky
had vanished. The sailors hauled down the sails and started
telling each other jokes. Even the topman allowed himself
the distraction of smoking some tobacco. It was as he puffed
on his cigar that he saw a caravelle flying past the prow.
He rubbed his eyes to see if he was dreaming, and when he
focused his vision again the boat was already almost crashing
into the *Argos*. The din was so tremendous and everyone on
deck, after rolling (briefly) on the ground, ran for their weapons against a more than likely boarding.

"Everyone get ready!" shouted the captain.

"This time I shant wane in my industry against these sea
dogs," said our hero, unsheathing his sword.

But they weren't boarded. Everyone remained with their
weapons at the ready, muscles tense, fingers on harquebus triggers or with their swords or lances in the air while
an anxious silence hovered over the deck. The ghost boat

floated beside the *Argos* in silence, its sails lowered and prow destroyed. It seemed abandoned. Captain Nino resolved to board the boat and when they landed on the other deck they found it scattered everywhere with sailor corpses.

"What a bloodbath . . ." murmured Martulina to our hero, who, hearing screaming from the hold, decided to open up its doors.

When he opened the hatch that led to the hold, Gregorio Izquierdo found a most atrocious, appalling spectacle: from the beams hung ten bodies that were swaying inert, beginning to rot. When they went down the stairs they saw forty or fifty people, skin black as coal, huddled in fear at the back of the room. Some of them were only half-alive, most were silently withering with hunger and thirst, others whined in pain. On the floor were excrement, urine, and amputated limbs. The stench was so horrific that some sailors had to run out of there to keep from vomiting.

"Who art these poor people in chains?" asked our hero.

"Most lik'ly African slaves abandoned to their fate," responded Captain Nino, who was coming up behind him. "And what a stench . . . bloody hell!"

"Who could bee responsible for such butchery?" said Gregorio Izquierdo, stepping over dismembered corpses on his way to the forecastle, where all the survivors were staring at him with terrorized eyes. "Let's see, who amongst ye speaks Spanish?"

A very tall and brawny man stood up, his torso covered in old scars, and he spoke. "I speak, yo glace. My name is Esteban, but evelybody know me as Estebanico the Blackamoor."

"Very well, Estebanico, tell all these folks to come up to the deck, where they shall be given food and care," said our hero. "And then thou shalt tell us what happened here, if thou will."

Once all the survivors were up on deck, the Jesuits tended their wounds while the sailors prepared some food for them. The bodies of the dead were tossed into the ocean, all the surviving slaves were transported to the *Argos*, and the ghost ship was burned. As it sank, Estebanico the Blackamoor began his story while he slurped his turtle soup.

"You al not going to believe the adventuls I'm about to tell you, Don Glegolio. I glew up in Azamor, near the African coast on the Atlantic, but I was acquiled as a slave at an eally age by a Spanish nobleman, Andlés de Carranza, who filst took me to Spain and then to conquer La Flo'ida, in the New World, in sealch of the Fountain of Youth."

"Herotodus spoke of it in the third book of *The Histories*," noted our hero. "Howe peculiar!"

"That I don' know because I don' know how to lead," continued Estebanico. "What I do know is that, even without knowing how to shoot a halquebus, I went deep into the vast extensions of Nolth Amelica following those clazy Spania'ds. We were moldan thlee hundled soldiels, but a month later we wele only fo' left. The Indian tlibes extelminated us melcilessly. Finally I was captuled by a tlibe with othel shipwlecks like Alvar Nuñez Cabeza de Vaca."

"Tis not possible!" exclaimed Gregorio Izquierdo. "Such a book was published in 1555, if mine memory serves, and we art now in the year of our Lord 1623! If you be truly Esteban the Blackmoor from his *Shipwrecks* . . . thou must be older than Methuselah!"

"You've got a point there," said Estebanico. "But it was in that tlibe where we found the Fountain of Youth. Keep this twixt us, but that's why I never age."

"Incredible!"

"Nay. What was incledible was escaping flom there, since once you dlink flom that magic fountain, you can nevel leave:

those wele the lules of that tlibe. Cabeza de Vaca pletended to be a doctol and, once we'd ealned the tlust of the Indians, we fled into extlemely difficult adventules. Eight yeals laer I was palt of an expedition in Pelu to find the Seven Cities of Cibola. I didn't find them but I got lich with a tleasule of umalked pieces of gold I found neal a volcano in the nolth. But when I got to Quito, a detachment of soldiels of foltune got wind of mine luck and excogigated against me, until they managed to lob me of my ealnings. One of them, by the way, had the same name as you: Gregorio Izquierdo, but he looked naught as thou. Othelwise, I would have had to kill you light this minute with mine bale hands."

When our hero heard that his heart made a triple somersault.

"A strange story, Estebanico. And now, let us speak in private, if thou don't mind," he said, pulling him to one side.

There our hero explains the entire real Gregorio Izquierdo affair to him and promises Estebanico the Blackamoor half of the treasure if they manage to find it.

"I'm no longel intelested in gold," he replied. "But you should know that tleasule is culsed, since those Castilian pigs took it, put me in chains, and sent me to the galleys. I've clossed this ocean mole times than anybody. I'm black by bilth and folced into slavely, sir. But I cannot live without my fleedom, which is worth mole than all the gold in this filthy wolld."

"I shall grant thee thine freedom, *ladino*[92]," said Gregorio Izquierdo. "And I vow that any man who tries to steal it from thee again will taste mine sword."

That night the Africans joyously celebrated their newly recovered freedom, dancing the macumba and singing songs,

---

92.  *i.e.* A form of address for foreigners who speak Spanish like natives.

and everyone was happily drinking grog, as our hero mused on the affair of Gregorio Izquierdo's treasure, which was actually Estebanico the Blackamoor's. It was all well and truly a fix, but he'd have time to ponder it further because, as no good deed goes unpunished, the ocean began to get choppy. The ship crashed against the water, which had turned from light blue to gunmetal gray, and increasingly rough. Gusts of wind from the west made the ship veer directionless, spinning on the crests of immense waves. The *Argos* was dragged out of control through the waters of that dark ocean sea.

"We shant escape this thunder-head," cried Captain Nino.

Since the ship was too loaded down and was leaking everywhere due to having been poorly caulked, they had to toss part of the cargo into the water. The rudder was wrecked and even the mast got cracked, and had to be chopped down, while the wind and thunderclaps destroyed the sails. Some of the crewmembers fell into the sea, including the three Capuchin friars, while Father Claver was saved from the same fate at the last moment thanks to our hero, who grabbed him by his Christian beard and pulled him back on deck. And that was how they all spent the night, without a wink of sleep, bailing out water to stay afloat, vomiting all the sirens they'd eaten because of the ship's bucking back and forth, and pleading with God for the mercy of making it out of that alive.

## Chapter *XVI*

On how the Argos arrived safely in port and "Gregorio Izquierdo" sees the New World for the first time

The next morning, the sunlight revealed a clear day, as well as the image of the *Argos* completely destroyed, bobbing adrift. The survivors gradually awakened from the nightmare, one by one, and what they glimpsed when they opened the blinds of their eyes was a miracle.

"Terra . . . terra firma!" hollered a sailor.

It was the Cape of Three Points on the Paria-Araya peninsula. After two months, three days, five hours, and nine and a half minutes of brutal sailing, the mountainous silhouettes of terra firma appeared on the horizon like a dream while the forest trees extended from one shore to the other. Only 8% of the *Argos*'s crew had survived, but it was a happy 8%. The sailors were singing, the soldiers were singing, and the civilian passengers were singing.

♪ 𝕶ind friends and companions, come join me in rhyme 𝄢
Come lift up your voices in chorus with mine
Come lift up your voices, all grief to refrain

*For we may or might never all meet here again*
*So here's a health to the company and one to my lass*
*Let's drink and be merry all out of one glass*
*Let's drink and be merry, all grief to refrain*
*For we may or might never all meet here again . . .*

And such was the rejoicing and mirth at life's triumph over death, that everyone burst into tears, and trumpets, drums, and lutes were brought out on deck and they danced and laughed like children, spinning in a celebratory circle around the main mast.

When they were closer to Margarita Island, a hundred natives appeared in their canoes, offering pineapples, cassava, guavas, and tobacco in exchange for trinkets. Some of the vendors, with tattooed faces, smiled in the shadow of their canoes and the gold coins with the image of the King glimmered in the sun as they changed hands.

"I like this barter sistem," said Martulina the Divina, as she swapped a straw hat made by the natives for her rat-eaten blanket.

Our hero, oblivious to the transcultural trafficking, was looking out at those lands and saw in them the possibility of leaving behind the decadent world of the Iberian Peninsula in order to start afresh, in a new Golden Age, a new beginning. It was the year of our Lord 1626 and the equatorial climate of that promised land made his little hairs stand on end.

"Indeed, so much mountain and so much green upon the horizon seem to be a Lost Paradise," said Gregorio Izquierdo to Father Claver. "I canst scarce believe we surviv'd this hellish voyage."

"Poseidon hath pardoned us, mine son," said the Jesuit, who wasn't arriving in the New World for the first time. "But don't think for a minute what thou seeth be Plato's Atlantis (whych, as thou knowst, was ruled by Poseidon, a distant ancestor of Plato's father himself). Newcomers believe this to be Eden, but tis the same or worse than the Peninsula."

The *Argos* ascended, drained and gutted, to Cumanà, towed by sixty native canoes and a *patache* that came out to greet them.

There the entire crew disembarked and after getting through customs they found that the few belongings they had were inspected by the Inquisition staff. Many of the books the crew was carrying, rotted by saltwater, were requisitioned, since they were banned to avoid setting a bad example for the natives educated in Christendom. Our hero, however, managed to keep his extensive library—more than a hundred volumes, their pages covered in mold due to the sea climate—from being confiscated because it was hidden beneath a pile of clothes in his trunk.

The port of Cumanà, which was not larger than the one in Seville, had constant commercial traffic: strange animals with even stranger names: popinjays, panthers, and pelicans (and others that didn't start with the letter P) were for sale, criolla prostitutes whose flesh trembled, but not with fear, as they approaching singing obscene songs, brushing them with their breasts toasted by the tropical sun, blacks selling pearls, *muleques*[93] trafficking in indigo dye and cacao, and Indian women dressed in their huipils selling flour, fresh fish, seeds, and giants' bones to the ships heading back to Spain. Many other vessels arrived constantly in that port, from Africa, their holds filled to bursting with black slaves from Mauritania and "white" Berber slaves from Morocco, who disembarked covered in wounds and lacerations from the terrible conditions on the voyage. Some of those *bozales*[94] died as soon as they set foot on terra firma and their corpses were burned on a small island near the port in two large bonfires that were lit each day, at dusk, and gave off a greasy black smoke.

"Ay, I'm so afflight'd!" said Estebanico the Blackamoor. "If I'm not caleful, these honkeys will fly me alive!"

"Worry not, mine friend," said Gregorio Izquierdo. "Stick by mine side and everything will be fine."

Estebanico the Blackamoor followed our hero as they made their way toward the city. The imposition of Christianity and the Latin of the Vulgate mixed in that region with all the autochthonous imagery, creating a bizarre, improbable blend. Churches and monasteries sprang up all over and the clergymen rushed to create schools to educate and convert the locals. Cumaná, a border city between the old and new continents, turned out to be a cheap knock-off of Seville, made of white clay houses and a church that gleamed on a hillock. Criollo actors recited meters and rhymes for a few gold ducats on improvised stages in the city streets, the *mulequillos*[95] offered themselves as servants to the newcomers, the hidalgos, sweating beneath outmoded dress coats, rested

---

93. African slaves between seven and ten years old.

94. *i.e.* Recently arrived black slave.

95. *i.e.* Slave child up to the age of seven years old.

in the shade of mahogany trees on their private ranches, while two *cimarrons*[96] were executed in a public square for insurrection and others were displayed on a stage with their ankles shackled to an iron rod, as punishment for refusing to work. What was once jungle was now a garbage dump where wild dogs fought over a piece of rotted, fly-covered meat. However, our hero could see that, beyond that hostile town, the true America awaited him, a continent of lush vegetation that he would soon explore.

The surviving crew of the *Argos*, meanwhile, was celebrating with a meal in a tavern.

"In this one, fer twenty-five maravedis, thou canst eat in the Sevillian style," said Captain Nino.

After eating turtle soup, Gregorio Izquierdo made the decision to desert the army in order to fulfill the promise he had made to Úrsula Pendregast: to collect the part of the treasure the real Gregorio Izquierdo had stashed in Caracas. But, when he patted down the pockets of his dress coat, he discovered that where he once carried the letter given to him by the Sevillian swindler, there was now nothing. He'd lost it! And he was just about to leave, when a squadron of soldiers for the Crown burst into the tavern.

"Not so fast, *chapetón*!"[97] one of them said. "Or hath ye forgotten ye be royal soldiers? We are being sent to Salinas de Araya to defend it from the Flemish, and we're expected there yesterday!"

Our hero had to obey orders or risk being written up and convicted for desertion. Followed by Martulina, the Jesuit Father Claver, and Estebanico the Blackamoor, they had to get back onboard again, when it hadn't been even an hour

---

96.  *i.e.* Runaway slave pursued by the law.

97.  *i.e.* A term for Spaniards who had just arrived in America.

since they'd come ashore and, bidding farewell to the captain and the remaining crew of the *Argos*, they were quickly taken along with a squad of eighty soldiers to the south of Venezuela. And here begins the true life of the soldier Gregorio Izquierdo, which will not be told here in this Book Two but rather in the third, which follows after a brief pause as . . . **[if you'll excuse me, I have to visit the loo!]**

**1714.** The captain has an important and profound
discussion with his soldiers:

The captain returns from the bathroom still buttoning up his
fly and realizes that his public has grown. Women, children,
and old folks are now huddled inside the theater to take
refuge from the Borbonic artillery fire, which is relentlessly
falling on the city of Barcelona. Proud of the sudden swell in
his audience, the captain sits down among his soldiers and
fills his pipe with tobacco, lighting it with a match in prepara-
tion of continuing his story. But he's interrupted before he
can start.

"Sir . . ." says the soldier who is acting as scribe, "I hath
some questions about the plotte of this story: what happens
to the princess Doña María, does she just disappear? And how
is the whole 'Gregorio Izquierdo' affair resolved? I mean, how
doth Joan Orpí recover his true identity?"

"All in due time, soldier," assures the captain, taking puffs
on his pipe in such a way that his face is enveloped in a cloud
of smoke. "Allow the mysteries to resolve themselves, following the plot like a river follows its natural course. As I was
saying . . ."

"But, Captain, thine story is too predictable," complains
the scribe, interrupting him again. "How doth thou expeckt

readers to identify with the protagonist? While we're at it, we could also critique the fact that the narrative voice is constantly interfering in the story, notte to mention the cacophonic pirouettes thou oblige me record, the dialectical expressions, the poetic amphigory, the constant linguistic ups and downs, and the impossible mishmash of archaic and modern language, etc. Thou art a rhetorical rebbel!"

"Shut thine trap, soldier!" the captain exclaims angrily. "Since when does the scrivener have opinions? What sort of *habitus* be this? What thou shouldst be doing is writing down what I say! And if mine words doth not illuminate all the paths of writing, tis because the relationship betwixteth signified and signifier—sorry to break it to you—will allways be arbitrary."

"Perhaps, Captain, but the way thou mocketh language itself leads to absolute ethical relativism and the impotence of ordering existential chaos," exclaims a different soldier. "I mean, I hope no pissed-off reader comes to me later complaining he's been duped by the back jacket copy, that it's all too parodical and scatterbrained, or that it's an attempt to write in a spoken Catalan or how they spoke in Orpí's time but without any sense of grammar, morphology, or syntax . . ." gripes the soldier.

"And so what is it that you want?" the enraged captain asks. "You want me to use more popular prose that fully respects the pact with the reader and the Aristotelian principles of realism? Would that make thou happy? Maybe you'd appreciate some sort of less autonomous literature, that takes part in the collective project? Come on, man, gimme a break! Your obsessions would make Plato himself laugh! You're worried they'll criticize thee for writing incorrectly? Well you tell them that you've invented a language that constitutes the topography of its own world . . . and that's that! Withal, as far as I knowe,

Catalan doesn't yet have any normative grammar—or descriptive, or prescriptive, or predictive, for that matter! And if we ever do, it will be like taxidermying the language and putting it in a museum, because everything's better when it's mixed! So just write down what I sayeth and quit yer jibber-jabber."

The soldiers looked at each other with a tinge of compassion. They seem depressed.

"Oooohkay. And when art we getting to the end of this story, Cap?"

"We're not far off," said the captain. "Book Three is the final and definitive of the adventures and misadventures of Joan Orpí, and they all take place in the Americas, except two or three Chapters. And now, if ye don't mind, it's time to shut your traps and prick up your ears."

The soldiers nod their heads and the one assigned as scribe prepares the pen and paper, the civilians get ready to listen, and the captain slowly opens his mouth, revealing a glimpse of teeth blackened by tobacco, about to continue declaiming his tale, amid the noises of war outside the theater.

*Book Three*

In which we learn of Joan Orpí's rise from a
low-ranking soldier to lieutenant general of the
Province of New Andalusia; and from lieutenant
general to royal representative in the city of
Caracas; and from royal representative to conquistador and founder of New Catalonia after
passing through both hell and high water in
the jungles of the new world, battling irascible
tribes and becoming bosom buddy to some and
nemesis to yet others amidst sundry milieus
throughout those there tropical and torrid latitudes and meridians.

## Chapter I

In which our hero engages in his first battle
as a soldier of the Crown and sketches out
a plan for desertion

With the servitude of all authors, we will fulfill our promises, not only those made in the title of this Book Three, but in the title of the whole book, since this is where our whole story takes off (complete with a surprise ending, like in all the best adventure stories), and will satisfy the patient reader who has reached this point.

Since 1593, the Dutch had been harvesting salt from a conglomerate of natural salt pans at the mouth of the Unare River, on the Araya Peninsula, and at the same time fostering contraband on the Windward Islands,[98] all in territory of the Kingdom of Castille. The Crown of Castille's only response had been to build, in a design by the famous Antonellis,[99] a

---

98.  *i.e.* Following the Union of Utrecht (1579) and the separation of the Kingdom of Castille from the provinces of the United Netherlands (1581), the Dutch went from stealing salt on the Iberian Peninsula to stealing it in the Castilian viceroyalties in the New World.

99.  *i.e.* Famous family of Italian military engineers who worked for the Spanish crown.

fortress above the beach, the ideal spot for defending the salt pan. But while it was still being built, a detachment of forty Dutch ships had arrived on the attack. The Castilians' situation was now a critical one. They were sitting ducks inside that lethal cage. It was only a question of time before the Dutch destroyed all the walls. Besides, the potable water had gone bad and the soldiers were drinking boiled sea water, sweetened with large amounts of sugar. On the fifteenth day of the siege, "miserere colic" showed up: the soldiers were losing their lives through their anuses while others were dealing with scenes lifted from the Book of Revelation. A soldier who had been reading some Chapters from *The Adventures of Esplandian* threw himself into battle, all on his lonesome, the day before, thinking that he was an immortal knight, and now his body, riddled with bullet holes, was resting in front of the doors to the fort.

And that is precisely where we find our illustrious hero, wearing a soldier's dress coat and armed with a harquebus that he is now firing from a watchtower onto the Dutch hordes who'd joined forces on the beach to the rhythm of drums. But Gregorio Izquierdo has only one thought: finding the original Gregorio Izquierdo's treasure in Caracas and leaving behind this soldier's life that was steadily leading him to certain death. There, in that critical situation, our hero makes a brave decision: to flee.

"People, tis highe time for me to go AWOL. As ye may hath noticed, those cannons art wreeking a considerable amount of damage here, ravaging the western walls whilst their soldiers attack us from the east. We're surrounded. We shall die here, indubbitably."

"Tha's not in oul best interest, sil," said Estebanico the Blackamoor.

"It's troo, I'm not putting my ass on the line," complained

a soldier of Jewish extraction, whom everyone knew as "The Scourge," who'd come to the New World searching for the ten lost tribes of Israel.

"What's thy plan, Gregorio?" asked another of the soldiers, a Catalan by the name of Jeremies with a long neck and a blond beard, who was shooting this way and that toward the beach from behind the walls.

"If we run off they shall hang us!" said Martulina.

"If we linger here we shall die for certain!" barked our hero, as he smacked a blood-sucking mosquito on his nape. "Perhaps we have a prospecte of survival if we pilfer one of the Dutch ships and beat a hastee retreat."

"Don Gregorio, thou art allways cogitating something!" said another soldier, an Andalusian known as "Octopus" who was a good egg, albeit very vainglorious.

"Thinking for one's self be a responsibility not all art willing to accept, but, mine friends, the greater the risk the great'r the victory," said our hero.

One morning when the bullets on both sides lay calmly inside their weapons, the soldiers were sleeping the sleep of the just, while their horses' ears were at rest and the birds chirped in the sky, Gregorio Izquierdo and Martulina, followed by Estebanico, Octopus, Jeremies, and The Scourge slipped through a side door unseen. Once they'd jumped into a small leaky shalop, they rowed along a low coast covered in swampland and mangroves and headed, armed to the teeth, toward the largest of the Dutch ships, where the enemy captains were sleeping. Splashing along the ship until they could grab one of its rope ladders, they climbed in silence to the deck. There they found three sailors on watch, and dealt them each a dagger blow to the abdomen.

"Now we just hath to take the boat and we canst hightail it outta here," ordered our hero.

But he'd scarcely gotten to the end of that sentence when the cigarette that Estebanico was smoking fell into a barrel of gunpowder. It went off with a big *BOOM!* and, immediately after, all the other powder kegs exploded.

"Ay, mamasita, this is hellich!" exclaimed Estebanico, his clothes burning like torches.

"Jump into the water, ye idiots!" bellowed Gregorio Izquierdo, as the ship resounded with a bulimic *BOOOOOMMMM* and all sorts of objects rained down into the ocean: shattered glass, split wood, sailors and soldiers tossed through the air. The explosion was heard from every point, from the nearest beach to the Castilian fortress. The main Dutch ship was exploding in a clap of gunpowder and licking flames, while Gregorio and his gang went back to the shalop amid the morning fog, having failed in their mission.

And then, since everything depends on who and how stories are told, an extraordinary bit of news spread through the Spanish soldiers' ranks: one of their own, a brave man named Izquierdo, acting of his own volition, had gathered a group of kamikaze heroes and blown up the biggest ship in the Dutch fleet. The Castilians, armed with renewed morale, opened the doors to the fort, storming out against the Dutch trenches. The enemy, horrified by the assault of the hotheaded Spaniards, rushed off to the dinghies and rowed toward their three remaining ships, ignoring their captain, who brandished his officer's saber in an attempt to hold them back. In the midst of that tumult, other Dutchmen emerged from the forest and ran scared down the beach, chased by the Castilians who, emboldened by that act of war, were shooting and insulting the enemy until they finally trapped many in a fierce battle beside the sea. Ferocious hand-to-hand combat had soldiers rolling on the sand, stepped on, sliced and diced, bloodied, split in two, choked, chopped into bits, bullets whistling to and fro and, every once in a while, bluntly entering an inert body lying on the ground like a doll. In the end, the enemy surrendered and the few Dutchmen still fighting were corralled against the twisted landscape of rocky salt pans and executed right there, mercilessly. And that was how, by mistake, Gregorio Izquierdo was honored as a hero and promoted to second lieutenant.

## Chapter II

### In which our hero becomes infuriated and has an outburst of righteous rage

Now, our hero—after defending the Araya salt pans from the sanguinary Dutch siege, where each side lost a few hundred soldiers—had seen with his own eyes the politics of conquest. His squadron had been sent further inland into Venezuela, a virgin territory filled with extremely dangerous native tribes, and he spent eight years there earning a salary of four escudos a month, advancing laboriously through the thicket, beneath tropical rainstorms. The scent of wet earth, humus and sap, reached the soldiers' bearded noses as they hacked through dense brush so they could advance their portable cannons. The expedition, made up of a hundred soldiers and fifty natives, fed themselves by hunting and fishing. There were many dangers in the forest, and a couple of soldiers died that very day, one from a rabid puma attack and the other from a fatal zebra-snake bite.

One day, while the troop was traveling up the Orinoco stung from head to toe by the *jejenes*,[100] the Spanish boats were riddled with holes from a rain of arrows. Despite being

---

100. *i.e.* Tiny but very vicious mosquito.

protected by *sayos*,[101] it turned out those arrows were poison-tipped, and anyone struck by the lethal arrowheads vomited black bile and died, and those merely nicked went mad and jumped from the canoes into the river, where they drowned in the current, or were devoured by piranhas and alligators. After unloading their guns into the tangle of trees, the soldiers landed their canoes and relentlessly pursued the natives, who were from the Tagare tribe, through the brush. The Spaniards soon had the upper hand with their firearms (bombards, harquebusses, and pistols), which were like thunder and lightning to the natives, equipped with very technologically inferior bows and arrows.

Once they'd arrived at the Tagare village, Gregorio Izquierdo and the rest of the soldiers saw the tribal women—bare-breasted with their arms painted red—weeping over the deaths of their warriors with bone-chilling wails. The king of the tribe, seeing himself defeated, offered his daughters to the Spanish captain.

"*Tobaya, tobaya*," said the tribal lord.

"That means 'son-in-law,' bro," said an army interpreter, a short, squat polyglot from the Guaiqueri tribe, whose Christian name was Luis Pajares.

"Hand 'em over," said Captain Domingo Vázquez de Soja, a fat man with the red nose of a drinker, who inspected the girls' teeth and flesh as if they were animals. "These wille do for bedding, not for labour. Proceedeth with the *requerimiento*!"

One of the soldiers unfurled a half-rotten parchment and began to read:

𝕴 𝖉𝖔𝖙𝖍 𝖍𝖊𝖗𝖊𝖇𝖞 𝖉𝖊𝖈𝖑𝖆𝖗𝖊 𝖙𝖍𝖆𝖙 𝖜𝖎𝖙𝖍 𝖙𝖍𝖊 𝖍𝖊𝖑𝖕 𝖔𝖋 𝖙𝖍𝖊 𝖆𝖑𝖑𝖒𝖎𝖌𝖍𝖙𝖊𝖊 𝕲𝖔𝖉
𝕴 𝖘𝖍𝖆𝖑𝖑 𝖊𝖓𝖙𝖊𝖗 𝖕𝖔𝖜𝖊𝖗𝖋𝖚𝖑𝖑 𝖆𝖌𝖆𝖎𝖓𝖘𝖙 𝖞𝖊, 𝖆𝖓𝖉 𝖜𝖆𝖌𝖊 𝖜𝖆𝖗 𝖔𝖓 𝖆𝖑𝖑 𝖘𝖎𝖉𝖊𝖘

---

101. *i.e.* Protective quilted tunic.

and manners that I can, and I shall subject ye to the yoke and yobedience to the Church and Monarchs, and I shall take thyne people and thine women and children and I shall make of them slaves, etc.

The proclamation, read without translation, made no impact on the natives because they didn't understand a simple word. Luis Pajares translated the moratorium as best he could to the tribesmen, so they would recognize the one God of the Christians, and abandon their own. The tribal leader murmured a few words to the interpreter and he said:

"The chief asks why do they have to abandon their gods, whom they received from their elders and who bestow good harvests unto them."

"These fuggin inverts . . . !" exclaimed Captain De Soja, cuffing the translator. "These sauvages go around in their birthday suits all day long with errybody getting it on with errybody else. Loathsome sin! Set the dogs uponst them!"

No sooner said than done, the soldier in charge of the captain's dogs, untied them, ordering, "Attack, Leoncillo! Sic 'em, Becerrillo!" while the two enormous mastiffs pounced on the women and children, tearing off chunks of their flesh.

Afterward, the captain ordered all the village's huts burned, killing all the children and elderly and turning the rest of the men and women into slaves. Our hero and his soldier friends observed that butchery, flabbergasted: babies were smashed against trees, children's throats slit, young women raped and old women burned alive.

The Spanish captain, who had come there to claim dominion, said, "Clear the lande!"

A scribe drafted agreements taking possession of the discovered lands and an inspector was careful to account for the expenses and the percentage of found gold that was due to the Crown.[102] The problem was that, as for what we call gold, there wasn't even a speck. That made Captain De Soja even more furious, and he burned village after village, murdering hundreds of innocent people and collecting slaves only to calm his fever for gold.

One day, when the soldiers were resting, after having set up camp amid the howling of the jungle, Gregorio Izquierdo confessed the following to his friends:

"I must say that I amm nowise in agreement with this policy of brutal conquest. These inquisiturient terror methods make this seem less like Paradise and more like hell."

"*Chumbamenea!* And I do not subscribe to the *malinchismo*[103] of these Indian chiefs, bro," added the native translator Luis Pajares, who happened to be passing by and had joined the meeting.

"I feele we should complain to the Crown," said Father Claver. "We hath come here to create a Christian republic, not to murder right and left. Bartolomé de las Casas hath already declar'd that these beings be 'neither evill nor duplicitous.'"

---

102. *i.e.* The famous "royal fifth."

103. *i.e.* A derogatory term derived from the name La Malinche for Doña Marina (ca. 1500-1527), a native Mexican noble daughter who was Hernán Cortés's translator and lover, considered by some to be the supreme traitor for helping the conquistador to defeat Moctezuma, but also the mother of all the mestizos in America.

"I wouldst give the valiyant captain a piece of mine mind," threatened Martulina the Divina.

Finally, our hero made a decision. And the decision was the following: to speak face-to-face with Captain De Soja, which was only possible since our hero had accumulated enough merits in those early days in the New World to be considered a captain by the soldiers, despite not having that actual rank.

"Mine captain," he said, before Captain Domingo Vázquez de Soja and all the soldiers, "as a lawyer I must warn ye that thine behaviour withe the Indians is illegal from a human standpoint as well as a juridical one, commensurate withe the 1512 Laws of Burgos."

"I knowe nothing of laws, I hath just comme to make just war," said Captain De Soja.

"Yeah, right, and I'm Virgil in the nine circles of hell," said Gregorio Izquierdo. "Having two hundred slaves and murdelating everyone left and right appears *just* to you?"

"On Aristotle's authority, slaves be natural born," defended the captain. "In the case of resistance, war is justified."

"Sir, I rather incline toward the Gospel of Saint Mark, who sayeth: *Praedicate Evangelium omni creaturae*. Besides, from what I doth understand, in his *Ethics*, Aristotle did say that the just man be he who respects the mandates of fairness, and thou hath been anythyng but just. Less than an hour agone you vilely murdered women and children. I request you turn in your stripes as War Captain."

"Insurrecktion!" howled the captain, unsheathing his saber. "Contempt! I shall report solely to my main man King Philip!"

"Well I shall report solely to the justice of the courts," said our hero, with typical lawyer's tenacity.

So Vázquez de Soja called for his personal guards and the encampment was soon divided in two: those who supported

Gregorio Izquierdo and those who supported the captain. The matter would have been resolved the way these matters usually are, which is to say by blows, but common sense prevailed in favor of resolving the issue via legal means. And it was in Santo Domingo where the trial would take place, before the Royal Audience of the Supreme Council of the Indies, as we shall see forthwith.

## Chapter III

### In which our hero defends himself before a jury
### and very nearly gets burned

Seems the trial took place in a room filled with crucifixes and holy oils and was presided over by three judges of the Council of the Indies. The courtroom was full of Castilian gentleman, except for the indigenous translator Luis Pajares and Estebanico the Blackamoor, who were sitting in a dark corner observing it all with their enormous black eyes. Further up, sitting in the second row, was the imperial administration of the lettered city with all the human instruments of its bureaucracy. Before the judges, to the left, was Domingo Vázquez de Soja, accompanied by other noble military men, all of them criollo sons of illustrious conquistadors who'd been born in the New World and considered it their own. To the right, was only our hero, defending himself, dressed in a black lawyer's robe. The judge spoke first:

"In the name of the King of the Islands and Terra Firma of the Ocean Sea, we openne this court of the first instance in order to reconsile the fyude between troop lieutenant

215

Gregorio Izquierdo versus the nobleman De Soja, both loyall servants of the Crown."

De Soja's lawyer began the trial with a dissertation on the savage figure of the native, before the smiling faces of the noblemen:

". . . and it canst be asseverated, without a shaddow of a doubt, that the natives are uncultured, inhuman barbarians, as they knowe not God nor recognise his law. Therefore, ours indeed be a just war, as declared by Sepúlveda in *Democrates Alter or, On the Just Causes for War Against the Indians*, where he recognises the right of the Pope and our Catholic King to enslave the Indians, being as they art natural servants of the Crown. Furthermore, it upholdes the right, under juridickal, theological, and political bases, for *iusta causa posesionis*, in other wurds, the legitimacy of our conquest, from the Capitulations of Santa Fe to the Laws of Burgos, gathered in the treatises *On the Islands of the Ocean Sea* by Palacios y Rubios and *Concerning the Rule of the King of Spain over the Indians* by Matías de Paz. And as syuch, our actions are justified and preserv'd by the law of those just treatises."

Two of the judges nodded, while the third scratched his curly white wig and gestured with one hand for our hero to begin his rebuttal.

"Much obliged, Your Excellency. All the arguments put forth hath been call'd into question by umpteen people," said Gregorio Izquierdo, pulling a bundle of books out of his satchel. "Fray Bartolomé de las Casas hath already refuted, in his *Apologetic History*, the savage nature of the Indians. As for their conversion to Christianity, that art a right of the Indians but not an imperative to be imposed bloodily."

The people sitting at the back of the room murmured some astounded "oohs" and "aahs" at the impertinence of our hero.

"Conquest for the Gospel, yes, *mero et mixto imperio*[104]," he repeated, reasserting himself. "Howsoever, the era of epics and novels of chivalry has long pass'd, my lords. Now tis registry and law which rule, the tangible and the rational. These natives are not the devil, they art human beings such as ourselves, and as such their treatment at Spanish hands be unjust, and based solely on the fact that they doth not believe in our God, of whom they hath ne'er before heard telle. The *plena potestas in re* of the Kingdom of Spain and its *dominum* over the Indians, derived from Roman law, cannot be absolute for were it so then the very Pope in Rome and his *Romanus Pontifex* bull must necessarily take sides in this trial!"

There was a considerable upturn in the courtroom's commotion when someone shouted out "heretick!" and the judge banged his gavel as he shouted, "Order . . . ! Order in the court!"

"Your Excellency, I invent none of this, it's all in the books," continued Gregorio. "Fray Francisco de Vitoria revisits the juridical & theological corpus of *De potestate civili* (1528) in favour of an international law grounded in natural right and not on force. Correspondingly, from a legal perspective, war against innocents goeth against natural and divine law."

"I object, Your Honor!" said the lawyer for the State. "The Eramist ideas of Second Lieutenant Izquierdo do not correspond with the reality of the colonies. Dost thou not concede that it should be preposterous not to oblige the Indians to labour for and submit to both Church and King?"

"Objecktion overruled," said the judge. "Allow the soldier Gregorio Izquierdo persevere with his defense."

"With all due reverence, counsel," said our hero, "what

---

104. In other words, with absolute power and jurisdiction over sentencing and punishment.

thou deemst 'preposterous' is verily the possibility of true justice."

"What art thou propounding? That the Indians simply do as they wish?" said the nobleman's attorney, adopting a surprised expression. "For tis it not also true that in another of Francisco de Vitoria's books, namely *De indis prior* (1539), he states that the Indians have no convenyent laws, no magistrates, and are not even capable of governance? The *Seven-Part Code* hath already establish'd the *ocupatio* and governance of these savages and their lands, being as they were *res nullius*, all became ours. And for that motife and none other, the Crown must acte as Father to these savages and, concurrently, govern them so as not to relinquish all that the Crown has achieved, the trade and economic benefits to our Empire."

"Whilst the aforementioned be veracious," said Gregorio Izquierdo, "in *De indis posterior seu de iure belli* (1539), Vitoria himself admitte that natural law prohibits the killing of innocents. Las Casas concurred, in his *New Laws* (1542), which state that slavery and the *encomienda* system must be outlawed in favour of a just treatment of the Indians. That an empyre of justice must be established through the use of reason, never force! Roman-Christian law, the *Lex romana visigotorum*, rejects slavery. In other wordes, the Indians must submit to the power of the King, but war canst be waged against them merely for not being Christians. Alexander VI's four bulls and the legal justification for the *Requerimiento* should not presume to sanction any massacre, because tis he who kills an innocent and is unable to admit to his atrocity who demonises that innocent in order to justify his demise. The Gospel leads altogether too swifth to the sword in these lands. And that be indubitably what nobleman Domingo Vázquez de Soja and his vassals did, dispiteous . . . setting the dogges upon an entire tribe for not submitting to their orders, converting that village into a veritable cemetery of Indians!"

The women in the courtroom gasped in horror and the men coughed and mumbled. The judges didn't know where they stood in the face of our hero's exposition, while the noblemen noted with discomfort that Izquierdo was gaining ground. But their lawyer had a trick up his sleeve and this was the time to use it.

"Objection! Objection, Your Excellency!" he said. "Be there perchance a witness in this courtroom to the supposed exploits of which my client is accused? Does perchance any man knowe beyond doubt that this soldier, this Gregorio Izquierdo, be truly who he claimeth to be? Who is this solider, who travells with a black slave as if he were a white man?"

The murmuring in the room grew shriller, becoming a constant soundtrack.

"Order in the court!" called the judge. "Carry on, barrister, and clarify this matter."

"Your Excellency, I hath heard telle that the soldier Gregorio Izquierdo, who today assumes all the riskes of defending himself, is truly named Juan Urpín and a Catalan national, in other words a foreign'r, and furthermore a lawyer by profession," continued the attorney, smiling triumphantly. "What bee the motive behind this learn'd man travelling through these new worlds with an assumed name? Be he a fugitive? Be he a runaway from prison or the galleys? Who is Juan Urpín and who is Gregorio Izquierdo? Is he, perhaps, a spy for the English or the Portuguese? This matter must be urgently address'd!"

Our hero, whose face had blanched more and more as he listened, his body sinking into his chair, wanted to die. The crowd in the courtroom erupted in a commotion, each person giving his opinion. He patted down the pocket of his dress coat, searching for the letter from Úrsula Pendregast, but then he remembered that he'd lost it on the high seas. Amid the commotion, Luis Pajares, the native interpreter, stood up from his chair and walked to the middle of the room. The throng, upon seeing his slight, dark figure, was suddenly quiet.

"Your Excellency, witnesses and jury, all assembled bros & hos: mine Christian name be Luis Pajares and I didst right verily eyewitness all these massacres in the jungle," he said. "And I doth swere, in the name of God Our Father and the Holy Spirit (can I git an amen!), that Gregorio Izquierdo allways comported with honour and kindness among the Indians, while the enraged nobleman Domingo Vázquez de Soja didst murder entire tribes. *Carajo!*"

"Ti'th tlue!" exclaimed Estebanico the Blackamoor, emerging from behind Luis Pajares. "And ath fo' the tlue identity of the soldiel Gregorio Izquierdo, do not be led astlay by lumols and tlust mole in the tluth of leason: thi' vely Don Izquierdo fleed me flom a slave ship and celtain death and that i' what count."

After the speeches made by the indigenous man and the African man, the courtroom was dumbstruck. A deafening silence hovered for a few moments over all the shaken faces of those present, until the judge coughed and then murmured a few words with the other judges before speaking.

"Ahem! Well, this court deems it just to dismiss the charges against the noble criollo Domingo Vázquez de Soja, as a recognised figure of great merit in these regions, with a forewarning of possible charges on crimes and misdemeanours shouldst he commit further atrocities. And we shall adjourne our review of the strange 'case' of Gregorio . . . or Juan whatever-the-heck and his suspected dubble personality, whilst considering in accordance with common agreement to ceast and desist all further crimes and misdeamors. Session adjourned!"

While the judge hammered out the sentence and the audience bellowed with rage and confusion at that strange ruling, Captain De Soja and the other noble hidalgos didn't know whether to laugh or to cry. And as for our hero, let's just say he got lucky that time, but a new fearsome enemy had appeared on the scene, as the attentive reader will see straightaway.

## Chapter IV

In which our hero meets a powerful lord
who makes him a unique offer, and then
encounters the Indian Araypuro

Our hero was celebrating his partial victory at trial, in a tavern with his friends Martulina the Divina, Father Claver, Estebanico the Blackamoor, and the soldiers Octopus, Jeremies, and The Scourge, drinking a wine made of fermented yucca. After their carousing, Gregorio Izquierdo walked back alone to the soldier's barracks. As luck or fate would have it, he ran into Domingo Vázquez de Soja and the other criollo noblemen. Upon seeing them, he greeted his opponents, politely removing his hat and even bowing.

"Quit yer reverences and playacting, second lieutenant!" ordered De Soja. "Today, in that trial—or shall I say farce—you dug your own grave, Don Gregorio. Or was it . . . Juan Urpín?"

"I like both names equally, thanks," said our hero, sarcastically. "But I'm not nearly as fond of hypocrisy and injustice as thou beest, that's for sure."

"Nor am I fond of the Indians and black slaves you consort with as your lickspittles," said the criollo nobleman, with a disgusted expression. "Nor of *bretones*[105] and wooden nickels like you!"

"Only the lily-livered extermynate an entire village of women and children," said Gregorio, starting to get nervous. "Murderer."

"That's an affront!" exclaimed the nobleman, unsheathing his sword.

"Indeed!" said our hero, unsheathing his, and preparing to duel with that villain.

The other military noblemen also drew their swords and surrounded Gregorio, and soon a crowd—alerted by the shouting—had formed a circle around the soldiers, hoping to see blood.

"Halt!" shouted an elegantly dressed man, emerging from the crowd. "Four against one . . . not a verry gentlemanly battle!"

"And who in the hell art thou?" said one of the noblemen, pointing his sword at him.

"Diego de Arroyo, governor of Cumaná, at your service," he said, pushing the sword away by its tip. "And all of ye be under my jurisdiction and as such I canst send ye all to the clink with a wave of my finger. So . . . no more insults and break it up!"

The noblemen put away their swords and dispersed amid the crowd, their faces reflecting their rage, as Gregorio Izquierdo also sheathed his weapon.

"Second Lieutenant Izquierdo," said the Governor. "I attended thine trial today and saw thee to be a just and

---

105. Foreigners

learned man, precisely what I require for the post of second-in-command in Cumanagoto, in New Andalusia. Willst thou accept?"

"Thy will be done," said our hero, bowing until his nose touched the ground.

"Then come see me tomorrow and we'll do all the paper-work," said the Governor, and the two men shook hands. "By the way, I forgotte to mention that some fishermen have gotten word from some other fishermen who, in turn, heard yet other fisherman further up the coast say (basically, a bunch o' fishermen), that there is someone named Gregorio Izquierdo who's just arrived from Seville to reclaim his treasure. So now we have a fake Gregorio Izquierdo and a real Gregorio Izquierdo. Which one art thou?"

"Yeegads! Gregorio Izquierdo is alive? My real name is Juan Urpín," confessed our hero, embarrassed. "It's a long story. Pray allow me to . . ."

"I don't want to hear it!" said the Governor, cutting him off.

"Wherefor dost Your Grace trust me?"

"Thou art a man of letters and verily a personage of char-acter," said the Governor. "Just men are few and far between in these parts and thou shalt be of more use in my service than locked up in jail. But watch it with the whole matter of the bilocation, I assume twill catch up with thee at some point."

Having bid farewell to the Governor, our hero, on his way back to the hostel, ran into the native translator who had defended him in court, sitting on a corner beneath a weak streetlight, drinking a bottle of firewater all by his lonesome. He had taken off his white shirt and linen pantaloons and was dressed in the garb of the Guaiqueri tribe, amulets hanging around his neck. Gregorio approached him and asked, "Thou art the translator Luis Pajares, right? I have to thank thee for defending me at the trial."

"Darn tootin'! You owe me more than thanks, milord, I need a job after court today or I'll end up eating wood, since I'm flat broke and only want to tie on a big trial-tribulation with this here hot firewater," he said. "But mine name is Araypuro, not Luis Pajares. Luis is the name some over-the-top Christian *dima*[106] with horriblis bad taste gave me. I prefer my birth name, if it's not too mucho to ask. And as for name changes, bam! Methinks thou hath a little problem of thine own."

"What cheek!" our hero exclaimed in surprise. "Since when doth an Indian speak that way to an officer of the King?"

"Come now! I never did meet no injun, I only know Tasermes, Tomuces, Pírutus, Guarives, Guaiqueris, Xacopates, Coxaimes, Palenques, Caracares, and a bunch more who been playing *macumba tarumba* from long since before you guys showed up," said Araypuro. "The word 'Indian' is something you long-legged hairy moochers use to insult us. Guaquerí or not Guaiquerí, that is the question."[107]

"Thou crosseth the line, Luis, or Araypuro or whatever. But I shall grant you pardon maugre the fact that thou art a malapert Prince of Insolence. However do not forget that, as a mestizo, thine life is worth zilch."

"Not this again, bro! I thought you were a good guy, against slavery and all . . . Or at least that's what I thought I heard during the trial. Although you negleckted to mention

---

106. *i.e.* Father in the Guaiqueri language—Chotomaimur, which is very similar to Warao, an isolated tongue still spoken today, by the Waraos, at the delta of the Orinoco, in Venezuela.

107. Araypuro foreshadows here, by a few centuries, the famous "Tupí or not Tupí" of Oswald de Andrade's *Cannibalist Manifesto*.

that Bartolomé de Las Casas, in his *Twelve Doubts Treatise*, demanded abandoning the Indies and returning all the goods you *dosarao*[108] have been fleecing extralegally for two centuries. Granted, that selfsame huevón 'parently sed that 'steda injuns, you should enslave blacks, which isn't a great look for a clergyman. Yer all a pack of bewhiskered cretinos!"

"Goodness sakes . . . don't push thine luck and be more polite!" ordered Gregorio Izquierdo. "If I had said all that at the trial, I'd right well be execut'd now for insurrection . . ."

"You'll get your comeuppance sooner or later, bro" said Araypuro. "For those very same Laws of the Indies make any and all justice impossible, by authorising our enslavement and suffering, just so ye bearded dudes can throw your little Catholic shindigs. I dost favour a getty as much as the next dude, but your raping and pillaging blotted out the sun. But here, inland, even the most saintly has a scantling of the devil in him."

"I must admit thou art not wrong. By the by, how be it that thou knowst so much of laws and letters?" asked our hero.

"Because I'm a Southerner born in the Old Worlde, son of a Guaiquerí and a Spanish prostitute, the opposite of Inca Garcilaso, who was the son of a Peruvian noblewoman and an aristocratic Spanish conquistador," replied Araypuro, taking a long gulp of firewater before continuing. "'Course mine dear parents gave me up when I was a baby, for mestizo, left me in a Dominican—'the dogs of God'—monastery, and I was raised there by servants and educated by a friggin friar with a perfect bald pate, up to the task of any grammarian and extremely fond of nice-looking brown lads. But there were other young lads like me in that monastery and one day they rose up and burnt it down, roasting all the friars. From there,

---

108. *i.e.* soldiers

I was condemned to the galleys at the age of thirteen, where I rowed my way over to the New World, which I consider mine true homeland. I landed in Cumaná having fulfill'd my sentence and I enlisted in the Spanish army, but everyone didst give me side-eye for being a half-breed. So I sought out the Quaiquerís, but my father's tribe didn't accept me either, taking me for a foreign mutt from Carupa, blecch! Between one syde and the other, I began to fear for my life, so I put down my sword and picked up the books, studying grammar: Latin, Spanish, and some of the languages of my native region. Once I was able to *namina*[109] languages on my own, I put down the books and started working as a translator of the Spaniards."

"Thine bisarre story doth certainly bear some resemblance to Inca Garcilaso's, except thine voyage was in t'other direction," reflected Gregorio, smiling. "But then, to whom art thou accountable? To the Kingdom of Castile or to thine tribe?"

"At this point, I'm not accountable to nobody. I couldn't give two shits about the King of Castile or the King of Cipango. I only take orders from Sir Moolah Ducats and my female-half-moon and billy-goat-sun spirits and the *piracucú* and all the animals and trees in these forests that make up my world, and which I keep in this periapt hanging 'round my scrag, as you can see."

"I see that thine insolence be as sharp as thine pragmatism."

"*Chumbamenea*! That's because I'm a halfbreed mutt in this wretched world filled with assholes."

"Well, if thou desire a job as mine translator, I'll pay thee for thine services and thou'll be a slave to no man. On my word as a Christian. One condition: quitte all thine swearing."

"Friggin' *jokos*,[110] as if imposing the Castilian language on

---

109. *i.e.* learn

110. *i.e.* whites

us weren't enuf, then ye cume at us with the oaths!" complained Araypuro, drunk. "There's no truth in the word of youse bewhiskereds . . ."

"Bite thy tongue, Luis! I've killed no man for pleasure, and I'm no Castilian. I'm a Catalan. Besides, I consider mineself a just man and I shall pay thee well."

"*Alabao*! You're not being feezy, right? Cuz my feez are high, bro."

"Crikey! Be thou the one in charge now and I'm the vassal?" asked our hero.

"Giving orders to the one in charge, serving the servant. That be the true obligation between free men," said Araypuro.

"Quit it with the paradoxes, Araypuro. I'm starting to regret putting thee in mine service."

"Bro, if it makes you happy you can call me 'Indian' (or epsilon) and I shall call thee 'master' (alpha), and that way your conquering soul will be more assuaged and pious.[111] But don't be a skinflint and pay me well, if thou wouldst be so kind and just becuz, 'kay 'kay? Soun' like a deal?"

"Talk less and thou shalt live longer, Indian. And now, put down that bottle, you're beyond stewed and the Devil bathes in that stuff. Let's hit the road already."

"*Yakera*.[112] But when Imma liddle drunk I doth enjoy my job much more!" protested Araypuro, reluctantly putting down the bottle of chicha and following our hero down the

---

111. The figure of the mestizo Araypuro allows us to reflect here on the relationship between colonizer and colonized with a geometry of resistance to colonial power and knowledge, and at the same time go beyond the stereotypical image of the colonized as well as the (false) universal nature of the colonizer. After all, the colonizers were and continue to be a silent minority, scapegoats in the classic sense, subordinate to the dominant discourse of each nation and each nationalism.

112. *i.e.* "Okay" in Guayquerí.

avenue as night fell on America, and their silhouettes disappeared there where the sky meets the earth.

## Chapter V

### In which "Gregorio Izquierdo"
### recovers his true name and begins his new post
### as lieutenant in the tropical forest

Under the protection of the Governor of Cumaná, our hero
had to be sworn in before the Court of the Indies in his new
post, but this time with his real name: Joan Orpí, or Juan
Urpín as they called him there, obscuring the splendor of his
obviously Catalan origins. Oh, the indignity! Oh, the indecen-
cy! Anyhoo, one thing was clear: our hero was already quite
used to name changes. Once he'd been sworn in, he set out
to keep the peace within the jurisdiction of New Andalusia,
which extended from the Orinoco to the Caribbean, through
the mountains to the district of Caracas, covering a territory
of hundreds of leagues.

During the months that followed, Joan Orpí and his infantry regiment controlled the forests, islands, and plains of New Andalusia, through rock promontories, gently bubbling springs, rushing rivers, cliffs, sandy banks, abysses, ancient trees, metal beds, salt pans, and thousands of heads of cattle brought from the Iberian Peninsula filled with virus and bacteria that silently exterminated local fauna and flora.

As they moved slowly through the forest, Orpí had begun to teach Araypuro Catalan.

"Master, why doth thee have a different language from the Castilians?" asked Araypuro, upon his mule with the book open in front of him.

"Well because . . . because we're a different tribe," reflected our hero, riding on his Acephalus. "Dost thou understand what I mean?"

"Yes, master, that thy language is quite similar to Castilian. Although when it comes to *teribukitane*[113] it's more of a drag."

"Mind thy tongue, Indian, I love my language very much. What's more, I'm a Lieutenant now and thou mustest treat me with the respect due to my rank. Keep reading in Catalan, when thou hast learnt it we'll communicate better."

"With pleasure, but the mountainous regions in these sad tropics be verily a bitch, master," complained Araypuro.

"Thou canst address me as Joan, Indian, as that be mine true name," said our hero.

"Very well, I shall, unless some fearsome beast eats me or I fall off this mule," said Araypuro.

It was true. They were making progress. But it wasn't easy getting through that region. The horses and mules slipped on the muddy slopes and the soldiers had to keep helping them get back on their feet. One of the mules skidded and fell into

---

113. *i.e.* reading

a gully. The forest was teeming with life, and with death, at every step. One of the soldiers got caught in quicksand and there was no extricating him. Everyone watched as he sank in up to his nose and then was swallowed up by the deadly sand pit. The jungle seemed to devour everything and thousands of frogs croaked in the streams, blending in with the crackling of the ancient trees and the whistling, moaning, and howling of the creatures in a titanic cacophony. And thus Orpí's expedition marched forward until, in the course of one of their incursions through the Venezuelan geography, as they crossed the Macaira River, a tributary of the Manapire, the detachment came across San Cristóbal de la Nueva Écija de Cumanagoto. The town in question was a ghetto filled with cane shanties populated by some thirty-odd Castilians, with beards down to their ankles, ill with dysentery and depressed, surviving on potatoes and other tubers. While the mayor came out to receive them, Orpí observed the gray and khaki stains on the man's skin, which had become taxidermied, clinically dead flesh. Toothless, his eyes bulged from the sockets as if they were about to explode.

"Betwixt the attacks by the Injuns, the terror sown by the White Pygmy and the 'French disease' we keep getting from these eligible catechumen ladies, we're going to rot here, Don Urpín," said the town's mayor.

"The White Pygmy?" asked Orpí. "Whatchoo talkin' 'bout, Willis?"

"No one has ere seen him," explained the mayor, shaking with fear. "But legend has it that a wee evil being has a band of runaway slaves and they've formed a blockade not far from the Macaira River, and even the Injuns are afraid of them."

"The wee evil being!" exclaimed Araypuro in fear. "The spirit that governs the Dense-Forest by wielding its dark magick!"

Determined to investigate the intriguing matter, Joan Orpí, who had already learned that the mysteries of that new world grew in the imagination, ordered his soldiers down to the river where they splashed around a bit in the bogs until, amid the savage geography, they caught a glimpse of some Indians smeared with turtle grease: they were the Bubures. Araypuro asked them in their language whether they'd heard tell of a people led by a white pygmy and the Burbures pointed up the river with terrified expressions. While the soldiers travelled upstream, Orpí wondered if that pygmy was the same "Evil Thing" described by the chronicler and conquistador Álvaro Nuñez Cabeza de Vaca who, in Chapter XXII of his *Shipwrecks*, spoke of a small bearded being whom everyone feared. Focused on those thoughts, our hero, who was heading the expedition through the forest, came face to face with a man black as night. From deep in the forest resounded an uproar of popinjays and other shrieking birds. Then two more black men appeared. Then three. Four. Five. Then they found themselves completely surrounded by black men armed with sabers, pistols, and furious faces.

"Sky's gettin' mighty low," said Martulina, pulling out her sword.

"How 'bout if we just skedaddle?" suggested Araypuro. "We don't fit in round here."

"Button your lip, Indian. Soldiers, prepare thine weapons!" ordered our hero.

The runaway slaves were about to pounce on the soldiers when a voice was heard. "Halt! No fighting . . . I know this dude!"

From among the thicket emerged a stunted little being on a wild pony, and dressed in cow and goat skins and wearing some sort of cap made of piglet hide and covered in medals, a green velvet bodice, and black boots.

"I can't believe mine eyes . . ." said Orpí, mouth agape. "I would have never imagined being happy to see thee, Triboulet!"

"Halfman!" exclaimed Martulina.

After embracing his friends, Triboulet the Dwarf led them all to through the forest to a hidden village called Caracazo. The people there received the dwarf and his friends with trumpeting wooden flutes and shaking seeds inside dried gourds, which the locals call *maracas*, while dozens of mangy dogs barked at the newcomers. They were all invited to drink cassava beer and eat yam bread.

"I know what ye are thinking," said Triboulet to his friends, with artless smugness, "Ye are thinking 'what is Triboulet doing here'? I'll explain it as briefly and simply as I can: after fleeing that bar in Seville where we last saw each other, I was arrested and sent to the galleys. One day, there was a mutiny onboard and they blamed me for it (with goode reason). So they abandoned me on an island and from there I managed to reach the maineland, where I found some fugitive slaves and befriend'd their leader, Negro Miguel. They'd joint up with bucaneers who were illegally harvesting pearls in the Margarita sea. Since then I've been living like a pasha, without modern hustle and bustle or imperialist flights of fancy about world domination. One moment . . ."

The dwarf approached two monsters with rough hides, and threw them a bit of softened bread, "Here boys, come on over . . . !"

The two crocodiles docilely came over to Triboulet and began to roll over on the ground playfully, just like puppies.

"These creatures must be the *maniriguas*, as described by Juan de Castellanos in *Elegies II*," Orpí concluded literarily, shocked to see that those enormous reptiles with dangerous jaws could be domesticated.

"They're called *babas* here. Despite what many people think, they're quite tame little creatures. And thou needn't walk them, they walk themselves."

Triboulet the Dwarf seemed terrifically happy, since there, in that republic, blacks, *pardos*, *ladinos*, *zambos*, and mulattoes lived under the principles of liberty, equality, and fraternity.

"Good on thee, halfman," said Martulina the Divina. "By the way, whatever became of thine Homunculus?"

The dwarf pointed to a small figure seated beneath a palm tree. He was a strange being, with almost human features, tiny as a bottle of wine. When he saw Orpí, he started to sing:

♪ The soul hath its ups and downs ♫
the wave, don' let it make thou frown
all we ask for are eyes to see clearly
hands with which to cling dearly
a mouth with which to speak
feets ta keep us on fleek
and we be never ever stoppin'
always we be ever steady popping
yeah, that's right, never ever stopping
check out these beats we be droppin'
if things don't work out the way you plann'd
you can cross borders wit' yer contraband
(and mayhap ye'll find what ye seek)
Whilst leavin' yer enemies up shit's creek
Yes, we be constantly perforating oblivion
on beyonde that sick-ass post meridian
surfing fer pearls here in the Carribbian
Yeah, we half-split yer tir'd attitude
showing two faces amid all this solitude
don't play it safe, don't come unglued

there may be no morrow, by which I mean
please doth feele free to follow your spleen
The soul hath its ups and downs
the wave, don' let it make thou frown
all we ask for are eyes to see clearly
hands with which to cling dearly
a mouth with which to speak
feets ta keep us on fleek
and we be never ever stoppin'
always we be ever steady popping
yeah, that's right, never ever stopping
check out these beats we be droppin'
etc.

"Bravo! I see thine Homunculus hasn't forgotten how to sing in perfect Catalan!" said Orpí, applauding. "Out of respect for our friendship, Triboulet, I shant tell a soul that thou art here. But prithee, try to refrain from evil deeds and pissing off the settlements, or the entire Royal Army will come here and disstroy thee. The King is no fan of rebellious negroes or treasure-hunting buccaneers. Although given your gift for ubiquitousness, I know we shall meet again beneath other skies and in other guises."

"Speaking of treasures," said the dwarf, "a few sennight agone some guy named Gregorio Izquierdo came through here with a load of mules and Indians, heading to the city of Caracas. All I remember is that he was missing one hand and was all paranoid, going on about how his wife and her Cataloonian lover had tried to kill him and assume his identity, in order to go to America and claim the gold he'd amassed in Trujillo. And, from what I've heard about thee in these lands, thou dost also go by the name Gregorio Izquierdo. Tis not thee who hath the talent for being in two places at one time?"

Estebanico the Blackamoor looked at Orpí.

"Brodel," said the African. "Please deal with this mattel once and fol all, to cleal my name and youl own. I want aught mole to do with tleasures."

"What?" asked Orpí. "Wonst thou come with us?"

"No. I've decided to remain hele, with these negloes who are blood of my blood. Hele I shall be a flee man at last."

So our hero bade farewell to Triboulet the Dwarf and Estebanico the Blackamoor, and returned to Cumaná. Pragmatic as few men are, and with permission from his mentor Governor Diego de Arroyo, he resigned from his post as lieutenant in order to resolve the "Gregorio" matter in Caracas before it shot his whole career to hell, as we shall see anon.

## Chapter VI

### In which Joan Orpí arrives in Caracas and confronts an unpleasant surprise

Accompanied by Martulina the Divina and Araypuro, our hero set sail on the first ship heading out of Santo Domingo to La Guaira. After advancing along the coast, past the Unare Depression, where the coastal mountain range is interrupted, and crossing Cordera Cape, beyond the two mountain crests along the Aroa, the Valley of Santiago de León de Caracas stretched out before him, at the 67th meridian.

Everyone said great things about the city, but when Orpí arrived, he was tremendously disappointed. Caracas was just a bunch of ugly adobe houses, home to around three hundred souls including the two dozen gentlemen who spent their days lounging in hammocks and living off the work of others. The noblemen—failed conquerors or simply freeloaders—had discovered the comfort of a life of leisure built on their own boredom.

The next day, thanks to Araypuro's investigations, Orpí discovered that the true Gregorio Izquierdo had indeed been through Caracas but had now moved on. He was like a ghost.

In any case, after little more than a month, Orpí had made a name for himself in the city as a lawyer resolving legal disputes, even winning the favor of the Governor of Caracas, Juan de Meneses, who named him Lieutenant General, thus elevating even further our hero's good name.

One day, as he was in dealings with two merchants in the middle of the street, he heard a voice behind him shouting, "Good afternoon, lieutenant! Or perhaps I should say . . . Don Gregorio Izquierdo?"

Hearing that, Orpí was silent, and his skin turned white as a corpse. When he turned he saw a shriveled, toothless woman who had long since lost the gleam of youth. A tatterdemallion, her hair everywhichway, she looked at him with demented, furious eyes, waiting for a reply, as she picked her nose. Orpí, thinking she was mistaking him for his double, responded, "That be not my name, I sweareth to God. Thou must believe me, ma'am, you have the wrong person. I know that I am not Gregorio Izquierdo. I have authentic documents that certify the Catalan origin of my name and personatge, son of a large family of old Christians, the Orpís . . . I am one of four siblings and we all look alike: the same aquiline nose, the same bulging eyes . . . twould be easy to mistake us. And all because of the intermarriage in our great family . . . ! I have more than two hundred cousins and they're all half retard'd from the intermingling . . . anyhoo, these things happen in every family! Mothers are confused about who to nurse . . . fathers are muddled up and don't know who to scold . . . and in the end it's all a huge mess! But let me assure thee that I am not the man thou seeketh, since I know nothing anent this Gregorio Izquierdo . . . I mean . . . I am not him. Take a good look at me! Shed some light on mine face, open the curtains of thine eyes. Dost thou still believe me to be him? Dost thou seest his mustache on my face . . . ? Canst thou be sure this ear is not mine? Art thou sure this is not my chin . . . ? Take a good look, for thou art mistaken. I am not whom thou seek . . . I am altogether someone else!"

"Ha, ha, ha . . . !" laughed the woman, clapping. "Fabulous. Brilliant. Marvellous. Estupendous. Incredible. Phantastic. Go on and tell, essir, all the estories and lies you weesh, for no matter how well the esstory be told, tis nothing without truth in it. No matter thine elegance and position, I know who thou art. But now wise up and take a good look at my face, look at me and then look again . . . and try to jog the memory in that mosquito brain of thine."

Our hero approached the woman, who stank of rotten eggs, and his eyes grew wide as saucers. "God help me . . . Úrsula Pendregast!"

Exactly. Before our hero was none other than the woman who had gotten him mired in the whole "Gregorio affair" in Seville. Dragging her out of the middle of the street, our hero and the crafty woman walked in silence to his house. Then he sat her down in a chair and began his interrogation:

"What in God's name art thou doing hither? Why dost the shadow of Gregorio Izquierdo plague me still? And why art thou lain so vile and misshapen of face? This entire story of doubles is too baroque and oppressive . . . Prithee to explain!"

"The tale is long, cohort, so I recommend thee essit," said Úrsula, running her fingers through her natural dreadlocks. "Nothing is what it esseems. If you thought that my Gregorio were a cadaever, thou art mistaken. In fact, we both were mistaken, esince he didn't kick the bucket atall, but rather awoke the following day with nigh more than a bump on his crumpet. After beseeching him a thousand pardons for the evil deed (and taking a harsh beating), he forced me onto the first esship headed to La Española with him, to recover his treasure and unmask thee for false appropriation of name and titles. But, no matter how much the rogue hit me, I didn't give him thine true name, essince twere I what got thee into this mess: I am a viper, but mostly an honest one."

"I appreciate that. I did already know, from other sources, that Don Gregorio did not die but rather return'd hence. And I also did learne that his treasure be not his, that although a story composed of lies often ends up being true, the accursed treasure, in this case, was stolen from a good friend of mine named Estebanico the Blackmoor. But anyway, hath thou been on this side of the pond long?" asked our hero.

"Near nigh two months . . . (Who couldst believe that! The Lord only knows how much misfortune and peregrination I've suffered over that treasure!) As I was esayin', two days after reaching La Española we came without delay to Caracas, through jungles filled with cannibals, to gather all the gold my husband had estored esafely here, before thou couldst claim it in his name. Gregorio's melancholy grewe considerably over our journey to the New World and by the time we arrived in this city, he had completely lost his mind. He was constantly convinced that esomeone was trying to esteal his gold. One morning he disappeared into ze mountains with the entire treasure loaded onto four old mules. I haven't seen the bastardo essince."

"A right bizarro tale!" exclaimed Orpí. "I am soothly glad to have lost the letter thou gave me, and I was hoping to meet up with thine husband here, in Caracas, and settle this malignant matter once and for all. Thy plan ne'er would have worked, by the way. Furthermore, tis well known that encountering one's double is a sign of bad lucke. To be sincere, I also thought I had lost my reason with all that name-changing. Now I can finally put the matter to rest and make the factum of reason the logos of my life hereafter. Never again shall I be anyone else's cheap imitation."

"Prithee, don't get philosophical on me, Cataloon," said Úrsula. "But to answer thine ultimate question, that bastardio Gregorio ruined my life. After coming to this horrible country and esquandering all hopes of becoming rich, I esspend my days grinding coffee on the plantations and part of the night fornicating with estrangers to earn a few lousy ducats! Pray put paid to mine quest for vengeance, I hath become a FFFF (fugly, fierce, false floozy) . . . tis a long fall from hustling in Seville to two-bit whore!"

"Thou hast made thine own bed, milady," said Orpí. "With all the evil thou brought upon thine husband and mineself with thine machavellian plans. Tis the Devil who twists all that should be straight, like the very road to heaven."

"Estuff it!" bellowed Úrsula, making as if to leave. "Twisted, eshmisted, the just and the esinners are one and the same, I'll have ye know. Now, farewell. We eshall meet again in the helle at the end of this life!"

And thus, cursing at a few of the saints, Úrsula disappeared from our hero's life, and he found he had finally recovered his name for, lacking a better word, eternity. And while Orpí continued to exercise his post in Caracas with the utmost diligence, it wouldn't last much longer, since he heard tell that the Royal Audiencia in La Española had opened up a public grant to become an *adelantado*[114] and set out to conquer terra incognita in the unexplored jungles of Venezuela. That made our hero's gray matter tingle, as he had always identified with the adventures of Hernan Cortés, because they had both studied Law (and, truth be told, they were both terrible students). He began to dream of riches in the New World and flaunting a noble title that would allow him to return home to Catalonia dripping in gold and live like a sultan, and because

---

114. *i.e.* conquistador

he was already thirty-two years old and not wanting to live out his days in Caracas. Or to put it another way: since he could no longer get rich via Gregorio Izquierdo's treasure, he would become a conquistador and climb the ranks, following the formula of El Cid: honor and profit. If he applied for that grant he could escape that depressing, sordid city, whose history was nothing more than a succession of epidemics, raids, massacres, mass agony, and envy. And so he left Caracas, with Araypuro and Martulina in tow, just as quickly as he'd come and without a word, heading toward Santo Domingo in the manner we shall see forthwith:

## Chapter VII

In which Joan Orpí heads out toward La Guaira and,
along the way, is captured by a tribe of
very fierce warrior women

Orpí, Araypuro, and Martulina left the city of Caracas one
morning headed to La Guaira and they went through the
mountains, where the dense, sweltering forest began, with no
clearings or pause, and then they went down amid the banks
of the Orinoco and the Amazon Rivers. Tribes and regions
with strange names appeared and disappeared amid the
perpetual shadows of a tangled landscape covered in trees
that devoured each other and vines twisted into impossible
spirals, with nasty swamps that swallowed up knights whole
who dared to traverse them, where secret bogs drowned anyone who sought to pass, and which abounded with outlandish
reptiles and felines who could rip your head clean off.

While Martulina the Divina brought up the rear, Orpí and
Araypuro took the lead, advancing through the jungle. The
Indian chewed *hayo*[115], an herb placed against the gums that
slowly, slowly numbed the mouth.

---

115. *i.e.* coca leaf

"That is a vice, Araypuro. Thou must just say nay to drugs."

"Hayo is good for the *buba*.[116] Seems like since you honkeys showed up we never have any fun anymore. This herb helps me work, master," he said. "I'm ne'er tired and squirrelly squirrelly all around."

"You are my employee, Injun. I pay thee to interpret, not get high," said Orpí, businesslike, extracting a handkerchief to wipe his dripping forehead in the torrid heat.

"Hot damn! So what ye smoke is not a drug?"

"*Touché*," answered Orpí, rolling up a dry leaf and lighting it, so that his face was clouded with smoke. "This Barinas tobacco hath been a great discovery."

The Venezuelan climate was muggy as all get out. While Orpí cooled off by the Cuchivero River, in the Tamanaco jungle, after sweating like a butcher for hours, two-hundred warrior women appeared amid the vegetation, aiming long arrows at him and his friends. Most of the warriors were nude, covered only by long hair down to their knees, and they had each cut off one of their breasts so they could handle their bows more skillfully. They stood still as statues.

"*Dale*, bro, let's bolt, it's the *aikeam-benanó*, the badass *tida*[117]!" cried out Araypuro, running up into the mountains, howling all the names of his jungle spirits like a lunatic.

"Are they the *maniriguas* of which Juan de Castellanos spoke in his *Elegies*? Or what Pierre D'Ailly described in his book *Imago Mundi*? Or mayhaps they are the Amazons Christopher Columbus told of?" said Orpí, pulling a book from his satchel and opening it up. "On 6th of January, 1493, he wrote that: 'The Indians speak of the Island of Martirio along this route, said to be populated by women without men, of whom

---

116. *i.e.* syphillis

117. *i.e.* Women, in his language.

the Admiral of the Ocean Seas very much wish'd to deliver five or six of them to the Monarchs.' If tis written, it must be truth; and if it is truth it must be this island."

"This is no island, Orpí, come on," said Martulina. "We're on *terra firma*."

"Zounds, you've a point there."

Quickly deprived of their window for reflection, Orpí and Martulina were captured by the armed women, who bested them in number, arrows, and estrogen. Araypuro was also captured a few minutes later, despite crouching stock still and hoping to be taken for a bush. The were all three brought to the village, made of palafittes built on platforms supported by wooden beams, in the delta of the Unare River.

"Now I understand why Vespuccio diddst call this country Venezuela," said Orpí. "Tis indeed the very picture of rural Venice!"

"More like the very picture of a military matriarchy, master!" exclaimed Araypuro. "These beatches are women warriors, bro! They allow dealings with *bembas* once a twelve-month, for fertilization purposes, but they kill the boy babies and just keep the little girls."

Martulina the Divina was brought before the tribe's queen, while our hero and Araypuro were stripped naked and tied to stakes by the warrior women as they prepared a bonfire beneath their feet.

"Shit luck, master, they're gonna fry us up alive!"

"That one they refer to as the queen could well be Queen Calafia, a character in *The Adventures of Esplandián*, and her Californian warrior women," said Orpí, thinking out loud and not even listening to Araypuro. "Or perhaps not, as California is further north. Perhaps she's Queen Coñori, of whom Father Carvajal spoke in *Orellana's Chronicles*. Or perhaps . . ."

"Spirits of the jungle, I beseech ye, come to my aid and get me outta this getty!" pleaded Araypuro. "I don't want to be grilled up in this here barbeque!"

"There is no call for melancholy, Injun," mused Orpí, as the Amazons lit the fire beneath him. "Whyfore dost thou weep?"

"I'm weeping because I'll ne'er again fornicate if these bull-dykes cut off my *joaika*."

"Of the whole anarchic pile of mestizo bastards in this paynim paradise we call the New World, thou art the worst, injun. A New World picaroon, that's what thou beest. If you abandoned sex and drugs you would see that, on the road of our existence, we are constantly exposed to death in all its horrible forms, and only in the next worlde will we be sav'd with the help of our Lord."

As Orpí continued giving Araypuro that sermon, Martulina showed up, half-naked and wearing a crown of laurel.

"Y'all, I spoke with the queen of the tribe and she deigned to free you both, once I had convinced her that, despite being of the male persuasion, ye art good folk."

When they'd been released, they hugged Martulina and thanked her for saving their lives.

"Perfect! And now we're gonna get the heck outta Dodge," ordered Orpí.

"Wait a sec," interjected Martulina. "I'm done playing little soldier boy."

"What doth thou mean by that?" asked Orpí.

"I'm going to stay with the Lionzas tribe and their queen, María Lionza[118], who is a sort of goddess of the forests and the waters."

Meanwhile, the goddess herself appeared, and Orpí's face fell so out of joint that he almost suffered a jaw fracture right then and there. Princess María Lionza, a tall woman with

---

118. *i.e.* Venezuelan goddess

incredibly long hair, her delicate zones covered only by a belt of leaves and flowers was none other than . . . Doña María Fernanda Esmeralda Brunilda Isegarda Sigismunda Regenta Magdalena Grande de los Cerros Medianos de la Onza. In shortened form: María de la Onza!

"Good heavens!" exclaimed the Queen when she saw our hero. "I imagined you well dead, little soldier man!"

"And I thee, Your Majesty . . . !" Orpí said, getting down on bended knee. "For God's sake, how is it possible that I find thee here, alive, in the middle of the jungle?"

"Well, alloweth me to give you a quick rundown," declared Queen María, "once taken prisoner on the English corsairs' boat, all we women were repeatedly violated by all the men on that vessel, night and day, incessantly. Those swine took turns twixt our legs, one after the other, interminably, until I lost all sense of tyme and swore uponst my life that, should I survive such ignomy, no man would ever again put his filthy hands on me, or anything else inside of me. One day, the corsair boat was beset by two Portuguese ships that opened up an enormous, gaping hole in the vessel with their cannonballs, and we were all sent headfirst into the drink. Believing mineself to be dead, I imagin'd my fate was fish food yet, somehow, I awoke on a deserted beach the following day.

As I say, I was alone & naked, so I covered my immodesty with palm leaves and headed into the jungle. There I met a tapir, and befriended him and tamed him and rode him like a horse. Upon that animal, I crisscrossed the jungles, eating berries and other fruits I didst gather, until I reached a cave where there lived a group of indigenous women, whom the Spaniards had violated, burning their villages, and killing their men and children. When the women saw me, they took me for their goddess (because of my lighter skin) and, since we hated all men, we resolved to form a matriarchy of women warriors, and later we were joined by nuns who'd escaped convents and jails, and other runaway women who'd fled detestable marriages."

"What a tale! But, Doña María, if you won't marry, you'll live in sin for not respecting the sacrament of matrimony and be condemned, on Judgment Day, to erelasting hellfyre with all t'other sinners!" Orpí informed her.

"Spurious," clarified María Lionza. "How couldst I marry these noblemen when they be as bad if not worse than the rovers, since they have their wives and also take up with barmaids or slaves who practice prostitution, adultery, and concubinage. *De facto* unions between Indian women and Spanish men art an everyday occurrence around here. In short: out-and-out patriarchy."

"Thine logick be not unsound," confessed Orpí. "But . . . I'm still in love with thee, Doña María!"

"Do not tell me that thou dost love me, little soldier man," insists the Queen. "In our village we merely wish to remain chaste, far remov'd from phallocentric powers. I beseech thee respect our decision, prithee."

"Thou hath my word," accepts Orpí. "And what shall become of our friend Martulina?"

"I shall remain here, Orpinet," Martulina replied. "I hath

finally found my place, far from that farce that the society of men hath constructed to deprive us of all but lives as submissive wives or consecrated vyrgins, thus depriving our bodies of their natural desire. Fare thee well, friends."

"Very well, as thou wisheth, then," said our hero. "I'm sure thou shalt be very contented in this tribal gynocracy. I wish thee much luck in your new life as a warrior."

"And just gimme a call if these Sapphic mamacitas need a real pinga to liven up the long full moon nights! Adioh!" said Araypuro.

"Depart anon, ere the Lionzas change their minds and impale you both on the spot," said Martulina. "And you, Indian, watch that tongue or one day they'll tear it out and choppe it into bits!"

Thus, while Martulina the Divina, happy as a clam, remained behind with Queen María Lionza experiencing a true matriarchy, our hero and Araypuro trotted off to the port in La Guaira, and nothing worthy of note happened to them along the way. So, on to the next Chapter.

## Chapter VIII

In which Joan Orpí makes a
very belabored request for a
public grant to become a conquistador

While our hero drafted his proposal for the grant aboard
a hulk, Araypuro drank some *chicha* and watched him in
puzzlement.

"What dost thou writ in that *karata*,[119] master?"

"A planne for obtaining a *capitulación*[120] from the Council
of the Indies."

"Come again?"

"A public competition for the right to conquest, injun. That
is why we are going to La Española."

Araypuro looked at the papers and screwed up his face.

"If thou listened to me instead of fornicating like a rabbit
all daye long with all the *índias de cama*[121] thou mightest

___

119. *i.e.* Book, in his language.

120. *i.e.* A public legal document awarded by the Crown to designate conquest
expeditions.

121. Term used to designate native women who were for sex, as opposed to

learn a thing or two. Here it says that I am requesting official permission to conquer and populate Cumaná, and that I, Doctor Juan de Orpín (in other words, me) shall be conceded the title of Governor in Perpetuity of whatsoever I discover. What that means is that I'm requesting a grant of *encomienda*— legal tribute and labor rights in exchange for indoctrinating and protecting the natives—over everything I find, in order to have complete autonomy over the government I establish, without having to answer to the royale taxman."

"Damn, bro! You gringos just love to discover stuff, wage yer little battles, claim rights to everything, and everyone," complained Araypuro, adjusting his straw hat. "Two centuries and counting we've been made to worship yer *diris*[122] and swallow yer prevarications. Pero like yer nothing more than petty thieves, lying and cheating and embustering pell-mell and helter-skelter."

"Don't bring me down with thy sermons, injun. Furthermore, I canst grasp nigh half of whatfore thy speak (whenever will thee finally learn Catalan!). I am only attempting to follow in the footsteps of other discoverers, who were following the first discoverer, in order to earn riches and honours. And now, silence! I must concentrate."

The two men continued on their way to La Guaira, where they boarded a caravelle setting sail for Santo Domingo and La Española. Once they reached the Council of Indies to request the grant, Orpí found that three criollo noblemen, descendants of conquistadors and founders, were also there making their applications. One of those noblemen was none other than Vázquez de Soja, his old archenemy. All three of the gentlemen had more riches, titles, and crests than Orpí,

---

labor.

122. *i.e.* Boats

and that was a hiccup for our hero, who was not even close to being noble. But he only had to play his cards right and he would be on the path to fame and fortune, for wasn't Pizarro a pig herder before he was a marquis in the Indies?

So Orpí, always thinking ahead, had already drafted an extremely long list of white lies to make him sound like he was of higher lineage: claims that he was pure of blood, that he was descended from old Christians, etc., designed to give his bureaucratic paperwork the necessary patina of pedigree to make him stand out among his competitors. He had reviewed the works of ancient orators, and prepared an extremely eloquent defense of his grant. So eloquent in fact, so extensive and concrete, so well fashioned that, thanks to his literary arts (shamelessly plagiarizing the prose of Bernal Díaz del Castillo's *True History of the Conquest of New Spain*, which circulated in a manuscript edition in that era), the Council, seeing that the lawyer/conquistador had expressed his project so articulately, awarded him the grant.

Thus, on that very 20th of December, 1631, on the cusp of forty years old, Orpí was named "Governor and Captain General of the conquest, pacification, and population of the Province of the Cumanagotos" before the entire Council of the Indies and the stupified indignation of the three criollo noblemen. The Council invited Oprí up to the dais where he carried out a display of thanksgiving to God and the Crown, kneeling and bowing and curtseying. Then they bestowed the Capitulations upon him, saying things such as this:

As ye, Doctor Juan Urpín Adelantado, related unto us, of thine worthy and loyal services furnished in defense of the Araya Salt Pans and as Lieutenant in the City of Cumanagoto and its corresponding province, populating it with Christians and pacifying the entire region with the Yndians in peace, and willingly serving the Christians, and that now, ye desire to serve the good and growth of our Royal Crown, as ye have always done, ye may now go forth and populate new lands to bring us much service and benefit, and for such ye need be provided with sufficient armament and well supplied with all necessities, and ye shall enter these lands with four hundred Christian men, on foot and horseback. And as ye hath deemed from thine experience that expenses shall exceed forty thousand castellanos, and in order to fulfill and complete ye incurred expenses, ye requested by grant license to conquer said lands, and bestowing and allowing the grants and conditions of usage contained therein, regarding which I order ye to take the following capitulation and seat: [ . . . ]

Orpí's success enraged the three noblemen who, led by Vázquez de Soja, plotted a scheme to eradicate that escutcheon-less Catalan. As is widely known, envy is a virus that extends rapidly, and Captain De Soja was infected from head to toe. The noblemen of Santo Domingo turned out to have dangerous, far-reaching tentacles, and our hero was arrested for no apparent reason and tossed in the clink. But the following day he was released for lack of charges. Unable to stop our hero by force or by law, his archenemy Domingo Vázquez de Soja decided to place a scribe in Orpí's expedition so he could keep tabs on his movements and cause him harm with authentic evidence. Meanwhile, our hero visited an affluent man, Juan Sedeño de Albornoz, and drew up a contract of "fraternity and repartition" in order to finance his expeditions inland and named him General Alferes. Orpí also gathered up his former cohorts, the soldiers Octopus, The Scourge, and Jeremies, who had served with him at the Araya Salt Pans, and he named them Captains of the guard, of the steeds, and of the infantry, respectively; he convinced Father Claver to accompany him, as well as a few colonist families who would be tasked with populating the conquered lands; he hired foot soldiers and bought provisions, beasts of burden and of saddle, foodstuffs, and arms. And when he had it all prepared, his conquest expedition waited for the rainy season to end, and when it had, they set out along their way in the manner detailed posthaste.

## Chapter IX

In which Orpí heads over to inland Venezuela
and is soon embroiled in battles
with the hostile tribes found there

Thus, in 1637 (give or take), the expedition led by Joan Orpí headed up the Orinoco to the sound of trumpets and drums. Our hero, mired in his thoughts and with a map out in front of him, guided the procession through the brush, followed by Araypuro.

"Now that thou beest verily a VIP, what doth the master ruminate thus?" he asked.

"Mexico was taken by Hernán Cortes with four hundred soldiers and thirty-five thousand native subsidiary troops, whilst our detachment only disposes of some two-hundred persons in total, not even the three-hundred we were promised in Santo Domingo."

"Pero, like, master, here there be no empire to attack!"

"Ah, dear injun! I find thine brutish logick a lighthouse, illuminating me. What's more, I find myself swervening with my eyes open," exclaimed Orpí, looking at his map. "At times

I think I can see my beloved Catalonia in these lands, and as such I've decided that the conquered territory should bear the name New Catalonia."

"But that map of thine is a dog's dinner, can't you see that, master?"

"Without a map there is no discovery, and without discovery there is no map, Araypuro. And we are travelling with three highly professional *baqueanos*[123]. That said, Columbus set out with his primitive maps of the mythical Seven Cities of Cipango; Ponce de León always had a map in hand as he searched the Antilles and Florida for the legendary Fountain of Youth; Orellana descended the Amazon River and Pizarro and Aguirre (who was two sandwiches short of a picnic) were looking for El Dorado, every last one with a map in front of their noses, too. And if they were searching for it, there must have been something true in those maps. Gold favours the bold, they say. I exist, ergo I discover."

"You guys haven't exactly discovered anything, in point of fact," declared Araypuro. "This continent existed long before you ever set foot on it. Since before the Aztlanecas[124] of the north conquered territories in the south while the Incas, who came from the south, conquered the tribes in the north, like the Aymaras, and errybody was runnin' amok, cockeyed and panicky. And in the middle of all that rampage you guys showed up, you gun-happy leeches, and from the frying pan into the fire with your get-gold-quick schemes."

"Thou art verily an unlicked cub, Araypuro. Were I like Captain Vázquez de Soja, I would have already had the dogs rip thee limb from limb."

"For all the spirits of the forest, don't get all chafed—use

---

123. *i.e.* guides

124. *i.e.* The Aztecs

yer head, master! Just as you all discovered our *wamma*,[125] we too could say that we discovered Europa."

"I will not allow thee such a diabolical inversion."

"We didn't even get to choose the name! Amerigga . . . what kind of numbnuts name is that?"

"Even though Columbus was the first colonizer, it is called America due to a misreckoning on the part of the cartographer Waldseemüller," clarified Orpí, "who, on his 1507 map *Universalis cosmographia*, thought that the continent *inventa est per Vespucci*. But it was Columbus who was predestined to his taske of 'discovery.'"

"Yeah, yeah, we've all heard that fairy tale, bro," said Araypuro, haranguing his master. "Pero, according to Inca Garcilaso's *Royal Commentaries*, neither of them discover'd this land, but rather it was a superlost, friqueado sailor in the year of your Lord 1484 who, *a posteriori*, explained the route here to Columbus. Pero, like, it's the powers that be throughout history who decide who takes the credit, even though Columbus def took some hard knocks from them later on in life. Whatevs, all I've seen is you guys on such a mission to kill, burn and sic dogs on women and children alike for no reason I can see, and killing our spirits for your one God."

"Stop trying to make me feel guilty, injun!" said Orpí. "Thou art not even a pure native, but a bastard son of the two worlds. Thou passeth thine days communing with spirits and the like but thine Spanish is better than mine! Why must thou persist in pretending to be what thou art not?"

"Bueno, cuz I feel like it . . ." Araypuro murmured angrily.

Orpí, ignoring him, stopped the expedition between the Macaira and Tamanaco Rivers to establish a settlement he named Santa Maria de Piera, to honor his hometown, and

---

125. *i.e.* land

there he left some colonist families and heads of cattle, governed by Captain "The Scourge." Then, travelling up a mountain from which he could survey the vast territory, our hero considered it a good place from which to look out for possible attacks, and he also left some men there, governed by Captain Sedeño de Albornoz, who set down the beginnings of some crops and a town named San Pere Màrtir, being that it was an April 29th. Once they reached the plains, he founded a third settlement: Nostra Senyora de Manapire, along the Manapire River.

They constantly ran into tribes in the course of all those incursions into hostile territory. Father Claver, who served as the chronicler of the conquest, explained it thus:

The adjacent faithfull all didst arrive thatts same day from all around, for they desired to sette out and conker despite the perrils of war with the natives & other skirmishes. Doctor Urpín didst leed the charge, follow'd by his labour Indian Luis Pajares, and then came the kaptains, Jeremías and the one they call Octopus. And they also together form'd what seemed to be an armee of invincibles, like the horsemen of the Oppocalypse, entering withe yndustriousness and facing any & all enemees. And subsukwent wee advance'd long most of the river and war a days journey of four leagues wense we arriv'd at some very lovely plains; and all cross that lande there wer many large trees and bald hills and many ducks and falcons and many other fowle. And therr werr also many good meddows for the livestock. There was fog and drizzle, and walking we didst camest upon very wiry, verry strong, but very uglee Indians, by the name Cumanagotos. Whenc they did see us, the natives flee'd to forest'd hills and proeceed'd to rain arrowes down uponst us. Urpín & his men didst defende themselfs without flagging and with vigour the attack'rs war thwarted. Then Doctor Juan Urpín, who allways dealt with good words toward all the caciques in that there lande, didst emerg whensc we hidd with nary a weapon and affearing no death and he drewe neer the natyves and sayeth he be sent by his Emperor and that thay too shouldst obey the Emperor, and that in returnne he wuld aide them in whatsoever way needffull & cure theyr aillments and that thay woode all lyve in peace. And the Cumanagotos, who dist appeer so verry fierce, look'd with favour upunst Doctor Urpíns golden words and ye diss become goode friends and nexxt those same Indjians were recognised as citisens of the Newe Catalonia.[126]

126. Unfortunately, Father Claver's *Chronicles* are lost to the winds of time. If they were to be found, they would shed new light on Joan Orpí's biography and the history of New Catalonia.

## Chapter X

### In which Joan Orpí has a heavenly vision and founds the future New Barcelona

After advancing through the immense territory for one long month, Orpí's caravan stopped in the midst of a lovely green meadow covered in palm trees, on the southern end of Cerro Santo, near the sea, to rest a bit and drink some *guarapo*[127] out of calabash bowls. Suddenly, a furious rain began to beat down on our protagonists and, a few moments later, it stopped just as suddenly. The sun gleamed through the trees and they all took off their jackets, sweating from the heat. As soon as they'd taken them off, and with no warning, it began to rain again, incessant and overwhelming: the earth grew swampy, mud covered their boots, and even their bloomers were sopping. When everyone had found shelter beneath the palm leaves, the rain stopped again in the blink of an eye, and a scorching sun again beamed down, so hot it could roast a live lamb in two shakes of its tail. When they'd all changed clothes they took up their forward march once more, but

---

127. Sugar cane juice with lemon.

again the rain came down without warning and, in a matter of seconds, the entire troop was soaked again.

"Zooterkins!" exclaimed Orpí. "These drastic weather changes be verrily the Devil's work!"

As a scorching sun beamed down and everyone was cursing the climate, a wondrous occurrence occurred. The moon, which was not yet scheduled to be out, moved over the sun and obscured it from view. That supernatural phenomenon, known scientifically as a solar eclipse, sent the Indians into a panic; they all ran off screaming and shouting: "doome and gloome!" and "tropical apocalypse!" Some ran to confess while others threw themselves to the ground, dug holes, and buried their heads in them, while yet others tried to commit suicide by punching themselves in the face.

Father Claver tells of the strange phenomenon in his *Chronicles* as such:

> A true accounting wurthy of being beknownst to all, of some chilling and marvellous signs glimpst in the skye and herd in the mountains . . . as all the Christians in our accompany in the conquest and pacifickation of the natives werr resting there in that very wilderness . . . and at that momment the light of the sun beganst to darken and, *Stupor Mundi*, the horses begunst to runne mad and a silense extend'd throughout the worlde unlike any heard befoure til all war dark as if some sorte of prodygious occurrence and all the soldiers & colonists cryed and threwe themselfes onto the earthe and pray'd, affearful of God's wrath, excepting Don Juan Urpín, who stoode standing, looking up at thee sky . . .

In fact, Joan Orpí had just heard a voice from beyond the grave saying: "Looke at the heavens, looke up at the heavens . . ." After blinking violently, before our hero appeared none other than the Virgin of Montserrat, levitating over the meadow. Upon seeing the apparition, he got down on his knees, clasped his hands together, and murmured, "Miracle, miracle!" as he repeatedly made the sign of the cross.

"Quit thy song & dance," ordered the Black Virgin, "and harke what I've come to say. Thine glorious destiny hath brought thee here, just as I predicted some thirty-odd years hence. Here is where thou shalt found New Barcelona (and for conceptual continuity, New Catalonia). With three conditions *sine qua non*: 1) that all the natives learne Catalan; 2) that they are all baptised with the grace of the Divine Creator; and 3) that ye eat grass from that meadow o'er yon!"

And, having delivered her esoteric message, the Black Virgin disappeared and then reappeared in the form of a wooden engraving the size of a key, which fell from the heavens into Joan Orpí's hands as if by art of magic.

"Friends," said our hero, after his divine vision, "this be the sign I was awaiting. Here we shall establish the city of New Barselona and here we shall live far from all evill."

They began to build the city's first homes, made of wood, in the Venetian style of the indigenous villages, since they were in swampy territory. But after a week's time they realized that the area was infested with ants and terrible fungi that ate away at the wood. Not to mention a plague of mosquitos that arrived one day in the shape of a terrible, gigantic cloud, assaulting their ears, noses, and mouths, penetrating their clothes, and stinging all the flesh they came into contact with, and neither the incense smoke nor their mad running about could scare off that throng of winged vampires that bit legs and arms, making no distinctions of age or gender. The territory's perilousness also included war-mongering Indians all around, wild beasts, scorpions, poisonous snakes, and various tropical diseases. After holding out for a couple more weeks, Orpí (tormented by mosquitoes) gave in to defeat and they decided to found New Barcelona at some remove from those fearsome swamps. To be more specific, according to Father Claver's *Chronicles*:

In greene fields, where Don Juan Urpín didst heare the cry of the fatherland, did he establishe the city and ydeal Church in the month of Febyuary year of our Lord 1638.

Thus, on the feast of Saint Eulàlia, patron of the original Barcelona, the city of New Barcelona was founded. Standards blowing in the wind, drums redoubling, trumpets sounding, the honor guard in formation, a troop of harquebusiers shooting salutes, and captains Jeremies, Octopus, and The Scourge followed Orpí and Araypuro all decked out in fancy dress and swords. The celebration was precise and sincere, but we won't go into further details because that would require writing more pages and we'll leave that bit for another occasion, since it's high time we moved on to the next Chapter.

## Chapter XI

In which Joan Orpí teaches a tribe
to count to ten and they
quite nearly eat him alive

Soon word had spread that a conquistador was making that region flourish and Spanish and criolla families from Caracas, Cumanagoto, Cumaná, and Margarita joined him there, until the population of the burgeoning New Catalonia had quadrupled. It should be noted that our hero was more fond of speaking than of waging war, and that was his strategy for most of the indigenous villages he came upon. Thus he arrived to an understanding with the Tagares, Tasermas, Tozumas, Guarives, Guaiqueríes, Chacopatas, Cocheimas, Palenques, Caracarares, Cores, and Cumanagotos, with whom he set up an exchange of consumer goods such as hens and the fruits offered up by that fertile land. However, some of the more bellicose tribes, such as the fearsome Caribes, weren't so keen on being governed and required special attentions on the part of our hero.

The Caribes lived in the southern plains and were famous for eluding pacification by any military detachment and for their unwholesome habit of eating their enemies. Orpí made his way to their village, with Araypuro alongside him, through a twisted landscape covered in deep gullies and dark swamps, near the San Juan River, with a message of peace and brotherhood. As he drew nearer to their territory, he came across dozens of human skulls on stakes, lined up in perfect rows. When he reached the village, made of conical houses arranged in a circle and surrounded by a wooden fence, the locals were preparing to chow down on some prisoners from a neighboring tribe they'd just defeated on the battlefield. Men and women, with rings hanging off their faces, feathers on their heads, and their bodies painted black and red, were sharpening their knives and forks for the occasion.

Orpí recklessly approached them, since he had recently read a book, *The Indian Militia and Description of the Indies* (1599), which gave tactics and tips for dialogue with the natives.

"Wan esegond," spake the tribal leader, stopping their preparations in his cacologized Spanish, while his men surrounded our hero with poison-tipped arrows. "Ow meeny arth ye?"

"What you see: 2," said Orpí.

"Ah, dis iz pokitos," said the leader.

"And if we were more? And if we were ten?" asked Orpí, mathematically.

"Wee ownlee kownt two 8," answered the tribal leader, politely.

The Caribes had a nebulous numerology. For example, if they gathered more than eight coconuts from a tree, instead of saying "we hath nine coconuts," they said "we hath a lot of coconuts." If, for example, it hadn't rained for twelve days, instead of saying "it hath been twelve days since the last rain," they said, "it hath been many days since the last rain," etc. Anything over eight just got lumped together. Furthermore, they didn't have the number zero because they didn't believe in the absence of numbers, nor in absence in general, of anything: everything, in their world, possessed a complete organic meaning and that was enough to keep them happy. That, and noshing on human beings. Our hero attempted to explain how to count to ten by placing ten tobacco leaves one beside the other, but the Caribes lost their patience and grabbed our hero and Araypuro and tied them up to an artisanal stone oven, prepping them for the next meal, while polishing off their enemies, whom they had gutted and grilled over hot embers.

"Tis a sad fate to ende up in someone's stomach," said Orpí, watching as the natives sprinkled condiments on their feast. "I knowe of a case, from the *Chronicles*, in which five soldiers of the Crown, lost in the jungle and famish'd, eventually devour'd eache other, save the final one, who didst lay hisself to rest, alive, so as to have a Christian burial.

"From a strictly nutritionall perspective," said Araypuro, "the Caribes are in the right: humanoids art omnivorous little mammals with flesh that tastes *bajuka sabuka*[128] (a bit too sweet, ackording to the finest gourmets) but with highe nutritional value. Tho' I prefer arepas."

---

128. *i.e.* just okay

"Yuck, injun. If thou insistest on this line of talk, I shall puke."

"This guy. Don't ye Catholics, in yer self-same mass, receive the sacred host while yer *wisidatu*[129] drink the bloode of the son of God?"

"If mine hands weren't tied, I should give you a goode smack, blasphemer!" muttered Orpí.

"Don't gette all pissy on me, master. Some of us over here have had to adopt cannibalism in order to absorb, dygest, and process your refi culture, just to survive."

"In this particular case, I shall grant you that, injun," conceded Orpí. "Thou doth surprise me more with each passing day. Tis verily true that the *topos* of the cannibal has been a constant since Herodotus, Saint Isidore, Marco Polo, and Mandeville, and is related to the ancient peoples who didst symbolically devour their Gods so as to acquire their powers."[130]

"Criminals and saints, errybody ends up in the same hole when booked by the Gravesend bus," reflected Araypuro.

"A very positive logick," smirked Orpí. "And now kindlee desist with the philosophical debates, these folks are gonna eat us."

Indeed, when the Caribes finished their repast, they approached Araypuro to cut off one of his legs. But just as they were about to stick a fork into his thigh, Martulina the Divina appeared out of nowhere, wearing a quiver filled with lovely arrows and brandishing a bow, leading two hundred

---

129. *i.e.* warlock, in his language

130. Native American anthropophagy is a recurring theme in colonial literature, constructing a type of representation of the indigenous population, a *topos* that Columbus himself, among others, contributed to perpetuating in his 1503 letter from Jamaica, despite the fact that various modern researchers believe there is no conclusive proof of this cannibalism. On the other hand, there is reliable evidence of Columbus's exploitation of the Indians through forced labor.

Lionzas, who promptly freed our hero and subdued the Caribes.

"Ye art lucky we were hunting in the area," said Martulina, tanned and muscular from her new jungle lifestyle. "Otherwise, ye'd bee hamburger."

"Thanks," said Orpí, as he untied himself and hugged his friend. "Now we musteth convince these flesh-eaters to unite with New Catalonia."

Orpí assured the Caribes that they wouldn't impose any more numbers on them and they could live just as they had been on their lands. The only condition was that they had to stop eating people:

"And, on my worde, there art more ethically nutritional things to eat," our hero explained, "like, for example, *panbolibo*."

"Pan-boli-bo," repeated the local chief.

"Exactley, bread with a splash of oil," elucidated Orpí. "Or otherwise, 'eat grass' as the Black Virgin spake us."

"*Aya-huasca*," said the Caribe leader, as he ran to find some vines, chopped them up, and boiled them into an almost solid liquid—a liquor so strong it could walk—and offered it to our hero.

"When in Rome . . ." said Orpí, drinking that grass down and, after vomiting a little and less than two minutes later, it seemed to him that his mind was separating from his body and he felt himself endowed with magical powers to speak with animals and plants, and to turn himself into a jaguar or a coconut palm if he so desired. Then his body lifted off the ground and, floating, floating, passed over the forest's canopy and shot up into the heavens, while the earthly atmosphere throbbed with life beneath him and, after two voyages around the sun like an Icarus, he returned, flying over the tops of the nearest trees and landing once more inside his earthly body.

"Lookie lookie! Now I understandeth why the Virgin of Montserrat wished for me to eat grass," said our hero, when he regained consciousness.

And that was how Orpí made friends with the Caribes and since then there were no more problems of violence in the recently inaugurated New Catalonia.

## Chapter XII

In which Orpí does the general accounting
for New Catalonia and discovers a spy

Once the region was pacified, Orpí and his officers changed
their army jackets for linen suits, much better suited to the
scorching sun. They let their beards grow out and spent long
days laboring in the new lands: they chopped down trees,
prepared the firewood, gathered potable water, sowed the
fields, and, with the help of hunting and fishing, waited for
the first harvest. In short: they subjugated nature. And, with
the fiercely rebellious American landscape under control, the
newcomers felt sure they could make that region a more hos-
pitable place, and more similar to the homeland they had left
behind on the other side of the Atlantic. In the months that
followed, soldiers and Indians felled the trees that bordered
the small region like a firewall, and laid down dirt paths that
interconnected and headed in every direction. That bit of land,
located between the Unare and Neverí Rivers, was chockfull
of God-given riches: a thousand different fruit species, easily domesticated livestock, fresh, clean water, everything.
Furthermore, since there is no spring, autumn, or winter in

the Amazon forest, soon the crops—maize, yucca, *auyamá*, sweet potatoes, and yams—began to sprout. They planted fruit trees, sugar cane, cotton, and smoking tobacco (which they would register under the brand Almogàvers Tobacco™) and they raised the first few wooden homes. The construction work was carried out by carpenters, painters, men of hammer and saw, and artillerymen who transported old cannons for the city's defense. The first homes in New Barcelona were made of wood and cane, and our hero built a small rancho he named House Orpí, like the one back home in Piera. Soon they built a capitol building in the city and a small church in which Orpí hung up the engraving of the Black Virgin (since he had no larger effigy), and prayed a very intimate, heartfelt Our Father.

One day, as our hero was checking to make sure no one was loafing, he found Araypuro with his pants down and his hands beneath the petticoats of a criolla girl. Angry, our hero approached him and dealt him a slap.

"Whatever art thou doing, giant swine?" he said, grabbing the Indian by the ears, leading him to a desk, and sitting him down in front of a large pile of papers.

"Aaayyy, don't abuson me, master! I was all cozy with that lovely lady, reciting from *The Dialogues of Love* by León Hebreo: 'The penis be analogous to the tongue in position, shape, and power of extension and retraction; both art centrally placed, and the tongue works in much the same way as the penis, whose movement generates physical progeny; the tongue is spiritually generative of specific speech, and gives birth to spiritual offspring just as the penis does physical. The kiss is common to both, one often provoking the other.'"

"Sssh! Silence, how ungodly! And thou art drunke! Abandon the spirits and listen to me: since thou hast study'd as a scribe with the monks, pick up the quill, moisten it—the quill, minde you!—and write out all these inventories that are bedeviling me, before one of those greenly envious governors comes to hook his clawes into what ritefully belongs to New Catalonia," our hero ordered, accountably. "Come on over and don't look at me like that. Thou shallt be in charge of the accounting for New Catalonia, in the following manner:

**First Column:** gross national product.

**Second Column:** transnational sales produkt (when there be surplus).

**Third Column:** 5% of proffits for the church, the crippled, and the olde.

**Fourth Column:** legall costs for shipping of goods to the Peninsula.

**Fifth Column:** preemptry rights to all future leaseholders in these lands.

**Sixth Column:** the approv'd percentage to be used to pay the *anata*[131] to the Crown of Castile.

**Seventh Column:** restitution of private assets, including honours, dignities, etc, etc.

"Is that clear, injun? Continue on, now that thou knowst how it's done."

"Come on, bro," complained Araypuro. "That shit is super boring. I'd much prefer to assist Father Claver. That poor priest lit'rally gets more laughs than converts with his terrible prununciation of the native tongues. His improperlee used verbs & nowns, undetter'd by much saintly intent, rather than saving souls for the Christian cause, mere maketh the lokals burst into houls of laffter."

Indeed, Father Claver, by then known as The Saint because

---

131. *i.e.* A fixed amount paid to the King.

he always begged for victuals that he carried around to give away to the poor, was performing baptisms and giving catechism to hundreds of Indian neophytes from all over to convert them to the Catholic faith; however instead of these being ceremonies worthy of the divine design, most of the Indians were rolling on the floor, laughing like lunatics and pointing at the poor priest with one hand while clutching their bellies with the other.

"Very well," said Orpí. "Once agayn, much as I hate to, I musteth agree with thee, injun. Go and help him translate his sainted words. And, while thou be at it, teach some basick Catalan with these old codices. Tally ho!"

While Araypuro went to help Father Claver, a scribe sent as a mole by Domingo Vázquez de Soja approached our hero.

"Good afternoon, milord," said the scribe, a deformed man with a serpent gaze. "I see that thou dost not comply with the ordinances—"

"With whom do I have the honor of speaking?"

"Don Calixto Conejo, scribe of the Court," informed the scribe. "And I must informe thee, by royal decree, that each conquistador with exploratory license must order the *Requerimiento* be appositely read to all, inclusive of women and children. And thou hast failed to do so. Proceeding *plus ultra* be not legal without fulfilment of the decrees of the Holy See & our belov'd King. Anon I must inform on such conduct to our Majesty!"

"Do what thou will, *maistre*. Howsoever I shall do no suche thing, since the *Requerimiento* bringeth me only bad memories and I refuse to force anyone ynto submission, all whosoever come here do so at their owne behest!"

"That is verily contempt of the Crown," pointed out the scribe.

"I didst not hire you for my expedition and was tolde of no

scribe," said Orpí, drawing his sword. "Therefor I have reach'd the conclusion that thou beest none other than a spy! Am I mistaken? Speak, Conejo!"

All the scribe said in response was a hasty "c'ya!" as he fled down the street. No one ever saw him again, nor did anyone miss him. But the news of Orpí's successful conquest and his humanistic skills spread like wildfire through the regions, contributing to the aggrandizement of this story, in such a way and to such an extent as will be revealed in the Chapter that follows.

## Chapter XII

### Joan Orpí and Father Claver draft the constitution of New Catalonia and are interrupted with bad tidings

Matters were going along increasingly swimmingly in the burgeoning New Catalonia, since our hero had managed to achieve peace between the various tribes in his territory and some of them had come to live in New Barcelona following the rainy season because the rivers had overflowed their banks and carried off whole villages.

After mass at his brand-spanking-new church, bells still ringing, Joan Orpí paid a visit to Father Claver, whom he'd named provisional superior religious commissioner since there was no bishop, and who was working on an *Arte*[132] of the regional indigenous languages at his desk made of palm wood.

"Goode day, Father."

The Jesuit looked up from his desk with inquisitively furrowed brows, searching for the party guilty of that intellectual distraction, while Araypuro, who lay in a hammock beside him, lazed contentedly.

---

132. *i.e.* a grammar

"Ah . . . good daye to thee, Don Orpí," said Claver, placing his quill in the inkwell. "Pray tell . . ."

"Father, I wish for us to draft an official constitution for Newe Catalonia, cojoinedly," explained Orpí, placing a page filled with inked characters on the priest's desk.

"Very well," said the Jesuit, willingly. "I do expecte the first item shall be that New Catalonia must become a munificence of Christian love, ethics, and universall human morality."

"Well, furst of all we shall invoke Lady Justice."

"Bizarre faith, yours," said Father Claver, dipping the quill and starting to write. "And how wouldst thou desire to baptise the flocke? As the Dominicans, like Bartolomé de Las Cases, do, with complete indoctrination beforehand, or as the Franciscans like Motolínia, who preferr mass baptisms, without any pryor catechisation?"

"The only sacred baptism be that of educating just people," clarified our hero. "The vulgar preceedeth the divine, Father; first we must thinke of their material needs."

"Thine hintentions art clean, fresh, and honorable, but I know not this baptism of which thou speak, Milord Orpí," said the Jesuit, reluctantly taking dictation. "We must resuscitate nascent Christianity, live a true theocracy as in Plato's *Republic* and Campanella's *City of the Sun*, and as prescribed by the Jesuit José de Acosta in *De procuranda Indorum salute* (1588), viewing colonisation as a (re)invention of Christ in the New Worlde, a repetition of history in the guise of an hevangelisation very akin to Christianity's initial expansion led by Sainted Paul."

"Don't get ahead of theeself, Father. We'll have none of that Platonic collectivism or theocratick despotism," said Orpí. "No shared goods, like in Augustine's *City of God*. This be no Xanadu, but rather a business of progress and objective reason."

"Avarice is *pecatus* . . . !" complained Father Claver, now copying so rapidly that a thin line of smoke emerged from the page. "We must fairly distribute goods, as in Christian monasteries!"

"And share all the *tidas[133]*, like in Campanella's *Politics*?" asked Araypuro, who had been smoking calmly in his hammock up until then.

"Never!" said the Jesuit, smacking him on the behind with a *macana*.[134]

"Mmmm, these chubby little light-skinned tidas, so chévere-chévere with their luscious booties . . . make me so horny! Spicy like sofrito . . ." continued Araypuro.

"We shall abide no *barraganeria*!"[135] bellowed the Jesuit. "Intermingling religion and eroticism leeds to the unification of opposites and the wastering of time . . . Lucifer!"

"We shall promote usury (in other wurds, interest on loans)," continued Orpí, ignoring them both. "As well as the building of homes by the local inhabitants dependent on our interest-yielding loans. Write, Father . . . write!"

"Be heedful we aren't undone by thine vision of progress!" the Jesuit, who was having trouble keeping up, pointed out. "I am of the view that we should promote a subsistence economy. Abolish money in favor of a barter system, in which the wealthee art obliged by law to give to the poor.[136] Slavery of

---

133. *i.e.* Women, in his language

134. *i.e.* Hard, long wooden rods, used by the Indians like large swords.

135. *i.e.* Concubinage between Spaniards and indigenous women.

136. In this declaration we see Father Claver's attempts to convert a virgin, marginal space into the *axis mundi*, creating the possibility of transforming the colonization process in order to create a Paradise on Earth, an autarky where otherness was a constant, a providential third space of salvation, making possible a new—hybrid—society that minimized the processes of acculturation that erased differences, and transformed both the Spanish colonization and the

both indigenous peoples and blackes must also be prohibit'd. New Catalonia shall be a true Eden, an Arcadia, a Garden of the Hesperides! We shall learn from antiquity and progress!" philosophized Father Claver with encyclopedic frenzy, dipping the quill in the inkwell and staining his habit. "Where no man is above another, like in Lucian's *Saturnalia*, where masters and serfs art one and the same! Pray let us abolish the exploytation of the workers! Let us create a commonwealth in whych equality reigns! Fame, honours, titles, be they by law or social condition, allways create distinctions!"

"Very well, Father. But forgetth not that equality entails epicurian and pagan bliss and we're here to make coin, not pies in the sky," declared Orpí. "I'm the one in charge here, but I shall be impartial and in keeping withe God. This is no *In terram utopicam*, no Golden Age, no El Dorado. Many are those who hath told us about the New World: Aristotle, Averroes, Strabo, Pliny, Solinus, Marco Polo, Mandeville, Pierre d'Ailly, and obviously, Columbus himself in his *Book of Prophecies*, but, as thou hath surely noticed, this be a far crye from paradise, what this be now is a business adriven by a mightily strong kapitalist ideology."

"Yes, clearly, but the purpose of life in community is to shed vices and increase virtues . . ." said the Jesuit, his nerves making him wrinkle the pages in front of him.

"Mayhaps, Father. Notwithstanding, I came here to conquer in name of the Crown of Castile!"

And having said that, Orpí signed the constitution that had been drafted, while Father Claver and Araypuro discussed the whole affair, drawing severe philosophical conclusions on the inequality of the races and the greed for power.

"One moment, keepe calm, milord Orpí," said the Jesuit.

---

pre-Colombian civilizations.

"Let us be realistic, rather than mystic. Let us think logically, not pieskyly."

"Whatsoever dost thou mean, Father Claver? Don't beat about the bushel."

"Well, just that when the Castilians find out that thou hast sacked a royal scribe thusly, beleefee me, the Crown will soon retaliate."

Just as the Jesuit said that, two men on horseback arrived from Santo Domingo. One was Alonso de Amadís, and the other Álvaro Narváez, both tax functionaries for His Majesty who had come to make an inspection for the Royal Chamber of Castile and demand the tribute due to the Castilian Crown. After our hero hastily forked over the royal fifth to them, one said, "And that's not all. We come bearing two *pedimentos*[137] for thee, Doctor."

Orpí opened the first letter, which was from his old enemy, Captain Vázquez de Soja, and said things like "thou hath recruit'd outlanders & vagabonds . . . (and that) thou hath neither the knowledge nor the provisions to populate said lands . . . (and that) thou hath dismissed improperly a Court scribe and that is a crime . . . (and also that) thou art not only a furr'ner but also reside here without permission of His Majesty." In short, Captain De Soja had managed to get the Council of the Indies and the Audiencia of Santo Domingo to revoke his title of conquistador, fairly won by our hero a year earlier in the grant. Vázquez de Soja and other likeminded noblemen had managed to take from our hero everything he had achieved. And what's more, said the letter, everything he owned now belonged to Vázquez de Soja himself! The second letter left him even more nonplussed, as it was from none other than King Philip IV. Among other things, it said:

---

137. *i.e.* royal letters

*. . . I hath been informed that ye haveth bestowed uponst Doctor Juan Orpín, a man without fortune, experience, and without titles, powers, nor faculties to enter in that land of Indians as a conquistador, causing much harm, and as such I order ye, as soon as this letter be received, to revoke and nullify the commission endowed uponst Doctor Juan Orpín.*

*Signed: Philippus IIII*

"Blast! Thou shouldst spake sooner, Father," our hero lamented, as the royal functionaries rode off. "I canst rid meself of those criollo noblemen and their trickery. The only recourse to ensure mine undertaking is to speak personally with the King. I shall leave today on the first boat bound for the Peninsula. This vile affair shall not go unpunished!"

"And whom shall be left in charge?" asked the Jesuit.

"Piece of cake: I name thee First Lieutenant General of New Catalonia in my absence, if thou donst mind. And, well, even if thou dost. And I shall leave my loyal horse Acephalus in thine charge, to care for as a distinguished personage, since when we say that all human beings, independent of sex, race, or creed, are equal, without hierarchies, the same goest for animals."

"Very welle. May God be with thee," said Father Claver in farewell, returning to his *Arte*.

Receiving the King's letter and setting off for Spain were two sides of the same coin for our hero who, accompanied by Araypuro, set off on a merchant ship that very morning to Cumanagoto, where they embarked on a *nave de aviso*[138] headed for the Iberian Peninsula.

---

138. *i.e.* Ships that carried correspondence and dispatches for the royal court.

## Chapter XIII

In which Joan Orpí encounters
some freebooters who speak strangely and is
nearly murdered by a mysterious hired assassin

It had been more than ten years since Joan Orpí's arrival in America and now he was returning home against his will. However, this time, he was no longer traveling as a royal soldier but as lieutenant general of his own territory and, as such, he was entitled to a private berth befitting his rank. Less than ten hours after setting sail, our hero noticed a man dressed entirely in black who didn't take his eyes off of him. Thinking that perhaps he knew him from somewhere, Orpí approached to make conversation but the man slipped away and hid among the crew. Not thinking much of it, Orpí locked himself in his berth to meticulously prepare his speech before the Royal Audiencia in Madrid. But the calm voyage was soon brutally disrupted. When the Spanish vessel passed by the island of Tortuga, located near Hispaniola, a small brig cut off their access to the open sea. The passengers saw only one thing. The thing was this:

"Quotha! The Jolly Roger!" exclaimed a sailor. "Pirates!"

"Worse . . ." said the captain of the vessel, dodging the cannonballs that tore through the sails, shattering the mizzen and part of the prow. "They be freebooters . . . ! To yer weapons!"

The freebooters' boat was lighter and therefore swifter, and soon had the Spanish ship trapped. From larboard, they launched their grappling irons and proceeded to board extremely professionally. The assault was quick and brutal. Harquebus and musketoon bullets flew in every direction. Once the firearms were empty, both sides entered readily into hand-to-hand, face-to-face combat without further ado, armed with daggers and swords.

Joan Orpí, lost in the pandemonium of screams and bullets, was loading powder into the pan of his pistol when he heard a voice behind him amidst the clamor of the battle.

"Halt, barrister, thou beest a dead man!"

Those words were spoken by the mysterious man in black, whom our hero had seen when embarking on the ship. He was now pointing a gun at him, and pulled the trigger. Orpí was hit so hard that he fell backward, his legs out from under him, as he emitted a horrific moan. A pool of blood stained his shirt. His gaze befuddled, Orpí didn't seem to understand what was happening to him until he realized he had a hole in his abdomen. Before the man in black could shoot again, Araypuro, who'd seen it all with tearful eyes, pounced on the assassin, who managed to slip away and crack Araypuro over the head with the butt of his gun, leaving him flummoxed. When the executioner drew close to our hero to finish him off, Orpí asked, "Who art thou, gunslinger?"

Just as the mysterious man was about answer, he was shot and dropped onto the deck, dead. Our hero was bleeding out in a corner of the ship and, as his vision blurred into a nebula of blacks and grays, he managed to make out a small figure pressing a dirty shirt to his wound to stop the hemorrhaging.

Meanwhile, the skirmish had ended and soon the freebooters had taken over the ship. Quite a few men on both sides had died. The freebooters towed the battered Spanish to Tortuga Island, where they ordered the surviving crewmembers off. Curiously, and going against all prognoses, none of the crew were executed. Quite the contrary, those who were wounded, like Orpí, had their injuries attended to. There was no explanation given. Our hero was patched up by the freebooters' surgeon, who was just then sharpening his machete on a rock.

"Allouns'y 'ave a looksie at dere wound," said the surgeon, slicing open his belly as if he were a roasted boar, in a room filled with the injured and a horrendous stench of coagulated blood.

An hour later, our hero was already sewn up and on his feet, as if nothing had happened, standing beside that surgeon, who went by the name of Exquemelin and had been in the service of l'Olonnais and Henry Morgan, among other famous pirates, and who let Orpí have a look at the first copy of his memoirs among these pirates and buccaneers, with the provisional title *De Americaensche Zee-Rovers*.[139]

---

139. *i.e.* Alexandre Olivier Exquemelin, French writer known for his work on seventeenth-century pirating, *The Buccaneers of America*.

"Interesting, too bad it's in Dutch," lamented our hero.

Later, Orpí was happily reunited with Araypuro, who had been left stunned by the attack. They had no time to catch up before the captain of the victorious freebooters, some guy named Rock Brasiliano who wore eight loaded pistols around his neck and a parrot on his shoulder that sang in French, introduced himself to the crew:

"Nous no estamos nourrir por ningún boss, ni rei ni ná de ná. Tripeando por estos mares, guachimanamos & cachamos boten eben doh da draiba del timonero se le fue la têtê y neerly nos tuer. Nous belong to da Cofradía o'da Bróders de la Costa, of da Ille de la Tortuga, y we raid por rechts propio. Dropeando dejo por escrito que todo cuanto findeamos en este boot es ours and los survivors van a morir ol tugeder."

"Listen, injun, to the manner in whych these ruffians speak. What a dynamic language! What fabulous entropy . . . What be that jabberwocky? I understand not a scrap of what he speaketh," whispered Orpí.

"They speak *pechelingue*, a super chévere tongue," whispered Araypuro, "a kooky mix of English, Spanish, French, and Dutch. They're saying that basically they want to kill us all, because as is well-known, dead men doth tell no tales."

"There be no need for them to kill me," lamented Orpí. "I'll push off any minute now if that surgeon fail'd to do his job aright."

Then, Rock Brasiliano, polite as can be, introduced his band of freebooters:

"Ik presenteer a my équipage: El Manco, Rompepiedras, Barbanegra, Exterminador, Triboulet Dvergar el Distasteful . . ."

When Orpí heard that name, he bellowed, "By Neptune's beard! I knowe that guy!"

When our hero found himself face to face with the

dwarf—who was limping, drunk, happy, and irascible, dressed in rags and with a cane in his right hand and a pistol in his left—he laughed so hard he almost had a stroke.

"Triboulet! Don't thee e'er tire of playing the chameleon?"

"Nouus destinies vuelven a crossing!" exclaimed the dwarf, tipping his hat. "Verdad: ja no suis bucanero, ara suis filibustero. Bamoj a bacilal y truhanear por ahi pa bujcal tezoros pa chasser e vender."

"Stop making up wordes! You seem to care not a fig for whole *Gramàtica Castellana!*[140]" barked Orpí. "What be this tommyrot?"

"Que salimos a uerkaut por el zee con lo puesto, okey?" explained the dwarf, who was missing one eye and one ear from the kerfuffles inherent in that violent lifestyle.

"Are you stoopid or what, halfman? Prithee . . . speak in Catalan or in Castilian . . . but not in that horrific hodgepodge that no one can understand!"

Triboulet explained to our hero that he had been kicked out of the town of Carazco, because the *cimarrones* no longer wanted any white men among them, preferring to establish a realm of absolute negritude where Estebanico the Blackamoor was king. Triboulet and the other buccaneers had then joined up with the few pirates remaining on Tortuga Island, and that was the birth of that new race of sea dogs: the freebooters. When Triboulet found himself on Orpí's boat, during the skirmish the dwarf had seen a man try to kill our hero, but Triboulet was able to shoot him before he could finish the job. When the dwarf saw that Orpí was truly dying, he spoke with Rock Brasilero, who agreed to spare the survivors of the Spanish vessel and treat the injured in exchange for keeping

---

140. *i.e.* He is referring to the first ever Spanish grammar rule book, by Antonio de Nebrija, published in 1492.

half the spoils. And that was how, instead of more war, there was peace.

"So who in tarnation was that killer?"

"Je nai sais pas," said Triboulet, "the man who wanted to massacrate you wasn't one of ours, or one of yours. But you know what they say, he who liveth by the sword, dieth by the sword."

"Be mindfull, Orpinet, someone wishes you harm!" said the Homunculus who, following in his creator's footsteps, had also become a freebooter. The being had grown and now was as tall as Triboulet (which is to say, not very). He was like a child in a costume. Upon seeing our hero, the Homunculus sang a ditty that went something like this:

♪♪ Despite thine obsessions with territory ♪♪
yar siempre getting maltraitered, Orpi.
If you break out in hives or the clap
Put on some cream and that's that,
But if they plottin to murderlate-vous
Then yar best be realistique, sacre bleu!
Buck up, tis normal that yar downplay
Yar yearning for ye olde liberté
Hasta wakin' up in da cachot,
Just north of Barstowe
Yar yearnin to row row yer boat
not to be just a footnote
It be tyme for ya ta even out the score
Wake up, stop actin' like a sophomore!
Dose noblemen refuse vous dineros
--and I know, I get it, it blows--
But yar gotta look to make ya own way
Releaseth all yon spiritual decaye
Dost thou graspest what I'm trying to say?

"Bravo, Homunculus! Great song! But what canst I do? Living is slowly dying," declared Orpí in a somber tone.

"Arrrt yar insane in the left brain? Don't say quelquechose, Orpinet," said Triboulet. "Enjoya la vida, qu'es très short and don't megaworry tu mutx!"

After spending a night of revelry with those soldiers of fortune, including a dreadful "bathtub" rum, Orpí and the rest of the Spanish crewmembers sailed calmly to the Peninsula without any further piratetechnic scares. But our hero remained uneasy about the mysterious assassin who'd tried to murder him, and he gave explicit orders to Araypuro to keep his eyes peeled thenceforth. The only way, he figured, to have the same power as his rivals in the Spanish Indies was to win the favor of the King. But first he had to get to Madrid, as ye shall learn whereof in this next Chapter.

## Chapter XIV

In which Joan Orpí travels from Seville to Madrid,
where he encounters an old friend

The ship on which Orpí and Araypuro were traveling docked
in the port of Guadalquivir one morning in the year 1620,
with the Giralda and the Torre del Oro rising undaunted over
Seville as a heavy scent of burning human flesh greeted them.
The Holy See had begun a veritable crusade against the Devil
and hundreds of heretics were burned each day throughout
the Peninsula, up into France, and beyond, as black smoke
from the mortal bonfires darkened the European skies. Many
things had changed since our hero had left that city, years
earlier. The architecture of the buildings and cathedrals pre-
sented new shapes, twisted and darkly gilded, just as obscure
as the grotesque faces of the Spanish people, white and with
heavy shadows under their eyes, like cadavers, always looking over their shoulders as if Death was waiting to snatch
them away at any moment.

"*Carajo*! These irregular stones doth remind me of the
trees of the spirits in mine jungle, master," said Araypuro,
contemplating the Spanish architecture.

"Indeed, injun, they do," said our hero, wrinkling his brow, "but everything here is much more *destrudo*. I prefer the positive jungle energy."

From Seville, the two men rode on horseback to Madrid, but since requesting an audience before the Royal Council was a slow, bureaucratic process, they had to wait almost a month for their turn. So Orpí and Araypuro found themselves tourists, marveling at the buildings in the Spanish capital and the industrial quantities of white people in the Old World. The denizens of Madrid, on the other hand, regarded the two men like something out of a circus.

"We are not dressed in the latest styles, injun. We are eccentric, here," said Orpí, looking at the people. "I have to say, injun, thou stickest outest not only for thine darkness, but for thine bisarro native garments with feathers, and the amulets that hang from thine hair and scrag."

"Well, thou aint so hot thineself," noted Araypuro. "Thou resemblest a taxidermied hen."

"Insolent!" exclaimed our hero, moving to smack Araypuro but stopping suddenly when he saw himself reflected in a shop window: his big eyes were hidden in a dry, wrinkled face that was partially buried beneath a sparse beard turned yellow by the Almogàvers™ cigars; he wore torn trousers that were stained either by sea salt or excrement; his once-white shirt was just a memory; his hat was old and had no cord; and his shoes were pathetic sandals that clung to his feet out of pity. When Orpí saw his bedraggled image, he decided to visit a tailor. There they decked him out in some short black breeches with green silk stockings, immaculate white shirt, red velvet vest, stiff-necked doublet, and top hat. Elegantly dressed, our hero soon after ran into a character seen earlier in this story: none other than Grau de Montfalcó,[141] who it turns out was living in the capital at that time.

"I'm right contented here," Grau said. "I work mornings as a doctor in a hospital and I sing in a choir of *castrati* in the church in the afternoons."

"Good for thou," said our hero, who, when passing by a shop selling folkloric paintings, spotted a *retablo* engraved with the sad figure of Don Quixote and his loyal squire Sancho Panza. "Look at that, my friend. They are characters created by Miguel de Cervantes, from the book I gave thee when we met there in the kingdom of Valencia years ago. Dost thou recall?"

"And how! In fact, a second part hath already come out, Cervantes's highly intelligent response to a student of Lope de Vega who had the temerity to write a sequel to the Quixote (which wasn't half as good, truth be told), before Cervantes himself had a chance."

"Too many bad books in the worlde," said Orpí. "Diego de Saavedra, in his *Republic of Letters* doth declare that, with the invention of the printing press, 'everyone drags into the light what would be best kept in the dark, because, just as there be few whose actions are worthy of being record'd, there be few who write something worthy of being read.'"

"Tis true, and technology is everything these days," said Grau, showing him a French pocket watch. "Beholde, the universe is like this device, made of hands and numbers, more precise than a rooster's crow. What once was impossible to do no longer is: measuring time, controlling nature, ergo controlling peoples. Arms and letters no longer go together. The era of mythical kingdoms hath come to an end. Reality and progress rule. Everything is bureaucracy, here and in America."

---

141. See Chapter III, Book Two.

"I doth still believe in magic, my friend, as this conquest looks more like a step backward than progress, by any measure: astrolabe, sextant, hourglass, north star, or the minutes and seconds on thy watch. Howebeit I shant allow these rascally noblemen with the king's ear snatch from me what I've earned with my blood & sweat. Those virgin lands must be my economic salvation."

"Remember that Felipet is absolute sovereign of an empire on which 'the sun never sets,' as Charles the Fifth dared say."

"I've no intention of tossing in the towel," declared Orpí, gazing out at infinity. "Furthermore, Philipus IV is a two-bit monarch compared with the ones in the jungle. I've seen kings who knowe the language of magical plants, who can transform into birds and fly through the skies on whim, and whose armies obeyye them with the cohesion of a single man. Those be true kings."

After strolling along the Castellana, the two friends, followed by Araypuro, stopped to watch a sinister *auto-da-fé*, where repentant sodomites forswore their sins before being carried off to die by fire.

"I see tis yet fashionable to burn and hang people," lamented Orpí, as he glanced at the peninsular news on the cover of *La Gazeta Nueva.*[142]

"Yea, things haven't changed much 'round here," said Grau de Montfalcó. "And this Inquisition is positively soporific!"

And thus the two friends continued chatting, followed by Araypuro, until they start stuffing their faces at one of the capital's *merenderos.*[143] And there we will leave them as we move on to the next Chapter.

---

142. *i.e.* A Madrid magazine of the time.

143. *i.e.* outdoor eating areas

## Chapter XV

### In which Orpí meets with the King and demands legitimate dominion over his lands

Finally, after three weeks of waiting, our hero's day before the Royal Audiencia arrived. Orpí, dressed like a duke and accompanied by Araypuro, admired the palace square. They both watched the fish swimming in the pools, and were greeted by the fanfare of out-of-tune trumpets as they entered the long royal halls. The two men walked along an endless patterned carpet, through drawing rooms and chapels, taking in the royal sumptuousness: the royal library, the royal pharmacy, the royal armoury . . . everything there was royal, and a hustle and bustle of pages and courtiers dressed in finery who looked at the strange pair, lifting their hats. It turned out that the news of our hero's arrival in court had spread far and wide, as had his fame as a conquistador following the article printed up about him in a *pliego suelto*[144]:

---

144. Fanzine-style format of popular short writing of the period.

**Noteworthy.—New discoveries in America.**

In the Society of Jesus much has been written about the solar eclipse that last year occurred in the Indies, with terrible and strange aspects and signs. We have also heard news that a Catalan captain 'as founded a large province, called New Catalonia, and founded new towns, and seeks to place a bishop. And now this captain, the attorney Juan Urpín, has come to pursue audience with the King, accompanied by his eccentric Indian sidekick.

Orpí introduced himself to the Royal Council, ready to save his honor and recover his New Catalonia. He had prepared concise proceedings to rectify the royal decree, which he read aloud before the entire Council. First he recited a list of his accomplishments to demonstrate his more than justified ascent from rank private to Conquistador and Governor:

"I wert in many battles like the one in the Haraya Salt Pans against the Dutch, when we killt fifty-seven soldiers and were all injur'd, even meself, and we didst wage war of our owne volition and were vicktorious ; and in another verry dubious battle when we went after some Indians and Captain Vázquez de Soja set the dogs on them, and I didst bringe up judicial proceedings for his infraction; and another battle with the warrier womyn called Amazons, who art nowadays our friends; and another with those they call Caribes who desir'd to eat our bodies and now we're friends with them, too, since we did teach them to eat only grass."

After that he defended himself against the bureaucratic attacks by the Venezuelan noblemen, enumerating all the good things his New Catalonia had brought the Crown:

"And tis true that I'd a dispute with the very noble Vázquez de Soja over that dubious battle in the jungle, but the Indians didst suffer vile, cruel deaths for rejecting enslavement, whych be not legal in compliance with the Laws of the Indies, which was the motiv for myne opposition towardst Captain Vázquez de Soja, and I was named Lieutenant General for sayd achievement. And as for mineself, I must say that the journey I undertook in Terra Firma was entirely for Your Majesty. Altho' my honour was called into question by Vázquez de Soja and other noblemen from Cumaná and Caracas, I should wish to here clarify that all I didst do in mine province was trade in merchandise for the Crown. And in those regions I dist deal in cacao, cotton, and tobacco, register'd under my brand Almogàvers Tobbaco™, and in a positive, not negative, colonization. Furthermore, I hath allways led the natives to the knowledge of our fayth and service to Your Majesty and for said reason no one shouldst speak ille of me, because I assure ye, Sire, that it's all a load of codswallop."

Finally, Orpí ended his speech before the Royal Council thusly:

"Withal, as the fate of man is a struggle betweenst free will & chance—as Machiavelli says, Fortune is the mistress of one half our actions, and yet leaveth controll of the other halphe to us-selves. Withal, either I must be paid for the expenses incrued on said endeavor (upward of 10,000 pesos) or I must be compensat'd for mine services with the restitution of mine government, for, as much as I hath had, I'th spent much more in the aggrandizement of Your Highness's dominyon and assets, by meanes of conquest and placing mine personage in all manners of danger and risk all for new and novel kingdoms for Thine Highness."

His petition was so bold that it succeeded. In February 1636, a troupe of powdered wigs from the court nodded, and our hero once again held the title of Governor and Captain General of the Province of the Cumanagotos of his New Catalonia. Orpí had reached the peak of success. However, as far as money was concerned, they didn't give him back even a thin dime. The Royal Court did ratify all his military promotions, supported his appointments and decrees, and announced imminent reinforcements of troops, arms, and ammunition, and promised him his own ship for business dealings with the Peninsula. And there was more. After approving those decrees, our hero was granted a private audience with King Philip IV himself, lasting two minutes.

While he was left alone for a few moments in a vast waiting area, with large stained-glass windows and a majestic carpet, he saw a shape moving behind one of the curtains. As he approached he could make out the gleam of a dagger held by a man dressed in black, identical to the one who had shot him on the freebooters' ship. Orpí swiftly unsheathed his sword and began to silently advance on the hitman, when trumpets rang out triumphantly. Alarmed by the burst of sound, the mysterious man opened up one of the windows and leapt through it, before disappearing down a narrow alleyway.

Before our hero had a chance to react, the King arrived, followed by a page and two trumpeters. The monarch languidly made his way over to the royal throne as he waved off the brass section, and our hero ran to kneel before him, scrambling to remove his hat to bow down before his king.

"Blatsthed muthithcianth, playing that infernal muthic into my ear all the livelong day . . ." complained the King. He suffered from an alarming case of mandibular prognathism, poorly concealed by an insipid beard, that kept his upper teeth from ever meeting his lower ones. "Pleathe, sthand, Thir Urpín, and regale me with the thory of thine conqueth. But make hathe, for I've an appointment with the doctor."

Orpí explained his adventures with more imagination than truth, and as a result the King was quite contented with the story, despite the fact that his face reflected a thousand aches and pains, as the monarch was suffering from gout, arthrosis, tertian fevers, dropsy, and a host of other ailments that left him there sitting on the throne half dead, partly due to having suckled—by royal decree (which also meant he had a considerable collection of "milk brothers" scattered throughout the peninsula)—a band of Asturian wet-nurses rather than his mother's colostrum, and partly due to the constant concubinage with all manner of whores, as was the royal custom.

". . . and therefore, Your Excellency," concluded Orpí, looking directly into the monarch's watery eyes, "I be in most urgent need of the ducats invested in said enterprise."

"We hath no ducath in our cofferth, our debthth to German bankth art tremendouth, and profith from the Americath, diminithing. Withall, thine landth art newly thine againe," said the King. "Now thee muth religiouthly pay thine royal taxeth, ath put forth in mine mandate, theeing ath I am Philip 'the great.' Worry not, boy, twill all be fine & dandee. Goe with God."

Our hero knelt in multiple reverences before the monarch and left the palace infuriated by the King's lack of empathy with respect to his delicate situation, but pleased to have recovered what had cost him so much to achieve and what had been so vilely taken from him: self-governance. The following morning, he and Araypuro left for Piera to visit the Orpí family, as shall be revealed in continuation.

## Chapter XVI

### In which our hero returns home triumphant,
### yet irked by a strange sensation

Orpí and Araypuro covered the route from Madrid to Barcelona in less than eight days and in relative tranquility, excepting their encounter with a group of criminal bandits in the woods of Catalonia.

"God 'av' mercy!" their leader, by the name of Serrallonga[145], tipping his hat. "I seeth, from your appearance, that you must be a lord of great lineage, respected and affluent. So, if you wood be soe kind . . . your money or your life!"

Our hero, who had become a person who was quite difficult to frighten after years of waging war in the jungles of the New World and with little time to lose, unsheathed his sword and killed six highwaymen at once. Then he approached Serrallonga, who awaited his fate with eyes and mouth open, and Orpí exclaimed—with a gift for words and vast experience with bloodsplattering: "Sir, I hath seen many a highwayman such as yerself in the course of my life and I shant lie when I offereth up this advice: get a new job."

---

145. *i.e.* The legendary highwayman Joan Sala Ferrer (1594-1634).

But Serrallonga didn't heed Orpí's words, and some years later he would end up hanged. In the meantime, Orpí and Araypuro finally reached the town of Piera. Our hero was anxious to see his family, or what was left of it, since his sister Joana had died in 1623, and his mother had passed on just a few months prior. Arriving at the hostel on Raval de Baix and seeing the fields and the castle as he came over the ridge had our hero in a tizzy, and he regaled Araypuro with detailed stories of his childhood and the family business. When they reached Piera, the townspeople stared at the strange pair as if they were characters from fiction. It was well known that the eldest boy of House Orpí had become a conquistador on the obscure continent of America and had fought and pacified the natives like something out of a fable. Our hero, now forty-three years of age, had come home a veritable splendid man of fame and fortune.

His younger brother Jaume was now in charge of the lands of House Orpí, and had become a successful trader in Piera, surrounded by weights and scales that he used to count the money of their growing family business. In his first two days back in Piera, Joan was impressed to see how the town had prospered, with its new white-washed belltower, and flourishing agriculture, and he watched the bulls working in the fields and the shepherds leading sheep with their whistling. He enjoyed the sensation of seeing nature domesticated from the surrounding woods and strolling along the paths he'd spent so much time on as a child. He smiled to see the young artisans carrying on the trades of their ancestors: the blacksmith hammering a hoe at the forge, the cobbler sewing a hide to a sole, and the vegetable sellers setting up a stand in the market in the town square. And yet he felt strangely distanced from the atmosphere. He missed the remote province of New Catalonia and his life in the tropics. All that had once been his home was now only the memory of an idea that didn't fit with the current reality. His childhood friends, whom he met up with at the town tavern, were now strangers with whom he scarcely exchanged a word. Gisela Coll de Cabra, whom he had once found pretty, was now a fat woman deformed by cheap wine who hawked fish at the market with the voice of a drunken sailor. All the nexuses to his past were broken.

"I feel as a stranger in my own land, brother," he confessed. "After so many years in the Indies, this no longer seems like my home. Either everything is very changed, or tis I who hath changed too much."

"Verily, King Phillipus IV hath created a national state with extremist structures of centralised government, and people are abandoning the countryside to goe to the city in serch of work," complained Jaume. "To boot, his viceroys are siezeing, extralegally, Catalan powers and they no longer even take cognizance of the Constitutions of the Principality. The war between France and Castille have brought Felipet's soldiers into our homes, and believe you me they're a pain in thee ass, behaving like right beestes whereversofare they arte. Our Catalonia, in the longe or the short term, shant have an easy time maintaining its freedoms, and we'll ende up like everyone else: duking it out. I shall need all of Godde's help to keep the business afloat . . . at least ye'll gette rich, in the Amerrricas."

"Ye think that it be some Promised Land, eh? Turns out the vices of a sick society travell faster than goode intentions!" clarified Orpí. "However that distant chunk of land is my great opportunity, since it gives me the possibility of making my fortune. And at the same time it is the safe-conduct to your own future, mine brother, with the yields I hope to gain from it. It be a rich land, and unexploit'd, where the treasures are not gold but the soil itself & its fruits & its livestock."

As our hero asked his brother for funding for New Catalonia, effectively mortgaging his home and family assets, so sure was he of his favorable outcome, Orpí glanced out the window and saw, up in a tree in the garden, a man dressed in black, identical to the ones he'd seen on the ship and in the royal Court. Leaving Jaume mid-sentence, he went out brandishing his sword and shouting, "Where be thee, hitman? Draw near and we shall end this once & foreall!" After searching frantically through the garden for some trace of the assassin, he went back inside the house with a panic attack.

"I be increasingly convinc'd these men in black be spies for the noblemen of Cumanagoto, payd and trained to do me in."

"Art thou quite sure of these hallucinations, Joan? For I can see no one."

"Hell's bells, brother! They've already madeth two attempts on mine life! The governors of the viceroyalties in America hold mee in infinite envee. Those cretins are out to steal mine lands what I've earned with mine sweat and, being pedigreed *hidalgos*, they employ the Crown against mee to the point that it seems I'm battling against all the viceroyalties."

"And what dost thou plan to do, declareth war on the King?" asked Jaume, in jest.

"For Godde's sake, on the King, no! May Godde hold Him and keep Him. But the criollo noblemen of Santo Domingo and Caracas wante to rob me of what I've worked so hard to earn!"

After a few days with his brother, our hero had to leave. Jaume, seeing that Joan was now a man of royal fame and institutional worth, didn't hesitate to mortgage the lands of their family patrimony, and lent him 12,000 escudos for the conquest of New Catalonia.

"Bon voyage," said Jaume, embracing his older brother for the last time.

"Best of lucke, Jaumet," said our hero.

And that was how Orpí and Araypuro came to travel south once more, smoking and singing to the rhythm of their trotting. When they reached Seville they bought provisions to bring to New Catalonia, and embarked on a galleon headed to the Americas, the Indies, the New World, or whatever the fa-boop you want to call it, dear reader.

## Chapter XVII

### In which Juan Orpí sees a play
### he finds very disconcerting

The caravelle with our hero on board departs and travels away from Old Europe for the second time, toward the remote provinces of America. By now, Orpí's headaches over the criollo noblemen's plotting had turned him well and truly paranoid and he kept looking over his shoulders for men dressed in black. "Tis no time to lose ye 'ead," our hero told himself, filling his lungs with sea air, while the sailors went up and down the ship's masts, unfurling sails and hoisting the anchor, amid popular songs. Now they would set sail on a dicey new voyage through ocean seas populated by enemy ships and subject to metereological inclemencies that struck all nations and flags with equal force. Luckily, the water was so calm that they could see flying fish diving into the crystalline depths past corals on the sea floor.

On deck everyone was in good spirits and they now gathered around an improvised play. A theater company called Il Gran Teatro di Broccoli, comprised of Italians trained in *commedia dell'arte* and some Castilians who were headed to the New World in search of work in theaters there, performed a *naumachia*[146] with caravelles made of paper and actors in sailor costumes.

Orpí and Araypuro approached the imminent spectacle, joining the audience and watching as an orchestra made up of soldiers and actors lugged scores and cardboard set pieces to and fro. Then an actress transformed into a Mademoiselle by a gleaming tunic appeared, to the strains of a *copla*, and was received with an ovation as she began to declaim:

> ♫♪ Gather ye round to hear the tale ♫♪
> Of lawy'r and his holy grail
> Seduced by a saucy lass
> In Seville he gave up his past
> Betwixt the two they did kill
> Her husband (just for a thrill)
> Twas in error . . . oh, the horror!
> He took the name of the cuckhold
> Off to the Indies, seeking golde.
> Along the way he kiss'd sirens
> Oer to his new environs
> But not all was honky-dory
> For all of his fame and glory
> Twas in error
> Allways in err-orr,
> oh, oh, what an "honor"!

Our hero furrowed his brows and widened his eyes maniacally. "Araypuro, answer me thusly: art they singing mine exploits or be I hallucinating?"

"No master, get over theeself, thatz just a made-up little ditty," said Araypuro, impassive, scratching his inner thigh.

---

146. *i.e.* A mock naval battle.

"How is't possible yond the story of mine adventures is known on the other side of the globe? Could it be the King hath spies in every corner of the worlde?"

The choir was now singing beside an actress being seduced by an actor dressed as a low-ranking soldier, and Orpí didn't know whether to hide somewhere or jump directly into the ocean to be devoured by fish.

Urbín, Urtín or Urbín
(who giveths a whoop, I mean)
Like a pig to slaught-err
Did foind himself in hot water
When his very double he met
And was working without a net
Zoinks, how his hopes were abash-ed
Oer the riches safely stassh-ed . . .

"My God, Araypuro, what sort of terrible metalepsis be this?!" Orpí exclaimed in a whisper, his paranoia reaching new heights. "How canst these ydiots know my history so? If news of this reacheth Drye Lande or the Court I'm a dead manne!"

"No problemo, master, simple coincidence," said Araypuro, lighting an ounce of Almogàvers™ tobacco.

"How couldst thee, buffoon! Canst thou not see they speak of me? What sort of intrigue be this? Perchance a fisherman spake of the 'istory of New Catalonia with an innkeeper on Espaniola, and he, in turnne, explixt it to some soldiers what returrned ere the Peninsula, and so onne and thus . . ."

"De pinga, bro! You bestest check that ego, master. Thine delusiones of grandeur nair grow."

"Insolence!" barked our hero. "Thou art verily like a stubbern mule, comprehending nothing!"

The nucleus of the chorus, made up of sailors and some of

the audience members themselves, were now reciting verses that went fast and loose with the chronology of events, while the actors depicted a battle:

♪♫ Ruses and cunning arguments, ♪♫
The occasional armaments
Allowed him conqu'r yon lands
Freed the slaves with a shake of hands
Along with Jesuit ideal
And thirty-five pinches of zeal
There be men who think with the groin,
But this one: of coin to purloin!
Challeng'd his king and government
to some halffcoxk'd covenant.
Rogue plusse 'is mestizo sidekick
Verily as some bromance flick
Dey conquistador'd & found'd
And oftentimes they flound'r'd

"Wait up!" exlaimed Araypuro. "Am I the mestizo sidekick?"

"Aha! Now that they mentione thee, dost thou finally believe me, ya thick injun?" asked Orpí, smirking. "In any case, we hath not employed the word 'conquer' since 1573, but rather 'pacify' or 'populate.' These dramatists are behind the tymes."

"They're talkin' about me, massa!" said Araypuro, doing a happy dance. "I'm famous!"

"Very well, injun, hush thine mouth a while so I canst hear the play . . ." ordered our hero.

An actor playing a fortuneteller was now delivering a prediction, in the voice of a countertenor, about the apocalyptic future of a mythical territory, amid the crew's general jubilation:

𝔜et that new civilization
Is a repetitive nation
Of all that he doth reject
Mirror'd bye a new architect
The hatred and envy and greeds
No gold to show for his misdeeds.
Urbín, Urtín, Urpín, Urpine
Be the name o' this jewy canine
And the cries of noblemen
Were nary as Greek to him.
Twas a big mistake on his part
Since no single man can outsmart
Our great ruler, the Planet King.[147]
Especially on a shoestring...

In a fit of paranoic delirium, our hero leapt up, determined to multiply his allegoric and hypostatic legend and, moving through the audience, plants himself amid the actors, exclaiming: "Ladies & gentlemen, I be the sole manne what knowth the veritable story told here! For I beest the veritable Juan Orpín and this story be mine pure life!"

"Say what?"

"Juan . . . who?"

"What sayeth this nutman, this play is by a mightily famouz playwrite!" exclaimed the starring actress.

"Zat so?" asked our hero. "And what be the name of this capricious hack?"

The actors stammered for a few moments and, after gathering in a circle and murmuring among themselves, one said, "Ahh, no, tis an anonymouse work!"

"And what be the title, then?" asked our hero.

---

147. *i.e.* One of the names for Philip IV.

The actors gathered in a circle again, whispering secretively.

"So ye knowst it not, hucksters? I shall tell ye who wrote this play, and who strives to drive me battsky with all these theories of conspiration, which with each passing moment I doth see more and more clear before mine eyes!" bellowed Orpí, beside himself. Then he spied a man dressed in black and, thinking him one of the murderous hitmen, began to chase him all over the ship with his sword drawn. In the end our hero had to be reduced by a group of five soldiers. After everyone swore up and down that the man in black was merely an actor, our hero calmed down a little bit.

"Damn'd if I canst understand any of alle this, injun," said Orpí, stretched out on his bunk with a lime blossom infusion to calm his nerves. "Thee canst see that I be not mad, right? We must remain alert for I canst trust no-man. Take the first watch turn, then wake me and I shall take over, agree'd?"

"I knowst not whether thine madness is real or feigned, master," said Araypuro, drinking down a slug of firewater he'd found in the hold. "But thou footests the bills, and I follow thine orders without rolling mine eyes."

Having said that, when less than five minutes had passed since our hero had fallen asleep, Araypuro was already snoring his heart out and in danger of falling from his chair. But even if Araypuro were to fall, that would not stop the historian from continuing his telling of these adventures (despite no one asking him to) thusly:

## Chapter XVIII

### In which Joan Orpí is shipwrecked in a highly literary manner and questions the meaning of life

That selfsame night a storm unleashed upon the high seas and, while the ship surfed gigantic waves, a monstrous figure emerged from the depths and appeared before the caravelle:

The giant squid of colossal proportions moved its tentacles, glued to the keel, tossing the vessel to and fro. The entire crew came up on deck to see the creature, including Orpí and Araypuro, who looked upon it in horror.

"Bejabbers!" exclaimed Orpí, trying to remember his readings. "This creature must be a *physeter*, as described by Torquemada in his *Garden of Curious Flowers (Book VI)*!"

"Jesus, Maria, and José! Either that monster's gonna eat us all, or we're surely bound for the black depths!" exclaimed Araypuro, crying in desperation.

As was written in the immutable, eternal legends of centuries past, some of the sailors ran for weapons to hunt that sea monster. "To the kraken!" they shouted, "Launch the harpoons!" Seeing the threat, the enormous cetacean squeezed the ship's hull and it collapsed with a loud wooden crunch. The crew was exiled from that false kingdom of secure timber and thrust into the black depths without time to even think twice.

Our hero, who had also leapt into the sea as sportingly as he could muster, found himself suddenly swimming upward from the bottom of the ocean in search of oxygen, dodging a stream of blows, barrels, arms, and fabric until finally he was able to surface. In the distance (but not as distant as he would have liked), he saw the sea monster swallowing up sailors by the dozens, and himself managed to cling to a wooden plank that floated adrift. With his body numb from the cold water and his mind fixed on all the mythology of shipwrecks, watery graves, and legends with horrible endings that he had read or heard tell of, out of the corner of his eye Orpí saw the boat's stern sinking in a swirl of water and the giant squid diving into the nadir. The few surviving crew members were floating in the night and getting lost in the darkness, shrieking as long as they could before drowning in the waves. Our hero searched for Araypuro, but it was impossible to see a thing with the saltwater creeping into his mouth, nose, and ears. He tried to climb up onto the plank he was gripping and, after a few frustrated (and frankly pathetic) attempts he pulled it off. Using his arms as oars, he navigated those fearsome latitudes guided by Polaris, sailors' fundamental astronomical point of reference, which hid beyond the horizon. And thus the hours passed, as he observed the night sky until the effort wore him out and he fell asleep with the swaying of the plank floating in that dark ocean.

Believing himself to be dead, he had the horrible sensation that demons were tickling his toes. When he opened his eyes, he found that he was stretched out on the sand of a beach, with two pyschopathic seagulls nibbling on his feet. Waving his arms and legs and shouting like a lunatic, he scared them off and then stretched out again on the sand, watching the luminous clouds slowly sketch out the shape of a whale in the blue American sky. All was now calm. The speed with which the incident had occurred the night before, plus the coldness of the water, and the effort he'd expended to save his own life provoked in him a sensation of inebriation similar to madness. "What designs doth this twist of fate hold in store for me?" Orpí wondered. "And what symbols, presences, messages, or warnings must befalle me in order for me to comprehend my mission here?" His questions received no answers. In part because they had none and in part because our hero was distracted by a body floating near the shore, not far from him. Thinking that it was his Araypuro, he struggled to his feet and ran over to it. When he turned the body over, he recognized the lead actress from the theater company, dead, swollen, her skin black from stomach gases about to explode. "No man ever said the life of an artiste war easy," he thought. Then he saw how, along the beach, the corpses of his vessel's crew swayed back and forth in the shallow water, inert and jumbled amid a scramble of guts that came out of their open mouths. A prolonged shriek from the sky was the prelude to the predatory symphony of a group of vultures spurred on by the rotting flesh, who flew down in increasingly tighter circles in search of gifts from King Neptune. Horrified, Orpí ran away from the shore and into the jungle, scratching himself on the brush and the skin on his feet bleeding as he advanced along streams filled with pointy rocks. Lost in the tropical vegetation, our hero embarked on the adventure of scampering up a tree in order to look out on the horizon in search of some trace, however faint, of civilization. Scraping his body against the bark, scratching himself on the branches, he finally reached the crown and, once there, all he could see was a carpet of treetops extending endlessly. Losing hope, he clambered down and took off, without a specific destination, into the thick lattice of the jungle as the afternoon shadows surprised him along his erratic wandering. Starving, and with his stomach grumbling, Orpí watched as ants gathered tiny pieces of fruits, transporting them in a chain to their hills, until his mind grew cloudy. Frightened by the giant butterflies that were following him, he fell onto all fours in an enormous puddle of mud wearing no more than some torn bloomers, his torso bare and all his ribs jutting out in relief. Hallucinating from his hunger and with his face marked by terror, he discovered that even his own shadow had abandoned him and that night was falling filled with the sounds of ferocious beasts, devouring each other in the darkness, until our hero embraced a sensation of belonging to the eternal circle of life more than to any particular period in history. Dragging himself along like a larva, his bloodied hands now gripped the trunk of a fallen tree and his dilated pupils remained fixed on the absence of reality. His skin dirty and white, he resigned himself to the monstrous death of his earthly life, waiting for the end, which he was sure would not be long in coming. Just as he was about to give in to his fate—either devoured by one of those famished beasts or dying of pure desperation—the tree he was clinging to disappeared as if by the art of magic and our hero found himself in the midst of a desert of white sand.

"This lyfe is unbearable!" Orpí complained in desperation as he fell to the ground. "I require a divine sign!"

No sooner did he pronounce that invocation than a figure materialized right before him. Orpí fell to his knees, prepared to die.

"Quit yer drama!" roared a familiar, deep voice.

"Beest thou angel or devil?" said our hero, his head in the sand like an ostrich.

"Less lip and look mee in the face, halfwit!" said the voice.

Orpí lifted his head and saw the ghost of his father before him.

"Father . . . ? Art thou true?"

"Indeed! To mine dismay. Look what hath become of thee, goldbrickster!" said the ghost, with a voice from beyond the grave. "Thou hast ever been a spineless gyrl!"

"Thanks. Thou donst look too bad thyself, Dad," murmured our hero. "One query: be it veritable that beyonde death lyes only emptyness, blackness, and the abyss?"

"Quit thy foolishness, mine son," said the apparition. "All what thy seeth is thee work of God, who ist All and is in All."

"Ah, okay then. So forsooth, what must I doeth now, Dad? Must I die and enter the kingdome of Heaven or wut?"

"Thou hast more doubts than Hamlet, my sonne . . ." he replied. "Thy thyme hath not yet come. Follow the dog and there thee shall find thine sidekick. And now fare thee well, they art calling me from up in the heavens . . . so, gotta run!"

Having said that, the ghost of his father disappeared and our hero found himself face to face with a dog that was attentively watching him. Orpí had no idea where that animal had come from but, after sniffing at the air, it approached him wagging its tail. It was some sort of mutt, an impossible mix of Spanish water dog with American coyote. Our hero gave it the name Friston, in homage to the magician in *Don Quixote* and because he thought it was the reincarnation of his father's ghost. The animal seemed to know the route and Orpí followed it until, a few meters on, he found Araypuro sleeping under a tree, just as his ghostly father had predicted.

"Idle injun . . . wake up!" he said, delivering a swift kick to Araypuro's rear end.

"What . . . ? How . . . ? Señor Urpín?" said Araypuro, opening his eyes and looking at the dog. "Shit . . . what's that?" he asked, pointing at the canine.

Friston sniffed the two men and trotted around in circles wagging his tail. While Orpí explained the story of his shipwreck, Araypuro noticed something gleaming on a promontory. As they approached it, the two men were amazed to discover a gigantic round building, shining like a mountain made of solid gold. Both men had heard (and read) stories of realms where the chairs, pots, and helmets were made of gold, where nature's miracles offered the prodigious metal as if it were marjoram water. Now those mythical stories, accumulated in their genetic memory over centuries, were becoming reality.

"Now I understand the exact meaning of my hallucinated adventure," reflected Orpí, scratching his beard. "It was fate what brought me to the City of Gold . . ."

"Let's not waste time thinking . . . we're rich! Filthy rich!" said Araypuro, running up the promontory toward the enormous geometric mass, driven mad by its blinding gleam.

"Halt, idjot!" shouted Orpí, wary.

Too late. Araypuro had already gone inside and our hero and the dog Friston had no choice but to follow him, as detailed in the following Chapter:

## Chapter *XIX*

In which Joan Orpí and Araypuro find a treasure
and other unexpected things

While the two men walked further inside that mysterious
structure, lighting their way with some palm leaves they
burned like torches, they saw a series of strange symbols covering the walls. It wasn't written in the alphabet imported by
the Castilians to America, but they weren't the typical native
glyphs either. Those inscriptions, in some unknown language,
were accompanied by primitive paintings of short little beings
with enormous heads, emerging from an ovoid house that
seemed to be elevated in the heavens.

"Where we at, massa? The City of the Caesars?" asked
Araypuro, as he contemplated the mysterious graffiti.

"Nay," replied Orpí, advancing along the hallway.

"El Dorado?"

"Nay."

"The Empire of Prester John?"

"Nay."

"The Valley of Cinnamon?"

"Nay."

"The Seven Cities of Cipango?"

"Enough, injun! Shut up for once and for all!" ordered Orpí. "I knowth not the cause behind all this Egyptianism, but I hear voices. We art not alone."

Indeed, as the two men continued, their surroundings shone brighter and brighter until they found a room that was not illuminated by any natural light but rather by mountains and mountains of gold that glowed like stars in the night. And amid that whole gilded promontory, there was a man rolling around, happy as a child. He was dressed in stinking rags. Orpí approached him, pinching his nose, while Araypuro stayed back, and Friston the dog growled, baring his eyeteeth threateningly.

"Who be thee, sir?" asked Orpí.

When the man saw him, a string of drool fell from his lower lip, which hung listlessly. His palate was a conglomerate of bleeding gums and rotten teeth. His eyes were bloodshot and revealed him, clearly, as demented. His face was tinged with blue, surely brought on by some unknown tropical disease or perhaps a liver infection. But the most important detail, which did not escape Orpí's eye, was that the figure was missing a hand. His left hand, to be precise.

"It canst be . . ." murmured Orpí, drawing even closer. "Thou art . . . Gregorio Izquierdo!"

We have no way of knowing whether the man was listening to our hero or not, but we can say that he did not react when hearing his own name. Instead, the numbskull merely repeated one word, over and over:

"Nyargocs, Nyargos . . . nya-nya-nya-nya-nyargocs!"

"Poor thing, he hath lost his marbles," said Orpí.

"Gangsta done flipp't the wig, bro," confirmed Araypuro. "Let's grab the gold and hit it!"

"Nay, one moment, injun. We canst just abandon a Christian. Mine brain ist cloud'd with mysterious questions. How hath Gregorio Izquierdo arrived to this here place? Why is this treasure here? And, above all, why is a bizarre, slimy being tugging on mine trousers?"

Orpí and Araypuro, pulled from their gilded moment, jumped back in fear when three tiny figures appear out of nowhere. Friston started barking and refused to stop until Araypuro gave him a swift kick.

"Who be ye?" asked our hero, who received no reply. "We espeek no Inglish, comprenden?"

"They be not Spaniards, nor of any known tribe," said Araypuro, analyzing them. "They be mightily ugly & ill-humoured but do not seem to be Englishmen. Their strangest aspect is the fact that they have no butts."

Indeed, the three mysterious creatures were standing there like dolts, looking at our hero blankly. They were short, poorly put together beings, wearing green leggings and, as Araypuro had said, had no butts whatsoever.

"Who be theese monsters, Sir Gregorio?" Orpí asked the demented man, while keeping one eye on the strange beings.

"Nyargocs!" shouted Gregorio Izquierdo, kneeling before them.

"Nyargocs?" said our hero. "Must be some sort of Oriental tribe . . ."

"Oriental or not, massa, let's get outta here," said Araypuro, pricking up his ears. "I hear war tam-tams."

"I hear nothing," said Orpí. "Quit thy inventions, injun."

Too late. Our hero's disbelief (or deafness) was swept aside as dozens of indigenous locals armed to the teeth came in along the hallway they had entered through not long before.

"There be no end to this pile-on!" complained Orpí.

"They'll slaughter us like rabbits! Shit just got real," exclaimed Araypuro.

Indeed, the natives on the warpath would soon reach the large room, pointing their bows at Orpí and the others. When the natives saw the gold, they didn't think twice and began to shoot. But—miracle? Or not—when the arrows dipped in curare seemed about to pierce the body of our hero, they stopped suddenly, slowly veered and traveled back whence they came to kill the archers.

"Pinche me to see if I dream, injun . . . What artifice, miracle or rich mystery be this?" said Orpí. "Didst those arrowes retorne to their bows, verily a Zeno paradox?"

"I knowst not from Ceno, massa, but that's what it looks like!" said Araypuro, whimpering and hiding behind our hero. "It be the buttless beings and their hocus pocus!"

"Life itself seemeth unreal, injun."

Indeed, those three beings that Gregorio Izquierdo called Nyargocs extended their arms against the natives, who shot arrows at themselves or stabbed themselves with their own daggers, and died with believable expressions of surprise and disbelief. The problem was that more and more armed Indians kept arriving, entering *en masse* in a jumble, to the point that the three beings were having trouble containing them all. Arrows flew everywhere chaotically, and one of them hit Gregorio Izquierdo, making him collapse on the floor.

"Listen up . . ." he said, with that gust of lucidity typical of the moribund. "Grabbe all the golde ye can and escape thru the backe. There be a door that leeds outside . . . aaaa aaaaaaaaaaaaaaaaaaaaaaaaaaaaaaaaaaaaaaaaaaaaaaaaaaaaaaaa aaaaaaa- aaaaaaaaaaaaaaaaaaaaaaaaaaaaaaaaaaaaaaaaaaaaaaaaa aaaaaaaaaaaaaaaaaaaaaaaaaaaaaaaa-aaaaaaaaaaaaaaaaaaaaaaaa aaaaaaaaaaaaaaaaaaaaaaaaaaaaaaaaaaaaaaaaaaaaaaaaaaaaaaaaa- aaaaaaaaaaaaaaaaaaaaaaaaaaaaaaaaaaaaaaaaaaaaaaaaaaaaaaaaaa

aaaaaaaaaaaaaaaaaaaaa-aaaaaaaaaaaaaaaaaaaaaaaaaaaaaaa
aaaaaaaaaaaaaaaaaaaaaaaaaaaaaaaaaaaaaaaaaaaaa- aaaaaaaaa
aaaarrrrrrrrrrrrrrrrrrrrgh."

"This be the seconde time I see thou diest, Sir Gregorio," said Orpí, tossing him over his shoulder. "This tyme I shall save you. Grabbe all the gold thou canst, injun, and let us blow thar pop stand, anon!"

And as our hero carried the wounded man, Araypuro filled up three sacks high with gold and they both fled, followed by Friston the dog, through a small side exit, as hundreds of arrows pierced the door they were now closing. Once outside, what they'd assumed to be an ovoid city began to shake as if it were alive, spinning, and two of those strange buttless beings stood in a door waving goodbye.

The golden geometric object rose up, floating through the air, and after buzzing over the jungle treetops with an earsplitting hum, it disappeared into the extraterrestrial outer space. Everything was left in darkness and only a first-quarter half moon illuminated Araypuro, who smoked sitting alone now on the promontory, while Orpí scratched his head, not knowing what to say over Gregorio Izquierdo's pale, inert body. After a short while, the two men buried the deceased in a Christian grave and prayed a very heartfelt ourfather as the crickets chirped *ric-ric* in the obscurity of the jungle. But the stillness was shortlived because from a distance again they heard the war tam-tams. It was the tribe who had come to find the treasure that belonged to them. A few brief, brave words emerged from the lips of our hero:

"Erry man fer hisself!"

## Chapter XX

### In which Orpí and Araypuro come down with gold rush fever and it very nearly ends in homicide

Not without much effort, Joan Orpí and Araypuro dragged along with them all the gold they'd managed to save from that floating temple, walking arduously through the jungle and crossing vast harsh deserts, rough mountains, rivers, marshes, and great lakes. And all that while hearing, night and day, the shrieks and drumming of the Indians, who continued to stalk their prey. During six days and their respective nights, they advanced with their precious cargo until, on the seventh, they stopped in a forest clearing, near a grotto that served as their temporary shelter.

"I can take no more, massa," said Araypuro, dropping two sacks brimming with gold. "I quit . . ."

"Never, injun!" bellowed Orpí. "Don't get persnickety with mee or I shant pay thine wages!"

Araypuro suddenly burst into laughter.

"I seeth not what the gleek is, injun."

"The gleek is that we're filthy rich! But the way this gold is slowing us down, those Indians finna eat us alive!"

"Very well. We shall camp here this night," said our hero, sitting down. "On the morrow we shall decide what to do."

While Araypuro went hunting for some game, Orpí prepared a campfire with dry brush. The two men ate in silence, watching the flames rise and spark into the sky, as they tried to digest the impossible adventures they had recently lived through.

"I recall reading *The Adventures of Esplandián* as a boy," our hero said sadly, "where tis recount'd the dream of El Dorado. We hath made that dream a reality, injun."

"Pero, bro, what use to us is this pure gold?" he asked, gnawing on an iguana drumstick.

"It shall finance New Catalonia," said Orpí, looking into the fire. "We no longer must waite for financing from the Crowne. If all the coin we hath forked over as the *anata* and the royal fifth were retornned to us as aid, these lands would have long been prosperous and booming. Yet those Castilians ere want more and more, and the King hath alreddy saith he shant helpe me againe. This here treasure means the ende of begging for scraps. We shall live in abundance! From the fountains shall spring gold! No one will ere go hungered!"

"And what do we want wid dat? We'd be better off headin' to France to live like lords, off the fat a da land, like kings!"

"Thine be a trick question, injun. Is it that . . ." said Orpí, picking up a red-hot ember, ". . . thou wishest to catch me unawares and steal mine gold?"

"Master, don't get thine bloomers in a twist, thou knowst I am sensitive . . ." said Araypuro, frightened.

"Inveigle me not, injun . . ." said our mad hero, threatening him with eyes aflame. "I shant allow thee to purloin this treasure!"

"Master!" said Araypuro, leaping up and running toward the jungle. "How now!?!"

"Thou canst run, but thou canst not hide!" bellowed Orpí, completely bonkers, chasing after him, while Friston barked without knowing exactly why he was barking.

"Don't crosseth that line, massa, for I hath done nothing wrong!" whimpered Araypuro, running in circles amid the trees. "Quit thy aggression against me!"

Crazed, Orpí chased Araypuro for a good long while through the forest thicket until he finally caught him and threw him to the ground. When our hero was about to bash in the Indian's head with the torch, he stopped, hesitating, in a state of shock. He threw the red-hot branch far away and kneeled beside Araypuro, crying disconsolately.

"Mine Godde . . . apologies . . . !" he said, his nose dripping with snot. "Mine Faustian ambition be repellent . . . ! I did wend crazy for a moment, as if Satan himself had possess'd me . . . ! Canst thou ever forgive me, injun?"

"*Dale*! Have I any choice? All ist ever forgiven to the massa if he pays enuf," said Araypuro, hugging our hero.

"Forgive me, injun, mine greed got the best of me, but I'm cured now," begged Orpí. "I shall tell thee what we will doo: bury the treasure in this clearing, near this cove, and that way we may verily escape these Indians and stay alive. Once we reach New Barselona, we shall retornne with horses and soldiers to recover it, what say thee?"

"I darent say no, for fear thou wilt go all mandinga on me aginn, and send me straight to hell, hence . . . *dale*."

After hiding the gold in the darkest corner of that cave and drawing an improvised map on a piece of paper, Orpí and Araypuro continued on for New Catalonia. Three days and three nights they traveled, lost in the mountains, until finally losing the tribe that was on their trail and, on the fourth day, the two men reached the shores of a river, where they found a detachment of New Andalusian colonists, made up of twenty people living in deplorable conditions in a few straw houses around a wretched garden patch. A man of syphilitic appearance, who seemed as if he could drop dead at any moment, emerged from among the townspeople, prepared to challenge them, but our hero, who had kept a few ounces of gold from the treasure in his pocket, exchanged one for a ship. And that was how our hero and Araypuro set sail in a small canoe, with Friston sitting in the back, vanishing into the fog as they traveled down the Orinoco. What happened to them on that river no one can rightly say, however what remains of our outlandish story will please all who wish to persevere with it.

## Chapter XXI

In which our hero returns
to New Catalonia, founds New Tarragona
and cuts a rug

In Cumanagoto, news of Joan Orpí's return quickly spread. After various rumors that included murders, pirates, monsters, and shipwrecks, the steadfast attorney had come back victorious from his audience with the King and now was fully invested with the power to govern his New Catalonia. When Vázquez de Soja and the other criollo noblemen heard that, their envy multiplied and they doubled down on their efforts to defeat that "Doctor Urpín" who so enraged them with his achievements, moving all the strings they had in reach, which were many. They spread tittle-tattle among the people of Cumaná, Cumanagoto, and Caracas, saying that our hero's lands were a breeding ground of outlaws and notorious miscreants who were getting rich at the expense of the livestock of other viceroyalties such as New Andalusia, and that Orpí himself was a frequenter of taverns, a cardsharper, and a swindler who was cheating the King out of taxes. This vile rumorology resulted in furious letters sent by the criollo noblemen to King Philip IV, only snowballing the nefarious lies.

Meanwhile, nearly a year after leaving Spain, Orpí and Araypuro rowed their small canoe until they reached the first traces of civilization: trimmed lawns, straight trees, and a small dock announced they were close to New Barcelona. Once they had eaten and were dressed, they took stock of the progress made in that tropical city, filled with the smells of oil, roasting coffee, incense. Almost all the homes were now two stories high, with wide balconies and arched doorways, decorated with colorful flowers. The businesses had prospered and now one could find a tailor, a carpenter, a hairdresser, and even one man from Seville who had opened up a bookstore—Suspicious Books—with one of the few printing presses in America, furtively publishing all the works of fiction (by Lope de Vega, Quevedo, Moredo, etc.) banned by the Spanish authorities in the New World. The cultivation of raw materials had yielded bumper crops, particularly tobacco, and they saw large bales tied with hemp cord of the Almogàvers™ brand, giving off a perfumed scent.

After a few days of resting at his ranch, our hero continued with his plan of populating the vast wild regions of New Catalonia. Astride his steed Acephalus and followed by Friston the dog, Orpí led a small expedition of thirty soldiers and twenty Indians, plus Father Claver and Araypuro, up the Unare River in a *felucca*[148] to unknown lands yet to be conquered. When the river became too narrow, they continued on foot through the jungle, first in a straight line, then in circles, and finally zigzagging through the thick brush, and they soon had no idea where they were.

---

148. *i.e.* Vessel propelled by oars or lateen sails, or both.

The following account is part of Father Claver's *Chronicles* of this voyage:

> Aving advanced oer three days and three nights we came upon a very fertile and clean plain & Doctor Urpín deemed that place good territory for populating and decreed New Tarragona be found'd there. And in the fifteen or twenty days of work that we were there that city of New Tarragona was constructed, under the unerring leadership of Lieutenant Jeremías, and such a peaceful land was nere before seen and the Indians aided us with the task and cooked us fowls, pheasants, tame geese, reed birds, hares, and rabbits. And having done so . . .

"What be that which thou scribest, Father?" asked Orpí, interrupting the Jesuit's writing.

"Some *Chronicles of Conquest*," said the friar, who sat beneath a tree with Friston curled up beside him. "Someone must leave written documentation of thine exploits and all what happens here, is that not so?"

"The tyme for writing is passt, Father. Tis time for action and labor, not intellectual daydreaming and leisure."

That night the natives and the soldiers ate *moriche* and bitter yucca *casabe* and together drank and sang to the freshly founded New Tarragona. Our hero gathered with Lieutenant Jeremies and Araypuro, who danced arrhythmically in a circle. Their eyes gleamed because they had imbibed the "magic grass" that allowed them communion with the world of the dead and they now danced like men possessed, in honor of fertility and life, while some Indians blew bamboo flutes, repeating the same tune over and over, accompanied by the recurrent beating of a drum.

Orpí approached them and asked, "What be this dance, injun?"

"*Areyto*, Indian dance," said Araypuro, his eyes bulging out of their sockets.

Then our hero taught them a dance of his land, done in a circle, everyone holding hands, making little hops and gazing up at the moon.

"This dance is called Sardana."

"What a bore!" complained Araypuro. "I much prefer zarabandas, zambapalos, and chaconas! *Chumbamenea!*"

Seeing that they were all dancing like wild beasts, Father Claver wrote the following in his *Chronicles*:

> . . . and t'day the grand party twixt Indians and soldiers was celebrated, all conjointlee, and Doctor Juan Orpín put forthe the idea of a dance with many peoples all round & in circkler formation and round that cirkle there were four fires in the sine of the cross and the musicians didde play and the people leapt and ate magick grass and thus passt the lifelong night & all in attendunce felt content'd and Doctor Urpín, who also danced with his beloved dogge Friston, didst relate to the Indyans that the dance doth goe by the name Sardana and thuslee the Indians adopt'd it and made it their own, yet they didst Christen it The Dance of the Crazed Snake altho the whole kit & kaboodle was ekwal heathen for twere better to praye the Our Father.

"Be thou scriptulating again, Father?" asked Orpí, coming out of the circle. "Pray dance a while, Godly man!"

"I must confessor, milord Orpí, that I findeth these dances highly sinful," complained the Jesuit. "As the saying goes: Lead us not into Sardana, for it be mightily profane."

"Come now, where tis it written that one mustnt dance?"

"Back in 1552 twas banned in the *Liber Consolatus* of the city of Olot and Father Benet Tocco, Benedictine monk, Abbot of Montserrat, and Bishop of Girona, in 1573, did write edicts against dancing sardanas at the church, for it be a rite of witchesses."

"Now, Father, leave off the sermones. Would thee like to dance or not?"

The Jesuit, seeing that everyone was having fun except him, abandoned his *Chronicles* and, crossing himself a couple of times and hitching up the skirts of his habit, entered the throng of dancers as someone gave him some magic grass to eat. The festivities grew to such a joyous fever pitch—with the Jesuit dancing wildly, laughing and leaping—that the circle broke and they all took their partying to the street of New Tarragona, and not a soul ceased dancing during the entire blessed night.

# Chapter *XXII*

In which Joan Orpí and Father Claver
search for the treasure whilst engaging
in a debate on economics

Orpí was anxious to set in motion his enterprise, this New
Catalonia, for he was nearing fifty years of age and those
lands had yet to bear him any material fruits. All the petitions
he had sent to the King, asking for ships to allow him to do
business with the Peninsula and other neighboring regions in
the Americas, had been ignored and he now found himself
completely isolated. The industrial quantities of products
such as cacao, leather, and tobacco that those lands produced
had no way to travel, and that was an impediment to acquir-
ing financing to make New Catalonia prosper. Orpí named
Lieutenant Jeremies governor of recently inaugurated New
Tarragona and left him in charge, heading off on his trusty
steed Acephalus and followed by his dog, with Father Claver
and Araypuro on a pair of mules. They resolved to go find
Gregorio Izquierdo's treasure, which, according to their cal-
culations, couldn't be too far.

"Those nobles from the viceroyalties aim to halt mine

progress, bye legall or illegal means, and they ne'er shall cease untill they hath seiz'd our landes," lamented our hero. "Yet the trezure shall allow us to face up to such injustice. Perhaps purchase an entire shippe for trade with the Pininsulla."

"Be wary what ye wishe for," advised Father Claver, "for golde doth unhinge the wizest 'mongst menne."

"Ya dont say! I know it all too well, Father," complained Araypuro, "ole Massa here near nigh burn't me up right crispy fore it."

"Bee not unappeased, injun!" exclaimed Orpí. "That war a passing delirium. Now I comprehendest the utility of that golde, far fromme its initial purppose."

"Prithee explain," said Father Claver, his curiosity piqued.

"Let us suppose," began our hero, "that in these lands there war a man what wanted the selfsame as I, the right selfsame, and furthermore, he bore the name I once did have, Gregorio Izquierdo. Or more precise, I bore hizz name. Let us suppose that we sought the selfsame thing, our hopes identical, and we both call'd this thinge 'trezzure.' Very well, the question is whether the veritable Gregorio Izquierdo and I doth refer to the selfsame thinge when we speak of 'trezzer.' *Ex hypothesi*, our brains, while identic, thinke on different thinges when pronouncing that word. Gregorio Izquierdo, in thinking of the word 'trezzure,' thought of being able to live without working like a noblemen foreremore henceford. I, when thunking on dis very word, think of prosperating the entire territory of New Catalonia."

"Thine objective is true and thus honorable," said Father Claver. "Yet I know not how thou canst elude the royale dominion."

"The conquest hath passt into handes of private entrepeneurs," explained Orpí, "to whoms the costs defray'd must grant rights and prerogatives regarding the exploitation of the

Indians and the new territories. The gelded trezzer shall aid us in our tasks."

"To pay the Kings *anatas*?" asked the Jesuit. "Or mayhaps to create an Aristotelian-Thomist *autarkeia*?"

"Nay, to buyye shipps fore import-export!" replied our hero. "Mine intent is to create a region based on calculation and reason."

"Take heed, milord, for we alle must make an accounting with Our Lord on the day of Finall Judgment," warned Father Claver.

"Fear thee not for I be a learn'd lawyer and I canst defendd meself befor the courts, be they earthily or divine," said Orpí. "Furthermore, I hold noe evul in mine hart, tis the others what wish me harm."

"Hath thou lost thine Faith, milord?" said the priest, repeatedly crossing himself.

"I hath seen tribes what art not of ourn unclean world," said Araypuro.

"Shaddup, injun, thou turnst mine stomache," said Orpí, raising an index finger to his nose to request silence, not wanting to continue that conversation.

The weather had changed and now a solid rain fell on the three men, who struggled to advance along the muddy path. Father Claver, on his little burro, pulled a notebook from his satchel, placing the quill and inkwell on his lap, and jotted down the following in his *Chronicles*:

> . . . and Sir Urpín bade us speak no more and thusly put payd to the conversation. Then we climb'd arduous seeking a cave wherce suppos'd said treasure war. Yet having reach'd the pointe indicated neither Sir Urpín nor his Indian of labor encountered anything rezembling the treasure sought, tho' much smelling about by hiz dog didst ockur. Aformentioned episode made Sir

Urpín scream many sinfull werds & even hit his dog, what no blame hath in the matter, may the Lord hold 'im und keep 'im. And then, enraged at not finding said treasure, he chasd me and his Indian of labour all round the jungle, wishing to kille us both with his sward. But, fortunately, he regain'd his good sense just in the nick of tyme & then bust into teers like a wee child & the Indian and I hadd to console him verily like his blessed fathers. And then he wished to take his own lyfe with his owne sward and we had to grabbe him fore he couldst kille hisself right there & all on account of that blasted treasure & soon we three all werst crying like wimmin. Doctor Urpín then wanted to retrace our path and retornne home, but no befor leaving a sign in that place, thus he order'd his Indian of labor to done so, who took up a knife and mark'd a stone, thus and so:

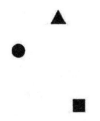

And then our lord Urpín made proffecy, vaticinium ex eventu, what said that in that land a cave and its treasure would be found by future generashuns, brought to these parts by a merchant in letters, alongside this field diary like an ancient scroll, what those who knoweth the language shall decipher with much effort. And that said, we three menne travelld down the mountain and returned to our belov'd New Catalonia, hands empty but hearts fill'd with joy for the treasure was safely stor'd in the mountains of . . .[149]

149. *i.e.* This fragment of Father Claver's chronicles is smudged beyond

"What be this mad passion for writing, Father?" asked Orpí, as they all headed down the mountainside.

"In case some day some one reads thine adventures, milord," replied the Jesuit. "The written word is the only way thee shalt bee remembered, for good or for ill."

As the three men passed a high plateau covered in dry brush, they came across a small settlement of colonists mixed with natives who, in that very moment, were celebrating some sort of Carnaval. They approached our hero to the sound of trumpets, cymbals, and flutes. Most were dressed as knights with strange names such as the Unfortunate Knight, the Knight of the Forests, and the Panther Knight. A man, dressed in black with (fake) gold flourishes and topped with a cavalier hat with a long feather plume, mounted on a horse adorned with a (fake) pearl-encrusted saddle, and accompanied by four pages dressed in striped uniforms, headed up the procession. He went over to an altar where simulated chivalrous feats were being performed. Then, from amid the crowd, materialized a character who fascinated Orpí and his companions. Father Claver, surprised, noted the following in his *Chronicle*:

> At that pointe the Knight of the Sorrowful Countenance Don Quixote of La Mancha appeared, searching for his Dulcinea, as natural and true to life as he be depicted in his book, and twas a great joy to beholde him. The knight-errant came on a skinny horse very much like his Rosinante. He was accompanyed by the priest and barber with their own suits and Princess Micomicona, as welle as his squire Sancho Panzo on his saddled ass. Don Quixotte approach'd an improvised altar wherce ther war

<hr/>

recognition in the original manuscript. Truly a pity, since surely the part that is missing would have given us the geographical coordinates indicating the location of the treasure.

sum jutges and Don Quixotte awarded a prize to Sancho Panza, and gaveth him instructions to lay said troffy at the feet of the mistress of 'is heart, Princess Dulcinea, beseated amongst the laydees at the reception. And erryone laughed and applaud'd.

"Incredible," exclaimed Orpí, as the carnavalesque character thrilled the audience, which shouted, clapped, and laughed like crazy. "Cervantes's character hath crosst the Atlantic! And to thinke that I mette that famous author!"

"And that be not all, milord," said one of the locals. "Tis sayd that the liver of the true Don Quixotte canne be found in Trujillo, in Perú."

"Yet . . . he is mere a literary character!" exclaimed Orpí in surprise.

"Mayhaps for thee," replied the local man. "For here we all suffer from a mite of oneirataxia, like poor ole Alonso Quijano."

That colorful incident worked to brighten our hero's existence and improve his mood, and thus, along with Araypuro and Father Claver, they spent that night in company of those affable locals, enjoying the festivities and a nice Tinta de Toro,[150] which all three friends drank happily, forgetting for a time their bad fortune at not having located the golden legend of the New World.

---

150. *i.e.* Wine imported from the Kingdom of Leon, famous for tolerating long voyages without arriving as vinegar.

## Chapter *XXIII*

In which is recounted a battle against the Dutch
and in which Orpí carries out a pharaonic labor

The day after the inauguration of New Tarragona, Governor Jeremies went running into Orpí's house, bellowing, "Milord, there be a shitton of Dutchmenne at the Unare making trobble . . . !"

And indeed, a troop of Dutchmen, who in that era were at war against the Kingdom of Castile, had disembarked on the beach of New Catalonia and were stealing salt from the salt pans at the delta of the Unare River. Orpí sent a messenger to request urgent aid from the noblemen of Cumaná and Cumanagoto, but there was no time. Our hero, adorned in a metallic cuirasse, his sword on the left side of his belt and a dagger on the right, resolved to head there with forty soldiers from New Barcelona, twenty from New Tarragona, and some fifty-odd Indians from various tribes, to engage in battle. When they arrived they found twenty hulks and five-hundred Flemish soldiers armed to the teeth.

"Let 'er rip, boys, fight these Flems to the very death!" ordered Orpí.

Shots hither and thither, the battle was bloody, and would have gone to the Dutch side, due to a sheer question of numbers, if not for the fact that a caravelle with an English flag happened to be passing by, and seeing the kerfuffle, joined in the battle alongside Orpí without thinking twice.

After the Dutch captain's death and the retreat of his troops back into the river, our hero offered his thanks to the English captain who'd come to his aid. The days that followed were a frenzy of trading merchandise between New Barcelona and the hold of the British ship, a highly profitable exchange for both sides: one sold cotton, tobacco, leather, and Venezuelan pearls, while the other sold oil, wine, cinnamon, and many other basic necessities that were much needed in New Barcelona.

Orpí struck up a friendship with a pleasant Swedish sailor, who went by the name of Jonas Jonassen Bronck,[151] who was on his way back from Jamaica and headed for North America, to the territory controlled by the Dutch West India Company. The two men shared a fondness for smoking and the gift of the gab. One evening, as they were sitting on the porch of Orpí's house, eating a papaya, Jonas pulled out some dried branches from a little bag and rolled a cigarette.

"What be thee smokin', sailor? Uat du iu smokin'?"

"Marijuana from Jamaica," said the man, who had three enormous dreadlocks hanging from his head. "This noted weed, as Shakespeare said, makes a journey in your head. Do ye wanna try? Fire it up, man, and inhale-exhale."

Orpí took a good long hit on the joint and suddenly found himself floating above his ranch and seeing everything through a strangely-colored lens. It even seemed to him that

---

151. *i.e.* A historical figure who traveled from Sweden to North America and settled by the Bronx River (which bears his name), in the state of New York.

his dog Friston was staring at him, his head cocked as if to ask, "You okay, master?"

"Lorde in Heaven, what a lonng strange trippe its be-iiin-niiin . . ." said Orpí when he returned from his psychotropic journey.

After smoking that wacky tabacky he felt depressed, since what with those new attacks by the Dutch to control the salt pans of the Unare, our hero had had no time to further the cause of New Catalonia. And if he had to depend on the aid of the Castilian administration, it was going to be a long haul, because they were harder and harder on him with each passing day. He explained all his concerns to Bronck, who—also high as a kite—had a madcap idea:

"Översvämning[152] the salt pans!" he said, gesturing with his hands to get the idea across.

"Gute aidiah!!" exclaimed Orpí who, after burning off a few more brain cells with some more tokes, had grasped the concept.

Our hero put into action the pharaonic project of flooding the salt pans so that no one would ever again have the crazy idea of trying to steal them. He notified all his allied indigenous tribes in the region and, in less than three days time, he already had more than five thousand Indians prepared at the entrance to New Barcelona. Jonas and his crew also offered to lend a hand. Everyone rolled up their sleeves and prepared to work together. They opened up a vast ditch from the Unare to the salt pans, with hoes and their bare hands. It was so vast that it could have held more than ten heads of cattle. The work got off to a bad start since it entailed leveling a part of the virgin forest and, on the very first day, a tree fell upon

---

152. *i.e.* Flooding, in Swedish.

two soldiers, killing them instantly. We have no record of the exact number of laborers involved, nor how many of them died of thirst, attacks by other tribes, or execrable exhaustion. Under the beating sun and over two months time, they all worked to expand the channel, digging out that reddish earth, amid caimans, boas, and carnivorous ants, making their way through the various clay stratifications along the morass. It was hard, back-breaking work and hundreds of Indians, whites, and blacks fell ill with fevers or enervation. But finally, one day, the river's water ran down through that wonder of artisanal engineering to the salt pans. That entire enormous promontory of smooth, sterile, violet rocks that extended in a display of mysterious geometric shapes, formed by the action of the ocean water, spirals and twisted barbs that looked like the surface of an unknown planet, were submerged forever beneath the river's surface. And, with that strategic move, Orpí was free from having to worry about any more Dutch incursions.

Once the epic task was completed, the festivities began in New Barcelona, complete with theatrical representations paying homage to Jonas Broncks and his invaluable help, who then continued on northward, until he reached New Amsterdam, near the island of Manhattan, where he bought some lands he named Broncksland. But that's a story for another day. When Orpí returned to his ranch, there on the table, he discovered that the Swede had left him his little bag filled with magic grass. As he lit up one of those magical cigarettes, under the watchful eye of his dog Friston, he saw a shadow behind the tree in his little garden. When he went out, armed with his sword, he found himself face to face with a man dressed in black who came rushing toward him, arm held aloft, brandishing his own sharpened blade. Luckily, Friston sank his teeth into the hitman's leg, and he fell, like a dead weight, to the ground. Once the mysterious man was captured and his wrists tied, Orpí interrogated him:

"I war just following orders . . ." he said, bleeding from the blows received during the interrogation. "But tis true, sir, that milord Domingo Vázquez de Soja and other criollo nobles from Santo Domingo and Caracas wish thee harm and t'wont end well, for they hath munch more power than thee."

The hitman was freed while our hero seriously reconsidered what to do about the criollo noblemen and the rest of the viceroyalties surrounding New Catalonia.

"For this I hath worked so many years in service to the Crowne? I doth refuse to allow New Catalonia to falle into the wrong hands. Cannot somethinge be done?"

# Chapter *XXIV*

In which our hero finds himself besieged by enemies
and realizes that history is an endlessly
repeating circular path

Well, yes, something was done. Not in the Americas, but
rather on the Iberian Peninsula. It was the year of our Lord
1640 and France declared war on King Philip IV in the well-
known Thirty Years War. The Spanish monarch strategically
situated his troops within the Principality of Catalonia, which
fueled the population's discontent, to the point that many
Catalans ended up rebelling against the royal army itself.

That remote political reversal in the distant fatherland
triggered unknown forces and devastating consequences
for the colonies across the ocean and, particularly, for New
Catalonia. Orpí's territory bordered New Andalusia, whose
old Spanish populations were abandoned and malnourished,
and so they gradually moved into New Barcelona, which was
growing with each passing day. That worried the Castilian
authorities in Caracas and Cumanagoto, who observed—with
a combination of envy, disgust, and stupefaction—how the
Catalan was growing strong in his region, which even—to top
it all off—bore the name Catalonia in a direct tribute to the

peninsular one. The governor of Cumanagoto, Arias Montero, was spurred on by his friend Vázquez de Soja to complain that everywhere Orpí "*sentaba Real*"[153] was soon filled with "slaves and outlaws." This calumny spread like wildfire through the Spanish nobility of the region. And all that was exacerbated by Orpí's legal fights to end the enslavement of Indians and Blacks, which the Venezuelan nobles felt impinged on their rights. Furthermore, our hero had engaged in trade with the English, considered heretics by the Castilian crown, which only hammered the point home. None of Orpí's efforts to protect the salt pans, construct canals, and make his region more prosperous and habitable for the profit of King Philip IV had done him a lick of good. Orpí and his name were completely surrounded by rumors, snares, lies, and letters back and forth filled with mortal loathing, unfounded envy, twaddle, and calumny amid a heat that poisoned the humors and a mugginess that made everything a sticky mess.

Our hero, seeing what was his lot, acted quickly. In a letter addressed directly to the King, he requested that Cumanagoto and the rest of New Andalusia be annexed to New Catalonia, which was much more prosperous and gentrified than the former. He received no reply. Considering the precedent of the original Catalonia, the one on the Peninsula, neither the King, nor a single noble, nor those on the Council of the Indies were now looking kindly upon the project of New Catalonia. Quite the contrary, in fact. What those nobles were wanting, actually, was for Orpí's lands to be annexed to New Andalusia. The campaign against our hero brought together the most fantastic gathering of illustrious noblemen in Santo Domingo and Caracas, who all saw the Catalan as a secessionist danger to crush.

---

153. *i.e.* Settled new population in a territory.

"These noblemenne be worst than bloodsucking mosquitoes and cannibalous ants!" complained Orpí. "There be no way to get them off mine back. They be greedfull and sellfish, with some sort of institutional delirium against me, despite the fact that I be as pro-King Philip as they art, if not more. All this gluttony for land merely rotts souls."

"We shall get nowhere with that pessimistic logick, master," said Araypuro.

"Life is but a theater, dear injun. And just menne such as I, lemme telle ya, allways get the short straw in this crazed *trompe-l'*œil. Tis better just to dream: tis free and no-one gets hurt."

"Man does not live by dreams alone."

"True, my injun. Yet all this greed for conquest hath only broughten me great misfortune," said Orpí, as his blood rose to his face. "Belieffeeme, man wasteth away laboring for these noblemen, who live off the fruits of others, and miss not a chance to get backstabby. And I, somehows, musteth extricate mineself from all this or I shall end up ill, for I am near nigh fifty-one & tortur'd by dis 'ernimated disc."

Araypuro tried his darnedest to cheer him up, but Orpí could now only see the futility of all his efforts.

"All these yeers of travell & wandering hath made mee see how wrongheaded mine venture hath been. All the things of this worlde be mirror doubbbles, to infinity and beyonde. Godde be prais'd, yet ne'er shall He forgive mineself."

"I don't know about God, massa," said Araypuro. "But I forgive you."

"Thank thee, my injun, yet it be not enuf. If thou couldst see the lyes writ against me by those sonnes of snaggletoothed whorebuckets," swore Orpí, pulling out a stack of letters. "The inhabitents of Cumanagoto in New Andalusia, afeared of their governor, keep sending complaints to the King, difaming mee publickly. Listen to these callous fiends: 'Aforementioned Mr. Orpín, sinister to de core, never hath done had any nown wealth and thusforth and so he approprimagated the fals name of Gregorio Izquierdo.' And what bout this one: 'He hath disappropriate dealings with the Indian ladys and even rite befor the Indian mennes theyselfs & he dances impiouslously round fyres with the natifs' . . . canst thou belief this? And, as if that warn't bad enuf, theyve the gallish balls to pulleth out the olde canard that they be 'Spaniards & loyal vassals of Your Majesty whilst said conquistador be a native o'the Catalan nation, and as such we groweth quite alarm'd, be he not another Aguirre, in whomse footsteppes he be followeing!' Sooth be told, these criollo noblemen art greatly enviegious and wish to have New Barcelona under their control. Desire be a slipperee thing and everyboddy want what others doth possess. Domingo Vázquez de Soja desireth mine desire, which is to saye mine very viceroyalty and the usufruct of all mine labor. On mine life, if they want a piece of mee, they verily knowe where to finde mee!"

After that speech, our hero headed off with his dog Friston to rest at his ranch, because he'd gotten his blood pressure up. However we, at any rate, must proceed with this story, which continues in the following manner:

# Chapter *XXV*

## In which Orpí's patience runs out and he rebels against the injustices of the criollo noblemen

With the Reapers' War in Old Catalonia, everything took on a doubly dramatic edge due to the distance. But events taking place in the Principality could easily turn against our Joan Orpí's personal pet project. The increasingly skimpy loads of gold and silver being exported from America to the Court in Madrid had intensified the hatred toward the rich, lush region of New Catalonia. Every day news arrived of Administrators and Officials landing from Madrid with serious expressions and dire faces, carrying mysterious orders to the criollo noblemen against our hero. And as if that weren't worrisome enough, he also knew that some of his admirals had betrayed him, switching sides for the promise of ignoble gold. While Orpí's complaints to the monarch were systematically disregarded, the criollo noblemen of Caracas had begun a brazen policy of boycotting New Catalonia, and now refused to sell or trade any products with the region.

Our hero's solitude increased in proportion to his growing historical significance. Revolted by all that plotting, Joan Orpí reacted by putting the final touches on something he'd been cooking up for some months. The political shift that events in the Principality of Catalonia had taken had emboldened our hero, who was now seriously considering how to break off relations with the Crown of Castile.

"I canst even!" he shouted one day, losing his temper in front of his generals, in the offices of the War Council. "If those dogs of the Crown cometh back yon with their redde tape and estupid laws, I shall knocke them all on their shit-covered arses! I hath not gone bougie nor calm'd, but rather I be prepared for watsoever trouncing of those jobbernowls."

"Do not blaspheme, milord," said Father Claver, trying to calm him down. "Let not the Devil guide thine steps in lyfe."

"Basta wit' the sermons, Father," Orpí replied, as he passed an *arbitrio*[154] to the priest. "I know fulle well that our two-bit monarch has sette his sights on New Catalonia. We doth generate too much wealth compar'd to the other Venezuelan vice-royalties, and the Crown is bankrupt. They art not prepar'd to relinquish the golden gooser eggs. However, they shalt not strippe me of it so readily!"

"We must create state structures, establishe a strategic planne, self-gobern, redefine our cultural autonomy in a separatist State and beginne the process of sovereignty!" advised Captain Jeremies, nationalistically.

"I think we should leave all that be in hands of the Court . . ." suggested Captain Octopus.

"And, if possible, without waging war . . ." added Captain Sedeño de Albornoz.

"There be no tyme for any of all that!" said Orpí, banging

---

154. *i.e.* Name given, in the first half of the seventeenth century, to the fiscal reform treaties designed to save Spain from its economic ruin.

his fist on the table. "Those nobles hath left me broke as a joke and tis not funnily! There be tyme only for brave resolutions, deare friends, and now I must listen to mine heart and not mine head. Look out the window: the Neocatalans art hoppin' mad o'er the boycott impos'd by King Philipito and the criollo noblemen of New Andalusia."

It was certainly true that the city of New Barcelona was filled with antimonarchical refugees from everywhere. One of them was just then singing a song about the political situation, making jabs and taking swipes at Governors, Corregidors, Mayors, Justices in the Audiencias of the Courts of the Indies, the royal Administrators and Officials, and—generally—with every accomplice of the Crown:

> ♪♫ We art so weary of the King ♪♫
> his coin obsession it doth sting
> False justice his perogative
> We doth find it pejorative
> So no more señor nice guy
> Long live our fatherland!
> Refrain: Which fatherland?
> New Catalonia, of coooourse!
> For every king be a tyrant
> Our new nation sempervirent
> And barring any sleight of hand
> We shall never leave our homeland
> Long live our fatherland!
> Refrain: Which fatherland?
> New Catalonia, which else?

"The reapers hath mutinied in the original Catalonia, we should verily be apt to push back all these Espanyolades," said Orpí, lighting his pipe after listening to the ditty. "The tyme hath come to challenge the Court. I shant allow those green-eyed puttocks to take what I hath earned over thee course of so many adventures. They can verily sard off!"

"They shall send in the troops!" said General Octopus.

"Not if we act speedy and industrious," reflected Orpí. "The Crown is in neede of menne to wage war with the French and the Catalans, they shant spare many contingents in the defense of a remote colony. If we challenge the nobles of Caracas and Cumaná, we hath gots a chance."

"Thou dost venture most high," lamented Jeremies.

"They shall slay us like wee mosquitoes!" said Captain Scourge.

"Tis easy to see thou hath read myriad imaginative books . . ." added Father Claver, grabbing the cross that hung down his chest. "Challenging the Crown is suicide! Furthermore, it entails losing thine human condition, sullying thine soul, and becoming cruelle."

"Have faith, Father," said our hero. "Chance to die every last one, yet we shall winne fame and honor. Tis better to be in disaccord with the entire world than in disaccord with one-selfe, as Plato said."

"Dost thou ween that the Catalans of the Principality or the American larva shall give two hoots if thou be Joan Orpí or Pepet dels Horts as they devour thine cadaver in the sepulture?" asked Father Claver. "As far as I hath learnt the wurms hath no awareness of 'istory and couldst care no less for 'eroic ephemerides. Repeat not the brouhahas on the Pininsula."

"I no longer hath a thinge to do with the Pininsula," exploded Orpí. "New Catalonya is mine sole fatherland and its virgin taigas, mine home. Gather everyone! Bring them all to New Barselona! The tyme hath come to appointe an army!"

Orpí had a triumphant halo as he and his captains traveled to every end of New Catalonia, gathering up all the tribal leaders in the region, promising them legal citizenship in New Catalonia. They hailed him proudly and aggressively prepared for war to the rhythm of their tam-tam drums. Soon five hundred men assembled in New Barcelona, armed with harquebusses, swords, daggers, bows, and arrows and all sorts of killing devices. The spies of New Catalonia, trained in the art of occultation, went from province to province to learn the criollo noblemen's plans and, while they were at it, conspiring the secret revolution among the antimonarchical comrades gathered in private taverns, carrying secret missives under their hats, hiding instructions that were passed from hand to hand in dark alleys or the depths of the jungle, convincing discontents stealthily behind a barn, in the back rooms of any town, in the caverns beside the cliffs, in clandestine speakeasies filled with soldiers of fortune surrounded by large clouds of tobacco smoke, beneath tables filled with people to impregnate the rebel seed in their minds and nourish local revolutionary attitudes where least expected.

One day, our hero went to Santo Domingo in disguise to meet up in secret with Governor Diego de Arroyo, the nobleman who had helped him ascend in his military career, and seek out an alliance.

"Urpín, thou dost alreddy know how much I value thee, but what you proppose is crazytalk," said the Governor. "Rumor tells me that thou art forming militias with hopeless malefactors, and fans of infamy & crime to wage war against the Crowne like a Pizarro or a mad Aguirre, be that sooth?"

"Some say Aguiree was a devill, others consider him the first great liberator rebel of the Americas. Yet I be neither one nor the other, Governor Arroyo, but rather a simple businessman who doth not desire the intervention of the state when it merely intervenes to rob what doth not belongeth to it. I be not guided by any external aut'ority, rather I demand the unconditional freedom of my own self-rule."

"I understand," responded the Governor. "However I canst not give thee the alliance that ye seek. As fond as I be of thee, and as loathsome I findeth Domingo Vázquez de Soja and his band of noblemen, my loyalty is to the King."

"I too understand," said Orpí, tipping his hat. "Then all that be left is to thank thee heartily for all thee hath done, Arroyo, for thine stance now maketh thee mine enemee. It remainth to be seen who shall laff last."

## Chapter XXVI

### In which Araypuro earns a Chapter
### all to himself
### in this bizarre story

While New Catalonia prepared for war, Araypuro was swimming contentedly all by his lonesome one day, in the waters of a bright blue stream, when he suddenly spied a squadron of royal soldiers amid the jungle's trees.

"How goes it, mestisso?" called one of them from the shore.

"Caint complain," he said, practicing the crawl nonchalantly.

"Splishitty splashitting like a caiman?"

"Sumpin like dat . . ."

Without further ado and just for the fun of it, the squadron charged and shot their harquebusses at him. Yup, you heard right.

"Mudderfuggers . . . these bros are lookin' for a fight!"

Araypuro seethed with hatred as he made his way out of the water, doing the butterfly stroke. Then he started running through the jungle as the royal soldiers chased him the way one chases a game animal of very high caloric value. And Araypuro seethed even more. All told they ran a league and a half. And then they kept running. In the pursuit through the forest, they were all attacked by stingetty-sting-sting red ants, gonorrheaic ticks, and somewhat murderous hornets. One of the soldiers shot his weapon and a bullet, smoking with diabolical gunpowder, dodged a surprised bird, coconut palms, vines, and couple of carnivorous plants that whistled out an exclamation, until finally landing on Araypuro's right ear. He howled with pain, grabbed a round rock and *catacrack!* threw it at that same soldier who, with helmet and all, fell to the ground loosening sphincters.

"Bullseye! Na-na na-na poo-poo!"

That infuriated the soldiers even more, and they ran more rapidly through the brush, while Araypuro kept looking back instead of ahead of him, until he found himself at another stream where, just then, an Indian lass with a marvelous smile was washing her braids.

"Allo? Who be this impertinent jackanapes?" she asked, frightened.

"Yoooo . . . what dey do, jit! No time for all that!" exclaimed Araypuro. "Da bearded abominations are coming!"

And so they both, holding hands and holding their breath, dove beneath the water and swam amid wiseacre anacondas, dwarf whales, catfish, tambaquis, and grinning piracucus. The soldiers attempted to grab them, but one who was bleeding from all the bramble scratches ended up devoured by three hundred dancing piranhas, while another spasmed and fell, electrocuted by a very rare, fluorescent electrical eel. They ceased their pursuit. Meanwhile, the pair of swimmers continued diving and the Indian lass with her braids sang, aquatic and divine, to convince the river to not take their lives:

♪♫ How! Beloved amapuche riverlife ♪♫
Who ever give-um and never take-um
Embrace-um us with thine life waters
Pure spirits and good vibraciones, dale?
Lead-um us not to macumba happy hunting ground
For many moons, make-um us heap glad
Oh riverlife, may thine waters protect-um
Take-um to pure sun gardens, hey!

A giant river turtle who had listened to her little song invited them aboard his shell, allowing them to traverse the underwater algae and make it back up to the surface, far from all danger. As they dried off inside an enormous sun-flower-house, the Indian lass formally introduced herself amid real tears:

"Me name Ta-Ipí and me tribe, the Tarumba, live here since birth of sun, among flowers and birdies, but now paleface come—what thee call Castilian, destroy our jungle and our all. Very distressing."

"Please cry not, fine squaw," said Araypuro. "Let us expel them forthwith!"

Ta-Ipí, seeing that Araypuro was fearless and brave, wanted to play with him, and he did not object seeing as he was quite taken with the princess. They ate guanabanas and chirimoyas, flown in by the aviary fauna of troupials and Pantepui thrush, and they snuggled up beneath the leaves and branches they were gifted by the Samán and Camoruco trees. And thus they spent the evening, sighing, kissing, and giggling, until they fell asleep in each other's arms, superhappy and head over heels.

"Me feel all cuchurucho," he said.

"Me right there with you, my hallaca," she added, making almondy eyes.

When they had finished their playing for the time being, Ta-Ipí accompanied her new friend to her village and asked her father, King Ma-Naa-Cri, for permission to marry Araypuro. The King, seeing that he was a mestizo, wrinkled his nose. But the Queen Mother, Tra-La-Rà, who was really the one wearing the pants, consented. The wedding was celebrated that very night and the entire village was invited. The party lasted for hours and Araypuro was happy: "Oye, broder, what a shindig! Y'all sure knowe how to throw a getty that never stops! But . . . there still be a bululú of soldiermen out there, and they do not have pure love in their hearts for us."

To put paid to that farce for once and for all, the entire tribe armed themselves to the teeth and went out to face up to the soldiers. With their arrows tipped in mortal poison they forced the Castilians to retreat to the border of New Catalonia. Araypuro fought like one of the tribe, finally winning the affection of his king-in-law, who still wasn't sure about the victory:

"Will palefaces return, hero-in-law?" asked King Ma-Naa-Cri.

"Supposably. And in spades. We must now leave for where my boss waits. There ye shall have protection and live in peace."

"And what shall become of tree and river and piracucu, which give all and to which we owe all? How shall we live without our motherjungle? What care me about paleface wars?"

"While the worlde keepeth turning, all thinges change . . . oh king-in-law. The bearded palefaces be trippin' wid this here gold and land, and they not goin' nowhere. Hasta the most buzzard fopdoodle among us will suffer at their hands. Soon there shall be no jungle left for no-one."

And thus the village of the Tarumba packed up and moved to the recently founded New Barcelona. When Juan Orpí saw Araypuro, he exclaimed, "Wherefore hath thou been at, injun?"

"Do not getteth all angry bird on me, massa. The spirits hath gifted me a wife . . . and I put a ring on it!" he said, introducing Princess Ta-Ipí.

"Commendations! Thou wasteth no time!"

"Dassit. Why live in this worlde without love?"

"Verily," said Orpí. "And who be these: Tagares, Tasermas, Tozumas, Guarives, Guaiqueríes, Chacopatas, Cocheimas, Palenques, or Caracarares?"

"Tarumbas. Not Catholics, not Baptists, not passive, not addictive . . . very active. Cuz it don't matter if you're black, Indian, white, or yellow polkadot. We all be together on mine piano keyboard here in this macroterritory, therehence we musteth live in peace and harmony."

"Dulcet words, injun," said Orpí. "But if thou hast wag'd war against the soldiers of Vázquez de Soja in Neocatalan landes, that meaneth that the final battle approacheth, and tis too late for all else. The Tarumbas & their King be welcomed hither, there be room for all who aid in our fight."

King Ma-Naa-Cri swore friendship to Joan Orpí and the Tarumbas were soon beloved within the New Barcelona community. Araypuro and Ta-Ipí looked deeply into each other's eyes and, after sighing, retired to play their version of the rumble in the jungle, all blessed evening long.

## Chapter XXVII

In which the war between men and the battle
between Heaven and Earth confound Joan Orpí

During those days our hero was tense with nerves. He paced
around the round table of his War Council, stopping in front
of his officers, who were perusing broadsides that announced
a more-than-likely imminent civil war between New Catalonia
and its neighboring viceroyalties. Orpí had an army of five hundred men, who were satisfactorily trained but poorly armed.
Their entire arsenal consisted of harquebusses, swords, daggers, native bows and arrows, and a few rusty cannons. They
managed to cover all the vulnerable points on the coast and
in the jungle by erecting fortifications for the defense of their
small homeland.

The criollo noblemen of Santo Domingo ordered a royal
commission be sent to mediate the conflict. When the members of the commission arrived at the Council office, they
found our hero sweaty and with his hair awry, while his dog
Friston snarled and scratched at the fleas on his scruff.

"Negotiate thy surrender anon & thine lyfe & that of thine
citisens shall be pardouned & granted preeminence," advised
the Commissioner. "The King hath decreed that thee shall be

ceded an *encomienda* that shall allow thee and thine captains to live like kings in thine *haciendas* in Caracas or Cumanagoto, and thou couldst even return to the Peninsula, to thine home, and retire as a gentlemann to live off the fatt of the lande . . . with riches few menn hath ere seen!"

"I refuse to negotiate!" bellowed Orpí. "Tis precisely the institution of the *encomienda* what shelters the Crown's policy of slavery! If thou dost think that I shall sell out to thine King like a veritable strumpet thou bestest think agin . . . I be the slave of no man!"

"Well then prepare to die," warned the Royal Commissioner, "for I seeth not much of an armee to protect thee in this city."

"Mindeth thine selfsame beeswax, Commissioner. Tis sooth I hath few men yet they be all devoted to a cause, and if they perish they shall do so with honesty & justyce, and it be not thy place to call their honor into cuestion. Now, get thee to helle!"

Our hero's speech had been clear, concise, well-delivered, without excessive rhetoric, and the soldiers applauded as the Commissioner galloped off amid hoots and whistles from the Orpian troops and fierce barking from his dog Friston.

"Those serfs of the King wish to scare us, however I canst telle ye now they shant achieve said goal," said Orpí. "Altho' tis indeed sooth that we be four-hundred against four t'ousand."

Two weeks later they heard the news: the noblemen of Cumaná had gathered up an army and were coming across the border of New Catalonia, advancing toward the capital of New Barcelona, flooding the surrounding mountains with armed men. War was nigh. Our hero went out into the streets of the city, ordering his lieutenants to gather the troops. Some soldiers, however, impelled by fear, had fled to the Castilian side the night prior, waving a white flag. Our hero realized that he was leading into certain death soldiers who had too long hence become farmers, and farmers who had never been soldiers. It was a war lost before it even began. Depressed, Orpí was about to tell them all to return to their homes and await surrender when, suddenly, from the beach, a ship fired its signal cannons. Everyone ran to their weapons but when they reached the beach, they found it was merely an old, decrepit boat with patched sails, like one of those ghost ships in pirate stories. At the stern was a small man waving hello.

"Triboulet!" exclaimed Orpí happily.

They set out their small boats and soon Triboulet the Dwarf and his entire gang of gap-toothed freebooters, their skin gleaming with sundry diseases, stepped onto the beach and limped over to our hero and his army.

"Didst thou think I wouldst miss this soiree?" said the dwarf.

"Helles to the nay. Yet thine hundred freebooters shant suffice to defeat the enemee."

Having said that, from the depths of the jungle came the terrible shrieks ("yeeeee-haaaa!") of the Lionzas, led by Queen María Lionza and Martulina the Divina, who now arrived on wild horses, nude as ever and armed with bows and arrows. Behind them came various tribes such as the Caribes and the Cimarron community, captained by Estebanico the Blackamoor. They had all come to offer their sworn loyalty to New Catalonia. Our hero straightaway granted them the same standing as VIP citizens.

"Wee soldier boy of mine heart," said María Lionza. "For the first time we shall fight alongside men, however this shall be the expection, not the norme."

"I verily appreciate, mine queen, thine ferocious aid," said Orpí, kneeling before her while Martulina the Divina, beside him, winked complicitly.

Our hero organized his attack formations, placing his captains at the head of each detachment, while an insistent rain fell increasingly harder. It was typical for those lands to be besieged each year by a cyclone from the coasts of Mexico that laid waste to everything in its path like some sort of collective purge. The fishermen had officially announced the impending cyclone, and it was approaching land. As Orpí trotted hither and thither atop Acephalus, organizing trenches and advising his soldiers, he found Father Claver deep in prayer, standing in the middle of the street, staring up at the sky.

"Father, art thou quite right?" asked our hero.

"Betwixt Heaven & Earthe there be much invisible to the human eye," said the Jesuit, pointing toward the ocean. "Divine punishment approacheth!"

Everyone turned to look at the Atlantic and saw ten columns of water forming over the ocean's surface, heading toward dry land. The wind howled monstrously and made the churchbells chime out of rhythm. There was no time to protect the homes and livestock. Spirals of air and salty rainwater came down from the sky and crashed to the ground, shaking doors and windows as everybody ran to prepare for battle, which was announced by the enemy troops' signal cannon. Domingo Vázquez de Soja's army had arrived at the gates of the city. Enemy cannons were soon launching their terrible balls, and terror gripped those beneath the projectiles falling harder and harder upon the streets of New Barcelona, hammering the roofs of houses, collapsing walls, perforating stone and wood, sending balconies and double doors flying through the air, bouncing down the street and rolling, between cracks of thunder, into anything and everything. Each new round was a butchery of bodies turned cadavers. A scent of discharged gunpowder swathed the city and dried out the throats of the people running helterskelter, breaking formation. The fires produced by the bombing spread throughout the entire city, and as most of the homes had roofs made of braided leaves and fibers, they burned by the dozens. Orpí, atop his loyal Acephalus, with his cape soaring behind him and one hand clamped down on his hat, rode all over the city gathering his soldiers and emboldening the cowards, amid that cataclysmic setting. More than a thousand but less than two thousand armed men and women awaited the enemy troops: blacksmiths, butchers, jewelers, prostitutes, monks, soldiers, scholars, and vagabonds gritted their teeth over the impending combat.

Twas shortly after midnight when the squadrons of royal soldiers entered the city brandishing their musketoons. The two sides came face to face. Orpí guiding his, and Domingo Vázquez de Soja leading the royal army, which was much better armed and more numerous. The two men's gazes met and they scrutinized each other's faces for any symptom of weakness or disillusionment. While the two armies awaited the order to charge, a silence had imposed itself atop the rain and the heavy winds from the north.

"Unleash the beast!" screamed Orpí, lifting his saber over his troops as his voice boomed across the plain and his war cry blended with Friston's barking. Or perhaps it was the dog's barking that sounded like his voice. Man and beast had both influenced each other.

Before either of the two armies moved an inch, and after a few moments in which time and motion seemed to have stopped, an immense bellowing was heard advancing along the streets of New Barcelona. Suddenly, a diabolical wind picked them all up and dragged them: the cyclone was touching down in full force. Several columns of whirling air came down from the heavens and swept up everything in their path. Soldiers rolled along the ground, houses collapsed, horses neighed as they floundered, eyes panicked. Those who could fled and hid in the jungle as from the heavens rained down pieces of beams, roofs, glass, wood, doors, and windows, and a moment came when the entire ground trembled, opening up a rift that shook the church belltower and, as the bell sounded amid the roaring winds, the tower cracked and fell, crushing some soldiers beneath it. Father Claver and a few Jesuits witnessed the spectacle, their arms outstretched like the savior on the cross, observing it all like an illustration of the End of Times. Everything was dragged, pushed, rolled, thrust forward by the mercilessly inclement weather, and the cyclone's strength didn't wane until everything was well and properly smushed, flattened, and razed.

A few hours later, it seemed the army of clouds in the sky decided to break file and retreat, following the wind. The cyclone also seemed to pacify, fading in increasingly weaker and sporadic gusts as from the sky fell only a harmless, cold, intolerably sweet rain. Hundreds of inert bodies rested in the rubble of New Barcelona, and the royal army—or what was left of it—had withdrawn before ever attacking. Peace reigned, after so much raging weather.

"*Chumbamenea*! We won!" shouted Araypuro, who had spent the entire evening hidden inside a wine barrel playing with Ta-Ipí.

"Do not believeth yond, injun," said Orpí, "for those noblemen shall anon return with an army double grand. We hath birthed a stillborn New Catalonya. They shall hang me for insurrection and thee, for following me. I surrender."

"Yeah, no . . . thou canst poop our fiesta now, literally. We mustnt abandon ourn ranchito, master," insisted Araypuro.

"Hath thee beenst smoking mine magick herbs, injun? Dost thou ween the Castilians shall stop here? Thou be wide-eyed & artless! All what hath been blighted today shall pass to the possession of the Crown. Leave aside thine folly and tell everybody to return home and pray forgive me for mine sinnes. I ne'er wish'd harm upon a soul, mine aspiration war to build a more meritorious worlde."

"Go forth and build it somewhere else! Whither thou goest, we all shall go."

"Whyfore doth I dearly ween that tis I who allways follows thine orders, when in sooth it oughtest be precisely versa and vice?" asked Orpí warily.

"For I be thine lackey, furthermore I be so by free obligation."

Orpí, spurred on by Araypuro, organized the exit from the flattened city. They built stretchers to transport the wounded and, with no time to bury all their dead, they left that ghost city *en masse*: Caribes, Lionzas, colonists, freebooters, and Cimarrons, amid tears of sadness, traveling deep into the darkness of the virgin forests until they disappeared forevermore from those lands belonging to the Crown. Once Orpí and his motley crew were gone, New Catalonia was finally annexed to New Andalusia by royal decree, just as the criollo noblemen wanted. New Barcelona was dismantled and as for New Tarragona, it was abandoned, and its wooden houses were soon overtaken by ants and fungus. And thus, in that brusque, stupid, and indecent way, Joan Orpí's dream of founding a New Catalonia in the New World drew to a close. Or did it? Dear readers, do not rush to judgment. Dear critics, accuse us not of a facile *deus ex machina*, for the final Chapter will put all things in their right place, as called for in a fine adventure of these characteristics.

## Chapter XXVIII

In which, in this here final Chapter, Joan Orpí's death and New Catalonia's final destiny are revealed

We could very well have titled this book *The Outlandish Peregrinations of Joan Orpí*, since our hero spent half his life on the road, both on the Iberian Peninsula and in the New World, and we beg leniency for any errors of our pen, whose ink flows with the kind goodness and clever wit of its author as our story nears its end.

Joan Orpí, dressed in the finery of the Guaiquerí Indians and riding bareback on his loyal Acephalus and accompanied by his faithful dog Friston, headed up that final desperate, desgeographied expedition, deep into the heart of the thick jungle where no white man had ever set his stank feet, fleeing everything. More than six hundred people—men, women, and children—wounded by the cyclone and the bullets of the Spanish army, followed him for months, advancing up the mountain and down the mountain in their adventure north into uncharted territory. One fine day, the expedition came across a particularly green and florid area, made fertile by the gifts of a nearby volcano and river.

"Holey Saint Pancras!" exclaimed Captain Scourge when he laid eyes on that beautiful landscape. "Is this is or is this aint a veritable Paradise on earth?"

"Veritably," agreed Orpí. "And thusly I name this place Saint Pancras of Paradise, and here we shall found the Brand-new New Catalonia."

Orpí left a quarter of his expedition members there to lay in crops and begin a new life, with Captains Octopus and Scourge in charge, along with Triboulet the Dwarf, his free-booters and his Homunculus, while the rest continued along the banks of the Antuvi River to a red field where poppies happily sprouted, surrounded by imposing mountains.

"Here, amid these fancyful mountains and this valley of fresh spryngs, we shall found skools," said Orpí, daydreaming. "And teech Civill Law to all the Indians, as I learnt in Ole Catalonia, so they may defend themselfs from the injustices of this lyfe."

"I swear to thee I shall," said General Jeremies. "Twill be the most rheumily intellecktchuell acaddemy ere seen!"

"Jesus, Orpí! Mayhaps building a monastery be more urgent," ordered Father Claver.

"Monastery and academy," ordered Orpí, "both places art ideal for the habitus of study and contemplation."[155]

Then the expedition arrived to a valley filled with black rocks, which our hero named the Valley of the Bronx, in honor of Jonas Broncks, the Swede who had helped him in the liberation of the Unare salt pans. Captains Jeremies and Sedeño de Albornoz stayed behind there, along with Estebanico the

---

155. Here we see the birth of what would become the University of Saint Jeremies, although it first began, according to Father Claver's wishes, as a monastery. In the early twentieth century the building was destroyed by a missile during the Great War of the Thirty Tyrants. It would not be rebuilt as a university campus until 1946.

Blackamoor and his Cimarrons, as well as the Lionzas, with María Lionza and Martulina the Divina, who soon forsook their matriarchial exclusivity to join forces with those men. Finally, the expedition arrived at the frontier where the Castilian Crown's property ended, there by the mouth of the Antuvi River. From that point on the landscape and ocean were unknown. The region, perfect for agriculture, was filled with fruit trees, and fields of fresh grass so pleasing to the sight and so perfumed with the scent of wildflowers. Seeing that the area stimulated everyone's five senses, Orpí decided to establish his city there.

"Pero, like, what shld it bee call'd this time: New Barselona, Brand-new New Barselona, Ultra-Mega-New Barselona?" asked Araypuro sarcastically.

"Shaddup, injun, thou giveth mee a migraine. Twill be callt just Barselona, for the previous one no longer exists in mine mind. I hath no past, merely future."

For our hero did not want to reproduce the rational world he had already left behind, but rather forge an authentic jungle city. He founded it in a virginal *tabula rasa*, a marginal space free of tariffs, laws, and borders. When it came time to establish the configuration of the new city, Orpí sketched lines that weren't always straight, but more often curves that wound back upon themselves, and the engineers and architects were incredibly stressed out trying to follow his antigeometric blueprints. As a result, the new-new Barcelona ended up being a hieroglyphic of streets that led nowhere, inverted bridges, stairs that returned to the same place they started, and squares with no exits or entrances. Everything in that small city grew and multiplied organically, like a fungus, with no sort of logical planning. Farmers, office workers, shopkeepers, and customers frequently lost their way and often people would be spotted wandering with no particular destination, their eyes lost in the distance; when asked where they were headed, they had already forgotten. And in spite of it all, Orpí felt at home in that supremely antirational artificial homogeneity. In a matter of few weeks the town was bursting with life, families, and prosperous bartering businesses, with garden patches beside the river that were blooming green, relationships between white men and Indians that were improving, and our hero smiled happily seeing that he had devoted his best years and efforts to building that ultimate nation and that in the end it was bearing fruit. He must have done something right, he thought, over the course of that turbulent existence of his.

For a few years, Orpí lived in relative tranquility in that place and spent his days puttering in his private garden patch and long hours of reading that kept him amused, interspersed with walks with his dog Friston. Araypuro, who had a small ranch with his wife Ta-Ipí, studied Catalan and took up painting, devoting many hours to an enormous canvas depicting the most important episodes that he and Orpí had lived through—the kerfuffles with the tribes in the jungle, the Virgin of Montserrat's appearance, the founding of the first New Barcelona, the whole treasure affair, their trip to the Iberian Peninsula—immortalizing their adventures in an eternal manner.[156] And as for Father Claver, his days were spent finishing his *Arte*, the multilingual dictionary translating Catalan into Guayquerí and other local languages, and putting the finishing touches on his *Chronicles* of the conquest.

Everyone seemed to now be living in peace and harmony in that new secret territory, but as so much adventure can't be good for one's health, one evening Joan Orpí felt himself

---

156. *i.e.* Here we see the author (or authors) complying with the Horatian simile of *ut pictura poesis*, in which literature and painting are placed on an equal plane.

ailing and collapsed to the ground. Fierce fevers attacked our hero. His skin had turned pale, his belly swollen, his tongue black, and his wide-open eyes bulged at the very Gates of the Apocalypse. He lay prostrate in a bed as Father Claver acted as his doctor, performing two or three bloodlettings on our hero without a miracle. He delivered his definitive verdict to Orpí's captains:

"He is headed to the better place of daisy-pushing."

Joan Orpí felt his life slipping away and everyone in New Catalonia was of heavy heart. The sorrowful news traveled through all the tribes in the new territory like a flash of lightning and soon hundreds of people had come to Barcelona to pray in front of our hero's home, bringing palm leaves and lit candles, and watch over the dying man. All his captains came, the Ya-no-mama and all the other tribes, Martulina the Divina came, as did Queen María Lionza, Triboulet the Dwarf, and his freebooters. No one failed to show up. Some brought incense and aromatic plants to see if they could cure him. Others intoned strange prayers that were said to have extraordinary powers and even the Cimarrons, with Estebanico the Blackamoor dressed in white, sang in unison, decapitated a rooster, and held it aloft so that blood poured out, in an attempt to distract Death from his rightful duties.

Surrounded by his friends, Orpí spoke to Araypuro, who kneeled beside him, whimpering.

"Be not sad, injun, we all must go when it be our tyme," our hero said. "Mine *bajukaya*,[157] as thou callst it, be in the toilet."

"Pero, master! If thee injestest the *guarynara*, the sacred wood, perhaps it will cure the French disease, master," advised Araypuro, in perfect Catalan. "I've also made thee a

---

157. *i.e.* health

remedy employing *aranto*, from the *ojarasin* family."

"Leave off the balderdash & poppycock, injun, none o that will cure what ails me. Tis the anguishes I've suffered over the course of this life that slay me! There be no point to so much worry, nor art fame & honors worth the pain, for at the end of life all I hath to show for it be the four hairs on mine head. I forgive all the Castilian noblemen for all their grudges and may all those I've wounded or killed forgive mee as well. And now heed my counsel, Araypuro: bee happy and do not thinke too much, thou shallt live longer. And as thou hath been loyal, not as a serf but as a true bosom buddy, I name thee Governor General of the Brand-new New Catalonia and I gift thee mine dog Friston & mine steed Acephalus. And that concludeth mine testament, if it be poorly composed prithee forgive mee . . . for I suffer a bisarre paucity in mine body."

And with that, Orpí—his eyes rolling back in his head and his face out of joint—had a final celestial vision prior to the *de rigeur* rigor mortis: it was the Black Virgin herself come down from the heavens with her typical blinding brilliance and a chorus of otherworldly voices from beyond the grave:

"Orpínet, Orpínito, thine tyme hath come, seeing as the prophecy hath been fulfilled!" she said. "How was thine little adventure?"

"To be frank, I still hath many more thinges to doeth in this world, milady!" complained our hero. "Couldst thou allength-en mine lyfe a coupla years more?"

"Sure, no prob, and whilst I be at it I shall injecte some hairs on thine pate and find thee a twenny-year-old wench!" guffawed the Virgin before disappearing into the divine ether. "What thou must do, in this worlde as in the next, is eat grass, eat grass . . ."

"Sweet Black Virgen . . . halp mee!" exclaimed Orpí before expiring.

And thus passed on Joan Orpí del Pou, on July 1st of 1645, in his early fifties. The next day Father Claver officiated a mass in "the glorey of our Lord *ad quam nos perducat Iesus Christus Filius Dei, qui cum Patre et Spiritu Sancto vivit et regnat in secula seculorum Amen*" and then he sang a hoarse rendition of "Dies Irae," and left brand-new New Barcelona to settle in Cartagena de Indias, where he devoted his life to the protection of Black slaves. Meanwhile, Araypuro and the other Neo-Catalans presided over his burial, according to the local rituals, as the Homunculus sang a very heartfelt song that went a little something like this:

♫♪ Well, c'est la vie ♫♪
aint none o this new ta mee
aint nuttin but a cinnamon bun
meltin in the tropical sun
nothing sure but death and taxes
we all gotta face our axes
one State or another
my sister my daughter my mother
in the promise of a second
buildings and cities, I reckon'd
in perpetual motion

a fish jumping in da ocean
aside a ship pointing to the southern seas
an itsy bitsy ant down on its knees
toasting beneath the sun
of a northern land set to stun
that's cold, that's hot
aint none of this what its not
bees buzzing o'er a gilded bloom
vouz ferez le voyage outta this earthly room
eternal returns
infinite reincarnations
that's life, that's death
c'est la guerre, c'est la vie
that's the end of Joan Orpí
move on, nothing here to see
God glimmers in the white teeth
Of the devil smilin in the black heath
A distant star dancing in the universe
A wish that's risk adverse
A story that beginnes
Stories that have reach'd their "FIN"s
Legends gasping wid a wheeze
The chaos of a loud sneeze
Religions in left field
The Final Mystery revealed
A million strategick confessions
glimpsed in extraterrestrial expressions
Falling into the void
Eyes wide open
Eyes wide closed
That's life, that's death, c'est la vie
That's the end of Joan Orpí
Told as ne'er before heard.

Joan Orpí's body was laid to rest and his dog Friston kept watch over his gravesite day and night, ceaselessly howling until one day he too died of sadness. And that, dear readers, is how my licentious tale ends, and the moral of the story is: don't try to do it all in this life, or you won't be left with anything good to do in the next. *Vale.*[158]

---

158. *i.e.* Latin farewell.

## The infantry captain ends his telling of the tale and a great secret is revealed:

September 11th, 1714. A distant howl traverses Barcelona: Philip V's troops busting down the city gates. As the Catalans lay dying beneath the royal fire and artillery, a group of soldiers and plebes listen, mouths agape, to the end of the captain's tale, beneath the arch of the theater in ruins.

"The story of Joan Orpí concludeth," says the captain. "And were it worthy of the telling, tis because it hath allowed us mental respite beneath enemie fyre and bestowed a bit of lyfe to our bodys. Our earthly bodies, to be clear, for the Author of life shall take care of our souls."

"Dis whole fable hath been highly entertaining, Captain," said one of the soldiers. "But what war the true cause of Joan Orpí's demise?"

"Chroniclers and historians hath come to no agreement," responds the captain. "However there art three possyble theories: 1) neumonyia or untreated siffilis; 2) poisoning by Domingo Vázquez de Soja's assassins; 3) murder'd at the 'ands of a possibble large-scale conspyracy of American natives, in an attempt to kill all white men and restore sole native rule on the continent. There also be a rumor—little likely yet not ludycrous—that his body disappear'd and rests mummified in the cave where Orpí and Araypuro hiddest the treasure."

"And what befell the New Secret Catalonia following the decease of Joan Orpí?" asked another one of the soldiers. "Tisnt crystal clear, yet I've the impression you aint told us the hole sooth and nuthing but the sooth . . . Pray tell, of what art you trying to convince us? Or, better put, what art you trying to sell us?"

"I merely wanted to exxplain the story of an ordinary man who, through frekwent faylures, achieved great 'eroick feets. Now, ta be fair, one thing is verily sooth: Joan Orpí didst create his own previous future, as he thought up New Catalonia in advance and on his own. And with dis firm, clean, sincere, smooth, heroic, precise, and daring gesture, our hero left his definitive mark on history. And all de rest is merely myne figurative telling, for memory be not print'd like books."

"And what be so durn speshall bout thinking up New Catalonia, Captain?"

"That he thought it up on the very arse end of nowhere . . . that's what so durn special! But you are right, in fact, I still hath not told you the entire story . . ." acknowledges the captain, removing his hat and ripping off a fake moustache, thus transmuting into a strange being.

"Oh!"

"Ah!"

"Uh . . . miracle!"

"Tis science, not miracle. Gentle sirs, I be nun udder than the very Homunculus, created by the grace of Triboulet the Dwarf, and imbued with a talent fer immortality," said the faux captain, taking a bow. "Forgiving this final trickery, as discreet and amusing, ye all can be quite sure that there still be—in the middle of the virgin jungle—a wee community of mestizos, a mix of natives and white Quakers, who speak an odd Catalan, dance the Sardana, pray to the Virgin of Montserrat (because she's dark-skinned like them), self-determine as a (small) independent sovereign country: Independent from Spain, independent from Catalonia, from Europe, from the rest of America and from the world in generall. A republic freed of cliques and illustrious family names, where neither private property nor sovereign authority existeth, where all live in a communitas of absolute equality and where nature mobilizes the resources, as the economists say, or in udder wordes provideth all that be necessary. In short: a new Eden . . . and ye all be invited! My (secret) mission here is to bring back all the Catalans (specially Catalan women of marriagable age) I can to New Catalonia! A vessel awaits us in the Barcelona port. Tho' while I be here I also intend to plant mine seed amid the ladies of this Catalonia, to engender a new mestizo race in the jungle, because commingling makes da worlde go round, and because I doth struggle to keep it in mine pants."

"Incredible!" exclaims one of the soldiers.

"And what be the name of this new territory?" asks a woman.

"New New Catalonia," answers the Homunculus. "Listen, the shit here done already hit the fan. I'm off, back to the other Barcelona, folks. Would ye care to join me or doth ye preferr to die the proverbial and literal horrible death here?"

"Count me in!"

"Me too!"

"& me!" exclaim soldiers and civilians.

Shots are heard, and screams, and bombings, and breaking glass, and collapsing walls. Philip V's army advances into the city. Meanwhile, the soldiers and the throng of women, children, and the elderly leave the theater behind and follow the faux captain to the dock, where a small ship is waiting. It sets sail immediately for America, fleeing certain death. The

Homunculus, standing at the ship's prow, now in a more confidential tone addressed only to the soldiers, who look up at him with inquisitive eyes, unbuckles his sword belt and lets it fall to the floor, frugally fills his pipe with Almogàvers™ tobacco and slightly contracts his expression to accompany the gesture of his left hand lifting, and puts the pipe in his mouth, lighting it as he advances one leg forward to contribute to the desired theatrical affect and, with his eerie gleaming eyes fixed on a point in the distance, says: "Eat grass." The end.

**Max Besora** started his career as a poet, and has since gone on to publish four novels. *The Adventures and Misadventures of the Extraordinary and Admirable Joan Orpi, Conquistador and Founder of New Catalonia* received the 2018 City of Barcelona Prize for Best Catalan Novel of the Year.

**Mara Faye Lethem**'s award-winning translations include novels by Irene Solà, Albert Sánchez Piñol, Javier Calvo, Patricio Pron, Marc Pastor, Marta Orriols, Alicia Kopf, and Toni Sala. She is the author of *A Person's A Person, No Matter How Small* (Antibookclub, 2020) and the story "Twin Flames" in *Berkeley Noir* (Akashic Books, 2020).

**OPEN
LETTER**

**OPEN
LETTER**

Elsa Morante (Italy)
  *Aracoeli*
Giulio Mozzi (Italy)
  *This Is the Garden*
Andrés Neuman (Spain)
  *The Things We Don't Do*
Jóanes Nielsen (Faroe Islands)
  *The Brahmadells*
Madame Nielsen (Denmark)
  *The Endless Summer*
Henrik Nordbrandt (Denmark)
  *When We Leave Each Other*
Asta Olivia Nordenhof (Denmark)
  *The Easiness and the Loneliness*
Wojciech Nowicki (Poland)
  *Salki*
Bragi Ólafsson (Iceland)
  *The Ambassador*
  *Narrator*
  *The Pets*
Kristín Ómarsdóttir (Iceland)
  *Children in Reindeer Woods*
Sigrún Pálsdóttir (Iceland)
  *History. A Mess.*
Diego Trelles Paz (ed.) (World)
  *The Future Is Not Ours*
Ilja Leonard Pfeijffer (Netherlands)
  *Rupert: A Confession*
Jerzy Pilch (Poland)
  *The Mighty Angel*
  *My First Suicide*
  *A Thousand Peaceful Cities*
Rein Raud (Estonia)
  *The Brother*
João Reis (Portugal)
  *The Translator's Bride*
Rainer Maria Rilke (World)
  *Sonnets to Orpheus*
Mónica Ramón Ríos (Chile)
  *Cars on Fire*
Mercè Rodoreda (Catalonia)
  *Camellia Street*
  *Death in Spring*
  *Garden by the Sea*
  *The Selected Stories of Mercè Rodoreda*
  *War, So Much War*
Milen Ruskov (Bulgaria)
  *Thrown into Nature*
Guillermo Saccomanno (Argentina)
  *77*
  *The Clerk*
  *Gesell Dome*

Juan José Saer (Argentina)
  *The Clouds*
  *La Grande*
  *The One Before*
  *The Regal Lemon Tree*
  *Scars*
  *The Sixty-Five Years of Washington*
Olga Sedakova (Russia)
  *In Praise of Poetry*
Mikhail Shishkin (Russia)
  *Maidenhair*
Sölvi Björn Sigurðsson (Iceland)
  *The Last Days of My Mother*
Maria José Silveira (Brazil)
  *Her Mother's Mother's Mother and
    Her Daughters*
Andrzej Sosnowski (Poland)
  *Lodgings*
Albena Stambolova (Bulgaria)
  *Everything Happens as It Does*
Benjamin Stein (Germany)
  *The Canvas*
Georgi Tenev (Bulgaria)
  *Party Headquarters*
Dubravka Ugresic (Europe)
  *The Age of Skin*
  *American Fictionary*
  *Europe in Sepia*
  *Fox*
  *Karaoke Culture*
  *Nobody's Home*
Ludvík Vaculík (Czech Republic)
  *The Guinea Pigs*
Jorge Volpi (Mexico)
  *Season of Ash*
Antoine Volodine (France)
  *Bardo or Not Bardo*
  *Post-Exoticism in Ten Lessons,
    Lesson Eleven*
  *Radiant Terminus*
Eliot Weinberger (ed.) (World)
  *Elsewhere*
Ingrid Winterbach (South Africa)
  *The Book of Happenstance*
  *The Elusive Moth*
  *To Hell with Cronjé*
Ror Wolf (Germany)
  *Two or Three Years Later*
Words Without Borders (ed.) (World)
  *The Wall in My Head*
Xiao Hong (China)
  *Ma Bo'le's Second Life*
Alejandro Zambra (Chile)
  *The Private Lives of Trees*

**WWW.OPENLETTERBOOKS.ORG**